THE
KILLING
SPELL

THE KILLING SPELL

SHAY KAUWE

SAGA PRESS

LONDON · **NEW YORK** · TORONTO
AMSTERDAM/ANTWERP · NEW DELHI · SYDNEY/MELBOURNE

AN IMPRINT OF SIMON & SCHUSTER, LLC

1230 AVENUE OF THE AMERICAS, NEW YORK, NEW YORK 10020

For more than 100 years, Simon & Schuster has championed authors and the stories they create. By respecting the copyright of an author's intellectual property, you enable Simon & Schuster and the author to continue publishing exceptional books for years to come. We thank you for supporting the author's copyright by purchasing an authorized edition of this book.

No amount of this book may be reproduced or stored in any format, nor may it be uploaded to any website, database, language-learning model, or other repository, retrieval, or artificial intelligence system without express permission. All rights reserved. Inquiries may be directed to Simon & Schuster, 1230 Avenue of the Americas, New York, NY 10020 or permissions@simonandschuster.com.

This book is a work of fiction. Any references to historical events, real people, or real places are used fictitiously. Other names, characters, places, and events are products of the author's imagination, and any resemblance to actual events or places or persons, living or dead, is entirely coincidental.

Copyright © 2026 by Shay Zykova

All rights reserved, including the right to reproduce this book or portions thereof in any form whatsoever. For information, address Saga Press Subsidiary Rights Department, 1230 Avenue of the Americas, New York, NY 10020.

First Saga Press trade paperback edition April 2026

SAGA PRESS and colophon are registered trademarks of Simon & Schuster, LLC

Simon & Schuster strongly believes in freedom of expression and stands against censorship in all its forms. For more information, visit BooksBelong.com.

For information about special discounts for bulk purchases, please contact Simon & Schuster Special Sales at 1-866-506-1949 or business@simonandschuster.com.

The Simon & Schuster Speakers Bureau can bring authors to your live event. For more information or to book an event, contact the Simon & Schuster Speakers Bureau at 1-866-248-3049 or visit our website at www.simonspeakers.com.

Interior design by Lewelin Polanco

Manufactured in the United States of America

1 3 5 7 9 10 8 6 4 2

Library of Congress Control Number has been applied for.

ISBN 978-1-6680-5328-7 (pbk)
ISBN 978-1-6680-5329-4 (ebook)

Let's stay in touch! Scan here to get book recommendations, exclusive offers, and more delivered to your inbox.

For those who have lost their mother tongue or have had it stolen from them.

That was not the end of your story.

AUTHOR'S NOTE ON LANGUAGE

This novel has many Hawaiian words, so I've included the language's diacritical marks to help readers with pronunciation. An ʻokina is a glottal stop that looks like a backward apostrophe. It's pronounced the way you might say *uh-oh* or *butter* in a Cockney accent—that little hiccup in the middle is an ʻokina. There is also a line that appears above vowels called a kahakō. Letters with a kahakō are drawn out for an extra beat.

You might notice sentences that look *almost* like English. That is Hawaiian Pidgin, which, ironically, is a creole. Pidgin was birthed in Hawaiʻi during the plantation era, and since it's primarily spoken, may look a little funny on the page to those unfamiliar with it. But I wen do em anyway bumbai people tink it shame fo write lidat an dey wrong.

There's a fair bit of transliteration, too, which is just a fancy way of saying that I've tossed other alphabets into Latin to churn out something readable in English. It's how цветок became svetok and 水 became mizu. This is just how these words sound in my head, so don't take my spelling as law.

I'm sure that some people will be frustrated with my choices, offended that I haven't directly translated every "foreign" phrase used, or upset with how many times I start a sentence with *And* or *But*.

And to that I say, e hāmau!

Languages are wonderful, beautiful, strange things that change and shift as they please. The harder folks in ivory towers try to control them, the more they bleed outside the lines. Take comfort in the fact that there is no "correct" way to speak or write. So, speak more. Write more. Be loud about it, too. Because the only wrong way to use a language is to not use it at all.

LA CITY ORDINANCE #11358

As decreed by the Los Angeles Board, all prospective Guild members of any vocation, including Caster and Smith, must pass a licensing examination in order to practice magic within city territory. The examination shall be administered in the chosen regulated language: Latin, French, Italian, or Spanish.

Regulation shall be decided upon by the Board and reviewed every three years to include any language with a history of proven merit to be considered for advancement. A language may be considered three times for regulation before being permanently disqualified.

~

AMENDMENT 1: Arabic has passed its second attempt at regulation and been graded *exceptional* due to its profound influence on global literature. The language's proclivity toward storytelling, narration, and documentation is deemed invaluable to the study of magic. One seat has been opened on the Board for a licensed Arabic speaker of a recognized clan.

~

AMENDMENT 2: Cantonese, Mandarin, and Japanese have passed their first attempt at regulation and been graded *noteworthy* due to their contributions to culture and art. Cantonese and Mandarin's effects on good fortune and Japanese's manipulation of the human body are deemed worthy of further study. Two seats have been opened on the Board for licensed Cantonese, Mandarin, or Japanese speakers of recognized clans.

~

Tagalog has failed its first attempt at regulation. No amendment will be made.

THE
KILLING
SPELL

CHAPTER 1

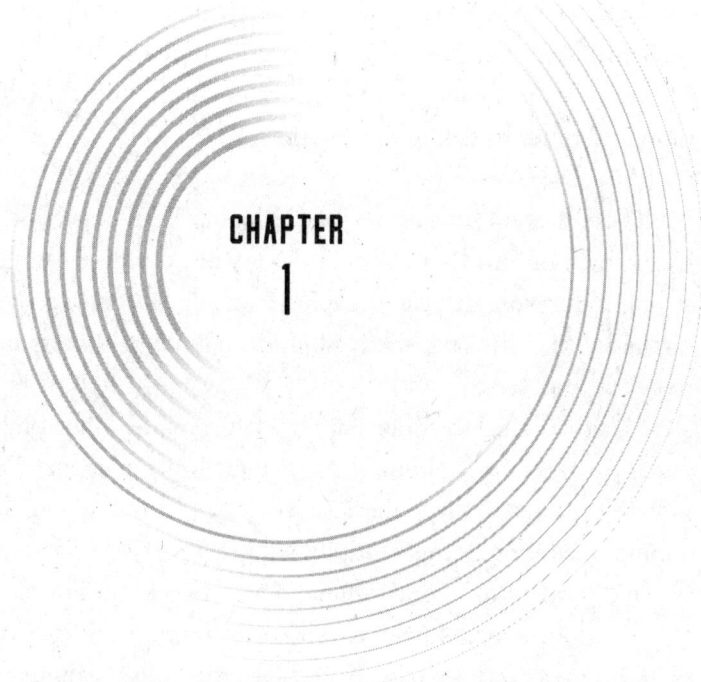

Kea, I need you.

I flinched at the sound of the voice in my head. Makani's sympathetic talent of telepathy, though benign, was always unsettling, like a pinch right at the temple.

Closing my eyes, I focused on sending him a response. *Your chores better be done if you're goofing off.*

Something followed me into the coop.

In a heartbeat, my irritation turned to ice-cold fear. I dropped the plastic basket of wet sheets I was holding and ran to the backyard, which overlooked the ocean. Our usually small house felt like a gigantic barrier as I sprinted across the dry grass toward the garden. The coop came into view, a ramshackle construction made of weathered wood, and one of our hens, Fiona, flopped out. She clucked disapprovingly at me; her leg twisted at a funny angle as she hobbled away.

The chalk of the ward around the entrance had been wiped off by the door, leaving a smudge of grayish residue on the wooden planks. Clearly Makani's handiwork. I swore under my breath. I'd told him a thousand times to stop pestering the birds.

I'm scared.

There was no time to be mad. I hadn't been expecting a fight, so I was stuck only with a leiomano in my back pocket. While relatively strong for a woman of my height, I wasn't *that* strong. If something big had gotten into the shed, I had little hope of success in beating it to death.

I gently tapped the door with my left shoulder while pulling out the flattened oval club, holding it at an angle in front of me. The sheen of polished wood and sharp shark's teeth looked intimidating, but it wasn't a hunting weapon. In the shed, I wouldn't have the space to move freely or build power into a good swing. I'd need to get it, whatever it was, *out*.

The door cracked open a hair's width, and I peered inside. A pair of hazel eyes stared back at me from my cousin jammed under the birds' perch. Feathers, blood, and dead chickens lay everywhere. A low, guttural hiss emerged from the darkness, irritated by the thin stream of light I had let in. The air, speckled with dust and fluttering pieces of stray hay, was heavy and hot.

Makani's chest rose and fell with quiet, strangled breaths. He squeezed his eyes shut and shot me a message.

It's behind the door.

Not daring to startle the thing, I twisted my head to look at the spaces between the bolts and spied a patch of scales hidden in the shadows. Stretching from the frame of the door to the wall, the creature was too large to be any normal animal. It had to be a magi.

The hissing stopped as the beast shuffled. I lost sight of it and became acutely aware of the blood rushing through my veins. Tensing my muscles, I leaned closer to the door, desperate to figure out what kind of magi it was.

A black iris flashed in the empty space, narrowing in on me, and the hissing turned to a growl. I sent Makani back a single command.

Move!

He crawled from his hiding place just as the magi lunged for him. I slammed my shoulder into the door as hard as I could, sending the beast squealing as it was knocked against the back shelves. Makani screamed. He squirmed forward on his stomach to the side of the perch that was protected by a metal grate. The magi's head swiveled to focus on his retreating figure.

"Hey, ugly!" I shouted, stomping my feet to attract its attention.

The beast snarled, stepping into the light from the open door. A mo'o. About five feet long, the lizard creature had sharp teeth made for rending meat, and smooth scales covered its entire body in a sickly Granny-Smith green that faded to pale white around its lower belly.

Just a baby one. I could take care of it.

Figuring my forearm would hurt less, I dragged the sharpest tooth of the leiomano down the front of my arm, wincing as I pressed in deeper to scratch up the skin. A trickle of blood welled to the surface and dripped down in a thin line.

The mo'o raised its head so that its bulging, white neck flared like a balloon. It sniffed the air. Once its beady black eyes found the source of blood, it stilled and turned its undivided attention onto me. Good boy.

Magi might be born from magic, but ultimately, they were just animals. They couldn't reason or use logic the way a person could. No talking dragons, or singing unicorns, or any of those other stupid stories you read about in fantasy books from before the Flood. Magi were dangerous but dumb.

I turned my back to it and ran.

Feral instinct took over as the magi smelled blood on my retreating figure. *Prey. Hunt. Food.* It rushed after me.

Running down the hill toward the beach wouldn't work as my blood would likely attract more creepy-crawlies from the water, so the front of our property was the best bet. My bare feet slammed against the dry grass as I lured it to the front lawn, but I wasn't fast enough. The moʻo was on my heels. My palms got sweaty around the wooden handle of the leiomano, and I swore to arm myself better next time I did the laundry.

Waving my arms wildly to keep the moʻo from ascending the back stairs onto the porch, I ran parallel to the rickety frame of our house. As I rounded the corner, I banged on the walls to make noise, releasing a shower of chipped dry paint in my wake. Sun-bleached flakes rained down around me, filling the air with the dissipating scent of sour milk.

It worked. The moʻo slithered in my direction with its mouth wide open, ready to chomp down as we made it to the front lawn. If it sunk its teeth into me, I'd get a nasty cut. But we didn't have any money lying around for stitches, so I wasn't looking to take chances. I'd have to cast something. My jaw locked as I planted my feet and pivoted to face the moʻo. Breathing deeply, I ran through a list of words I could use that could make this damn thing stop moving.

Russian could work. It was simple and effective when there was an obvious target and I didn't need to bother with definite articles, but I needed a word that rhymed with *begat*. Maybe run was the wrong idea though. Did lizards really run? At eight feet away, it certainly felt like it.

Scratch Russian. I didn't have time to figure out a rhyme to make the spell work. My other trusty language, English, was always a no-go on the fly. Any attempt on my end to be poetical fell flat no matter how many Shakespearean *arts*, *thous*, or *foes* I threw in, even though it was an established fact that a good sonnet would work wonders. Emphasis there on *good*.

Hawaiian it had to be.

Six feet away now, the moʻo crawled closer, a furious pace infecting its approach. Five feet. Hawaiian was so vague though. A simple *stop* might work, but it also might stop all the internal organs in both my body and the moʻo's from functioning. Only four feet left. Three. There was no time.

Keeping eye contact with the beast, I crouched low and dug my fingers into the lawn, entwining brittle blades of grass in my grip. With my other hand I dropped the leiomano flat to the ground and pressed hard on top of it for balance. The moʻo was nearly right in front of me, its breath warming the air so close that I could feel the heat on my nose.

Reaching for the mana from my core, I said the first word that came to mind. "E hoʻopaʻa." *Stick.*

Magic surged out of my hands and into the ground around us, rising up like a sudden breeze from the dirt. The lizard stopped moving. It writhed, tossing itself back and forth, but its efforts to escape were futile. My spell kept its legs glued firmly to the earth around it.

I breathed out a sigh of relief.

One-word spells weren't supposed to work, but they always had for me. Sort of. They had an effect, that was enough. Call it a quirk of my mana, an unexpected benefit to being absolute crap at all other kinds of magic. I tried to lift my left hand off the leiomano so that I could finish the job and found that my spell had worked a little *too* well. I was also firmly stuck to the ground.

Dammit.

I really should have stopped using one-word castings years ago, but when in a pinch, I had a bad habit of saying whatever popped into my head. The joke was on me, though, since they rarely worked how I wanted them to.

The moʻo spat at me, struggling against my magic's hold as I strained my neck toward the house. "Sisi!" I could hear the TV blaring inside. Giving it a minute, I baked in the afternoon heat, three feet away from a floundering giant lizard. "*Sicilia!*" I yelled again, louder.

The screen door on our porch swung open and Sisi, my teenage sister, appeared. Her hands were on her hips, and there was an irritated crease carved through the sun-freckled skin of her forehead. With Sicilia's light-brown waves and emerald-green eyes, people usually did a double take when I explained that we were related, though I never really understood why. She and I looked a lot alike.

We both had deep-set, almond eyes that turned down slightly at the ends, wide, flat noses, and full lips. Our features were nearly identical, but we were different in our coloring. While Sisi was fair, I had brown everything. Brown skin, brown hair, and dark-brown eyes that could only be described as *penetrating*.

Sicilia was chewing a piece of bubble gum, apparently oblivious to the spitting moʻo on our lawn.

"A little help?" I asked.

The gum snapped in her mouth, and she shot a disdainful glance at the magi. "What am I supposed to do about that?"

"Kill it," I explained through gritted teeth, trying not to let my irritation bubble out.

Sisi's gaze fell on the weapon below my left hand. "You do it."

"I can't," I stressed.

Sicilia's hair was wound into a lazy topknot that spilled precariously to the side. The tita bun was a nice complement to her attitude. "Doesn't look like that to me."

I didn't have the patience for this. "I'd *love* to take care of this myself, but I cast something and if I release the smithing, I'll end up unsticking the moʻo too. I'd be right back where I started."

To emphasize how bad that would be, the moʻo made a snarling noise and gnashed its teeth together, trying to lunge forward. Its feet didn't budge, but the beast did spit some of its saliva onto my cheek, making me recoil. Unfortunately, my spell held tight, and the only thing I could manage to do was jerk my head back a few inches. Gross.

My magic had a track record of fighting against every good intention I threw at it. At ten, I'd tried a common Latin spell to find my grandmother's lost keys and ended up with every pin, screw, and nail in the house flying at my face. I quickly learned that the only way to tame my magic into doing what I wanted was by using spells I'd smithed myself, but that took time, patience, and talent. Sadly, I was in short supply of all three.

Sicilia gave an exaggerated sigh. "Let me get my crossbow. I'm not getting lizard guts all over my favorite shorts." The screen door slammed shut and I was left alone.

As I waited for Sisi, I glanced around at our lot, trying to ignore the heat of the sun bearing down on me. A few generations ago, our family had built a single-story plantation-style house on the New Hawaiian Homelands, affectionately referred to as "the Homestead," which stretched across what had been Manhattan Beach. In the days before the Flood, this area had been packed with the homes of the wealthy, smashed together so close they almost touched. Nowadays, the residential area had been razed until nothing was left but hills, dirt, and sand.

The house, once a forest green, had faded to shades of dull sage over the years, but the wooden planks of our porch and stairs were still a rich mahogany. Out back, we'd planted mango, avocado, and banana. The trees seemed to grow taller and tastier from the trade winds that pushed in from the ocean and with a little help from Papa Ivan's green thumb. Our home stood on a grassy area at the top of the closest hill to the water, which, even by Homestead standards, was too close to the ocean to be safe. The sea was home to an abundance of magical creatures, or magi, and no sane person wanted to live near it anymore.

Despite the danger of roaming magi that regularly stumbled onto our land, I loved our home. The crashing waves were a soothing, steady backdrop for our daily chores, and more importantly, our house was on an apex of powerful mana. Mana, or magic, was all around us and streaming in rivers toward the depths of the forests and oceans. It pooled around beaches like the one we lived on, making us stronger. However, that strength came with the price of being in the middle of magi birthing grounds. It didn't bother us much. We were too small of a clan to be picky about the luxury of a safer lot farther from the shore. And magi were far easier to deal with than people.

Sicilia reappeared at the door, crossbow in hand, and aimed for its stomach.

"Shoot it in the head!" I shouted before she let the shaft fly. "We need the meat."

Sisi pulled a face but obliged, and the bolt whizzed through the mo'o's head, sending a splatter of blood onto my shirt. The oversize beast convulsed as the arrow hit true, then finally, it lay still. Its beady eyes went matte.

Willing my mana to rush out through my arm, I ended the spell. "E ho'oku'u." *Release.*

The snap of the magic breaking tingled as it let go of me. As I cracked my knuckles, I touched the tips of my fingers, feeling the mana disperse. I handed the leiomano to Sicilia, grateful that I hadn't needed to beat the lizard to death with a piece of wood smaller than my forearm.

Sisi took the weapon from me and flicked the tooth that was still red with my blood. "Are we desperate enough to start eating magi?" she asked, her face tight.

"It killed most of the chickens. The only one I saw alive was Fiona," I said. Eating lizard for dinner was the least of our problems. Without the coop, we'd be short on the meat and eggs needed to feed five hungry mouths.

Sisi grasped the situation quickly. "Did Makani try to chat with the birds again?" She popped her gum and made a hand puppet as she talked about our cousin's new weird hobby.

I planted a palm across my face in response.

"Great," Sicilia said, drawing out the word with a few extra syllables. She mumbled under her breath. "I'm going to smack him upside his head."

I dusted the grass from my hands onto my denim shorts. "You can have him when I'm done." First, I'd wring Makani's neck, then chop up the giant lizard for dinner. Perfect Friday night plans for any twenty-five-year-old.

~

I stomped over to the shed and kicked in the door to assess the carnage, counting five dead hens scattered throughout the coop. Our rooster was running around in panicked circles on the floor, while our most temperamental hen slept nonplussed on a top shelf.

A growing migraine pushed on my temple.

We'd lost the majority of our flock in a single afternoon. Two hens weren't going to be able to lay enough eggs to feed us all. Even if we could salvage some meat off the mangled corpses, it wouldn't make up for our loss in production. I mentally calculated how many more jobs I'd need to take on in order to replace the dead hens but soon gave up. Math wasn't my strong suit.

A soft cough came from the floor.

"Come out this instant, or I swear to god, I'll give you the dirtiest lickens' of your life," I said.

Makani crawled out from under the roost, covered in straw and chicken shit. His eyes were all fire. He sported a scratch on his head that was dripping blood down his cheek, and his arms were crossed defiantly at his chest. Other than the mean glare, he was a cute kid with copper-colored skin and a curly pouf of black hair.

"I didn't do anything wrong," he said.

"You know the rules. If you don't have an adult who can put the ward back, you need to stay out," I explained, struggling to keep my tone level.

He shrugged. "Whatever."

I bent to his eye level. "It's dangerous to remove the wards." I gestured to the coop. "Now, we won't have enough chickens to lay eggs for us."

"I don't care." Makani sniffled. "I hate eggs. If you like them so much, buy more birds."

"We don't have the money to buy more," I said.

"Then *get* more," he said flippantly. As Makani continued ranting, he began to cry. "You're the head, so it's your job to take care of our family. You were the first person I called but you didn't come in time. It's your fault they're all dead." Makani looked down at his bare feet and clenched his fists at his sides, refusing to look me in the eye. He wasn't talking about the hens anymore.

"Makani," I said hesitantly, reaching out for him.

He flinched away from my touch, his whole body shaking, and raised his hands to his face. I spotted from under the cover of his fingers fat droplets of tears as they hit the straw on the floor of the coop, fading to a darker shade of brown among the dirt. "I hate you, Kea. I wish *you* were dead instead!" He took off, dashing behind me.

I tried to grab the back of his shirt, but Makani was already running at full speed toward the edge of our property and down the hill that dipped to the beach. I covered my eyes with my hands and took a deep breath, which came out shakier than I wanted it to. My guilt and frustration had coalesced into a ball that made my stomach hurt.

Taking Makani in to live with us had been a given when his parents passed, but the extra mouth put pressure on the family budget that I hadn't yet been able to balance. His mercurial temperament was even more difficult to adjust to. I'd read more parenting books than a young woman ought to, and while I realized his mood swings were normal, even expected, it didn't make dealing with them any easier.

It wasn't that I was mad, exactly. I looked up into a sky so blue it was making my eyes water.

It's just so hard.

But I couldn't say that.

Makani was right about my responsibilities as his older cousin and, more importantly, his guardian. Yet, his cutting assessment of my own failings was a reminder I didn't need. I already knew I was ill-suited to being our clan's head. I saw it every time I looked into his eyes, eyes that were the same color as his mother's, my aunt's. I missed her. It left a gaping empty hurt in the pit of my stomach. For Makani, that puka was larger, deeper. It was a black hole that gnawed on him from the inside out.

I peered over my shoulder and looked at the remains of their old home about a mile away from our property. Half of the house was hollowed out from the blaze that had been set in the raid, and the white walls of what remained were stained with gray soot. Exposed beams in the roof had let in rain and sun in equal parts. Every so often, a piece of decayed wood would crack and topple to the ground with a *thud*. When Los Angeles had taken the Palakikos' plot, they'd pushed their border out to just beyond the perimeter of the house and on the edge of ours. The stones of the city's protective ward were shiny and new, unlike the decrepit Palakiko home that LA had never bothered to demolish, almost as a warning to the rest of us. I kept sight of it like a snake in the grass.

As Los Angeles grew larger and space became more limited, the city's sprawl expanded ravenously. They'd offered our people exorbitant prices for their properties, with the promise of Board protection and apartments hidden behind LA's powerful city ward. The Palakikos had had enough. They'd been moving back the city's ward stones little by little, pushing back against LA. Someone or something had tipped off the Board to their antics, and Los Angeles showed up in full force, wiping out most of the clan in less than an hour. Anyone left alive had either assimilated or been taken in by one of the other clans.

After that, I understood how things worked. Our treaty and two-hundred-year lease with the government didn't matter, nor did the pretty words that came out of the Board's mouth. The Homestead only stood because they believed this land too dangerous to be of any value.

"Girl!" A familiar voice caught me off guard and I looked up to see Nana Kūlia glaring at me from the back porch.

I took one look at my grandmother, her brilliant white hair flowing down her back in stark contrast to dark skin that shined like she'd rubbed coconut oil on herself—and promptly turned around.

"Are you walking away from me when I'm talking to you?" Her voice boomed, and despite being a grown woman, I grimaced. "Don't make me chase you down this hill! You know that I'm too old for that. I could fall and *die*."

I turned toward her slowly, sticking my forefingers into the loops of my waistband with a sheepish smile on my face. Nana used that line about dying at least once a day. Probably because it worked.

"Come here this instant, Kealaokaleo Petrova," she commanded, leaning heavily on her wooden cane. My full name stretched out on her tongue like a curse.

I marched back to the house as if walking to my own execution. As soon as I made it to the creaky stairs, Nana Kūlia smacked me on the back of the head with the flat of her palm. It didn't hurt. Much.

"Your temper will land you in deeper trouble if you don't watch your mouth, girl. You can't be running around yelling at Makani," she scolded.

"You used to do worse to me when I was little," I grumbled, rubbing the tender spot on my scalp. "How'd you even find out so quickly?"

She narrowed her eyes at me. "God is always watching, Kea."

I looked over her shoulder and spied Sicilia peeking from the kitchen. She lowered her head and began furiously chopping vegetables.

"God and Sisi, maybe," I muttered.

"Are you sassing me?" she asked.

I stopped my eyes from rolling and lowered them instead, knowing that my big mouth would just get me another slap. "No, Nana."

The expression in her brown eyes softened. "You better not be. Now, go make up with your cousin."

"I can't," I complained. "I've got to skin the moʻo and pluck the chickens that it killed." Not to mention fix up the coop, browse the online job boards for more freelance work, and pick up a few things from the store. Our to-do list was a never-ending battle that I was always on the losing side of.

Nana Kūlia made her hand into a fist and rapped me on the head with her knuckles, lightly this time. "Sisi and I will take care of the moʻo."

My cousin Newt rounded the corner as I was being scolded. "I can help, too. Do what you gotta do, Kea."

I glanced behind him at the dead magi splayed on the dining table. Newt must've carried it into the house when I was dealing with Makani because Nana hadn't been able to lift anything heavy since the last raid knocked her around. At the time, we hadn't had the money to see a proper doctor, so she walked with a limp to this day.

"You figured out how to cook it?" I asked my sister, over Newt's shoulder.

"Even got a recipe," Sisi said. "We're apparently not the only ones who've tried eating them."

I didn't know how to feel about the fact that there were magi recipes floating around the internet: kelpie soup, chupacabra tacos, baked chimera. The notion made my stomach churn, and I didn't know whether to be grossed out or relieved. I pushed away the nausea and settled on grateful. With my family's help, I'd have time to run to Bobby's for some groceries and ease the pressure of another chore from my mind.

I leaned in to kiss my grandmother on the cheek before scooting behind her, into the house, and grabbing my keys off a hook on the wall.

"Make up with your cousin!" she shouted at my back.

I hurried out of earshot without answering and shut the garage door behind me. I'd worry about Makani later. He needed time to cool down before I'd even be able to get within three feet of him without him shooting daggers at me, or in his case, throwing overripe bananas at my head.

My pocket buzzed and I pulled the phone from it, glancing down at the notification. Seeing the name, my heart dropped. Basilio.

> I really need to talk to you.
>
> Things have gotten complicated.
>
> Please respond.

Apparently, there were a lot of people I needed to make up with. A flash of molten lava lit up my core. My life was held together by spiderweb strands, and I didn't have time to feel responsible for a head who had willingly left the Homestead, who had given up, who had abandoned us. Abandoned *me*.

My finger paused over the message, my chest tight, and I pressed delete.

CHAPTER 2

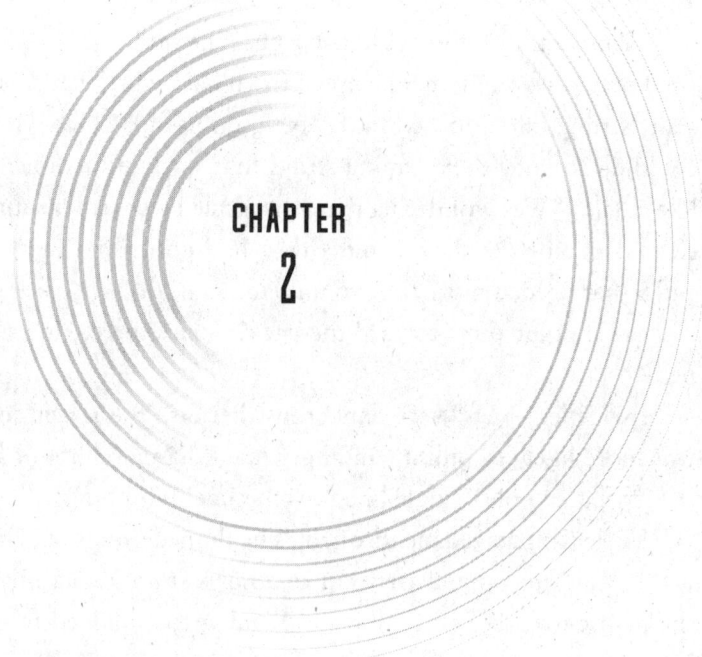

It took me less than five minutes to reach Bobby's, the battered convenience store that served as our fish market, grocer, meeting house, and barber for those in need of a trim. While the Homestead clans raided each other constantly, we still had to live together. Bobby's was one of the few spots where people stuck to basic civility. Partly out of respect for the unofficial hub of the store, and mostly because its owner, Uncle Colt, was a mean 'Caster with wicked aim.

Colt was a rugged old man who preferred to work at the chair out front rather than in his office. He claimed that sitting was bad for his back. Really, he was just nīele and liked being in everyone's business.

Uncle Colt waved at me as I walked in, setting off an ancient bell that rung a discordant note through the store. "Aloha e Kea."

I bent over the counter to the single-station barber's chair and gave him a peck on the cheek. Uncle had been here as long as I'd been alive. I imagined he'd still be here, sweeping up fallen hair and dust, long after I died, too.

"You look like you could use a cut," he said.

I patted down my wild, wavy brown hair, which had been haphazardly strung into a loose braid. "Nah, no need." There was nothing I could do to tame the escaping strays that sprouted around my profile like a halo. "Was wondering if any fishermen were still around?" Most cleared out before dawn unless they had gotten a particularly large catch that needed more time to unload.

Uncle pointed me toward the back. "Ben's there. He used a throw net."

I whistled. Nets were dangerous, because the larger surface area was more likely to pull up an angry magi than a school of fish. While riskier than a pole's single line, it sometimes paid off.

Uncle Colt waved me through as he flipped on the television on the wall. The scene immediately cut to a news story about Angelo Reyes, the man currently petitioning for Tagalog to be added to the official language registry and fighting for a spot on the Board. Though I didn't need any more reminders of my former friend, I couldn't help my curiosity about the man Basilio had left us to join.

Reyes was in his early forties with light stubble on his chin and the shadow of a mustache under his wide nose. He was giving a speech about the benefits of language expansion in Los Angeles, his whole body animated and his eyes shining. He had the aura of a leader. A changemaker. They were going places.

Or, they had been.

The scrolling text below the images announced in bold letters that the man had been killed. A suspected political hit. I recalled Basilio's text to me earlier and tried to ignore the weight of my phone in my pocket. I didn't give a damn about LA's inner mechanisms. That was city business, not mine. Even if he had been trying to contact me because of Angelo's death, as an outsider, there was nothing I could do.

I didn't want to feel bad for Basilio. In my mind he'd made his bed already, but pity was a little like a sore throat—it crept up on you when you least expected it. Things were going to be brutal for the Reyes clan moving forward, because even with such a popular leader, they'd been having a rough time making their case to the rest of the city. Without Angelo's mass appeal, it would be an uphill battle. There were many who didn't want Tagalog added to the list of regulated languages.

The last wave of expansion had been only ten years ago, when Cantonese, Mandarin, and Japanese were heralded into the ivory tower. In all fairness, though, that had less to do with diplomacy and more with sheer force. The camera swept across to Sora Kaiser, the infamous head of the Kaiser clan—and now Board member—who'd been at the helm of that push.

Sora's aura, in contrast to Angelo's, radiated menace. He was on the shorter side with a permanent scowl carved into his brow and a flipped smile. The man sported unusually long hair that fell past his shoulders, tied up into a tight bun at the nape of his neck. Sora looked up into the camera's lens, and his gaze, even through video, seared me. His eyes were dark rubies. The color of apples, the color of blood.

I unintentionally shivered and turned away from the footage. If I never met a member of the Board, I'd count myself lucky.

Trying to shake the image of that cold-blooded glare, I pushed farther into the convenience store under flickering fluorescent lights. Bobby's had seen better days. The walls were a brown cement, plastered with posters and old ads that were always inexplicably slightly damp. A wall of cigarettes and booze was set up near the bored cashier, secured behind a pane of plexiglass, and the shelves were jam-packed with local favorites like dried cuttlefish, cans of Spam, and stacks of canned juice that were more corn syrup than actual fruit.

I ducked under the plastic flaps that separated the front of the store from the refrigerated section in the back, where the morning fish market had forever imprinted its scent.

"Aloha, Uncle!" I called out, stepping over the slick puddles that coated the floor.

An older man with wrinkled brown skin looked up at me from one of the stalls. Most of the fishermen were gone for the day, but his area remained packed with fresh ice, and I could spot the distinctive stripes of a barracuda and the raised spines of a bright-red rockfish.

"You like buy?" he asked.

I frowned and poked at the skin of the barracuda. "Maybe. Manini this one, yeah?"

"Skinny but not small." He pulled up the fish by its mouth to demonstrate. Its long body hanging over the ice.

"You catch any aku or ahi?" Tuna was in season right now, and the deep-sea fish were bigger and better to eat than anything on display. He wouldn't have caught it with a net, but the top-quality fish was sure to be on hand.

He leaned over the counter. "You can pay? What clan you from?"

"Petrova," I offered.

He pulled a face, sending my own words back at me. "Manini, your clan. No money in the Petrovas."

"We get mana, though," I countered.

We bartered over the price of the fish, and I eventually agreed to give him a spell for eternal flame in exchange for some aku and the barracuda. I waited, leaning on my left foot while Ben placed the fish into a Styrofoam container, using a plastic shovel to pack ice around the sides. When he was done, he hoisted the lot of it over the counter into my arms, and I set the cooler on the floor. It was a good amount of meat that would tide us over until I could replace the hens.

Ben held out his hand and curled his fingers in toward himself until I shuffled close enough to reach over the piles of ice. Up close, he smelled of stale cigarettes and green bottles.

"You'll need to repeat after me and memorize the words," I warned. Since Hawaiian was exclusively an oral language, it was a tricky medium for Smiths to work with. While I could make notes, full spells could *never* be written down in their entirety or they'd lose their mana. It made selling and passing along Hawaiian magic particularly difficult. Most LA clans had family spell books under lock and key, but for us on the Homestead, those spells had to be taught and recited from memory. People guarded their clans' spells closely and stuck to longer incantations when possible, making them more difficult to steal.

"If you want the full demonstration, let me borrow a lighter," I said.

Ben shoved a hand into the worn denim pocket of his shorts and pulled out a chipped red plastic contraption. He dropped the lighter into my open palm while I searched around the stall and found a relatively dry newspaper. Flicking the fork, the lighter sparked and I held the device to the paper until it caught fire, but the flames were low and struggled against the moisture in the air.

I pointed to my mouth so Ben could watch as I formed the words of the spell I'd promised, waving my hand with the lighter over the fire. "O ke ahi i ka mea e 'ai i nā mea a pau, a hiki i ka pau 'ana."

The phrase flowed right out of me from diaphragm to mouth, as the vowels at the edge of each word blended subtly together. Below, the flame stretched to kiss the tops of my fingertips. Under my command, the small blaze grew stronger, and I gestured at Ben to take my place. He attempted to recite the spell and lifted his palm, face down over the fire, but it sputtered out as he mixed up the words. His pronunciation had been good though. At least he was familiar with the language.

Even though we lived on the new Hawaiian Homelands, where most of the Kānaka Maoli community had relocated after the Flood, speaking 'Ōlelo Hawai'i, or the Hawaiian language, was not common. English was the default because there weren't many native speakers left—only those who had made the effort to learn as an adult. Some of the older clans were able to do traditional magic in Hawaiian, using spells that had been handed down for generations, but I was unable to cast anything I hadn't made myself. Thus, out of necessity, I'd become the first and only Hawaiian Smith. Unofficially, anyway. Since Hawaiian wasn't regulated, I didn't exactly have my license.

Ben's forehead scrunched together, and his mouth tweaked down at an end. "How you expect me remember all that?"

"Don't focus on the length of it," I said, pointing out a pale cone-shaped squid lying face up on his ice. "We'll break it down to po'o, piko, and 'awe." I prodded the squid's head, center, and legs as I said each word.

"Got a lot of 'awe," Ben grumbled, but he obliged.

I repeated the phrase slowly and in small parts until Ben was more confident. By the third attempt, he could hold the fire on his own. The flames climbed higher, snapping at his hand. To demonstrate the spell's usefulness, I tugged on the edge of the lit newspaper near the ledge of his booth and carefully set it on top of the fresh ice near his wares. The man made a small noise of protest but quickly swallowed his complaint as the fire held true.

"O ke ahi i ka mea e 'ai i nā mea a pau, a hiki i ka pau 'ana," I repeated. "*Fire consumes everything, for a flame cannot say it is ever satisfied.*" I pinched a cube of ice between my thumb and forefinger, feeding the frozen water to the blaze. As if it were made of petrol, the flame jumped hungrily, licking the air.

Ben snatched his hand away and the fire went out. He squinted between me and the charred ice, back and forth, until satisfaction leaked out from between the spaces of his crooked smile. "I guess it's a fair trade." He paused a beat, eyes narrowing. "Manini young head."

"Grouchy old man," I snapped back.

Ben laughed, turning away from me, our deal finished.

I lugged the container to my car, still scowling. It wasn't a fair trade at all. That spell had taken months for me to put together, and its use extended from combat to agriculture. From a regular clan head, that kind of magic would've been worth a whole ahi, but the Petrovas had lost our status in the eyes of the Homestead.

My ancestor might have been one of the five heads who helped negotiate our treaty with LA after the Flood, but when she died before passing down her mana o ka mo'okū'auhau, or family spell, to her progeny, we lost our position on the council. There had once been talk that my Nana Kūlia, a powerful Caster, would be the one to reclaim our seat, but she wasn't much of a Smith and never succeeded in crafting a new family spell. I intended to do exactly that and put due respect back onto our name.

I slipped the cooler of fish into my truck and slammed the hood down hard before walking back into Bobby's to pay for some gas. I was riding on empty and would need at least a twenty-buck fill to breathe easy for the next few days. There wasn't a lot left over this month, so I had to be careful with what we still had. After cashing out and giving Uncle Colt a kiss goodbye, I went to fill my gas at the pump out front.

"Kea."

Hearing my name made me jump, and I looked over my shoulder to see Keanu Mahi'ai right behind me. His skin was the kind of rich brown that you only got from hours farming in the heat of the sun and he had pulled his thick, black hair into a low ponytail. In his late twenties with broad shoulders and a trim middle, Keanu wasn't what you would call sculpted, but there was a meanness to his muscles that let others know that he worked hard and fought dirty.

The Mahi'ai head stood with his hands on his hips, shirtless and shoeless. "You get money for expensive fish but none for your mortgage?"

This again. "I made a deal," I said defensively. "And more importantly, I don't owe you anything until the end of the month." I hung up the nozzle and went back to the driver's side of my car, jangling my keys. "See you then."

As my key twisted in the lock, Keanu crept up behind me, breathing on my neck. "Your smart mouth is going to land you in trouble. Speak nice to me, Kea."

"*Nicely*," I said.

I tried to yank open the car door and jump in to run away from Keanu and my big fat mouth, but he beat me to it, slamming the door shut with his elbow before I could get it open. Keanu pushed me so I was facing him with my back pressed against the metal of the door. I must've hit a nerve because his cheeks were puffed up with embarrassment.

"Apologize," he demanded.

"I don't feel like it."

I spotted his friends coming out of the store with a six-pack of beer in either hand. They dropped the boxes and slid behind Keanu, flanking him on either side. Dammit. I didn't realize he had backup today.

"We doing this now?" one said, bouncing on the balls of his feet.

My eyes darted to the front door of the shop, hoping to ward them off. "Uncle Colt will skin us all alive if we fight here." If I could distract them for just a moment, I could get away.

Keanu glanced at the entrance. He took a step back and then looked at me with a vicious smile. "So why don't we all hop in your car and go holoholo? Take this somewhere more private." He placed an arm above my head against the truck, leaning over me with an ugly gleam in his eye.

I headbutted him in his stupid smug face.

Keanu reeled back and crashed into his two friends, cursing and clutching at his nose. Using the opportunity, I ducked under his arm and ran. My feet pounded against the pavement as I took a back road up from Bobby's, making a beeline for the forested area nearby. Behind me, I could hear shouts as Keanu and his crew took up chase.

It wasn't enough that Keanu was already the head of the strongest clan on the Homestead, basically pissing money everywhere he walked. No. He was also going to get every nickel *I* managed to save for the next thirty years and then some. Couldn't the man just wait a few weeks to legally rob me blind?

I reached for my leiomano, came away with nothing but empty air, and swore remembering that I'd left it at home. A stupid mistake. Now, I was about to pay for it by getting jumped by those assholes. I pumped my arms faster and raced up the hill. If I could make it to the woods, I could hide long enough to find a spell worth using.

The fishmonger had been right. A head who had to sprint away from an attack was indeed manini. My body heated up as I ran, but I couldn't tell if it was the exercise, embarrassment, or shame fueling my speed. The trail narrowed as I reached the top of the hill, and I flew off the path and through the trees.

I slowed intentionally as I entered the deeply shaded part of the woods, navigating soundlessly over the fallen logs and forest floor strewn with branches. Keanu and his friends were close. At the mouth of the park, I heard shouts as the three men made it to the entrance and I used their noise as a signal to stop and lay myself flat to the ground behind a tree.

Keanu's voice rose above the others. "She couldn't have gotten far."

Their tones hushed, and I could hear their heavy feet as they crashed through the bush, searching for me. There wasn't time to waste.

With my adrenaline pumping, it was difficult to move slowly, but any wild motion, even by accident, was sure to catch their attention, so I forced myself to lie still. A bird chirped overhead, and I turned my face upward, peering through the blanket of leaves. Above the blue sky faded to shades of pink and orange as the sunset peeked back.

I wracked my brain trying to think if I had any spell specifically crafted for the forest. Nature-based Hawaiian magic would be ideal, but I couldn't risk trying something too combative or, with my personal jinx, I might end up hurting myself as well. There had to be a non-dangerous way to fend them off. I silently mouthed the words to several spells I'd smithed in practice, trying to find one that would work. Trees. Leaves. Roots. I touched a finger to my mouth. That was it.

A hand curled around my ankle and pulled me backward while I screamed in surprise.

"Found her!" the man shouted.

I kicked loose of his grip and jumped to my feet to run, but Keanu's friend muttered a spell under his breath in a language I didn't recognize, and a bolt of blue zapped toward me. I leapt out of the way, crashing into another tree so hard that the bark scraped across my left shoulder.

"E huli nā aʻa iā kākou!" I yelled in defense, throwing my hands out in front of me.

The man flinched back but nothing happened. We awkwardly stared at each other until realization dawned on him and a slow smile spread on his lips. Of all the times, my magic had decided to act up *now*.

"Better run, bitch," he hissed.

I ran.

Panting, I jumped over obstacles, still trying to be as careful as I could on the uneven forest floor. One misstep and I'd sprain my ankle, leaving me at the whim of these jerks. Screw that.

It should've worked.

Failure stung as I bit the inside of my cheek and scrambled away from my pursuers. All the spells I'd smithed were well tested. They'd worked before, so there was no reason this one should've died like that unless I'd missed something big.

Casting required three fundamentals: intention, incantation, and utteration. You had to know what you wanted the spell to do, have the spell crafted to fit that intention, and then you simply said it out loud. I hadn't missed anything essential. The last time I'd used that same spell, the roots of the forest had jumped up to trip us all.

Kākou, I realized, nearly hitting myself for how stupid I'd been. That word specified *groups*. My smithing hadn't worked because there'd been only one man in front of me and I hadn't adjusted the spell to fit. It was such a rookie error, I wanted to cry. Hawaiian pronouns didn't follow English rules. I should've realized. Should've known better.

I had two choices left: Tweak the spell on the fly or wait until all three of them were in front of me. Logic leaned toward the former, but my mind was a giant blank page. For the life of me, I couldn't remember the correct word that specified *two* people. Wait to get attacked by all three it would have to be, then. Fun.

My wish was granted sooner rather than later as I made an abrupt turn and slammed into Keanu. He grunted and pushed me off him so that I fell on my ass. In the distance, the rest of their trio scampered toward us while my heart matched their frantic pace.

"Just hand over your cash and I won't hurt you," he said.

"I *need* it," I said.

One of his friends came into view. "Not our problem."

I flipped them off and Keanu's expression turned like spoiled milk.

At this point his friends had both caught up and were strolling over toward us. I tried to scramble away, but Keanu grabbed me by my shoulder and dragged me back.

"Take her wallet," Keanu ordered.

I felt a hand smooth over my bottom and jerked away from its touch but was met by a rough pair of arms that held me in a chokehold from behind. The friend laughed. "She's a fighter, huh?"

"And a huge pain in my ass," Keanu agreed. I moved to the right side, bringing down my left hand in a fist to hit him in the groin. Keanu dropped to his knees, while I leapt away from him.

Now free, I raised my palm and repeated my failed spell from earlier. "E huli nā aʻa iā kākou!" *Turn the roots upon them.*

This time, the result was instantaneous. The trees around us groaned as their roots and branches shot from the ground toward my captors. One of the men screamed as a sturdy brown bough tangled itself around his ankle. He yelped as the branch pulled him upward, his body hanging limply as he dangled from the levitating piece of wood.

That wasn't right. I had wanted to trip them, not hold them above the ground. Something had gone wrong—again. The tree began tossing the invader from branch to branch, as if the forest had turned into a mosh pit and the guy was crowd-surfing. It was trying to throw the group out, rather than attacking.

"What the hell?" the other man asked. He stared after his friend for a moment too long, giving enough time for a root to snag him, too. He howled in protest as the same thing began happening to him.

I was too busy watching the whole ordeal to notice that Keanu had leapt for me. His body slammed into mine, and we went rolling down a hill. He was done talking now. His fingernails ripped across my denim shorts as he tried to reach my cash. I fought back, but Keanu had a good fifty pounds on me and a mean streak that no one alive could match. It ended a second later with his hand pressed against my cheek, pinning me to the ground. He pulled out my wallet triumphantly.

"You asshole," I squeezed out with the limited air that was left to me. "That's mine."

Keanu grinned. "Not anymore."

A root shot toward him as if pissed at the insolence, but he dodged it and took off. Keanu didn't spare a glance back at me as he ran down the path, expertly vaulting over the branches that tried to trip him on the way out.

I stood to chase after him, when the air in my lungs was torn out of me, as a swift pull on my ankle hoisted me above the ground. I shouted in surprise as I was swept up in my own spell. My magic had somehow decided I was also a part of its curse.

"No!" I yelled in frustration as the branches tossed me back and forth. But it was useless to protest. I'd made a mistake and included myself in my own spell. *Turn the roots upon* us. Dammit.

The forest moved faster than Keanu did, and as I passed overhead, he laughed and shouted, "Thanks for the early deposit. I'll take it off what you owe me at the end of the month."

He had my money and pride in his fingers, and I wanted nothing more than to chop them off with a blunted blade. But all I could do was scream in frustration as I was hauled away. At the edge of the glade, I was discourteously dumped out of the woods, where I landed in a belly flop on the hard earth.

I dusted myself off, swearing and shaking as I plucked leaves out of my matted hair and surveyed the various scrapes that had imprinted across my body like I was a pincushion. The side of my stomach where I'd fallen had it the worst. A big green bruise was beginning to form on the left of my abdomen.

Rest and an ice pack would have the mark ugly yet healed by tomorrow, but still, this stung. Knowing there was squat I could do in my current state, I wiped a hand across my scowl and trekked back to Bobby's.

Keanu and his friends were nowhere in sight. I spotted my car, sitting where I left her, and pulled my keys out. They hadn't taken those at least. I reached for the front door handle, and it pulled open in my grip. My eyebrows shot up. I hadn't locked the car.

Hobbling over to the back, I tugged on the trunk until it popped open. My heart dropped the second I saw the overturned cooler. Chips of ice had melted into a puddle on the felted fabric of the back of my car, which distinctively did not smell of fish.

It was all gone.

Fish was pretty high up on the list of things for folks to steal, and I had left several meals' worth packed, chilled, and unguarded at the busiest part of the Homestead.

Tears pricked at the corners of my eyes, but I wiped them away. No one was around, but the hills had eyes around here, and the last thing I needed was a rumor whipping up around town about the Petrova head crying like a baby because she'd been careless. Because she'd gotten jumped. Because she was *weak*.

Since there was nothing else to do, I dumped the rest of the ice out onto the road, loaded the cooler back into the trunk, and drove home in silence, ready for the day to be over.

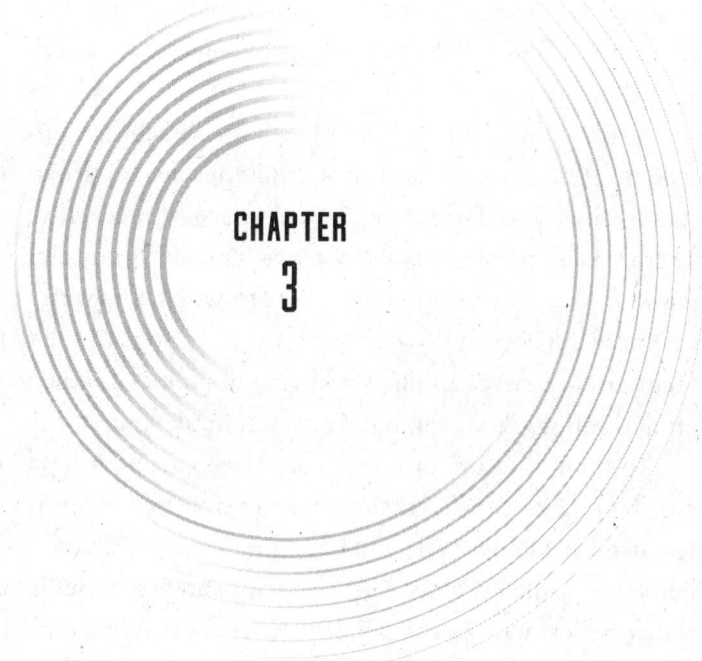

CHAPTER 3

The next day, I pulled into the driveway of our home after a long morning in LA. My usual clients had all grown cold feet, and I hadn't made a single deal.

Keanu hadn't stolen much, but it was enough to hurt. I'd need to find extra work, which meant more trips into the city.

I clenched my fist until the knuckles on my hand went white then relaxed, noticing the slight tremor in my fingers. There was nothing I could do to get that money back and stressing about it would only drive me up a wall. I needed to focus on what to do next and keep moving forward. Calm. Collected. Head of our clan.

Maybe if I repeated that enough, it would become true.

I opened the small door in the garage that led to our smithy and pulled on the hanging cord for the light. It flickered on and I rubbed the jeering headache rioting in my temples. A foggy head meant my work would be that much more difficult. I looked up at the corkboard nailed over the worktable and stared ruefully at the only order I had left to finish. With yesterday's cash gone, my deadline had been moved up.

A townie would pay good money for a spell that made his plants bloom faster. Luckily, this person just needed to grow flora of the stand-still-and-look-pretty variety. A waste of space, if you asked me. There was no point in plants that weren't edible or medicinal, but people who lived in the city didn't seem to worry about things like that. LA's near-impenetrable wards kept magi out, so people had the time to focus on their never-ending whirlwind of politics and petty feuds. The Homestead was rougher, but it was also more honest.

To the left of the order was a whiteboard with my notes. I refocused on the test spell, rubbing a finger over the ink until I smudged a few lines. Although Papa and I had messed around with a similar idea before, we called it quits when the fruit and veg came out tasting like soda crackers with skim milk. If Papa couldn't wring out a half-decent spell with his green thumb, then no one could. Magic was finicky. It didn't like giving away things for free.

I picked up a notebook, scanning the jotted variations I'd already attempted, written in my own special shorthand. I'd been playing with this spell for days with no success. None of the phrases I'd cobbled together had made the cut, and we needed the cash now.

Using Hawaiian had been my gut instinct since Hawaiian was an inherent catalyst for spells that altered natural elements, but I couldn't guarantee the buyer would get the pronunciation right. The oral limitations of Hawaiian made it less than ideal as a product. Unfortunately, it was also the language that worked best for me, so despite crafting some amazing formulas, selling them outside the Homestead was difficult.

It didn't take me long to realize I'd need a written spell. With my limited repertoire, that meant English or Russian, both of which were a problem. Written spells were too clunky for me, often leading to things going *boom* by accident. I wasn't the most poetic, a key quality for any written spell. Since magic fundamentals dealt heavily with intent, casting a spell without a very clear idea of what you wanted to happen usually went awry. In English, iambic pentameter or a few good bars worked wonders, but I wasn't lyrical enough for that, so I had switched to Russian. So far, the Slavic language had yielded the best results, but it still wasn't quite right.

I grabbed a pen off a shelf and pulled a chair over to the table. Situating myself off-kilter with one ankle under my butt, I bit on the tip of the pen while I scribbled some ideas down. Scattered across the table were various dictionaries I'd been perusing that were earmarked with notes in the margins. A copy of *Advanced Russian Grammar* was face down on a chapter about participles, the bane of my existence.

My head continued to throb, and I scrunched my mouth into a sharp frown while tapping my pen furiously against the page. In its current form, the spell *did* make flowers grow faster but seeds still took days to sprout. I needed something immediate to prove to the buyer that I wasn't scamming him. Identifying the problem—in this case, timing—was helpful, but the words I needed didn't fit the rhyme I had already built. If the spell didn't rhyme, it'd flop—every language had its quirks, and this was the challenge with Russian.

I chewed again on the pen, ruining the cap, as I felt out the right sounds. "O divnova krasa stsvetok raspucty luchectiy . . ." I mumbled, writing down the words I needed to use. The word *flower* was killing me. "What the hell rhymes with *svetok*?" I asked aloud.

"You're thinking too hard. Try *lepestok*," someone at the door said.

I scratched my head and turned to see my grandfather, his eyes squinting at me over his spectacles.

That would work. I crossed out what I had written, putting down his suggestion instead. The words ran through my mind as I dragged my fingers along the text, the magic buzzing familiarly under my touch, a little *click* going off in my head like the turning of a key in a lock. That word was the missing piece; now it all fit together like it was supposed to.

Papa Ivan patted my shoulder. "You should've come to me, vnuchka." Tall and fair, Papa was the opposite of Nana Kūlia in every way. Nana Kūlia still had softness in her physique, but he was like a rock wall. Despite his advancing age, he had muscles like cantaloupes running down his arms. Papa's gray hair and beard were always well groomed, so he never looked scruffy, even if the rest of him was typically covered in dirt and sweat from the gardens.

"I didn't want to bother you," I said as I finished writing the spell on paper, then tucked it into an orange envelope.

He winked at me, his light-blue eyes wrinkling behind his round frames. "There's no shame in asking. Russian is my mother tongue, after all."

I nodded, but the muscles in my neck tensed. Despite what Papa Ivan said, I always swallowed a prescribed dose of humiliation every time I turned to him or Nana Kūlia for help. Nana could joke about dying but the thought of them gone made me sweat.

When my ancestor had died before passing on her mana o ka moʻokūʻauhau, we'd lost more than just our family spell—we'd lost our connection to the past. Every head since had done their best to reclaim bits and pieces in their own way, but it was never enough. Nana Kūlia, for example, had sought wisdom in the words of our ancestors and used ʻōlelo noʻeau as the basis of her casting.

That hadn't worked for me, though. The old proverbs' mana ran like a river through my veins, more likely to let loose a tempestuous storm than a gentle rainfall. The time I'd accidentally summoned a tsunami when trying to bring in slightly higher surf for the summer, Nana stopped instructing me in casting and sent me to Papa instead. Papa didn't speak Hawaiian but he understood the mechanics of language. In time, I learned that magic could work for me, as long as I was exacting and specific. However, Hawaiian still had my heart. I was determined to learn my true mother tongue.

It wasn't easy, and I still wasn't fluent. Part of this was due to my lack of formal education and training. Bigger, stronger clans, like the Mahiʻais, had pronunciation schools, where they taught their own family spells. I'd never be allowed in unless I ceded my rights as head and joined their clan. Frankly, I'd rather be bashed in the head with a canoe paddle. And even if I'd had lessons, no one *smithed* in Hawaiian anymore. It was deemed too unpredictable, and people didn't care to mess with it when the spells that they already had worked just fine. The Homestead didn't fix what wasn't broken.

The other part of my failure, though, was lack of talent. Papa Ivan was the best teacher one could ask for, but I was a terror. A simple translation took me hours, and each new word I committed to memory was a struggle. I'd seen other Smiths—licensed ones—hop effortlessly between languages like breathing. Must be nice to be so gifted.

Papa Ivan noticed the curtain of doubt fall across my brow and pulled me to my feet. "Have you been working on our mana o ka moʻokūʻauhau?" he asked.

"No," I said, though I was sure he knew it was a lie.

I spent any spare time I had trying to craft a family spell that would be worthy of a great clan. All real clans had a mana o ka moʻokūʻauhau, a secret smithing that was handed down from generation to generation. In LA, they graded family spells on power alone, but here in the Homestead, they were required to aid the land we lived on. So far, my attempts had been futile.

He chuckled. "Don't force things, Kea. Smithing is not only about all the words we know but about a deeper feeling of *rightness*; the right word used at the right time in the right place. You feel this connection between our language and the mana around us better than anyone I know. It's your gift."

I snorted and pressed my face into Papa, smelling the dirt and grass that seemed to permanently stick to his skin. "I'd rather be fluent."

Sympaths were those born with innate magic that worked regardless of whether or not they casted. They could feel mana on another level, making it possible to sense attacks before they landed or use others' own mana to influence their state of mind. At first, people had thought the ability hereditary, but researchers slowly realized it was nothing like that. Sympathetic abilities stemmed from one's name. Once that became common knowledge, there was a sudden influx of little baby Herculeses and Storms, but mana wasn't so easy to control. Kids named Hercules ended up with the ability to speak to snakes, while others were supernaturally good at clearing clogged pipes, and Storms found they could influence people's anger rather than the weather.

Makani, for example, meant "gust." I'm sure my aunt didn't think that would translate to telepathy. Or not exactly telepathy, but something close. Makani said he gave his whispers to the wind and let it carry them to who he wanted. As for my name, Kealaokaleo meant "the path of the voice." Very pretty and all, but all it meant in practice was that I could feel the flow of mana around me acutely. It gave me a nice little heads-up right before people cast, though I couldn't do much to avoid getting hit.

Papa Ivan sighed and patted the top of my head, just like he'd done since I was little. "Fluency doesn't guarantee that one is adept with mana."

"It helps," I argued, my voice whinier than I wanted.

Papa spoke like a Smith, like he had all the time in the world to tinker with words. But that was an unrealistic goal. I wanted to be able to fight, to protect my family.

Nearly all Smiths could cast, but since the title of Caster was more closely associated with combat, the professions required different skill sets. Magic users typically specialized in one or the other. Talented Casters like Keanu might not be able to make up their own smithings, but their encyclopedic knowledge of regulated magic on command was far more desirable in a pinch than the slow, methodical work of a Smith. Especially a Smith who cobbled together spells from a patchwork of different languages with only half an understanding of each. I had no doubt that Keanu saw himself as a better leader than me. He was so convincing that even I wasn't so sure that he was wrong. The bruise on my stomach ached and I flinched.

Papa's eyes clouded with worry, and he shut my notebook for me. "Eat. You'll feel better after."

He guided me along back to the house and we entered from the side door that connected the garage to the kitchen, where the regular chaos of mealtime was in full swing. Makani had been scrubbed red and was sitting on the couch in the living room while Nana Kūlia yelled different half commands to the kids, slamming down plates of rice, salad, sautéed vegetables, and moʻo on the table.

"Food's ready!" she chirped as she took a seat.

Papa Ivan sat next to her, kissing Nana on her cheek. My grandmother giggled and blushed like a young girl. Makani rolled his eyes at them and stuck his finger in his mouth to fake gag while Sisi sat across from Papa, leaving the chair to her left empty, which I claimed. My other cousin Newt shoveled food into his mouth with an alarming speed that didn't match his wiry frame. Teenagers were terrifying creatures.

Makani pinched his mouth together when Nana dropped a piece of fried moʻo on top of his rice. "Gross. I'm not going to eat that."

The smell from the heavily spiced meat wafted upward, and I caught the scent of shoyu and sharp ginger. "It's not that bad," I said, emphatically taking a large bite. The texture of the meat was like chicken, but the flavor reminded me of a bland white fish. It was unnerving to have the taste of both chicken and fish on my tongue, but I forced myself to swallow. It wasn't bad, just weird. Lizard leftovers were going to be on rotation for the next few weeks, so it was better to get used to it.

Makani hadn't touched his food and instead pushed the meat, rice, and salad around his plate, sticking his tongue out at me when no one else was looking. I ignored him as best I could, but he wasn't exactly being subtle. After a few minutes, I wasn't surprised to feel Nana's glare on me.

"Something you want to say, Kea?" Nana prodded. I looked down at my food while my grandmother sucked in her cheeks and tapped her nails on the table.

I don't want to was a poor reason to disobey, so I set down my fork. "Makani, I shouldn't have yelled at you yesterday," I said.

His eyes were glued to a particularly interesting grain of rice. "It's okay."

I took a deep breath. "No, it's not."

I meant it. Getting the first words out had been the dam breaking, and it took all I had to contain the overwhelming feeling of drowning. I cleared my throat and caught his gaze. "I'm sorry."

Nana Kūlia nodded approvingly then rolled up the left sleeve of her shirt so we could see her shoulder tattoo, our family crest. The image was of an alkonost, a mythical Slavic creature with the head of a beautiful woman and the body of a bird, her feathers the color of fire. Our family saying swirled on the scroll wrapped around her body, which was grasped tightly in her right talon. Unlike the other clans on the Homestead, ours was a matriarchy, which meant our surname changed with every generation. As a tradition, so did the crest, to better reflect the heritage of our head's spouse. However, the ʻōlelo noʻeau that we lived by was never altered.

"I ka ʻōlelo no ke ola, i ka ʻōlelo no ka make," Nana read out loud.

Roughly translated: *In language there is life; in language there is death*. For me, the proverb was a constant reminder to watch what my dumb mouth said. Especially since I had a nasty habit of accidentally casting spells that turned dangerous.

"Kealaokaleo Petrova," Nana continued, using the force of my full name, "with our magic, we can't afford to be careless with what we say." She turned to Makani, her eyes sharp. "You too, Makani Palakiko. Or do you really want Kea to drop dead?"

Makani met my eyes, pushing quietly into my thoughts. *I don't want you to die, Kea.*

That was as much of an apology as I would ever get from him. He didn't say anything out loud, but he did finally take a bite of dinner.

We ate in idle chatter. The soft hum of Sunday supper lulled us into complacency when suddenly, Sisi shot to her feet. My sister stood up so quickly that she tipped over the salad bowl, sending lettuce and balsamic vinaigrette tumbling over the rest of our meal.

"What's happening?" I asked, seeing my sister's green eyes haze over to white as her sympathetic ability took hold. I reached for her hand, and the taste of Sisi's magic filled my mouth with sweet orange. My own ability wasn't nearly as useful as Sisi's, since all I could manage to do was experience mana with an extra sense. I could taste people's sympathetic magic, if they had any, and was better than most at feeling the flow of mana.

"Someone just stepped over the ward around the property," Sisi muttered, her brow furrowed as she focused on the intruder's presence. Wards either protected you from people or magi, unless you were rich enough to afford the stuff that worked on both, which we weren't. We were lucky to have one at all.

The family froze. Only someone who didn't mean us harm could get over, but we weren't expecting any guests tonight. An uninvited nighttime visitor never boded well.

"Is it a raid?" Nana asked, the words tight.

Sisi's brow furrowed as she delved deeper into her latent magic. "No. There's just one person."

"Who?" I asked, getting to my feet.

Sicilia closed her eyes, and I felt the mana around us prickle slightly against her skin. The air tingled with static. Finally, Sisi's eyes fluttered open. "Ha'aheo."

And I thought this week couldn't get any worse.

~

Ha'aheo Lin called a short hui as he walked up the steps to our house, but that was as far as he'd get. I met him on the porch, blocking his entrance.

In his thirties, Ha'aheo sported black curls that flopped haphazardly across the crown of his head, angled hazel eyes, and sun-kissed skin. He sat on the Homestead Council with Keanu, the only two remaining heads after Basilio's withdrawal and the Palakikos' demise. Between the two, I preferred Keanu. The man might be an ass, but at least he was honest about it.

"It's late," I said shortly. "And you're interrupting dinner." I narrowed my eyes and crossed my arms tightly around my chest.

"Nice to see you, too," he drawled casually. "You look good."

That was a lie. I didn't look good. I was bent out of shape, like a

Slinky that had gone off the steps and rolled to the bottom of a staircase. If Haʻaheo was paying compliments, especially false ones, that spelled trouble.

"What do you want?" I said, refusing to take the bait.

Haʻaheo pulled a single curl from his head until it unwound then let go. A childhood habit that had never left him. "Someone from the city dropped by the council today," he began, "looking for Smiths that worked with Hawaiian."

I kept my face perfectly neutral. "We don't have any Hawaiian Smiths on the Homestead."

It was technically true. There were only three registered Smiths here, all of whom specialized in either Mandarin or Japanese. And while I did smith in Hawaiian, none of my spells were official. The smithing exams were notoriously difficult even for the exceptionally talented, which meant they were impossible for me. The exam could only be taken in a language regulated by Los Angeles, meaning Latin, French, Italian, Spanish, Arabic, Mandarin, Cantonese, or Japanese. I spoke a grand total of zero of those.

Most passed in Latin, the universal language of academia. While I'd had the same classes as any other kid in the States, I'd never been able to master even the basics. I'd taken and failed the smithing exam more times than I could count and eventually just gave up. I didn't need a license to sell spells on the Homestead, and the work I did do in the city was always kept under the table. Untraceable, or so I thought.

Haʻaheo's brows slanted as his eyes crinkled at the edges. "O ke ahi i ka mea e ʻai i nā mea a pau, a hiki i ka pau ʻana." He recited my spell so flawlessly that I was lucky nothing had been burning, or the magic would've snapped into place. Mana, for all its wonder, couldn't create something from nothing, and fire was one of those weird things you couldn't just make appear in spell crafting, at least not without some kind of spark.

"Pretty," I said, still playing dumb. I made a mental note to blacklist the old fisherman from Bobby's, since he was either in Haʻaheo's pocket or too chatty for his own good.

Haʻaheo hit me with a discerning glare, unimpressed with my ruse. "You're a terrible actress. We both know only a desperate person would even attempt to write a new smithing." He sniffed the air and smiled. "And you reek of it, Kea."

I bristled. To Haʻaheo, any slipup by another head was a golden opportunity, and I refused to shine. "I don't answer to you."

The Homestead Council was less of a governing body and more our arm of diplomacy that talked to LA and resolved clan disputes that dragged on for too long. Haʻaheo's power came from his clan, not from his seat on the council.

He pulled an envelope out of his pocket, holding it between us. "Maybe not, but I'm sure you'll listen to reason if it comes in a different tune."

I reached out to take the envelope and tore open the top, noticing the insignia that adorned the letter's stationery, a statuesque figure grasping a sword in one hand and a balancing scale in the other. The Board's seal. My eyes slid down to the text.

Dear Ms. Petrova,

You are hereby summoned to appear before the Los Angeles Casters Board for a deposition.

I crumpled the paper without reading the rest, my head spinning. The letter was a death sentence. I'd always known selling black market spells might come back around to smack me in the face; I'd just never expected the hammer to fall from quite so high. It felt like a setup. The Board never involved themselves in petty crime like this. I glared at Haʻaheo, suspicious once more of his late-night visit. My endeavor to rejoin the council was no secret and I wouldn't put it past him to drop my name to the Board in order to remove me from the picture.

Right now, the only saving grace I had was a technicality. "The Homestead isn't a part of Los Angeles. They can't force me to attend," I said.

Haʻaheo's mask fell, and he took a step forward, closing the space between us. He jammed a finger at my face. "You *will* show up. I refuse to let you endanger us all with your stubbornness. The treaty expires next year, and we need to maintain peace with LA. With the Palakikos' revolt, we're on thin ice. We need to gain ground to negotiate better terms."

"You can't let the Board do what they want," I protested.

He frowned. "This is a small concession."

My nose crinkled, and I pushed his chest, so he stumbled back. Haʻaheo's words meant that my going to LA was a small concession on my part, but his tone implied something larger. I could see the puppeteer strings of his plan. *I* was the sacrifice he was willing to make to keep the rest of our community safe.

"I'm sure it was easy for you—for you to serve my name up on a silver platter," I stammered, rage flushing my limbs with the jitters.

Haʻaheo's mouth tightened. "When the Board showed up at the council, they already had your name. Three guesses who's actually to blame."

I didn't need three guesses. There was only one person from the Homestead that close to the Board, and I'd just spent the last few days ignoring his messages.

Basilio.

The bastard had decided to get me involved, whether I liked it or not.

My expression must've given me away, because a look of vindication touched Haʻaheo's eyes. "You may not believe me, but I care about the Homestead as much as you. Not all of us can fight the storm; some of us have no choice but to play the game."

"A rigged game," I argued.

"Do you have a different proposal?" he asked dryly.

I snapped my fingers. "Burn the pieces."

"Then no one gets to play."

"Maybe no one should."

I stared at Haʻaheo, purple-black shadows of the night dancing across his face. His breathing was in time with crashing waves below our property. The sound served as a constant reminder to never turn your back to the ocean.

"Such a child," he taunted. "You're losing, so you want to ruin everyone else's chance to win."

"That's not true."

I didn't want Keanu or Ha'aheo or even Basilio to fail. It was just that we were all running a pointless race. The rules changed on a whim, and whenever anyone got close to the finish line a pole would sweep out to take us down. The saboteur would blame a competitor instead of the ones making the rules, and things would devolve into a fistfight. They might refuse to see it, but I wouldn't become someone else's pawn.

"Show up," Ha'aheo warned as he made his way down the porch and back to his car. "I'll be sure to let the other clans know that you were given the opportunity to avoid a raid, so you won't be able to rely on us if they come for you. After the Palakikos' fall, I think we both know that you wouldn't stand a chance against the Board." He pressed a button on his key to unlock the door, which beeped happily in response.

Heat rushed through my body as a rock and a hard place crushed me from each side. "Go to hell."

Ha'aheo flashed another smile my way, but it was all teeth. A great white was circling us and there was blood in the water.

CHAPTER 4

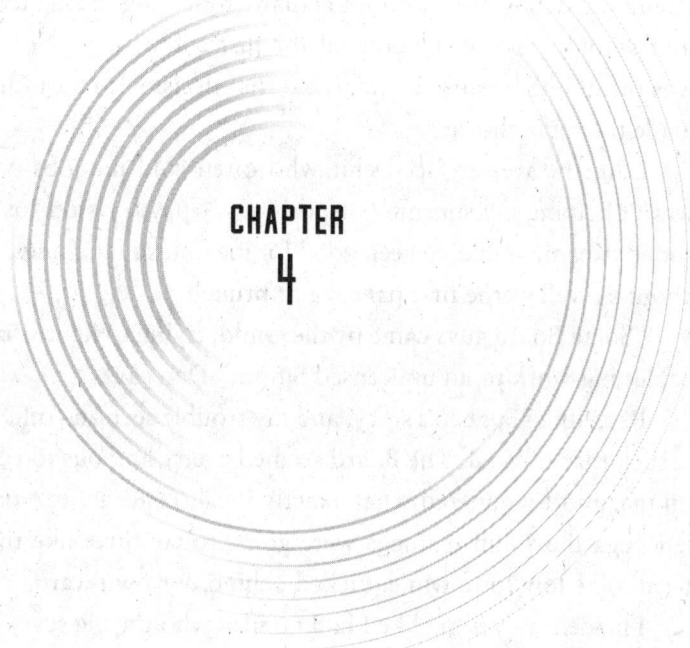

"What do you mean you can't hire me?" I asked Dan in disbelief.

Dan stuck his hands in the pockets of his worn jeans, and I felt my eye twitch in irritation. He only did that when he was taking a little extra off the top or laying down some bad news. We were meeting in the parking lot of a supermarket that was halfway between the suburbs of LA and the Homestead. The store behind Dan was a sullen gray block that stuck out in the otherwise flat land between the city and us. Part of what made LA's ward so effective was the large amount of buffer space between the border and any residential areas, so the gradation between the two communities was marked by the rapid growth of concrete. The closer you got to LA, the taller the buildings got and the closer they were squeezed together until cement was all you could see.

Ha'aheo's visit had ruined my beauty sleep, and I'd woken up irritable, deciding to head to town to make it look like I was going to attend the deposition, without actually following through. Hopefully, that would appease the council for just a few days. Now, my head was throbbing because I'd analyzed that decision to dust, unsure if I'd made the right choice.

Dan, the weasel-faced chit who often sold me jobs on the side, wasn't helping my sunshiny disposition. A payday after losing a large sum to Keanu would've been good for me but, so far, things were going about as well as the first pancake at brunch.

"Some Board guys came by the Guild, trying to figure out who was subletting work to an unlicensed Smith," Dan said.

Recalling Ha'aheo's story, and my trouble securing other contracts earlier, that tracked. The Board seemed pretty anxious to get its hands on me, and I wondered what exactly Basilio had done. Not my problem regardless, but if things were going to continue like this, I might need to lie low for a while, tucked behind our own wards.

I made my eyes big like I had no idea who the big scary guys were. "You think they were talking about me?"

My whole body hurt like hell. I had bruises up and down my torso from my tussle with the mo'o and the Three Stooges who'd jumped me at Bobby's. To hide my poor condition, I was currently baking alive in jeans and a long-sleeved T-shirt that my sweat was dampening at the pits. I was in no mood for fake flirting. The result was far more aggressive than I intended. Not sexy-aggressive. Just aggressive-aggressive.

"Could be," Dan said seriously. His buzzed head glimmered with sweat, and his plaid shirt hung limply off his wiry frame. Dan was an average-looking guy with a nervous streak that made him jumpy even when relaxed. Right now, Dan was not relaxed. There wasn't a single part of his body that hadn't fidgeted within the past five minutes, nether regions included.

"I—I don't think I can keep buying spells from you, Kea," he stammered.

Deep breath. Don't yell and scare him off.

I dropped my voice low, looking up at Dan from below my eyelashes and squeezing my arms into the sides of my chest in a way that made the goods impossible to ignore. "You aren't the only one buying from outside Smiths. They could've been looking for anyone."

"That's the thing." Dan gulped at my chest and blinked a few times before tearing his eyes away to nervously scan the parking lot. "They were asking about *unregulated* languages."

Languages were rarely banned outright anymore, as history had proven that incredibly challenging to enforce. Over time, the city had decided that elevating the few languages it deemed worthy was a far better policy. City regulation provided an incentive for Smiths to learn "preferred" languages, and after getting licensed, people rarely strayed from the "elite eight," though they could technically write in any tongue they chose. Unregulated languages came with liability, baggage, and the consumer perception of an inferior product when it came to selling spells. Meanwhile, regulation guaranteed cashflow, safety, and legal protection.

"There are plenty of unregulated languages. And Smiths," I countered. Part of the reason for that was price. Not everyone had the luxury of paying top dollar for spells from licensed Smiths. Moreover, every language came with its own quirks. Hawaiian, for example, was wildly inefficient at anything technology-based, and JavaScript couldn't be used for elemental manipulation.

Dan shifted his weight back on his heels, unconvinced. "They were asking about rogue *Austronesian* Smiths in particular. Someone who deals in death spells."

"I don't write death spells," I said. "That would be unethical."

Dan raised an eyebrow. "Like working without a license?"

"That's not the same."

"The Board would probably disagree."

I tried not to panic. I needed Dan as my middleman. With his name and license behind my work, no one looked twice. "Listen, no one will connect you to me. I've seen you piece together spells from Spanish and French, and you don't speak either language." The fake compliment tasted acidic on my tongue.

"I'm sorry, Kea," he said. "It's bad for business."

"This has been working for us," I protested.

"Things have changed." Before I could say more, he shoved an envelope into my hands and loaded himself jerkily into his car, the door catching on his shirt.

I tapped on the window, but he was already shifting to reverse and the vehicle ripped backward. It hit a speed bump on its way out with enough force to send his wheels bouncing, then he tore into the street. Yelling in frustration, I kicked the concrete parking curb with my foot and a sharp stab of pain shot up my leg as my toe accidentally hit the slab. I sat down on the cement block, head in my hands and the envelope in my lap. Dan had just driven off with all my remaining job opportunities in his shitty Ford Fiesta. I cursed again, up at the sky this time.

Could today get any worse?

Eventually, I calmed down enough to open the envelope. Nothing was missing. In fact, he had thrown in an extra couple bills. That was worse. It meant he felt bad and was easing the guilt with some cash. Bending the envelope in half, I put the whole of it into my front pocket, too paranoid to keep it anywhere but directly on my person.

When I lifted my head, I noticed someone across the lot from me, standing still among the swell of people pushing to enter the store, like a rock in a river. The contrast between him and the crowd was enough to make me stare.

He couldn't claim to be six feet tall, but he had enough lean muscles to make up for the height. Dressed sharply in a slim, black suit, the man stood out in the sea of T-shirts and jeans. His features were obscured by a pair of large sunglasses and he had long, straight, black hair tied into a low bun. He took a drag of his cigarette and flicked the butt onto the cement, blowing out a trail of smoke to his side before turning his attention to me.

His presence disturbed the mana around us in a way that made my sympathetic magic register him as a threat even without him using his power. I'd bet my life that he was a Caster. He walked into the road with large strides, and I admired the ease with which he moved, like a martial artist or dancer. His pretty face didn't hurt either.

He was about halfway across the parking lot when I realized that he was coming straight for me, staring at *me*. Jumping to my feet, I turned and walked a few quick steps to my left, darting in and out between parked cars that were near to keep myself calm. Surely, I was imagining it. I pivoted on my heels and turned back toward the entrance of the store, scanning for the man. That was a mistake.

In the few seconds my back had been turned, he'd advanced ten paces on me and was quickly closing the distance between us. He peered above the rim of his sunglasses, and my breath caught.

Mana came with a toll, and most powerful Casters had a physical trait permanently altered in some way from years of pulling large amounts of mana into their cores. Most just happened to be slightly taller than average or had nails and hair that grew faster than a normal person's. But if Casters specialized in one field of magic, their mana might warp around that element. Nana had known a Caster back in the day who'd primarily dealt with elemental wind spells. After a while, she said, the guy's hair just kind of always floated around him, like he was constantly being hit with a blow-dryer. It was a nice story. Cute, even.

Cute didn't fit this guy at all.

His magic had turned his eyes red. I'd heard of mana altering eye color to be brighter or duller, but I knew of only one person whose eyes were so vividly unnatural, having seen him on the news countless times before. There was no way Sora Kaiser—the youngest member of the Board, LA's most feared Caster, the man who'd single-handedly won the right of regulation for both Chinese and Japanese—was chasing me through a supermarket parking lot right now.

Impossible or not, I turned right around and ran, figuring that at worst I'd look like a nut. In this case, social norms be damned. Survival favored the cautious. The man broke into a sprint the second I picked up the pace and my fear escalated to a throbbing in the center of my throat. I hated being right.

He was fast. A second into our chase, and he was already close enough that I could hear his breathing at my back. I needed to get to my car. If I could make a false move and ditch him between the other parked vehicles, I'd have enough time to jump into the driver's seat and take off. A tingle sparked at the nape of my neck as I felt him pull for mana. Sparing a second to look over my shoulder, I saw the mana around us tunnel toward my pursuer. When it reached him, the magic swirled into his gut and he breathed it in, a natural siphon of the energy as he prepared to cast.

Casting required tapping into the mana that flowed through the world and drawing it inside oneself. Every person's capacity for holding mana was different—it was like everyone had a little jar of predetermined size inside them. If a Caster overextended themselves and tried to fill up with too much, their jar would shatter, and they'd go *pop*. This man had just pulled an ungodly amount of mana into himself without breaking a sweat. Not a good sign.

I stopped mid-run to square off, ready to divert his spell as best I could. His eyebrows curved up as I positioned myself to deflect the blow, but he didn't falter and continued to breathe deeply, arms raised and hands relaxed in half fists. Even more mana flowed to his center. I stuck out a palm, trying to come up with a word that would hold him back before he could release his spell, but I was too slow.

He reached for my extended wrist, reflexively grabbing onto my arm and shifting his weight as he spun, taking me with him. The ground came up to my face. Using my free arm, I tried to cushion my fall against the pavement. In that moment, his other arm pushed onto my back as he redirected his magic into a carefully timed attack that left me distracted and defenseless.

Fuyu no mizu
Ugoki ga tomaru
Shizushziu ni.

His voice was deeper than I'd expected considering his stature, and sent a bout of goose bumps down my arm. My body froze as the spell took hold. It locked me into place as I lay stiff against the ground, my cheek pressed against loose stones of asphalt. I wasn't even able to scream. The pressure of his hands against my skin lifted and I watched, furious, as his feet came into view, my eyes focusing on the shiny tops of his black oxfords.

He had a precise command over both movement and magic, as if his spell was aided by the control he had of his body. I'd seen a similar attack style a few times in televised duels. Kotodama was a method of breath, movement, and language that was specialized for close combat. A practice exclusively used by the Kaiser clan.

Above me, he sighed. "Finding you was unnecessarily difficult. Worse, you've made me run in a suit."

If he expected a response, he was going to be disappointed. My jaw was jammed shut and both my arms were stuck, pressed up against my body at an uncomfortable angle.

"If you'd bothered to listen to my very polite request, things would've been easier for us both," he continued. I felt his hands below me and my instinct to move away kicked in, but my limbs weren't listening; I remained completely limp. He hauled me up from the ground, throwing me over his shoulder in a fireman's carry. I wasn't a light woman, and he grunted under my deadweight. "Like I said. Difficult."

My mind raced as I struggled to process what had just happened. I was by no means good at casting, but I was excellent at defense. Yet in a single move he'd incapacitated me, using my own body against me. There was only one rational explanation.

Despite the mounting pile of evidence, I prayed to any and all the gods that this man wasn't who I thought he was. For one, he wasn't doing a very good job at carrying me. My nausea grew as I watched the pavement pass below. An engine roared behind my head, and then I heard the creak of a door opening. He heaved me off his back and into his arms, struggling to push me into the backseat of a car that had pulled to the curb.

"Mr. Kaiser," a pleasant baritone called from the front, "where to?"

Sora Kaiser, dangerous and irritating, gave me a disappointed look as he put my seat belt on. My stomach flipped as his scalding glare found mine. I'd known the Board members were strong but seeing that expertise on full display had been staggering.

"Griffith Hall," he said.

The door slammed shut, and the car sped off to Los Angeles.

~

After the Flood, the loosely structured feds claimed City Hall, but everyone knew they didn't have much power. The federal government was unable to adapt quickly to the changing reality of magic. They pushed the responsibility of defense and order onto the cities, and from the chaos, LA emerged as one of the strongest alongside powerhouses like New York, Chicago, and Houston. City-states were the true governing forces now, and the Los Angeles Casters Board was as strong as they came. The Board had settled on converting the former Griffith Observatory into their own official residence, expanding the structure to create several green copper domes that enclosed the park in a semicircle. Griffith Hall, as a shining city on a hill, was a fitting palace for the reigning Board and no expense had been spared.

The car pulled to a stop at the entrance, and my door opened with Sora Kaiser looming over me. He leaned into the car, took my hands in his and kneaded the space below my thumbs, moving slowly and deliberately upward. The motion was so intimate that I ached to snatch away my hands, but there was nothing I could do other than stare and blush. He pinched the end of each of my fingers while reciting his spell.

Harugakuru
Mizu gu mezameru
Umi ni nige.

The restraints of his magic faded, allowing me to move again.

"Are you going to walk or do I have to carry you in like a sack of potatoes?" he asked, righting himself after he'd finished breaking the odd trance that had kept me stuck to my seat.

"I—I'll walk," I stammered. I pushed his hands away and got out of the car.

Sora moved toward the building. I followed numbly up the steps, grateful that he hadn't looked too carefully at my face, which was still flushed.

Inside the main rotunda, a holdover from the old world decorated the ceiling. Even though I struggled to make heads or tails of the biblical mix of sepia-toned gods and angels, a pang of pity struck me when my sight landed on the straining Atlas. If he moved a toe, the balance would tip, and he'd be crushed under the weight. I could relate.

We walked through a circular hall with checkered floors and on to one of the renovated additions, an oblong room accented by an onyx table in the shape of an inverted teardrop. I scanned the faces of my judges, a mounting pressure building in my chest. The whole Board was assembled, now that Sora was here. Seven in total.

An older man with cropped black hair streaked white and thin lips glanced at Sora and me. He commanded that we sit and I obliged, falling into the seat at the tip of the teardrop. Reagol Stone. Nicknamed "the Backbone," Reagol was second only to the head of the Board and was about as cuddly as a sea urchin.

"This is Kealaokaleo Petrova," Sora stated as he walked to an empty seat near Reagol. The fact that he had said my name perfectly on a first try was disconcerting. No one ever pronounced my full name correctly.

A striking Black woman looked at me in disbelief as she tossed her intricately braided hair over her shoulder and scoffed. "*She's* the one that's taken days to track down?" A hint of a French accent, characterized by the softening of the letter *R*, tinged the woman's speech.

I wanted to feel indignant at her comment but couldn't. Every man in attendance was dressed in a crisp suit with a bold tie in primary colors. There were only three women, all immaculately dressed in neutral shifts and lethal-looking high heels. By comparison, I was still in a sweaty and now dirt-stained long-sleeved shirt. I didn't even want to think about the state of my hair.

"It's difficult to find qualified sources in unregulated languages," Reagol commented. "We must make do."

Not suspect. Not criminal. But . . . *source*?

Something was definitely wrong here. I glanced from member to member, trying to discern the nature of my summons today. I'd assumed that I was being charged with some sort of crime, but never in my wildest dreams had I imagined that I was being pursued by the Board as a language consultant. Even my nightmares weren't so bold.

Reagol cleared his throat and waved with his right hand, gesturing to a hall at the side. A door opened, and a uniformed bailiff led in another person in a suit. Basilio blinked as he shuffled into the room, adjusting his wrinkled lapel and smoothing down the front of his button-down. When he saw me, his face relaxed. Basilio was guided to a chair midway between me and the Board, and he sat.

I straightened to attention. This wasn't my trial. It was his.

A flood of emotions whipped through me. I'd known that Basilio was likely the one who had dragged me by the hair into this mess, but I'd guessed it was as cannon fodder. I stared at my former friend, fighting off pity for him.

"This is the woman you mentioned?" Reagol asked. "The one who can explain why it would've been 'impossible' for you to murder Angelo Reyes?"

"She's an expert in Hawaiian," Basilio agreed. "If you aren't willing to take me at my word, then please hear her out."

Expert wasn't exactly the word I'd use to define myself when it came to Hawaiian, especially given the recent fiasco with Keanu, but given the circumstances, I wasn't about to argue.

Reagol pointed at a perfect black circle at the center of the conference table, drawing my eye to its textured face. "Listen carefully," he commanded. He snapped his fingers and the device crackled to life, the audio half static. A mumbled voice echoed from the speaker, but the words were muffled and soft.

I leaned closer, straining to hear. The cadence and intonation of each vowel sounded distinctly Hawaiian, but it was impossible to discern specific words because the tenor was so low. At one point, I was certain I heard the word *au*, or *I*, but that was the only clear feature. Near the end of the recording, there was a cracking sound, a loud crash, and something like furniture tipping over. "It's difficult to make out," I said as the audio looped, replaying the incomprehensible spell.

"But it's definitely Hawaiian and not, say, Tagalog?" another man asked.

He was stout with dull gray hair and a short, neatly trimmed beard. He could've passed as someone's grandfather or an old man shuffling to a morning game of chess in the park, but I knew better. Matthew Greyson, the head of the Board, had a fierce reputation that made his bland looks a clever mask. Matthew sat at the center of the table, the dominating motto of the Board spread out behind him like wings, carved deep into the marble walls of the room, in imposing capital letters. FIAT JUSTIA PEREAT MUNDUS. *Let justice be done, even if the world must perish over it.*

The ancient Latin offered me no deep relief. In fact, it felt vaguely like a threat.

I nodded. Tagalog, despite being similar, sounded different from Hawaiian, with its sharp consonants a more prevalent thread through each spell. When you spent enough time with a language, even if not fully adept, it became a melody you could distinguish from others, even when the lyrics crossed over.

Basilio let out a deep breath, then slumped forward onto the table. "Like I said, my clan doesn't smith in Hawaiian."

His eyes found mine, and I held my breath. This was it. This was the moment Basilio would sell me out. I'd be turned into the Board as a rogue Smith and locked away in the desert, away from my family and the Homestead. All so he could save his own skin.

Basilio looked away. "No one does. The Homestead relies on spells passed down from generation to generation. Kea is the only one who's tried experimenting with the language beyond that."

My throat closed, and the tickle of a tear built at the corner of my eye.

I cataloged the seven people of the room again, noticing their drawn faces and curled lips. Disdain was an expression I was all too familiar with, but to see that vitriol directed at Basilio was new. His slouch deepened, and his hands on the table curled into tight fists. Once again, I was reminded of the merciless race in which we were pitted against each other, and the sour of noni fruit filled my mouth. In this game, we were all just pawns to those with power.

"You mean she's been smithing without a license," Sora countered.

"I don't need a license to sell spells on the Homestead," I argued, crossing my legs under the table.

Sora leaned back in his seat. "You *do* need one to sell in the city." He let the statement hang between us like litter, waiting to see if I'd stoop to pick it up.

"Which I don't," I challenged. Those red eyes searched for weakness, hungry and calculating, but I held his glare until he blinked.

"Mr. Reyes is a childhood friend of Miss Petrova. She might lie to protect him," a man said. He was blindingly handsome with severe black hair cut fashionably around his face, angular almond eyes, and skin so perfect he could've been wearing makeup.

"I can help with that," Sora offered.

Matthew's eyes slid to Sora, and gave a brief nod of approval. As commanded, Sora stood and cracked his knuckles as he approached me. With each step that he took, my body grew more rigid until I was as stiff as a plank. He reached out, fingers hovering over my head. "May I?"

I nodded and without any additional warning, there was a needle-like prick in my mind. Sora's eyes widened to the size of marbles. Though he never actually touched me, his hands dipped into my thoughts and feelings, swirling them around as he sorted through what he'd found.

His sympathetic magic was unlike anything I'd seen before, as if he could reach into the very heart of a person, laying bare their soul. He touched on the memory of the Palakikos' property, smoke rising from its ruins. Makani, standing with hollow eyes in our yard, tear stains dried down his round cheeks. I jerked away. There were some places one shouldn't tread.

Sora's hand lingered in the air a second longer before he withdrew it and calmly returned to his seat. "She's loyal, but not without reason. I'm confident in saying that she wouldn't cover for him."

"Which brings us back to the issue at hand," a woman concluded. She stood out, as she was dressed in a floor-sweeping beige dress with long sleeves and a sky-blue hijab draped gracefully across her head and neck. "The Tagalog clans had no reason to depose their own leader, especially when Angelo was so close to being admitted to the Board himself."

"Who says he was *close*?" Reagol muttered.

Matthew's sharp gray eyes found the woman who'd spoken. "Yet he's the only person with access, means, and most important of all, knowledge of both Hawaiian and Tagalog."

"I *don't use* Hawaiian," Basilio protested. "The family spell I shared with the Board to prove our loyalty was the only snippet my family had left, and we lost even that. That's why I asked for Kea to come. She, as a practitioner, can vouch for me."

Mana o ka moʻokūʻauhau were unique to each family and never shared outside of a clan. The only reason to surrender it to the Board was if you intended to join the city. New citizens were required to hand over their family's deepest magic to demonstrate fealty to Los Angeles. For Hawaiian, though, that very act would destroy the mana itself. The second a Hawaiian head wrote their mana o ka moʻokūʻauhau down in the Board's registry, every drop of that magic, mana that had been fine-tuned with each passing generation, would evaporate, its essence becoming no more than empty words. Basilio had sacrificed the one thing I craved more than anything in this world—for nothing.

The pain that stretched across Basilio's face hurt me more than I'd imagined. He'd tried to grasp at a brighter future and was now being punished for daring to want more. Basilio had never been like me, never willing to fight to the death or dig in his heels. He wanted comfort and safety for him and his clan, and I'd judged him for making that choice. In the end, it turned out the same for him, too. It wasn't fair. We deserved better.

Reagol clucked his tongue. "He's right. If the spell is Hawaiian, then the Tagalog clans are not involved. We're better off raiding the Homestead and taking each family's spell book until we find the murder weapon."

"A raid would be pointless," Basilio said. Hawaiian clans don't keep spell books. You'd need to interrogate each head and get them to recite it orally."

"The Homestead has always been a stubborn neighbor," the dark-haired Asian man argued. "I don't see their heads surrendering their magic unless pressured."

"Why not just eliminate the threat entirely?" Reagol suggested. "Our last expansion into their land gained us several dozen more citizens to help strengthen the city wards." Wards were built by a central power, be that a clan or a city, and used a process similar to a family spell in that they drew mana from every person in a clan. The more individuals one had, the stronger their wards and their collective magic became. "The universities have noted a sharp uptick in LA's magic reserves since, further protecting us from other city-states."

My jaw tightened. Reagol's casual categorization of the Palakikos' extermination as a win pulled my restraint taut. "You'd plough through an entire people to find a single criminal?" I asked.

The silence that fell on the room made clear that they'd forgotten my presence. To the Board, I was like the speaker on the conference room table, only expected to speak when someone else snapped their fingers.

"If the spell is Hawaiian, as you said," Reagol said, "then you are all guilty. Your people and language are representatives of your home. If you cannot be trusted to conduct yourselves in a manner that is civilized, then I see no reason to extend that same courtesy. The city demands fairness regardless of the price. Fiat justia pereat mundus."

"What you're describing isn't justice," I declared. "It's collective punishment."

The Board acted like they were the ultimate arbitrators of good, gifted with the right to punish or reward as they saw fit. As if they could grant us our freedom, then take it away whenever they deemed it necessary in the name of justice, safety, or whatever other incorporeal concept they'd landed on for the week.

I crossed my arms. "There's no need for such broad strokes. Just have your suspect recite in lingua veritas to ensure the spell belongs to them and punish the appropriate party."

In lingua veritas was one of the oldest magics known to man and a cornerstone of the smithing community. When recited, the magic of a spell became temporarily visible, turning its creator's tongue a metallic silver, thus proving ownership of any smithing.

"We have neither the time nor the linguistic skill to track down the assassin and re-smith the murderous spell," the Asian man argued. "The clans of LA are frightened and can only be quelled with *action*. They must see that we are taking Angelo's death seriously or there will be unrest. The Filipino clans have thousands of members and could flee to other city-states. Without their numbers and resources, Los Angeles's magic will wane."

"Let justice be done, even if the world must perish over it," I recited, throwing Reagol's words back at the entire Board. "Give me some time to find the culprit, and I'll decode the spell for you. You'll have your villain." And they wouldn't need to touch the Homestead in retribution.

Basilio's eyes went wide. "Kea, you don't need to—"

"When the only tool you have is a hammer, it is tempting to treat everything as a nail," Matthew said, settling the matter as he placed his hands flat on the table. "Kea has made her case as our scalpel." When he said my name incorrectly, pronouncing it *KEY-ah*, I did my best to not cringe. "We can put the notion to a vote. All in favor of immediately absorbing the Homestead?"

Three hands shot up: those of Reagol, Matthew, and the Asian man. The woman in the hijab kept her hands folded in her lap, as did the Black woman who'd spoken earlier, though she seemed conflicted. A third woman who hadn't spoken at all also remained still, her eyes red and cheeks puffy as if she'd been crying. Sora half raised his hand, even though he had just reached into my head. He knew I wasn't lying. He *knew*. I glared at him until he met my gaze and dropped his arm back to the table.

Matthew frowned as I breathed out in relief. I had won by a single hand—Sora's.

Across the table from me, Basilio swallowed and covered his face with both hands.

"We can't possibly trust this woman, an outsider, to put together this spell and find Angelo's killer!" the Asian man protested.

"This woman is the only known expert in Hawaiian," Matthew countered. "We have no other choice." His eyes flitted to Sora. "Mr. Kaiser will continue to lead the investigation. I trust that he will keep her under close watch."

"Hold on," Sora said. "You can't expect me to *babysit* in the middle of a murder investigation."

"Do you suggest we let her proceed unsupervised?" Matthew asked.

Sora swallowed. "No."

"Then it's settled." Matthew's gaze landed again on me. "You'll assist in finding the spell that killed our colleague."

"I understand but . . . Angelo Reyes was one of the most powerful Casters in the city," I said. "I can't imagine he'd just let himself be killed. Why didn't he fight back?"

Matthew shot me a chilly look. "We found his body, or what was left of it, right where you're sitting now."

I shifted in my seat as a shiver crept down my spine.

"He had, for lack of a better word, decomposed by the time he was discovered. Our best guess is he was ambushed at the end of the last meeting he took, which is why the room's mic caught the final moments of his life," Sora said.

I glanced around the bare room, noting the spotless walls and floors. Magical deaths rarely left behind any sort of residue that one could analyze, which meant the only clue both the Board and I had was the garbled recording of a half-formed spell.

"As for the why," Matthew said, "I believe that is now your responsibility to unearth, Miss Petrova—or we may have to return to a hammer as our solution."

My back stiffened at the implied threat.

Reagol agreed. "What we are asking is simple. Piece together this spell and reveal its maker." His mouth was drawn tightly across his face and his nose crinkled. Reagol closed his eyes and took a quick breath. When he looked back at me, his expression had relaxed, but his anger was palpable, brimming right under the surface. Whether he was pissed off at me or the Board, I couldn't tell.

I stared at my shaking hands until Sora's low cough brought me back to my senses and I found his red eyes burning into me like hot coals. To save the Homestead from LA's ire, I had just volunteered myself to find the assassin who had carried out a hit in the heart of the Board's operation.

Simple my ass.

CHAPTER 5

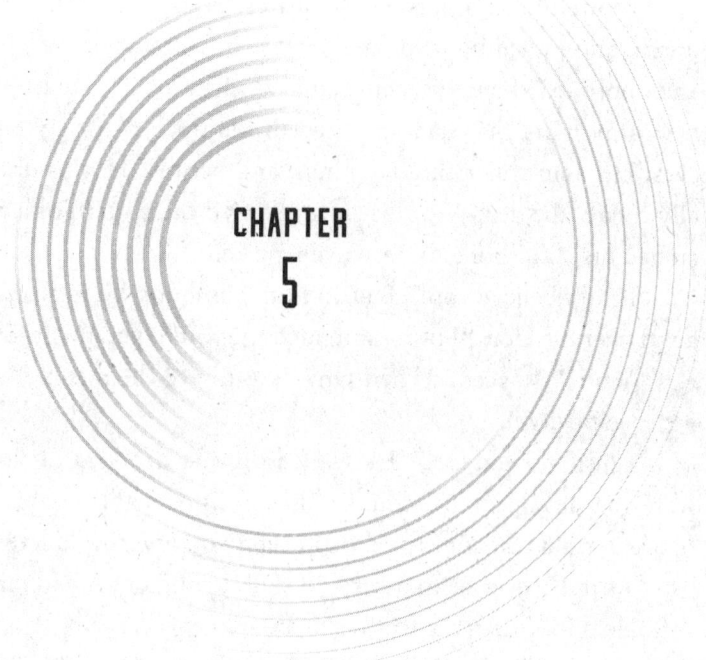

When Basilio had decided to join Angelo Reyes in the city, he agreed to give up more than just his seat on the council, his title as head, and his last name. Assimilation meant the entire clan leaving their home and moving into a suburb so that LA could claim their land on the outskirts as an additional buffer. I'd thought him a lunatic at the time, but seeing their new neighborhood in person helped me to understand why he'd made such a drastic choice.

The Reyes' new homes were crafted in a Spanish colonial style with high A-shaped roofs, floor-to-ceiling shuttered windows, and intricately twisted brass filigree in delicate arches above each opening. Each house boasted two stories, often with a cobblestone courtyard that spilled open into communal areas with a firepit or fountain so that everyone could gather outdoors. Their quarter wasn't the nicest area in LA, but it was a clear step up from the Homestead.

I spotted Basilio outside the nearest house, squatting on the front porch, and pulled up next to him. When I got out of the car, he stood and approached me, his steps tentative. I stared at his face, noting the new gray hairs that had sprouted in the thick black swoop over his eyes. His skin was rich golden tan, and because he was dressed casually today, the deep V of his shirt revealed the pattern of a tattoo that circled his collarbone like a woven basket.

"I can't believe you!" Basilio said. He shook his head, pressing his hand over his face. "I never intended for you to get involved like this."

"Yeah?" I asked. "Then why'd you have them come looking for me specifically?"

"I just thought . . ." He trailed off and dropped his hand. "You were the only person I could think of who might be able to help. I figured you'd just confirm it was Hawaiian, and they'd let you go."

"As if it'd ever be that easy," I said. Living in LA had made Basilio soft. He'd forgotten the truth: The Board never let things go. If I hadn't thrown myself in front of them, they'd already be on the Homestead.

We caught each other's eye, and he immediately looked away. There was so much we hadn't said yet. *Sorry. Thank you. I miss you. Why did you leave? Why did you ignore me for so long?*

I pushed past the bubble in my gut and said none of those things, instead placing my hands on my hips. "Can I talk to Vanessa?"

Vanessa, I'd learned, was the woman on the Board who hadn't said anything at yesterday's meeting. The acting head of the Reyes clan—and Angelo's widow.

His forehead indented with wrinkles. "Sora already spoke to her. Didn't he tell you?"

No, he had not. Sora hadn't contacted me once since the deposition even though I'd sent him multiple texts, left messages, and once even driven past the Kaiser estate until their security chased me off. The head of LA's Safety Commission clearly didn't want me anywhere near his investigation.

I ran a thumb down the side of my nose. "He doesn't really like me."

Basilio's frown folded into a smile. "For once, Kea, I'd say it's not your fault."

"Ha ha, very funny."

"Just try not to upset her too much," he explained. "She's been shouldering through, but she's delicate."

He waved me behind him, and I followed through the clan's village. There were more people than I remembered. Women hung laundry in the sun and a group of children kicked around a flat soccer ball as their feet flew down the main drag.

We stopped at a grand house that looked like a napoleon biscuit. The second floor was all in wood, complete with curved arc windows, while the first was made entirely of white stone. The large porch was bare, two ceiling fans spinning lazily to keep it cool. We ascended the sweeping front staircase and Basilio let himself into the house without knocking.

The inside of the home was just as stately as the exterior: dark wood floors, Turkish carpets, and redwood furniture inlaid with pearl. I could hear voices from inside. One was loud and male, the other more muted. It sounded like they were arguing, or at least, the man was. Whoever he was speaking to was incredibly quiet. Their conversation sharpened into focus as we got to the door of the main room.

"Vanessa, you have to see reason," the male voice said. "Your child needs a father."

There was the sharp intake of breath. "He already has one."

"I didn't mean—"

"Get out," the woman's voice said, thrumming with a quiet anger.

"Please, Ness. I wasn't trying to be rude. I just . . . hate to see you like this."

"*Leave*," the woman said, her voice cracking.

There was a pause, followed by the shuffling of feet. The door swung open nearly into us as a tall man barreled out of the room, his mouth set into a line and his eyes narrowed at the floor. I recognized him from the deposition the other day. The Asian man on the Board with dark hair—Charles Lam. He barely looked at me or Basilio as he left, muttering to himself on the way out.

With the doors to the room already flung wide open, Basilio entered and found Vanessa Reyes, his new clan head, sitting near the window in a stiff, tall-backed chair. She looked younger than me by a year or two. Plump and dark-haired, she sat with her hands clasped tightly in her lap. Her gaze was latched, unfocused, on a spot on the wall. Basilio approached and set a gentle hand on her shoulder to get her attention. She flinched, only relaxing when she recognized his face.

"You don't have to let Charles into the house," he said gently.

"He causes more of a fuss if I deny him," she responded, attempting to smile but faltering. "Our clan isn't in a position to alienate ourselves from someone like Charles. I can deal with his persistence. It's my responsibility." She sighed, though, making clear that despite the truth to her words, that burden was heavy.

Vanessa ran a hand through her hair, shifting her weight as she crossed her legs at the ankles. Under her long, figure-hugging dress, her stomach stuck out in a small bump. I hadn't realized yesterday since she'd been wearing a jacket, but she couldn't be that far along. I tried not to stare. She'd lost much more than just her husband.

Vanessa noticed me looking and averted her eyes to the ground. "Miss Petrova, thank you for coming. I apologize for the poor first impression. I'm not usually prone to hysterics."

It didn't sound like she'd thrown a fit at all. She'd barely raised her voice. It had been Charles who'd been loud.

"Please don't apologize. I'm the one intruding," I said, not knowing where else to start. I coughed, feeling the need to fill the silence. "Sorry for your loss."

Her lower lip trembled, and she wiped at her reddened nose. "I appreciate that." She reached out and patted the back of Basilio's hand as he'd remained standing next to her chair. "Has Sora filled you in on the investigation so far?"

"Sora hasn't been forthcoming with me," I admitted. "Though, to be fair, our interests are different. I'm not well versed in catching mur—" I caught myself and pinched the skin below my thumb. My stupid mouth. "In running investigations. My main talent is in smithing, so it makes sense that I've been asked to piece together this spell." *Asked* was a real polite way of saying threatened, but I was trying my best to be diplomatic.

Vanessa knitted her fingers together. "Oh. That's a shame."

My lips parted and I licked them, unsure. She wasn't talking much, and I was terrible at prying in a polite way. By the look of things, I needed to be gentle. Kid gloves. She was pregnant and grieving, and though she was holding it together, I had the impression that she might shatter at any second. Her eyes were clouded, and her fingers toyed with the slim gold wedding band on her finger, spinning it around and around.

She caught me staring at the ring and stopped. "Do you have children, Miss Petrova?"

"No," I said. "But I do look after my younger sister and cousins." She blinked and looked at me in the face for the first time, understanding without being told the how and why of my situation. There was only one reason that someone as young as me would be responsible for any kids that weren't my own.

"That must be hard."

"It is," I agreed. "I never thought it'd be my job to do homework and ground them, but sometimes we get tasked with things we never asked for."

Vanessa nodded and went quiet again, leaving me to stew. I never liked long pauses, but she had a habit of speaking only after thinking. "I, for one, never wanted to be head, though I was always supposed to be. Before Angelo and I married, I was set to inherit my father's title, but I left and joined the Reyes clan. My family cut ties, and even though it hurt, Angelo promised he'd handle everything. He kept that promise."

Directly related to former Board member Raul Ortega, Vanessa's family had perfected an offshoot of smithing that specialized in Spanish curses. The Ortega Syndicate was a hundred years old and one of the most respected spell publishing houses this side of North America. Curses were always in high demand.

"Now he's gone," she said, her eyes misting over. She wiped them and looked out the window. "If I don't finish what he started, it'll be like he never existed. I can't let that happen." Her hand curled around her belly.

"You still plan on pursuing regulation?" I asked, surprised. I'd thought for sure this would be the end for the Reyes' bid to advance Tagalog.

"This was his dream, and I intend to see it to fruition. I'm not fooling myself, though. I'll need help from Basilio and the others, since I haven't learned the language fluently. My specialization is still very much Spanish."

"Tagalog is healing-based, though," I muttered aloud. For Vanessa and Angelo, their magics would have been like oil and water.

I'd watched Basilio practice smithing a few times before he'd left the Homestead. Unlike Hawaiian, Tagalog thrived in the written form. He'd been enchanted by the Reyes clan's technique of combining medicine and magic, etching spells onto pills and bottles of tonics to create potent remedies. Their innovative approach was a major reason why he'd decided to join their clan.

Vanessa's mouth tweaked up at the end in subtle agreement. "Angelo and I were wholly incompatible." Her hand fell back to the top of her belly, disproving her assessment entirely. She exhaled. "I'm thirty-eight, which makes this pregnancy high risk."

I tried not to let my shock show. She looked so young.

"It's not just my age, though. The Ortegas have always struggled to conceive, each generation birthing two children at most. I'm aware of the irony. A generational curse on a curse-working family." She gave a humorless chuckle. "My grandmother theorized it was because of our magic. Casting ill-intended spells day in and day out ought to have some kind of effect."

Physical changes from frequent magic use were common, but such a major weakness in the powerful Ortega clan was likely guarded information. "Why are you telling me this?" I asked.

"So, you can understand why I would never hurt Angelo. He healed me and gave me the only thing I ever wanted," Vanessa answered, both her hands sat protectively at the sides of her stomach. "I know what the Board thinks about the Ortega Syndicate and their cursed magic, but I am no longer an Ortega. My father made sure of that."

"I'm sorry," I said.

She met my eyes for the first time, her voice thin but clear. "Don't be. I'm glad they disowned me. I'm more than my power, more than my family, and more than just a seat on the Board. Angelo saw that when no one else did."

"Everyone else will, too," I assured her.

She flinched and withdrew. "*That*, I'm less certain about."

"We believe that Sora sees Vanessa as the prime suspect," Basilio commented. He spoke as gently as possible, but when the words came out, Vanessa shrank back like they physically hurt her.

"I haven't written an original curse in over three years," she whispered, chin angled down at her chest. "And I wouldn't anyway, not when I'm this far along. I've been lucky, but there's always the chance that the child could . . . I wouldn't dare risk it."

"If you told Sora about your problems conceiving, it would help your case," I said. "He's difficult but seems logical. He'd understand why it would be impossible for you to do curse work right now."

She shook her head. "If I did that, he'd be required to report it to the Board. The Ortega clan would come after me for revealing the family's vulnerability. They'd ruin everything Angelo built."

"Surely, your father wouldn't attack your clan?" I had almost said *you* but held my tongue.

She gave a weak smile. "This is just the reality of LA, Miss Petrova. No one truly cares about finding the person responsible; they just want to use Angelo's death to their own advantage."

"You told me the truth," I argued.

Vanessa gave me a sheepish glance. "Well, that's because you are . . . er, impartial to city politics."

I was missing something. I looked over at Basilio for help. He sighed. "What she's trying to say, *politely*, Kea, is that no one here gives a shit what you say or think. Even if you did try to expose her secret, no one would believe you."

Ouch. I mean, he was right, but still.

"I need your help," Vanessa said. She squeezed Basilio's fingers, and he got up to pull a planner from the writing nook nestled in the left-hand corner of the room. He handed the book to Vanessa, who licked her thumb and opened it to a page with figures. "Miss Petrova, you have no ties to LA nor the Board and no stake in Tagalog's advancement. In fact, there wasn't much information to find on you other than one very noticeable detail. Debt."

Was she trying to blackmail me? I went stiff. "I don't know what you think—"

"I think that you are in a suffocating position," Vanessa said, still without raising her eyes. "I also know I'm not the only one who's going to dig into your background, just the first. All I'm trying to do is make sure that your vulnerabilities are covered before someone else can exploit them."

"I don't understand," I said.

She paused, taking a deep breath and gripping her hands together tightly. "If you can find Angelo's real killer—with definitive proof—I will ensure your family's debts are paid."

My heart pounded. "The mortgage . . . that's too much."

"I said *debts*. All of them. If that includes your mortgage, then so be it," she insisted.

The sum she was talking about was an impossible figure. With that kind of money, I'd have time to work on developing our clan's mana o ka moʻokūʻauhau without having to take odd jobs. Considering the pressure Sora had put on the Smithing Guild in order to find me, it was possible that there wasn't any work left there anyway. And the Board hadn't exactly offered to compensate me for my labor.

"I'm not sure I'm comfortable with taking your money," I said.

"This isn't just about you," Basilio explained. "Your clan's financial trouble could be used to manipulate you. In fact, you should expect attempts at it. Vanessa is kindly offering to plug this hole before it becomes a problem for everyone. Take her offer."

Vanessa nodded. "Basilio has assured me this will be mutually beneficial. I need someone within this investigation who will not be influenced by outside factors. You are my best shot at that. Please, Miss Petrova. I am begging you."

It was a good deal. A better one than I'd ever gotten in a trade on the Homestead.

Vanessa sat poised like she'd flee her chair at any moment, dark eyes scanning my every move. She closed her eyes for a beat, squeezing her brows together, and in that second, I recognized the same current I fought. A never-ending struggle to keep your head above water. Fear not just of failure, but of its consequences for loved ones. She opened her eyes, a hand unconsciously stroking the curve of her belly. "Someone close to my husband killed him. I don't trust the Board."

"Me neither," I said.

She looked sadly at her feet. "Had Angelo been as prudent, he might still . . ." Vanessa folded her hands back together, resting them on top of her knees, but didn't finish her sentence. "The Board has fought tooth and nail to keep the Romance languages a unified voting bloc—but with my marriage to Angelo and the addition of more Asian languages to the registry, that balance is starting to tip. Had Tagalog been accepted and Angelo joined the Board, we would've been the new majority faction."

"Are you saying you think the murderer is someone from a clan of the original four?" Latin, French, Italian, and Spanish—the city's first four registered languages, considered by some to be the crème de la crème of magic.

Vanessa shook her head. "I wish it were that simple. There are many new additions to the Board who carry the same beliefs of restriction over expansion. You'll need to look at everyone. Everyone," she emphasized.

"Including Sora?" I asked out loud.

She pursed her lips. "All I know is this. Angelo met with one of his colleagues right before his death. The Board immediately pointed the finger at me, Basilio, and then the Homestead—which makes no sense, since it happened at Griffith Hall. Someone on the inside is trying to manipulate this investigation to look *outward*. It could be Sora or someone who's keeping tabs on him. I'm not sure. Until we've rooted out the person responsible for Angelo's death, doubt about the future of our clan will hinder its advancement."

I reached through the space between us and tentatively held her free hand. "I'll do everything that I can."

She looked at our connected fingers and let out a breath of relief. "Thank you. Basilio says he will help, when possible, but they don't want him too close to things, since he and Angelo were so close." She examined my face. "You remind me a bit of him. Idealistic. Brave. Rough around the edges, but also very kind. I have no doubt that you'll do your very best," she said, turning her head to stare out the window. When Vanessa looked back at me, her tears finally won their battle, falling down her cheeks in pale lines. "I pray it's enough."

I tried not to dwell on Vanessa's foreboding parting words as I left the Reyes compound to drive home. But I couldn't shake the feeling that the Board had put me in the same chair that Angelo had last sat in on purpose. I hoped it wasn't an omen.

~

"Why are you wearing that?" Sisi asked, poking her head in around my open door as she unwrapped a lollipop. Her lips were a bright pink that matched the candy. Mornings here were always chaos. My grandparents had taken the car to the boat ramp, leaving me alone to wrestle Makani into clean clothes and fix him a bowl of cereal. Sicilia, however, ran on her own time. As always.

I looked down at the beige skirt suit, a peachy shade that looked ashy against the tan of my skin. The skirt was stretched a little too snugly across my broad thighs and rear, and the top button of my cream blouse had to be pinned down to keep it from popping open.

"I don't have any other professional clothes," I said. This getup had been my job-hunting outfit fresh out of high school. Needless to say, it hadn't gotten much wear. I was just thankful it still fit.

Sisi stuck the lollipop, which was probably her breakfast, into her mouth. "I asked why you put it on." Even though our faces had similar features, Sisi was stick-skinny while I had the kinds of curves that no diet or exercise would ever get rid of.

I tried to smooth down the fabric that pulled across my hips. "I was checking to see that it looked okay."

"I hate to tell you this but—"

"I *know*," I snapped. "It's tight. I haven't even decided if I'm going or not."

"Going where?" she asked.

I hadn't told my family about Keanu, the Board, or losing our only steady income. I didn't want to burden everyone with that, not yet. They were already worried about my ability to lead, and I didn't want to fan the flames. "I'm going to try taking the exam again," I lied.

"They didn't change the rules about regulated languages, did they?"

"No," I said shortly, not wanting to relive my previous failures. "Like I said, I'm not sure I'm going." That part was the truth. After talking to Vanessa, I wanted to track down the man I'd seen there, but getting close to Charles Lam was like trying to see the face of god. Sora could manage it, if I could persuade him, but the man had been adamantly ignoring me.

I pushed past Sisi and down the hall for breakfast, grabbing an apple and the jar of peanut butter from the fridge to snack on while I thought about my plan. Griffith Hall was limited to Board members and their guests, but I'd gotten clearance after the deposition. This meant I could get into the building, but I'd still have trouble entering each head's wing. Munching on the crisp fruit, I pulled a clean spoon out of the drying rack and wrestled open the jar, dished out a plop of peanut butter, and popped it into my mouth. I looked over at the clock. If I left now, I could make it there around lunch.

"Newt?" I called out for my cousin knowing he was likely around. Newt's father was Inert, non-magical, so for safety reasons they lived in LA as clanless residents, though during the summers Newt tended to camp out at our place.

A hand sprouted from the living room, and I spied him on the couch, tinkering with his computer while the news blared in the background. Newt wasn't watching the television, but he liked to have noise while he worked. It was another story on Angelo's death. The Board's assessment about unrest had been accurate. B-roll of shattered shop windows and grainy images of graffiti that was so hateful it had to be blurred flashed across the screen. Shaky footage of a cop charging a line of students with cardboard signs was suddenly flipped as the camera operator fell, leaving only the squeaking sound of sneakers against pavement. The internal turmoil was bound to weaken LA's border. Wards only really worked if the people inside wanted to keep everyone safe. *Protected*. If the community's trust in each other shattered, so would the ward.

"Turn that off," I said.

He looked up at me. "Why?"

At eighteen, he had lanky, gangly limbs and a mop of shaggy, brown hair. His dark eyes, glasses, and the smattering of freckles across his face made him look like some angst-ridden romantic. In reality, he still hadn't seemed to move out of the girls-have-cooties stage and would rather stay home and mess with his tech stuff than go gallivanting with other teens his age.

"Because I said so. Also, what's that?" I asked, peering over the couch's edge. He looked at me warily, and I glared back. "Don't give me stink eye."

"Trying to explain this to you is harder than actually doing it," he complained.

The kid was a Technic, able to weave together magic and computer programming with a level of skill that was beyond my comprehension.

As a smithing language, Technetic magic operated on a conditional process. Meaning spells required an input function to get the outcome one desired. *If* a user clicked on an extension, *then* a virus was released into their mind. *If* a user typed out a message, *then* it came out of their victim's mouth. The genius of Technics revolved around being able to predict standard user reactions and using them to trigger a specific outcome.

"Try," I pressed, trying to be a supportive, interested older cousin.

"It's nothing special. I'm in some gaming servers with this guy who, I swear, is the worst person on the planet. I'm making something that'll make him store up all the vile crap he says and then repeat it to his mom." Newt snickered. "He won't know what hit him."

Evil genius, applied to classic teenage drama.

Newt was getting ready for his last year of high school and had his eye on a Technetics college. I desperately wanted him to go, but his father and I had zero ideas about how to fund his education.

"That seems pretty harsh."

Newt shrugged. "You should hear the stuff he's said."

Personally, I thought his plan was a fitting punishment, but it was probably more responsible to steer him away from antics like this. "Don't you have any summer homework?" I asked.

He didn't take his eyes off his screen. "I finished weeks ago." Newt grinned maliciously. "Sisi hasn't even started hers, though."

"Shut up!" Sicilia yelled as she stomped to the couch and collapsed next to her cousin. That girl had supersonic hearing, I swear.

Sicilia *was* the type to go off gallivanting with her peers. Hell, she was the type to lead half her sophomore class out onto the ratty, dried-up football field and drive over the grass to perfectly form the letters *F U J O S H* to piss off an ex-boyfriend. And then, just for good measure, light it on fire. If that sounded incredibly specific, you'd be right.

"Take a break for me?" I asked. "I need a ride to the city."

He gave me a thumbs-up and closed his computer. I had one manageable kid in the house, at least.

The Board's Committee of Public Health wing of Griffith Hall was located underground, down a windowless corridor with walls the color of mushroom caps. Each Board member had their own committee dedicated to one thing or another and Charles's managed the efficacy and safety of Syndicates, organizations that wrote and sold spells to the public. At the end of the hall, a severe-looking secretary greeted me. His horn-rimmed glasses, slicked-down comb-over, and stoic expression told me he hadn't been hired for his friendliness.

"Name?" he asked, tapping the edge of his pen on the desk.

"I'm looking for Charles Lam," I said.

The secretary clicked his pen and repeated, "Name."

"Kea."

He blinked. "*Full* name."

"Kealaokaleo Petrova."

He scanned the computer screen in front of him, scrolling down a document with his mouse. "I have no appointment for a Kialo—" he stuttered, ruffled at his tongue's inability to form my name.

"If you call him, I'm sure Charles will agree it's important that we speak," I insisted with a confidence I didn't feel.

The secretary gave me a wary look but pressed a few numbers on his phone and picked up the receiver. A muffled voice came from the voice box, and he gave the person on the other end a brief rundown of my request.

The man's eyes darted from the computer screen to me and, after a second, he hung up. "Mr. Lam says he has no desire to meet with you. You may see yourself out."

His smug demeanor was infuriating. If I felt like it, I could easily launch across the desk and bend his reedlike body until he whimpered. But as he looked over his glasses and down at me, embarrassment burned through to the soles of my feet, made worse by the knowledge that Vanessa was the only member of the Board who believed I could figure this out. I was in the city now, where it didn't matter how hard I could land a punch. Power here was invisible, intangible.

Damn them. I'd find that death spell out of spite alone.

I turned on my heel and exited back to the main building.

Having already made the journey to LA, I might as well get something out of the trip. I retraced my steps, sneaking through Griffith Hall to get back to the boardroom the deposition had been held in. I passed the room with the beautiful ceiling, the one with checkerboard floors, until I came to the meeting room. It was exactly as I remembered, large with eight black chairs around a table in the shape of a teardrop. The speaker that had recorded Angelo's demise was still in the center of the table. I snapped my fingers.

On demand, the audio jumped to life, keyed to the same recording as before. Unintelligible words, cracking, and a crash. It ended and I snapped my fingers again. I listened to the tape about ten more times, taking notes of anything I could make out, even if they were wild guesses. There were definitely a few words with dominant *H* sounds. Hoʻi? Hoʻihoʻi? I wasn't sure. *Au* was the only word that was clear and that was a dead end. Meaning *I*, it gave no clue as to what the spell could be about.

That said, this person had used all the right tones, which hinted at someone who had experience with either Hawaiian or another Polynesian language. I looked up at the Latin blazed into the marble wall opposite from me, recalling Vanessa's warning about a mole. Could a member of the Board secretly speak flawless Hawaiian? My gut said no. Despite our alphabet only having thirteen letters, Hawaiian pronunciation was notoriously difficult for new speakers. None of the regulated languages were from similar language families, so I doubted I was listening to someone from the Board on the tape. This meant that someone from the Homestead was likely involved; at minimum, they had sold a spell to the culprit, and at most, they had killed Angelo themselves.

I went back to the chair Angelo had died in, inspecting the surrounding area for something important. Nothing. In a normal murder, that would be the end of the road, but there was a lot one could learn about what kind of magic *hadn't* been used, too. There were no burn marks or blood, which meant the spell hadn't been very violent. Possibly a quick death. Sora had mentioned something about the body sitting there decomposing; I made a silent wish that Angelo's passing had been painless.

I left the seat and approached their marble backboard, examining the words. *Let justice be done.* What a joke. When I touched the carved letters my sympathetic magic flared to life, shocking me. Withdrawing my hand, I frowned and hesitantly placed my palm flat against the text. Mana pulsed on the surface of the wall gently, like a heartbeat. I ran a hand over the Latin phrase, but it didn't spark again. Rather, the magic was an undercurrent, built into the stones themselves.

I closed my eyes, focusing on the flutter of mana under my touch and tried to follow it to the source. My head tipped back, and I opened my eyes to view the white cornice that framed the ceiling and walls. The plaster had been molded into an ornamental design and I squinted, trying to make out the contrast of the bas-relief. The swirls, I realized, were not abstract forms at all, but letters.

Arabic script.

I took a step back, following the lines of text around the room. The flow and form of the spell was so subtle one could easily miss it. Now that I'd seen it, though, it was impossible to ignore. Someone had intentionally placed a hidden smithing around the perimeter of this room.

An Arabic spell baked into the scene of the crime, and only one person with the background, skill, and access to attach such a smithing to Griffith Hall. The coincidence was delicious.

CHAPTER 6

Little Arabia, just west of the Anaheim stretch of Los Angeles, was renowned for its long, flat drags and towering Islamic architecture. The modular builds in central LA gave way to turquoise tiles, stone facades, and sunny courtyards lined with palm trees. The Amin estate was the largest property in the area and located closest to the central mosque, which boasted four minarets, one at each corner. A public hammam, that the Amin clan funded, lay a stone's throw away from the place of worship, and even at midday boasted a steady stream of customers.

Unlike Charles, Ivy Amin had been open to a chat when I'd called, and we'd made arrangements to meet the following morning. I pulled to the front of the Amin clan's ivory and gold residence, under an impossibly tall entryway that stretched up into a graceful arch. Coming to a stop, I parked behind another vehicle. Ivy Amin was outside her home, waiting, and greeted me with a warm smile when I stepped out of the cab.

In her thirties, Ivy had dark thick brows that drooped sleepily over her eyes, full lips, and a prominent hooked nose. Her features were distinct and made her easily recognizable from the deposition, but even if they hadn't, the hijab would've given her away. A peachy scarf covered her hair and draped over one shoulder, hanging to her waist. She had dressed for the heat, wearing casual linen pants and an oversize white shirt, buttoned to her neck.

"Miss Petrova," she called out in greeting.

"I appreciate you letting me drop by," I said.

"Of course," she said, leading me into the mudroom. "I only wish Sora had told us you'd be joining him. I was surprised to receive your call. I've known Sora for many years, and he's never sought outside help."

My brow creased. Ivy was speaking about Sora as if he was already here, but I hadn't told a soul I was coming. The black car out front wrestled its way into my thoughts, and I stopped in my tracks.

Sora knew about the spell, too, then. He'd figured it out first.

I smothered my curiosity. "I'm just trying to do what the Board asked," I said, playing into her assumption. Even if I disliked Sora, it was better that the others saw us as a team.

She led me through the Amin residence, and I couldn't help but admire the interior. It had been decorated with veins of golden Arabic text as art. The signature swoops of script were an unmistakable mimic of the ones at Griffith Hall, like a talisman against evil. Ivy opened the door to a small sitting room with a recessed sofa dug into the ground, promising that Sora would be along shortly. Snacks had been laid out on a shiny tiered platter, and I hungrily eyed the jewel-colored sweets, resisting the urge to eat them in handfuls.

Ivy departed, leaving me alone. Minutes dragged by, and I sank into the cushions of the couch, bouncing my leg. The size of their house brought a deep sense of discomfort to me. It was hard to believe anyone actually lived here, and the wait made me feel even more alone. Five minutes passed. Then, thirty. Just when I'd given up on Sora making an appearance, the door swung open and he stepped into the room, eyes aflame.

"Does your stalking know no bounds?" he asked bluntly, without any *hi, hello*, or *sorry for avoiding you for the past week*. "How did you even know where I was?"

I lifted an eyebrow. "I didn't."

We glared at each other for a beat, then Sora crossed the room in three strides and sat opposite me. "Then what brings you to Anaheim?"

"That's a stupid question," I remarked. "Same thing as you."

Sora's expression shuttered closed as he processed how I'd come this far. "You trespassed into our meeting room." It wasn't a question really.

"Whether you like it or not, I'm a part of this investigation. The Board gave me clearance to enter the hall, and more importantly, I wouldn't have needed to do any of this if you'd just *answered my calls*," I accused.

His right hand grabbed his knee. "I have no reason to tell you anything. Do not insert yourself into things, girl."

"I'm not *girl*," I snapped. "I have a name."

He took his time examining me, starting at my toes and moving his way up until he landed on my face. "Do not insert yourself into this investigation, *Kea*." Sora smoothed out the sound of my name on his tongue like he owned it, and I regretted making him say it.

I leaned forward. "I'm only here because I have to be. Stop getting in my way."

The surprise on his face was comical. "I'm in your way?"

"Yes. You went to see Angelo's widow without me, have blocked me from contacting you, are withholding information, and now you're interrogating me, when you should be talking to Ivy Amin," I stated.

His mouth drew into a tight line. "I would like nothing better. However, Ivy hasn't made an appearance once in the three days I've been here."

I stopped talking, sure I'd heard him wrong. There was no way that Sora Kaiser had been intruding on the Amins for three days. I raked over his appearance, noting the wrinkles in his suit, unkempt hair, and dark circles under his eyes. Sora expelled exhaustion in waves, but it was neatly hidden under his usual brutish demeanor. I blinked, astonished that he'd been so persistent.

"It's a miracle they haven't thrown you out," I said out loud, unable to stop my big mouth from vocalizing my surprise.

He scoffed. "They wouldn't dare. The Amins are far too proud of their old traditions."

"You're taking advantage of their hospitality," I said. "It's rude."

"Rude is their head avoiding me for three days," Sora corrected.

My leg stopped bouncing. "Rude is pushing the matter when Ivy clearly doesn't want to talk to you."

"If they want me gone, then Ivy needs to either remove me herself or give me an audience. It's her responsibility both as a head and as a Board member. Otherwise, I'm staying." He crossed his arms and sank deeper into the couch cushions.

"That's been working well for you, has it?" I asked. He scowled, but I moved on without skipping a beat. "You know, Ivy greeted me when I arrived. Looks like I have a better shot of getting her to talk than you."

Sora's nose crinkled, but he didn't say anything.

"That is, if I'm needed," I said, needling him.

He stubbornly kept his mouth shut.

Fine, he could have it his way. I stood to leave, rolling my shoulders. "Good luck on your own," I chirped. "I'm sure Ivy will break the stalemate soon."

He covered his face with his hand. "Wait. Just *wait*."

I stopped moving toward the exit and faced him, tilting my head to the side. "Yes?"

He frowned. "You can talk to her."

"Please," I said quickly.

"What?" he asked.

"Say *please*," I repeated, feeling petty about him calling me *girl* earlier. No one outside the Homestead, where they used the term with endearment, was allowed to refer to me that way, especially so dismissively.

He sighed and moved his jaw back and forth, a vein in his neck bulging. For a second, I didn't think he'd say it. I was more than happy to leave him here as the Amins' permanent unwelcome guest, but he eventually managed to get the words out. "*Please* talk to her."

"I suppose I could help," I said casually, plopping back onto the couch with a smirk. "Since you asked nicely."

Sora was so red, it looked like he'd given himself sunstroke. He sputtered out a few nonsense words before landing on actual human speech. "Arabic is protective in nature, which is why the Amin house is covered in their spells."

My eye was drawn to the gold seal above the door, then the tiles on the wall, which cleverly hid text in teal blue flowers.

"The one in the boardroom wasn't listed in any public records," Sora continued. "It's possible Ivy placed it there discreetly. I'm not sure why or what it does, but Ivy knows. Find out."

I paused, letting my smile stretch out.

"Find out, *please*," he said, correcting himself.

I relished in the small win. "If I bring you this information, you'll grant me access to everything you've found so far and anything you find in the future."

"Fine. But if Ivy tells you nothing, you get nothing," he warned.

We exchanged another rueful glare, and I let the challenge of a potential deal crackle. I'd get Sora his information, but then he'd have to give me what I wanted. If he didn't, I'd twist his arm until it broke. A part of me hoped he'd resist. Just a little.

~

Sora left, and before I had a chance to pop a rose-colored sweet into my mouth, an attendant opened the door. My hand lingered over the tray of candies, but I relinquished the prize and followed her down the hall. Ivy had promised tea, so I'd been happy to oblige. We ended up in the back garden, where bleached wooden posts held up a canopy of cream drapes. The stone floor below was arranged with burgundy pillows and a low table, no higher than my ankle, where a beautiful silver chess set was laid out.

Ivy invited me to join her on the cushions. Within seconds, another woman brought out a tray of curved glass cups filled with amber liquid and a small plate with more confections. I thanked her for the refreshment and took a gulp.

Ivy chuckled as she watched my face twist at the bitterness of the drink. "There isn't any sugar in that," she explained. "I prefer to have a small treat on the side instead, but I can call for a sweetener if you'd like."

I shook my head, reached for a pistachio-coated square, and ate the candy in a single bite. It melted on the tongue, and I tasted notes of mandarin, sunflower paste, and a soft nougat. The sweetness cut through the tang of the herbal brew nicely. "I hope Sora hasn't been too much of an inconvenience," I said.

Ivy took a polite sip from her own cup. "We enjoy hosting people."

It didn't slip past me that she hadn't answered the statement directly. The fact that Sora either wasn't aware of his behavior, or worse, didn't care, was embarrassing. I wanted to apologize on his behalf, but something told me that he wouldn't be pleased with that.

"He mentioned he hasn't been able to speak to you," I said, swishing the drink and disrupting the sediment on the bottom. "Yet here you and I are, having tea."

Ivy arched an eyebrow. "Would you prefer coffee?"

"I don't really like coffee," I responded.

"Me neither," she agreed with a smile. "And frankly, I don't see a problem in avoiding things that I dislike." Her underlying point was clear.

I picked up a small teaspoon and swirled the liquid in my glass, despite there being nothing to mix into the tea. There was a lot to dislike about Sora, that was true, but why would Ivy take a liking to *me*?

I hadn't done anything to endear myself to her and I possessed neither Sora's status nor family name.

I clinked the spoon on the edge of the cup and set it down. While I wished that my personality was winning enough to charm complete strangers, I wasn't stupid. Ivy was the head of the Amin clan, a member of the Board, and one of the few female leaders in LA. She hadn't gotten to her position by accident. Agreeing to tea with me, I had no doubt, was for her own benefit, not mine. My gaze fell to the chessboard on the table.

Ivy noticed my lingering eye. "Do you play?"

"My grandfather insisted on teaching me," I said. "He says shah-mat is one of life's true pleasures."

She looked at my face again. "What language is that? Perhaps an Indo-Iranian one?"

I shook my head. "Russian."

She let out an appreciative *ahh* in understanding. "I only ask because in Persian, shah is *king*, and therefore shah-mat can roughly translate to *the king is helpless*." Ivy paused. "Would you like to play?"

"I would love to," I said.

We set the board and flipped a coin. I lost, so Ivy selected white, taking the first move. Her pawn clacked as she jumped it two squares ahead. "I'm sure the Board's task has been hard on you. There's so much ground to cover and very little time. Sora is also notoriously bad at playing well with others."

I studied the board and moved my own pawn across from hers, so they faced off.

"When you called saying you'd drop by today," Ivy continued, "I thought it was to provide him with some assistance, but now I can clearly see that you are the one in need of support."

I struggled to control my reaction and made a move without thinking. Had she heard us or was she merely guessing? Sora and I had been careless in speaking so openly to each other while on the Amins' property.

Daring a glance at Ivy, I clocked her tight expression. She was completely focused on the board, her fingers hovering above the pieces without touching them, unbothered. Her forefinger stroked the back of her palm, and a small bubble of relief rose in my gut. Interrogating a head like Ivy was dangerous. If she knew my goal here, I'd be skewered, not having tea and playing chess.

Ivy's strategy reminded me of Sora's accusation that I had illegally sold smithings. She was baiting me with a piece of the truth, hoping I'd admit it. My confession would be all she needed to go in for the kill. Ivy moved another pawn, clearing out space for her figures to come out and play. A good battle was a dance, after all.

"He's prickly, but partnership requires balance," I said, taking another sip of tea, followed by a candy. "Bitter and sweet." I hoped the lie was as convincing as it sounded.

"Of course. But if you're ever in need of a sympathetic ear, I'm not far," Ivy mentioned. "Sora is a difficult man to trust." Her eyes were already almost black in color, but at his name they became a pit. His reputation preceded him throughout the Board, then.

I moved my knight aggressively, hoping to advance. "It's hard to measure a person's loyalty until a crisis appears. I've found that people who state their allegiance out loud are often the least trustworthy."

Ivy considered my words while she continued her defense against my push into her territory. "That's true. In the aftermath of a disaster, it is easy to see your true enemies." She caught my gaze. "Usually, they're the ones who are first to point blame."

I sat back and observed the board. Now I understood. Ivy saw it as an insult that Sora might even consider her a suspect. The Amins were a proud family. Irreproachable. Where other clans hoarded their wealth, the Amins spread theirs through philanthropy and community programs.

"I don't believe Sora is blaming you, per se."

"He is losing sight of the issue," Ivy said, and though her tone was level, her voice was sharp. She overtook my pawn and snatched it from play. "Someone on our Board is a murderer. So, for now, I must treat all guests with apprehension. I refuse to put my family's safety at risk. You understand."

I did. I would do the same for my own. "But you let both me and Sora in?"

"Information is a powerful tool in the right hands," she said.

My back stiffened and a creeping feeling that I was being monitored snaked down my spine, but I tried to ignore it. "Is that your strategy for pinpointing conspirators?" I asked. "Waiting and watching?" Ivy had taken my knight and I frowned, trying to find my next move. I took a chance and placed my king on a free square.

Ivy smiled and sat back in her seat. The curve of her lips made me nervous, and I leaned closer to the pieces, reexamining the game.

"It is a part of it. Though, when dealing with a traitor, it is better to draw them out," she said. "With a trap." Ivy slid her bishop across the board, successfully capturing my queen and revealing my error. "Brute force only works for so long."

My ears burned. Papa Ivan would've been disappointed.

"You lost because you were distracted," she said in consolation. "It's easy to lose track of certain pieces when bigger things are happening in the background."

"It's difficult to concentrate when I know I'm being spied on," I said.

Her eyes went wide, and then she let loose a laugh that was high and light. "What makes you say that?"

She was testing me, seeing how much I knew. "I imagine it's related to the smithings," I said, pointing out the ones I could see—a latticed window with small etchings in the wood and a stone wall with the text carved onto the perimeter. "They're beautiful, by the way."

"Calligraphy has deep roots in our culture, history, and religion," Ivy explained, settling herself into her seat comfortably. "Words are often lovelier than any image. More powerful, too."

"Is that why you placed a spell in the boardroom?" I asked. "To spy on the Board and use their secrets for your clan's advancement?"

She sipped her tea delicately. "I did not *spy* on them for my own gain; I was merely doing my job. I am the Board's archivist; we record history as it happens. It's better for our magic to be in the background unnoticed, like a piece of furniture in a large room."

"Then why not be honest about it?"

She shrugged. "When people know they are being observed, they act differently. And if anything, rather than risking anyone harm, it acts as another layer of protection."

Sora had also mentioned that Arabic was defensive. "If that's true, then how could Angelo have been killed?"

A storm cloud darkened her face. "Aside from observation, the spell I laid ensures that only an invited guest may enter or exit; it isn't a ward that prevents harm from befalling anyone in the room."

Meaning Angelo had known his attacker and expected their arrival. This provided a foothold for Vanessa's fear that the hit on Angelo had been internal, someone on the Board. Ivy had made the same assessment. I could understand Sora a bit more now. It did look suspicious to have Ivy retreat to the Amin estate after Angelo's death.

"I didn't kill him," she said plainly, beginning to pick up the fallen pieces. "The Amins don't condone violence."

I helped to reset the pieces of the chessboard, and something struck me as I laid a hand on the queen. She wasn't scared. She'd done exactly what she described: lay in wait. And we'd walked right into her trap. Ivy had only allowed us inside her home so she could keep tabs on us and determine whether we were friends or foes. If either Sora or I had failed her trial, I was sure we wouldn't have left the estate freely.

"Our spells reveal things that the eye or the ear may miss," she explained. I glanced back up curiously at the smithing in the walls.

Amin beckoned with her hand, and the woman who'd brought us our tea came out of the left hall with a heavy book. The chessboard was pushed aside, and Ivy settled the tome on the table, flipping to the last page with writing. The paper was worn with age, but the text was polished, written in gold ink that neatly filled each rectangular pane.

Ivy pointed to a section of the passage as she translated from

Arabic to English. "The women battled with sugar-tipped spears, jostling for the title of queen. The trap was laid; a victor emerged. Yet in the throes of war, recognition dawned on the white and black armies. Kinship in a world of men that believed a woman's worth hid under perfumed sheets."

I reached for the book but stopped myself short, unsure if I'd been given permission. In response, Ivy pressed the back of my hand so that my palm covered the page. The second my fingers brushed against the text, a familiar tingle of magic reached back for me. Mana.

"A chess game," I realized. I released my hold on the book and looked around at the spells in the crevices of the room. "It documented our match." Something my grandfather always said came to mind: Ya ne igrayu shakhmaty—v shakhmatakh ya srazhayus. *One doesn't play chess—one battles.*

"With some flourishes," Ivy added with a knowing smile. "The smithing does a wonderful job of capturing the nature of an interaction, but it takes a lot of artistic leeway. However, it gave me the clear understanding that you are not my enemy."

The Amins no doubt had a library that held their entire family history. Unlike the Homestead clans, they'd never have to wonder at black holes in their past, nor struggle to trace their lineage. A pang of bitterness coursed through me, but I swept it aside. I wouldn't sully another family's treasures because I was jealous.

My fingers burned. "Does this mean you have some record of Angelo's murder?"

Ivy nodded and turned the pages back as she read aloud, translating the passage.

> *When a blade tastes blood from one of its own, it cries*
> *Misfortune has brought death, arriving in twos*
> *The death of a hero, and the death of a dream.*
> *Wings broken, the angel fell to the forest floor, returning like a stone*
> *And the raven-haired king who'd shot him from the sky, wept.*

"Angelo was killed by a friend," I stated.

"Or an ally." Ivy shook her head, tossing away unclear thoughts. "Our smithing never uses names, which leaves us to decode the prose."

"Does the rest of the Board know about this?" I asked.

She ran her tongue across her lips. "They understand our spells seek to record but don't know the exact nature of our magic's final product. I have always refused to house our library at Griffith Hall, and now, I'm certain that was the right choice."

"You also didn't tell them you placed one in the boardroom," I said. "I'm sure they wouldn't be happy to learn they were being recorded."

"Probably not," she agreed. "Which is why after Angelo's death, I grew scarce."

I paused. "If anyone finds out what your spell does, the murderer might come after you."

"I suspected Sora when he first arrived for that exact reason. It was good that you followed, because if I hadn't gotten the gist of your earlier talk, life would've become unpleasant for him."

I raised an eyebrow. "How so?"

Ivy gestured to the doorway behind her, and I watched in awe as the smithing began to squirm; wood groaned and stretched at the hinges until an entirely new door appeared, this one made of solid bronze. It swung open to reveal Sora sitting in the waiting room, a look of surprise splashed across his features. "Kea?" he said as the door slammed shut.

For a moment, I sat too stunned to speak. The doorway had changed. In fact, the whole house had shifted. As I looked around at my surroundings, I realized that the light from the window was now coming in from an entirely different direction than when I'd first entered.

"As I explained, our spells ensure only invited guests enter *and exit*," Ivy said. "We've found it is a more humane way to deal with threats."

"A trap," I echoed and she smiled at me approvingly.

"I am glad things haven't come to that."

Had I not come, she would've kept Sora here for who knew how long. I'd be sure to hold that over his head. Maybe cast it in bronze and plant it in the garden as a monument.

"There must be others you suspect," I pushed.

Ivy adjusted her scarf, rearranging the drape so it looped over her neck and down her back. "I believe someone is trying to ensure Tagalog does not enter regulation. The same proposal was brought up three years ago, but the measure narrowly failed, four to three. I supported the amendment. The inclusion of more minority languages would tip the balance of power away from the classics. However, many others on the Board don't see that as a good thing." She held up her fingers, counting off the reasons. "The usual complaints: purists, members who think clans ought to 'prove themselves' before regulation, and those who believe that some languages are inherently more valuable. But the votes are sealed, so I couldn't tell you who exactly fell in either camp."

I needed those records as soon as possible. Sora might resist, but I'd be delighted to twist his arm. He owed me now.

"Maybe we can play another round in the future," I said, standing to leave. "I'd like to try again, even though it feels like I was fated to lose."

Ivy mirrored my movements. "The cure for fate is patience. You play like a wild thing. Impulsive, emotional, rash." Her eyes focused on the gold seal above the door as she strode past me. "If you learned to balance that with strategy, you would be magnificent." She glanced over her shoulder, her lashes lowered and a smile creeping on her face as she paused. "At chess, that is."

Swallowing the lump in my throat, I followed Ivy to the exit. A fire had lit itself on my cheeks, burning down to my core. I wondered if excellence tasted like the jeweled candies Ivy served for tea. I tossed the thought away and braced myself to reenter the heat of Los Angeles. It was better not to wish for impossible things.

CHAPTER 7

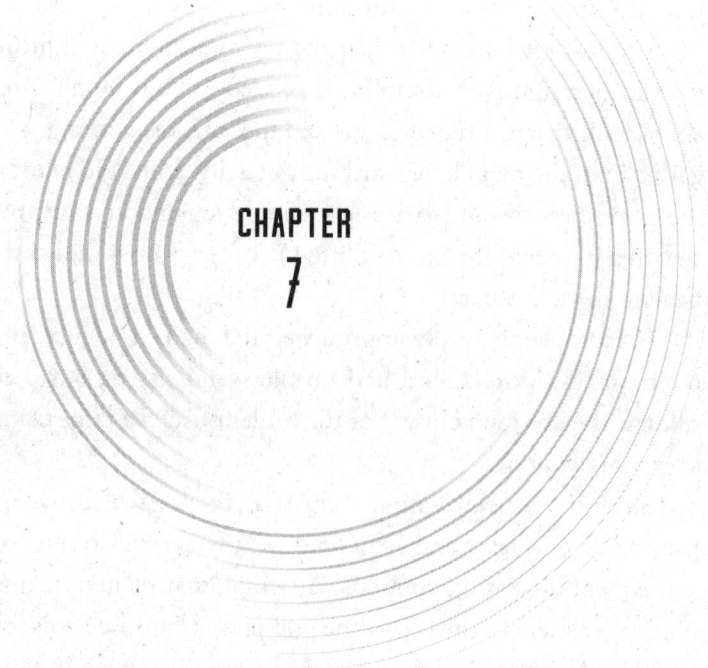

True to his word, Sora gave me unfettered access to the investigation and, by proxy, his home. I'd at first found that odd but quickly discovered why when I entered his wing of the Kaiser estate to find boxes and boxes of files stuffed full of papers and piled up to the ceiling. My jaw fell open at the sheer number of manila folders that he'd collected and cataloged.

"I don't like computers," he said by way of explanation when he noticed the look on my face.

"Are you a masochist?" I asked, stunned. Though the room was packed, everything was organized neatly, labeled with bold printed letters in alphabetical order. It would've taken him weeks to put it together.

He scowled. "I'm a realist. Technetics is a dangerous tool in the hands of a criminal. I try to keep my bases covered."

In other words, he was paranoid. I was both impressed and frightened at his commitment to his role as the head of safety and security for the Board. He was a natural fit.

The Kaisers had made their money by training and hiring out private armies, and that discipline extended to their home. Every day, at six o'clock sharp, a trumpet marked the start of morning, and a crowd gathered in the main courtyard for the daily drills. No matter the hour, there were always at least a few people jogging around the estate or sparring in one of the courts dotted between houses and cottages. Sora never joined, though.

In fact, people rarely approached the main residence unless it was for business. I knew Sora had brothers and sisters, but their absence told me they weren't close. For the leader of such a large clan, Sora was surprisingly alone.

Since the official voting records were still sealed, we'd spent the past week poring over hard copies of the Board's recent rulings and subsequent dissenting opinions. Anything that related to language regulation was sent to the top of the pile as we composed a list of suspects. Matthew Greyson and Reagol Stone were very much in the old guard and decidedly against expansion. Celine Vidrine, the seated representative for the French language, would also back them. Charles Lam—and admittedly Sora—could've gone either way.

I was useless at politics, so I spent most of my time reviewing the smithing from Ivy and trying to ignore how damn comfortable I was in the Kaiser home. It wasn't that the place was cozy, but rather that Sora had anything he could ever desire within arm's reach. The air was a perfect seventy-three degrees, fresh flowers appeared magically on his counter each morning, and any drinks I pulled from the fridge were restocked within hours.

I hated it.

The sheer ease of everything was unnerving. People shouldn't live like this, with no discomfort at all. I took to petty demonstrations of protest by being as messy as possible just to make the place a little more lived in. Situated at his kitchen island, I'd spread out files and clean sheets of paper, arranged so I could add notes as needed while I dissected the spell.

While reviewing my work, I felt a presence near my back and turned to find Sora standing over me, staring at the linguistic map I'd made. He leaned over, setting his arm on the counter, caging me in place, and tapped Charles's and Reagol's names.

I froze at his closeness, but Sora didn't notice and spoke directly into my ear. "Maybe you could translate the Board members' names as well, to see if there's a connection to the Arabic record."

"Their names are English," I stressed.

He left the table and returned a second later with a naming dictionary pulled from one of the bookcases that lined the wall on either side of his television. "English names have meanings, too." He flipped through the pages and called out the definitions as he came across them, prompting me to write them down.

    Matthew Greyson = Gift of God, Son of a steward
    Reagol Stone = King, Stone
    Sora Kaiser = Sky, Emperor
    Charles Lam = Free man, Forest
    Ivy Amin = Ivy, Honest
    Celine Vidrine = Heavenly, Name derived from a place:
        Védrine in France
    Vanessa Reyes = Butterfly, Kings

Sora grudgingly ended up pulling out an electronic translator to search for the ones he couldn't find a match for. For example, Lam was a transliteration common among families of the Chinese diaspora. It was derived from the Cantonese word for *tree*. The duplication of that character created the surname Lam, which meant *forest* or *woods*.

Armed with a new understanding, we pulled apart the rest of Ivy's spell, finding clear connections between the words *king* and *forest*, which helped us narrow our list. Reagol Stone, Charles Lam, and Vanessa Reyes all had names that tied into the smithing. Sora's name did too, but I made a mental note instead of saying so aloud.

I frowned, biting the edge of my pen. Nothing was really a perfect fit, yet the echoes of each person's name in the text were a map sketched in pencil: faint but hard to ignore. The smithing spoke of a betrayal, and Ivy's spell echoed that pattern, singing of regret.

The older members would have motive to kill simply to retain their status. Charles and Vanessa, though, seemed to have a more personal connection. Charles, from what I'd seen, was pursuing Vanessa so quickly after her husband's death that it seemed not just suspicious but inappropriate. I didn't know the backstory between the two yet, but he'd called her a pet name. Ness. Was his attraction one-sided, or had the two been having an affair? It warranted further scrutiny.

It was possible that Vanessa had lied to me, but it didn't seem likely. She was carrying Angelo's child, and it seemed she would give anything to find Angelo's killer. Frowning, I tapped the word *king* over and over until I finally realized what had been gnawing at me from the back of my mind.

"Arabic is gendered," I said, staring at *raven-haired king* before crossing off Vanessa and Celine. "I think we have to only focus on men."

Which left only three. Charles had built the Lam Syndicate up to a powerhouse in only ten years, rivaling even the Amins when it came to profits. His success was enviable, and it spoke to the hard work he'd poured into his clan. If he was still in love with Vanessa, perhaps he'd killed Angelo just to take his place.

Reagol did have a clear prejudice against any new language introduced to regulation, so that was a motive as well. And as for Sora . . .

Well, Sora was an enigma.

Sora's thumb tapped the back of my hand. I turned, finding his face close to mine, studying my expression. "What are you thinking?" he asked.

"That we need to talk to Charles Lam and Reagol Stone," I answered, fighting to keep a stammer from my voice. He was always so close. The man seemed to have no grasp of personal space.

Since I couldn't outright tell him that I hadn't yet removed him as a suspect, I instead walked him through my thought process, pointing out the connections I'd made between the spells and information we'd gathered while he listened aptly. Sora carefully considered each point, pulled along by my logic.

By the time I'd finished, Sora was on his feet, pacing the room. "The Board's between sessions right now, so we'll need to find another way to approach them."

"I don't suppose they're your friends?" I asked and was promptly met with a withering glare. Of course not. How dare I suggest that the great Sora Kaiser have friends.

"I'll figure out a way," he declared. His eyes scanned back over my notes. "This is very thorough. You've done good work here."

I drummed my fingers against Ivy's translated spell. "Anyone can analyze text. But writing a new spell? Now, that's magic."

"I've never written my own smithings," he said. "They don't work as well as the ones I've simply learned."

"That could be intention," I guessed. "You need to be confident in what you're smithing. Doubting your work would make it fail." I knew this well from personal experience. If it weren't for my weird little sympathetic magic trick, that *click* I felt when I knew the words fit together just right, none of my smithing would work either.

Sora grabbed the back of the bar stool I was sitting on and ran a hand over the pages of notes I'd made, much in the same way someone might pet a well-behaved dog. The shadow of a smile lingered on his face. "You're more perceptive than you look."

I launched the half compliment back at him. "Didn't realize you were looking."

He drew back abruptly and re-buttoned his blazer. Even when at home, Sora preferred to wear a suit. It had to be uncomfortable. "I'm not. Just observing."

In a moment of temporary insanity, I decided to tease him, leaning in closer. "And do you like what you see?"

Sora jumped away from me like I was made of hot coal. His mouth opened and closed, and then he turned on his heels and went to another room, slamming the door shut with a bang.

I laughed, filling the empty kitchen with gleeful sound. Leaving Sora speechless was going to be my new hobby.

~

"Why did your grandfather just threaten to beat me with a shovel?" Basilio panted over the phone.

"Probably because he didn't have a gun on him," I said. I'd expected to hear from Basilio sooner or later, but I didn't think he'd just drop by the house without letting me know first. "Was Papa in the garden?"

Basilio sighed. "Yes."

I finished painting my toenails, set aside the polish, and flopped backward on the floor near Sora's couch. I'd earned this small break—I'd been coming into the city daily to sort through files with Sora, meaning a long drive and even longer hours. "What did you expect?"

"You didn't tell them about all of this, did you?" he said with a groan.

"Of course not," I defended. "He just doesn't like you."

Ever since Basilio left the Homestead, and dropped us like a sack of rice, Papa Ivan had become his biggest hater.

Basilio, who was used to being liked, was immensely bothered by it. "I'm a *delight*," he argued.

I rolled my eyes. "Please."

"I never want to be on your grandpa's bad side," he said. "He's scary."

"Then you shouldn't have gotten me tangled up in this," I said.

"I tried not to," he said. "You wouldn't answer my calls."

"And that meant I was asking for this? The Board's collar around my neck, and Sora checking to make sure it's tight enough."

"Sorry," Basilio said. "I really didn't mean for all this to happen."

"It's fine," I dismissed. "I understand my part in this. Don't get all sulky."

Basilio laughed. I did, too, and we drifted off into a comfortable silence. "I missed talking to you," he said.

"Me too," I admitted. "The Homestead's different without you there. Just me and the Two Stooges. As soon as I get on the council, I'll pass a law that Keanu has to always be fully clothed."

Basilio cackled. The Mahiʻai head was notorious for taking off his shirt at any chance he got. "Watch out—if you try to force a shirt on him, you might get your eye poked out by his pecs."

The two of us wheezed in laughter.

"Are you close to figuring out a new mana o ka moʻokūʻauhau?" he asked.

"Define *close*," I muttered.

Basilio went quiet. "I shouldn't have pried, especially since you know what I did to join LA." To prove his loyalty to the city and fully dissolve his clan, Basilio had had to give up his own family spell.

"Can I ask you what it did?" I asked. Mana o ka moʻokūʻauhau on the Homestead were special in that they had to be not only extremely powerful, but also beneficial to the community as a whole. I knew, for example, that the Mahiʻais' spell somehow involved weather, but I was scant on the details. This was our most sacred magic and carefully guarded.

"Not like it matters anymore," Basilio said. "It's gone anyway." He took a deep breath. "You'd think the city would have better record-keepers, but the person who took down my spell didn't even know the basics of Hawaiian. Had no idea what I was writing. But to answer your question, our family spell was made for agriculture—more specifically for kalo, to build and irrigate loʻi."

In my mind, I could almost see the magic he described coming to life. Muddy, knee-deep taro patches with streaming fresh water filling each paddy. It suited Basilio's family perfectly. They were gardeners, growers, and most importantly, healers.

It was my turn to apologize. My throat seized up. "I'm so sorry."

"Don't," he said quickly, his voice stern. "I made my choice. Don't you dare pity me."

"I won't," I promised.

Basilio cleared his throat. "Anyway, I was worried about you. You basically dropped off the map after talking to Vanessa. When I asked your grandfather where you were, he got jumpy and pulled a shovel on me."

"I've been in the city," I explained, holding back a laugh as I imagined my Papa chasing Basilio off our property. Poor guy. I could pity him for *that*, at least. "It's been more convenient for sleuthing."

"I thought you were smithing?" Basilio asked.

At the mention of my task, I sat up from the floor and glared at the journals and papers spread out on the couch cushions, which were now eye level. I tapped the pages of my closest notebook. "Smithing. Sleuthing. Both."

"I hope Sora's been helpful, at least."

I snorted. Sora was being Sora. Though he'd promised to figure out a way to get in contact with Charles, he hadn't been very successful. The Chinese clan head seemed to enjoy holding something Sora wanted just out of arm's reach.

"Is there anything I can do to help?" Basilio asked.

I blew on the wet toenail polish. "Not that I can think of. Unless you can get me an audience with Charles Lam."

Another long pause greeted me, enough to make me stop what I was doing.

"What about a chance encounter?" Basilio asked.

My blowing turned into a sputter, and I sat up. "I'll take it."

~

Basilio was on the Asian American Cultural Center's directorial committee with Charles, and their annual gala was being held in a week. It was the perfect social opportunity to casually interview both him and

Reagol. It was also a fancy party with drinks, dresses, and unfortunately, dancing.

It wasn't that I was a bad dancer. Like anyone who had grown up around music, I could keep a beat. Whether it was late-night kanikapila sessions in the garage, hymns on the days that Nana convinced everyone to attend mass, or the soft humming of women washing up after dinner, I knew the motions required. Rhythm wasn't my problem. It was the shoes.

When I had danced before, it had been to the steady drum of an ipu being smacked against the earth or as I spun around the backyard with Sisi in hand. I liked the feeling of solid ground beneath my feet. For me, dancing required that close connection to the land, but whenever I slipped on a pair of heels, every step felt uncertain.

On top of everything, I'd be wearing an outfit that would weigh me down. Sora had explained that these events stuck to rigid dress codes. I'd need to look as extravagant as everyone else, which meant that I needed a custom gown. He'd seriously asked my opinion on Battenberg lace, hoopskirts, and chiffon versus crepe de chine while I stared blankly back at him.

I was too overwhelmed with smithing and memorizing handbooks on manners and city politics to decode his questions, so I left Sora to the task. It was on him if I ended up looking like a stuffed goose. In retrospect, that was a mistake. I'd snuck a peek at Sora's order, discovered that there was bound to be multiple layers of fabric, and literally choked. This was going to be a disaster.

Dancing, at least, I had some control over—being passable in the ballroom would help me blend in. Frowning, I took a few hesitant steps in the high heels that I'd bought for the occasion. While I was able to practice in the dance studio housed near the Kaisers' gym, today was my first time actually using it. I may have been the first to enter the space in years. The wooden floors shined like they weren't often stepped on, and the walls were mirrored from floor to ceiling, not a single smudge in sight.

Lifting my right hand to the air, I laid my left on an invisible partner, counting out in threes as I struggled to practice the footwork I'd learned from a video online. This was ridiculous. A step turn brought me back toward the door, where a shadow lurked, watching.

"You look stiff," Sora commented. The remnants of a smile were stapled on his face like I'd just missed him laughing.

I scowled. "I'm doing my best."

"Well, you can do better," he said. Sora came closer, circling me. His palm pressed against my spine, and I stood straighter while his other hand gently adjusted my elbow. "The crowd there will notice every mistake, so steel yourself."

"I'll manage," I said, distracted by his fingers as they grazed over my skin, working to fix the small mistakes in my form. He was too close for me to completely avoid his gaze. Even if I looked to the side, I'd see his reflection in the mirrors surrounding us.

Sora extended his hand to me with a snort. "I'd rather not leave things to chance."

I looked down, momentarily confused. When I realized he was offering to practice with me, I lost my footing and threw out my arms to catch my balance. "Do you even know how to dance?"

"Of course I do," he said with a huff.

There was no good reason not to accept, so I took his hand, letting him draw me to his chest. His thumb stroked the curve of my spine in a reminder to stand straight and I followed the command. He caught my free hand, placing it on his shoulder while his found my waist. "Don't look down," he said lowly.

Butterfly wings brushed the sides of my stomach, and I blew out a puff of air, trying to expel the feeling. Sora and I worked together every day, which meant I'd been close to him frequently, especially with his habit of invading my personal space, sidling up next to me while I looked over papers so our elbows touched. The thought made my face heat up, and I disobeyed his command not to stare at my feet.

Breathe, Kea.

I'd look up at his face and see the disinterest I'd come to expect. I raised my head, but when I met Sora's gaze, his red eyes reflected a barely contained wildness, like he was holding himself back at the edge of a cliff. My stomach clenched, but I was swept into his movements before I could think about what his expression had meant.

We spun around the room, but my footwork was clunky, and within minutes, I was digging my fingers into his arms to stop myself from falling over.

"Lean back," Sora instructed. "The momentum will keep us upright. Yes, like that. Relax your arms, too."

With each command he helped to guide my body into the correct motions, and after five songs, I was beginning to get a slight feel for the movement of a waltz. This was vastly different from the hula I knew. I felt like a new bird learning to fly or a top spinning out of control. Without a stable partner, I'd float off into space.

"Talk to me," he demanded, breaking my concentration.

"I'm trying to focus," I shot back.

He sighed and gave my right hand a small squeeze. "Don't be difficult. You need to be able to speak and dance at the same time. If someone asks you for a dance, they'll try to make conversation."

I scrunched my forehead together. "Why do I need to dance at all?"

He pulled me an inch closer then made an unexpected pivot to the left. "You never know when it might be useful for you to gather information. Let's start with something simple. What are the names of the two Spanish-speaking members of the Board?"

"Vanessa Reyes," I responded. "And Celine Vidrine." Everyone on the Board except for Charles was proficient in Latin, and most knew at least a few more languages. English, though not regulated, was the only true common tongue.

He continued to quiz me as we danced, and while I got half of his prompts correct, that still wasn't to Sora's high standard. I struggled to catch my breath and answer every one with a smile but quickly grew irritable.

"I'll just use my sympathetic ability. It'll be easier for me to remember their names and faces once I get a little taste of their mana," I remarked.

He stopped the barrage of questions and spun me out, then back in. "Your sympathetic magic can do that?"

"Nothing like your mind reading trick, though. I can just sense mana out in the world. It works on people, too. If I touch a bit of someone's bare skin, it'll help me discern their magic." I didn't know a better way to explain it.

He considered that as we did another turn around the room. "A dip would work best to get close to a dance partner. You can place your hand around their neck or chest. It's more difficult, but we can practice." He stopped moving and placed my right hand behind his neck, then guided my left to rest on his shoulder above the collarbone. His hands went to my back and pulled tight, so our chests touched. "This is the position you want to be in for better balance."

My mouth was dry and my jaw tight. I was afraid if I spoke, I'd stumble over my words, so I nodded dumbly and we reset back to first position.

Under his breath Sora counted in threes. "Just follow my lead."

He lifted his hand and I ducked underneath his arm, repeating the motion, before he guided me back. We circled the room in lockstep before returning to the door. He released me and I turned out, taking a spin to return so we were at each other's sides with my arms crossed over my front.

When I faced him, Sora was looking right at me, his arm around my back and hands tightly holding mine. Our faces were so close that the red of his eyes shone like a bull's-eye in a target. He suddenly spun me out once more. I gasped but had no time to think as I was drawn back again just as quickly. This time his arms dropped around my waist, and he leaned to the side to ease me into the dip. Remembering his instructions, I wrapped an arm around his neck and let myself fall into his arms, sparking my magic to life.

Candied ginger filled my mouth, sweet and sharp.

When I touched his skin, my ability took hold. His mana flowed into me, a wave of unbridled power. I knew I should pull away, but I was no longer in control of myself. I wanted more. My fingertips dug into his skin as his magic entwined with mine. Flashes of him poured through our connection. Not thoughts exactly. Fragments of who he was.

Sora likes dogs and hot chocolate with whipped cream, but he feels ashamed for enjoying it so much. He doesn't trust his family, nor the Board. He doesn't trust anyone much but that suits him fine. People are boring. Except maybe her. The girl from the Homestead, who is strange, ever present, and vastly irritating. For someone without much power, she never does what he expects, and he doesn't know what to make of that. In that way, she scares him.

Sora pulled me back up from the dip slowly. The thrum of our magics pulled tight, like threads weaving together. When I was standing again, he jerked away and walked to the other side of the room. Sora placed a hand against the mirror as he steadied his breath, leaving a handprint over his reflection. His chest rose and fell in deep pants.

"What did you just do to me?" he asked, his voice clipping at the ends.

I still felt strange, but it was manageable. A fizziness in my gut instead of the manic compulsion to spin in circles until I hurled. "I don't know."

He slicked back his hair but there was a shake in his fingers. "Bullshit."

I really enjoyed making him swear.

"It's never done that before," I said. "My sympathetic magic doesn't do much except give me a heads-up before others cast. I can also deduce another sympath's ability if I get close enough but that's it."

"I tasted . . . dark chocolate," he murmured. "And chili peppers."

"That's probably my magic," I explained, my cheeks burning. Hearing about the flavor of my own magic was oddly embarrassing. "I can taste people's mana. Maybe somehow, you used my sympathetic ability back on me."

Sora came to the same conclusion I already had. "If I accessed your ability, you must've touched mine, too." He didn't need to elaborate on his power. I had *felt* him. His likes and dislikes, his emotions, his essence. It wasn't simple mind reading like I'd assumed earlier, but something far deeper.

"How does it relate to your name?" I asked curiously. I knew very limited Japanese, but Sora was a common word, meaning *sky*.

"My mother thinks that the way I read people is like predicting the weather," he said. "I agree in the sense of how open the sky is; it eventually reveals everything, no matter how hard a storm might try to hide the stars. People lie all the time. My gift helps me see through that."

"That's why you have trust issues," I surmised.

His eyebrow raised. "Is that your assessment of me? Or something you saw just now?"

"Both," I answered.

A few tense seconds passed before Sora settled. He ran a hand through his hair, retying it out of his face. "I know you said this has never happened before, but we can't take that risk at the gala. At the gala, don't use any of your sympathetic magic. Just learn everyone's names like you're supposed to." He popped the button on his shirt at the nape of his neck, and my eyes were drawn down to the beads of sweat on his exposed collarbone. "You need more practice with footwork."

Sora exited the room as quickly as he could, leaving me alone in the studio. My face was flushed and my eyebrows reflexively drawn together. The taste of ginger lingered on my tongue, and I frowned at the empty doorway. He was such a jerk.

Sora was right about one thing, though. People lied all the time, but mana never did. He could hide behind his cold words and gruff attitude, but not from my magic. And I knew that what I'd seen was correct. He was afraid of me.

But how on earth could *I* frighten the great and terrible Sora Kaiser?

CHAPTER 8

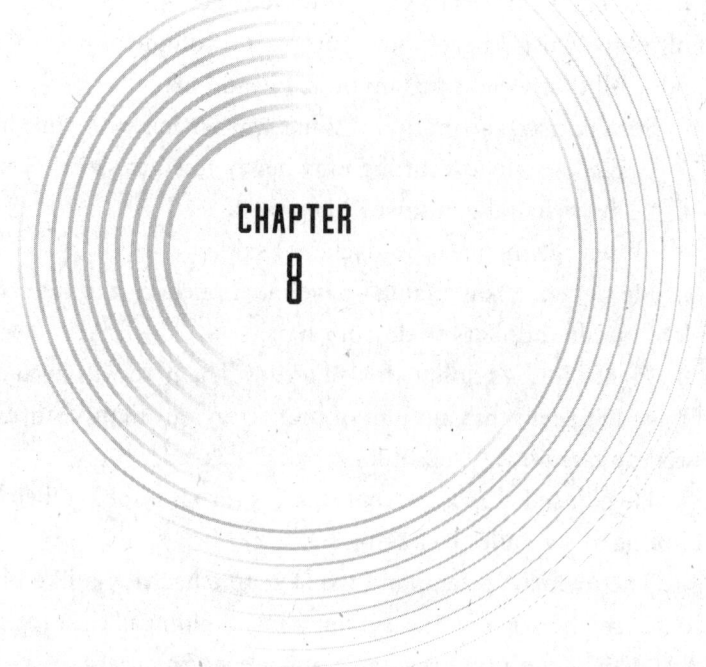

The day of the gala we drove to the event in dead silence, which for my usual chatterbox self was unusual, but I was consumed by nerves. When we arrived at the Asian American Cultural Center, I pulled on the handle of the door to let myself out just as Sora rounded the back of the vehicle. He extended his arm to me when I exited, but I just looked at it and stared.

He gave an exaggerated sigh, like he was dealing with the stupidest woman in the world. "Your heels. If you hold onto me, it'll help. All you have to do is walk in a straight line."

Yeah, right.

I let out a huff of breath and relented, placing my hand in his. He was right, unfortunately. I needed the support, because my feet already ached. My whole body was on fire, like I had a fever. As we walked upstairs toward the courtyard that led to the building, a cool breeze hit the back of my neck and I shivered. I needed to relax.

My scalp throbbed, so I untwisted the hair piled there, letting it fall to my waist. I never liked putting the volume of my waves into an updo. All that weight tied up on my head hurt.

Sora noticed the motion. "What was wrong with your hair?"

I raked my fingers through my newly freed tresses. "Nothing."

"Then why take it down?" he asked.

"It was giving me a headache," I said.

He sighed. "You couldn't have mentioned that to the stylist I paid eight hundred dollars to do your hair?"

Eight *hundred* dollars for a hairdo? The man was insane. I probably hadn't spent that amount of money on hair in my entire life, but it was too late now. "Does it look bad?" I asked.

He glanced at me, the center of his throat bobbing, before quickly looking away. "No. It doesn't."

The night was clear, and the sky stretched down like black velvet to touch the tops of the surrounding buildings. Unsurprisingly, the AACC was the same cement gray as everything else in Los Angeles, though it had an odd shape, built to look like a slice of cake cut out of concrete and glass. Rectangular pillars on the first floor hoisted the building above the red cobblestones of the larger plaza below.

Sora deftly pulled me through into the building's entrance and navigated through the halls until we came upon a lower room with glass walls that opened to an immaculately styled Japanese garden. At the front of the room, a slow line wound to check in weapons before entering the main hall.

The small motion of letting down my hair drew attention like a lit match. The other guests all had their hair in whimsical braids and swoops reminiscent of the Gibson girl era. Mine had already started frizzing on the ends, puffing up with humidity like a lion's mane. I began to regret taking out my updo, but even if I hadn't, I wasn't sure how much it would've helped.

People stared openly as we waited to enter the gala, their eyes landing first on Sora and then sticking to me. We made an odd pair. Though he spoke to no one, Sora fit in the way only a person who operated in this world could. He was untouchable. I, on the other hand, was an invasive weed in a rose garden. The gentle lilac of my gown clashed with my dark skin. A little reminder that no matter how much I studied or trained, I did not belong here.

Not that I would ever forget.

I caught the end of a conversation as we moved forward in the queue. "... why would the Kaiser head come with..."

I flushed scarlet, even without hearing the rest. I could imagine any number of unpleasant endings to that sentence. Sora, oblivious to my unease, nudged me forward.

Ivy's cryptic warnings were beginning to make sense. Wealth distorted people's perception of reality; it made everything sparkle, but none of it was *real*. In a world where people could play out their greatest fantasies with money, who needed to live on earth? Maybe there was something wrong with me, though, because all I wanted was to burn it all down.

At the entrance an attendant asked for our weapons. I hadn't thought to bring one but Sora had come fully equipped. He dropped his katana on the table, alongside a handful of knives that had been strapped to his leg and waist, as well as tucked into his socks, just in case his other eight weapons got lost. I shook my head at the young man and he shrugged, handing back a ticket. Taking the claim tag, Sora guided me by the small of my back to an empty cocktail table, swiping us each a glass of champagne along the way.

Shimmering gowns in white, gold, and pink spun across the floor. The delicate sound of clinking glasses and laughter floated like champagne bubbles around the room, beautiful but deadly. I suddenly craved the wildness of Homestead functions, colorful and playful, pā'inas that you remembered through a boozy haze. This gala wasn't a party. It was more like stepping into a role in a play where I was under pressure to perform flawlessly.

A small knot of fear filled my gut at the notion that I might get clocked as an imposter and hauled out. The people here would see right through me, and that would be the end of things. Sora must have finally noticed the tension in my back because he pressed the glass into my hand, urging me to drink.

I downed the champagne, enjoying the quick burn of alcohol as it lit me from within. It was so sharp and sudden that I coughed, needing to cover my mouth to stifle the noise. Sora's mouth twitched into the semblance of a smile, though he had the decency to ignore it.

"Do you see Charles?" I asked, setting the empty glass aside.

Sora nodded. "Don't talk to him on your own." He moved his eyes to the left. I followed his gaze with a small spin, noticing the other Board members here.

Sora grasped my elbow and led me over to the group of mostly men. "It's expected that I say hello. Don't antagonize them," he warned as we approached. "Just make polite conversation."

Reagol Stone and Matthew Greyson disengaged from their conversation as we approached and held out their hands to Sora in greeting, while Vanessa gave a short wave. Charles Lam, however, ignored both of us.

Vanessa shifted from foot to foot uncomfortably and kept her hands across her stomach as if to lift the weight off her. "Glad you could both make it." She gave a short huff. "Though regrettably, I might not stay long myself."

"Are you lightheaded, Ness?" Charles asked, laying a hand on her arm. His brow furrowed with worry; it seemed around her, his notorious viciousness fell away.

She shook her head. "Just tired. Getting dressed was an ordeal."

"I can take you home if you—"

"That won't be necessary," she said, cutting him off. "My driver is more than equipped."

He frowned. "If you're not feeling well, you should leave and rest. I'll walk you to the valet."

Vanessa hesitated, looking to me and Sora, but eventually gave in. "If you insist."

"Excuse us," Charles said, taking hold of Vanessa's arm. "I'll be sure to find you gentlemen later." They strode away together, his other hand pressed against her back.

Once they left, Matthew turned his attention fully to Sora. "Rare to see you at an event like this."

"The Kaiser clan intends to become more involved with the AACC moving forward." Sora's cool, disengaged tone made my head spin. I hadn't even noticed that he'd stopped using it with me. "We hope to help with the advancement of all Asian languages in LA."

"I suppose we have Angelo's death to thank for this sudden change?" Reagol grumbled, swishing down the last of his champagne and gesturing for a waiter to take it away.

"It may have had an impact," Sora agreed, eyes clouded. "Knowing your thoughts on such an expansion, I imagine you must have been feeling like the carpet was being ripped from under you before Angelo's demise."

"Don't misunderstand me." Reagol took a step back, waving his hands in front of his face. "The whole situation is tragic." He plucked another glass from the waiter's tray without sparing a glance at the man's face.

"Of course," Sora said, though his voice had already turned chilly.

The waiter offered more drinks to our group, and everyone declined but me. I gladly took one and thanked the man. Matthew and Reagol finally seemed to register my presence, staring disapprovingly. At my side, Sora lightly pinched the side of my elbow, and I withdrew back to the group, unsure of what misstep I'd just made.

Always the gentleman, Matthew smiled broadly and tried to smooth things over. "I think Reagol means that no one could've anticipated that the loss of Angelo would bring such a strong ally to the AACC and the Reyes clan. It's good that his death was not in vain." His thinning gray hair had been brushed unflatteringly over his head.

"Nothing like a martyr to win over icy hearts," Sora said. His fingers swept across my skin until they settled on my forearm, holding me in place.

I couldn't tell if the gesture was meant to hold me back, or himself.

"I didn't mean to start an argument," Reagol said. "Expansion can be good. But everything in moderation. I'm sure we can agree on that much. If change comes too quickly, the seams of our society will rip. Previously, Sora spoke out in opposition to the inclusion of oral languages. That's the same vein of thinking that I have, though my distinctions draw a tighter line."

Oral languages. Like Hawaiian.

I turned to look Sora in the face. His mouth was tight, and his eyes were narrowed, but that wasn't an unusual expression for him. His fingers pressed down more firmly on my arm. Was this the true cause of our disagreement regarding me using magic? Did he think I was inherently inferior somehow? I dropped my arm from his grasp.

"It'll take work to convince the public that Tagalog or any language aspiring to enter regulation has truly earned its place among the greats," Matthew concluded.

"What exactly are the qualifications?" I asked, riding a burst of barely hidden anger into the conversation. When the trio turned to look at me, I forced myself to stand straight. "To be considered a 'great' language, I mean."

"That's simple, my dear. Regulated languages are like clay. Easily moldable into whatever you want them to be, or to do," Reagol answered. "I'd also argue, on a more philosophical note, that they are the most beautiful."

I bristled. "How can you so confidently say that Latin is more beautiful than Igbo or Finnish or Hebrew?"

"It's not just beauty, but a combination of the two," Reagol argued, evading the question. "A *delicate* balance. Other languages are unwieldy. Rather than clay, they're blocks of stone."

"Statues can be carved of stone, too. Maybe it has less to do with the material and more to do with the skill of its sculptor," I argued.

An awkward silence descended on the group, and I opened my mouth to try and mend things, but Sora beat me to the punch.

"The Homestead has stood for two hundred years, pressed against the wild magic of the ocean, which even we avoid. Maybe we should trust that they have some special insight on how to turn rocks into arrowheads," he mentioned, effortlessly lifting me out of the pit I'd dug for myself. "But I think that's enough talking shop for tonight. Gentlemen." He reclaimed my hand, lacing our fingers together. "Enjoy your evening."

As we walked away, Sora poked me in the ribs. "I told you not to antagonize them," he whispered.

"They started it," I complained.

He set down his champagne glass. "Apparently, I'm going to need more to drink." He paused and eyed me. "Don't start any more fights while I'm gone. Don't disappear on me. Don't even breathe." He gave me a final tap on the top of my hand then left, striding across the geometric rug of green and gold.

"Ass," I murmured to his retreating figure. If Sora heard me, he made no sign of it. I watched him go, willing him to drop dead or spontaneously combust. Neither happened and I downed my glass in frustration.

A voice from behind me cut into my jumbled thoughts. "I never imagined that Sora Kaiser would show up to this with our little language expert as his date."

I turned around to see Charles return from the valet. He was usually movie-star gorgeous, but tonight he'd really leaned into the role, looking like a prince from a fairy tale. Charles was dressed in a cream-colored jacket, complete with a navy blue sash tied across his chest. An assortment of gleaming medals adorned the front of his outfit, which I had no doubt were real gold, and not plastic dipped in metallic paint.

His eyes traced over my body, taking in each frill and bolt of lace and lingering on my breasts, which had been propped to exaggerated proportions where the dress's corset pulled in my waist. Charles extended a hand. "Consider my curiosity piqued. Care to dance, Kea?"

"I'm not very graceful," I warned. Sora had told me not to speak to Charles alone, but I likely wouldn't get another opportunity.

He gently pulled me by the waist and adjusted my posture as we moved to the dance floor. "That's fine. I prefer to lead."

He caught my hand in his and swept me into the motions of the dance with the grace of a professional. He would be dancing with a wooden mannequin, but he didn't seem to mind.

Doing the waltz with Charles was different from practicing with Sora. He was technically perfect, and far more skilled; each turn was a precise movement that followed an expected sequence. I found him easy to predict, unlike the sudden spins and dips that Sora had urged me into, leaving me breathless.

"Are you nervous?" Charles asked, trying to decode the wrinkle of concentration on my forehead.

"A little," I admitted, though it had nothing to do with him, and everything to do with my heels.

Charles's eyes dipped to my throat, and pressure built in my gut like a swift kick. Dammit. He was disgustingly handsome, but I wasn't some addled teenager at prom. I needed to pull myself together and start using this opportunity to interrogate him.

"I'm surprised you're so involved in the AACC," I said. "Considering you didn't want the registry expanded to include Tagalog."

His smile was blinding. "I think all languages are wonderful, but not all are *exceptional*. It's not a problem as long as they stick to their lane. Tagalog and Angelo refused to." He tensed at having to say Angelo's name.

"That sounded personal," I said.

"Someone's nosy," he responded with the raise of an eyebrow and a slight grin.

"Not particularly," I said. "But we've met before. At Vanessa's house. You were rather loud."

His smile faltered. "Oh? I must've been distracted, because I make a point to introduce myself to beautiful women."

The attentive friend that had catered to Vanessa Reyes was gone, replaced by a shameless philanderer. It was such blatant two-faced masking that I wondered which persona was a front. The playboy or the puppy dog?

"Like Vanessa?" I pushed.

"Ness and I have known each other since childhood," he said quickly. "Other than that, we don't have much to do with each other. I was hoping not to speak about this awful business with Angelo tonight."

"We don't have much else to discuss," I said.

Charles's hand trailed down the bare skin on my arm. "Not true." He was speaking to me, but his eyes were focused over my shoulder, a smirk planted on his face. "Anyone that's caught Sora's eye is bound to be entertaining. I'm just trying to figure out what's made him so interested in you, and whether it's underneath that dress."

Before I could even open my mouth to snap back at the vulgar comment, a dark shadow flanked my side. "I leave for a moment, and you assault my partner. Typical," Sora snarled. His hand reached for my elbow and pulled me out of Charles's grasp.

"A single dance is hardly an assault," Charles protested.

"Not for anyone but you," Sora growled.

Charles's smile grew fangs as he passed by my keeper, placing a menacing hand on Sora's shoulder. "Forgive me, but it seemed the only polite thing to do when I saw her left alone. Sadly, Kea was only interested in talking politics, and I want to do nothing of the sort this evening."

Sora was visibly seething at being touched so casually. "Perhaps tomorrow, then?"

"Fine," Charles agreed lazily. "I suppose I can squeeze you in, if you bring her along." He winked at me, then walked away.

The second he disappeared, Sora laid into me. "What is *wrong* with you?" he asked. "Why would you speak to a suspect without me? I explicitly said not to."

"It was only a dance," I tried to explain.

"You should've said no," Sora said coldly. "Knowing Charles, he likely wrestled some vital piece of information out of you."

"I'm not a complete idiot," I said. "All he did was flirt a little. We didn't discuss the investigation." It was true that I'd let Charles go on longer than I'd normally tolerate, but only because I wanted him to tell me something. And I'd helped secure a meeting, hadn't I?

"You're wasting time here *flirting*," he said, shaking his head.

"I mean," I said, twisting a strand of hair out of my face, "he is handsome."

Brilliant. All my pretty spell-smithing words dried up the minute I needed to be quick-witted.

"Handsome?" Sora repeated the word back to me in utter disbelief. "All that critical thought." He stuck a finger against my forehead and poked. "All that caution of yours goes out the window the second a pretty boy flaps into view."

"Who said I was immune to good looks?" I retorted, slapping his hand away.

Truly dumbfounded, Sora's expression twisted as if he was embarrassed to look at me. "You were acting like an imbecile. Blushing. Holding hands." His mouth turned down at the ends. "You've never acted like that in front of me, and I'm objectively good-looking."

I let out a disbelieving laugh. He could not honestly be talking about himself this way. "And humble to boot."

"It's just a fact," he insisted, clearly not caring about the glances shot our way due to our escalating idiotic argument. "I am good-looking. *Objectively*," he restated.

"Who cares?" I shot back. "And you have no right to get on a high horse about liking someone for their looks when you and the rest of the Board treat anyone without enough power, money, or clout like they're disposable. Like they're worth nothing."

That stopped him dead. He reeled himself back and shoved his hands in his pockets, looking down. "I never said that."

"You didn't need to," I hissed. "Your record speaks for itself."

Sora's mouth tightened to a hard line, and he sucked in a quick breath of air, but he didn't try to correct me. He must've remembered that I'd been reading the same documents as him, looking into not just the other members' opinions, but his as well.

When we met each other's gazes, his eyes flashed a darker red than usual, mirroring the boiling rage I felt. I didn't care. He could stay mad.

Without another word, I gritted my teeth and turned sharply away from him to dive into the thickening crowd arriving for the gala.

~

More people had entered the gala since Sora and I arrived, filling out the main room with loud conversation and bodies. The stage was straight ahead, and the round white tables around me had become crowded as people claimed their seats. I didn't know where I was supposed to go, and the sense of being lost made my toes curl. I centered myself with a deep breath and scanned the room, my gaze landing on a wooden bar planted against the far-left wall. I knew I shouldn't drink more, but at least the bar was somewhere to go.

I wove my way there and ordered a vodka soda on the rocks. While the bartender made my drink, I settled onto a leather stool at the end of the counter, drumming my nails against the wood. The pop of a flash went off to my left, and I spied a small group of reporters and photographers swarming Sora as he tried to follow me. They'd cut him off and forced a camera in his face. He could barely contain his annoyance, and clearly was having a terrible time.

Good.

I took a sip of my drink and grimaced at the sharp sting of vodka. Tonight, we'd made minimal progress. Charles had toyed with me for his own amusement, and while I'd gotten a glimpse of the other Board members' prejudices, there was nothing particularly incriminating. If only people were as simple to analyze as spells.

So far, logic pointed to someone who knew enough Hawaiian to work its magic. But I couldn't figure out why anyone from the Homestead would care about LA politics. Targeting Angelo and Tagalog's advancement was especially odd, as it didn't align with our interests at all. The only dealings we had with the city were in relation to land rights, and with our lease up for renegotiation, it was a terrible time to antagonize the city.

My thoughts were interrupted by a blast of feedback from the stage. Across the hall, Basilio, dressed in a classic black-and-white tux, tapped the mic, the feedback echoing in the room. "Good evening, everyone, and welcome!"

His black hair was swept into an elegant coif and his face shone with his trademark smile. Basilio took a breath while the crowd quieted. "This is an amazing night for members of the Asian American Cultural Center and those of Asian heritage across LA." He beamed at his audience through a smattering of light claps. "Thank you to everyone who helped to pull together this event after our tragic loss. This night is dedicated to Angelo, forever our champion."

The room exploded with applause and Basilio left the stage, replaced by a band that quickly struck up a tune. He spotted me and made his way over.

"Never seen you in a dress like that," he teased. "You look like a cupcake that a kindergartner frosted over."

I rolled my eyes and took a sip of my drink. "The man wearing coattails doesn't get to mock my attire."

Basilio laughed and claimed the seat next to me. "Where's Sora?"

I clinked the ice in my cup together and pointed vaguely at the room. "Around."

"Guess he's been fun," he said.

"Want him?" I offered.

He gestured to the bartender, who poured him a dark-amber drink. "Pass. Anyway, I'm surprised he needed a date. He's a man in demand."

My eyebrows rose in disbelief. "I highly doubt that." Picturing Sora as popular with his sour disposition was like trying to capture wind in a jar.

"It's not his winning personality people want," Basilio said. He swirled his scotch and swiveled in his chair to face me. "It's his influence."

Wealth attracts flies like ripe fruit." He swept his hand across the room to gesture broadly at the guests dressed in frilly costumes that probably cost more than a month's food budget for our clan.

"Or like shit," I muttered.

Basilio laughed and tapped my shoulder. "Don't pretend to be above it all. You're also doing this for the money, or did you forget?"

"I'm doing this for *you*," I said, leaning back into him.

"I'm sure the cash doesn't hurt, though. We all have to be flexible when it comes to the rougher edges of life. Anything you have to do to survive is justified."

"I don't totally disagree," I said. "But there has to be a line. Validating survival at all costs feels wrong."

"The world is selfish," Basilio commented, clinking his glass to mine.

I downed my drink at the same time as him, then set it down firmly on the bar. "But that doesn't mean I have to join in. Things can change, but not if everyone's only looking out for themselves."

Basilio snorted. "Tell that to Keanu." He waved his hand at the bartender and ordered some kind of fancy cocktail.

I grimaced. "Keanu is a special case."

"He's not," Basilio insisted. "People like him are the norm. Why should I feel like I owe him something when he spent years beating the crap out of me and shaking me down for cash? Where was his sense of community then?"

"But was leaving really the answer?" I asked, then sharply inhaled, knowing I shouldn't have said that.

"Your reaction is exactly what I mean," he said, unruffled. "I didn't want to suffer and pinch pennies only to be brought down by Keanu or Ha'aheo, or even you, Kea. I wanted more. The Homestead is going to fall eventually, and I don't want to go down with it. Why can't you just be happy I got out?"

It wasn't just about wanting more; it was about wanting better—but by what measure? Most of the world used money as a metric of success, and by that standard, the Homestead was failing, but we had value in forms other than wealth. Living away from the Homestead meant living without mana underfoot. Leaving meant being away from all the vibrant things that made our home unique. Sure, there were flaws, but there was beauty, too.

"I am happy for you," I said. "But not because you left the Homestead. It doesn't make you better than those of us who chose to stay."

Basilio bristled. "I'm not saying that."

I waved a hand in the air. "No, I know."

I did know, but deep down, I think that Basilio pitied me. The reverse was true, too, and the irony was that we were both right. I enjoyed seeing him succeed in LA, but I also wished he didn't think less of me for not wanting the same. I didn't ever want to be a part of LA. I wanted to stay. To thrive.

The bartender brought us our drinks, and Basilio picked up his and took a sip. "We're struggling just to maintain a sliver of our culture. And for what? There's no prize for being Hawaiian in today's world. I'd rather be a part of something bigger and better."

"You gave up being head," I said. "That seems smaller to me."

Basilio got quiet, his face pinched. "Yeah, well, there are limits to where people like us can go." He brightened and clinked our glasses again. "But don't worry about me. I know how to survive. I'll eventually have even more power than Angelo did, just wait and see. *You're the one I'm worried about, Miss Hardheaded. What benefit do you get for resisting the changing times?*"

I didn't have a good answer for him, so I drank instead. My cocktail had an odd flavor, vaguely medicinal with an herbal taste from the fresh leaves seeped in the alcohol. Not a bad remedy for Basilio's cold truth. I knew we couldn't hold our own against the whole world; I just wanted to make sure there was room for us to grow, rather than letting it erase us completely. Each step was uncertain—tradition and change, a balance as thin as a blade of pili grass.

My head hung over the wooden counter, my thoughts cloudy. I had to stop drinking; this conversation was depressing, and the alcohol wasn't helping. "Ugh," I mumbled, scowling.

Ever the wordsmith.

Basilio chuckled and clapped a hand on my back. "I'm going to go look for Sora. Stay here and sober up a bit—you don't want the Kaiser head to have to carry you out of your first fancy party."

"Yeah, yeah," I said with a frown, swishing the contents of my glass with a straw. Basilio left me alone to stew and I followed his back, until my gaze snagged on Sora, who'd finally escaped the reporters.

Despite his abundance of good looks, he was noticeably alone. Although Sora was well known for his ability as a Caster, it was no accident that Charles, Matthew, and even Reagol often acted as the face for the Board instead. Sora might be *objectively* handsome, but he had a dark, sharp presence that threatened to consume the light around it. People at the party unconsciously maneuvered themselves warily around him like they might step over a puddle. They didn't even seem to realize they were doing it.

It was more pronounced now because Sora was visibly fuming. When he looked up, his eyes drilled into me like death, cherry red and unblinking. Basilio approached him, and annoyance splashed across Sora's face as he was forced to stop glowering to speak to him. They exchanged a few quick words and shook hands, but Sora's gaze didn't leave my line of sight the entire time.

Why is he watching me like that?

I picked my glass up from the counter and left the bar to walk in the garden and clear my head. Hopefully, the fresh air would be sobering.

CHAPTER 9

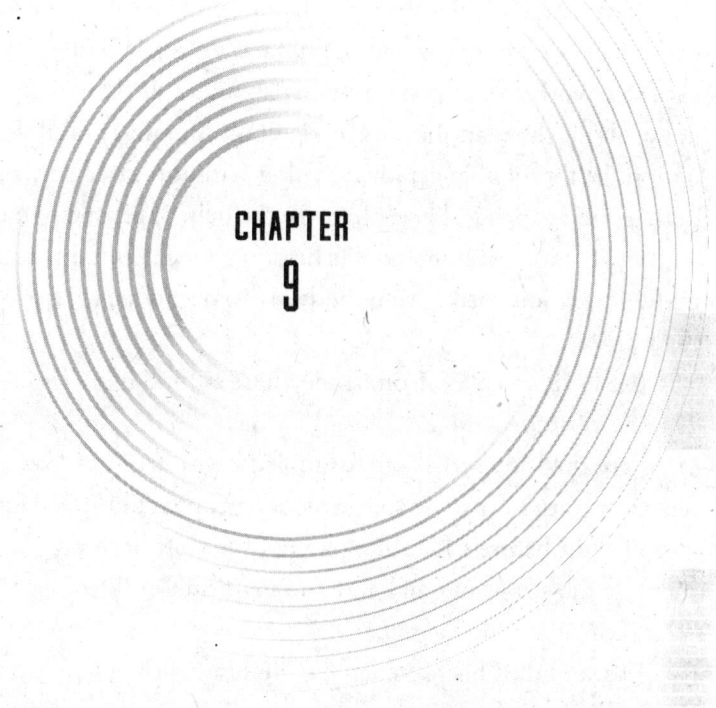

Outside, the summer night air felt like a warm hug. My skin prickled at the stark difference in temperature, and I walked deeper into the shrubbery until the open hall was concealed from sight and the sound of crickets buzzed around my head. Away from the bustle and cameras, I finally felt a bit better and continued to drink my cocktail while eating the spearmint that had been added to the concoction. It helped, but not much. My heart was still racing and my breath came out in quiet huffs, fogging in the night.

Sora was impossible, complimenting my work one minute and then ordering me around the next. I backtracked to Vanessa's warning and chewed on my bottom lip—I couldn't forget that Sora wasn't cleared as a suspect. If he was the person responsible for killing Angelo, he'd try to sabotage my investigation. Although that didn't require him being a stuck-up asshole.

Then I remembered that Sora hadn't tried to hide any of his history in the files we'd been examining. In fact, I'd read them in *his* house, on *his* table, with *him* leaning over my shoulder. If there was one thing I knew about the man, he was meticulous. Should Sora plot an assassination, he'd probably get away with it without leaving a trace. He was quite good at spying, especially with the help of his sympathetic magic.

My memory of him and I as he dipped me down, his breath on my neck, sent a jolt through my body. I shook my head, trying to dispel the image.

"Kea," Sora called from somewhere behind me.

Speak of the devil.

I groaned inwardly and stumbled away from his voice, walking deeper into the brush of the garden. I tripped and gasped as I caught myself right before I fell. In a panic, I took off both my heels, holding them by the straps in one hand and my drink in the other.

"Kea?" he called again.

The sound of his footsteps pivoted in my direction as I rushed off the path. Flushed from embarrassment and alcohol, I downed the rest of my drink.

Great, now I was literally hiding from him.

It was childish, but I couldn't help myself. I was so angry at him right now, at Basilio, at Charles, and god, it was so damn *hot*. Leaning against a tree trunk, I let myself rest for a second, dipping my fingers into my empty cup to pull out an ice cube and press it against my temple. I sighed and reached for another piece when something in the glass caught my eye.

The herbs in the cocktail were mostly gone, but there were a few leaves left in the drink, and there was something on them. Faint lines etched onto the surface. I dumped out the rest of the ice into the dirt and fished out the only remaining green bit, holding it up to the light while my breaths grew shorter and quicker.

I couldn't translate even a single word.

I'd chewed off one end, and the remaining writing was illegible, resembling squiggles more than any alphabet I knew, but my sympathetic magic didn't lie. It pulsed, and the letters faintly glowed under my touch, the mana in them unmistakable. A smithing. Or at least half of one, since I'd eaten the rest.

I opened my mouth to shout for Sora when the air rushed out of me in a whoosh like a sudden gust of wind. Gasping, I sank to my knees, holding onto my stomach. A sense of dread filled my gut like an inflating balloon. The shortness of breath, the feverishness—it hadn't been the alcohol, but a malicious spell worming its way through my body. Damn it! Couldn't I go a *week* without someone trying to kill me?

"Can we talk?" Sora continued, oblivious to the fact that I was being poisoned to death feet away from him. "I didn't mean to—" He sighed, clearly exasperated. There was a shuffling from the other side of the hedge as he retreated back to the party.

In all the times I'd been frustrated with Sora, this was the only time I truly hated him. The man was about to leave me here alone, slowly losing all the air in my lungs. I tried to shout again but only managed to open and close my mouth like a fish on dry land. I couldn't speak, couldn't call for help.

"I suppose this is the wrong time and place to speak about such things. Maybe after," he said, his voice fading as he got farther away.

Come back!

I made one last push and rushed after him, but the lack of oxygen made my movements slow. I wouldn't be able to reach him in time. I could hear him just ahead, a couple of cutoff paths from me—close, but just far enough that shaking a bush wouldn't be enough for him to hear. I looked down for something, *anything*.

I was still holding my heels. I took one and threw it as hard as I could in his direction.

"I just wanted to say that I'm so—" Sora's voice cut off with a yelp as the footwear smacked into his head. "Ouch! That *hurt*! You almost hit me in the eye with—is this your *shoe*, Kea?"

I tried to call out his name, but when I opened my mouth, I choked. I collapsed, wheezing as the spell's effect took complete hold of me. On my hands and knees, I sank unexpectedly into wet earth, which moments ago had been completely dry. The smell of decaying leaves hit me in a pungent wave, and I tried to ignore the stench. I needed to figure out a way to counteract the smithing. A written spell, since I couldn't speak.

I grabbed a twig from the ground, planning to etch it into the mud, but staring at the bare earth, I came up with nothing. Hawaiian didn't work when written, and I didn't have the time to come up with a Russian rhyme or an English verse. I sucked in another gasp, struggling against the magic as it pressed against my lungs. Every time I inhaled, the herb's spell squeezed the breath out of me even faster. Stupid Kea.

Suddenly, Sora was at my side. He took in my blue face and gripped my shoulders. "What's happening?"

I gripped my throat to show him, and he responded with a simple command: "Don't."

Sora was so irritating. Didn't he realize that not dying was *hard*? There was something magical clogging my windpipe, like a cork in a bottle. I wiggled my fingers in front of my face, frowning and wavering from side to side as I tried desperately to take a breath.

Sora held each side of my face, his fingers brushing against my neck. "Breathe, Kea. *Breathe.*"

I shook my head. *I can't.*

Sora's pupils got larger, his own breathing picking up. In a panic, his hands were suddenly all over me as if searching for a way to help, but even Sora, with all his power, couldn't do anything. He was a Caster, a combat specialist, not a Smith. "I—I don't know any counterspells for something like this!" he said, sounding more desperate than I'd ever heard him.

Maybe Sora's initial assessment of me had been right. Would a *real* clan head have been rendered helpless by something slipped into her drink? If I was a proper Smith, I would have written down a counterspell right away. I'd been fooling myself into thinking I was in any way equal to Sora or the others. Heroes had power to back up their actions; I was no goddess of fire like Pele, nor the warrior god Kū. If anything, I was like the demigod Kamapuaʻa. An outcast. A trickster, scraping by on shoestrings and charm.

"You need to break the curse," he said again, as if it were that simple. I tried to shake my head again, but he caught my face in his hands and held me still. "You can do this. Please, just try."

Sora pulled my head so close to his that our noses touched. Without knowing it, his motions mimicked those of a Hawaiian greeting. His breath was warm against my face, and he exhaled deeply as if hoping that we could share oxygen. The thought scratched at something in the back of my mind, and I lifted my head from his, the world's colors bright and intense even in my fading vision.

Breath was the difference between life and death, and I refused to have it stolen from me like this.

I focused on that spot in my piko, my core, where magic was housed, and I willfully ripped it open. Magic filled me until my skin buzzed with a riptide of power, washing over me in waves. Sora fell back, eyes widening as light seemed to pour out of my limbs.

Though people stored mana in their core, their piko, it wasn't something anyone could create on their own. Mana came from around us, and to access it, people had to pull it into themselves. However, everyone's capacity for magic was different, and when people overextended their limits, they tended to burst. Magic with no place to go, or without a wide enough channel to exit a person's body, built up like steam in a pressure cooker.

And here I was, filling myself with mana when I quite literally couldn't breathe, but it wasn't just some death wish. I had a deranged, brilliant, *beautiful* idea. It was either going to make me a mad genius or a dead idiot.

Folding both my hands together into a joint fist, I placed them at my navel and opened my mouth like I was going to give myself the Heimlich maneuver. I pushed in and up on my gut in firm thrusts, forcing the little air in my lungs out through my throat. It wasn't much, but the word I needed only required a little bit of oxygen, luck, and an open mouth.

Maybe legends preferred heroes, but magic favored tricksters.

"*Hā*," I breathed out, the vowel stretching long as I exhaled.

My lungs unclenched as every screaming muscle in my body was suddenly drenched with breath. I coughed until those gasps turned into wild laughter. It had *worked*. My crazy, one-word smithing had done exactly what I'd intended.

"But . . . how?" Sora asked, mouth agape. He regarded me with an odd expression. "You didn't say anything."

"I *did*," I insisted and laughed again, deliriously happy. For the first time in years, one of my risks had actually paid off. "Hā. It's a word in Hawaiian that you can say with just a bit of air and intention. It means *breath* but also *life*."

I inhaled deeply, leaning toward him again so our noses brushed together, our breaths intertwined. We stared at each other, then the Kaiser head stood and offered me his hand. "What happened?"

"Poison," I said and gestured to my abandoned cup on the ground.

His eyebrows shot up. "From the bar? Were you drinking alone?"

I rolled my eyes. "Yes, from the bar, where else?" Even I wasn't stupid enough to accept unknown beverages from strangers. "And no, I was drinking with Basilio."

We caught each other's eye as what I'd said clicked. Then, moving in unison, we turned back to the gala at a sprint.

"You find Basilio!" he ordered. "I'll get the bartender."

Usually, I'd give him shit for bossing me around, but I had more pressing matters this time. We ran back to the gala and burst in through the glass doors. Sora turned left to the bar and glared at the man behind the counter, who immediately clocked the menacing look and took off.

"I *hate* running in suits," Sora complained as he set off in chase.

I had to find Basilio. I'd eaten the damn poisoned smithing in my cocktail, likely speeding up the effects, but Basilio was oblivious. If the bartender had slipped something into his drink, too, then he was probably still sipping away. There was no telling how long I had.

Scanning the crowd, I looked for his stupidly coiffed hair while people stared at me. It wasn't hard to figure out why. I was barefoot, covered in dirt from the hem of my dress to my knees, and by now my hair had turned into a tangled mess. I bit my lip. I'd gotten myself into this mess *because* of that bastard. He wasn't allowed to die in the middle of this.

"Basilio!" I hollered over the music. "Goddammit! *Basilio!*"

The cellist made a terrible screeching sound as the band's song ground to a halt, and every eye in the gala turned toward me. So much for not causing a scene. "Basilio Reyes!" I shouted again, ignoring the pounding in my chest. "Where the hell are you?"

This was bad. My heart was racing and my head felt light, and I still couldn't see Basilio. The crowd parted, whispering about this wild woman in their midst who was making a fuss, when I finally spotted him next to the stage. His glass was still in his hand and raised to his mouth, frozen.

"Don't—!" I began to shout, but it was too late.

He made eye contact with me, then swallowed, his expression puzzled. "Why are you yelling?" He'd removed the cup from his lips, but the contents were totally gone.

Not good.

I lifted my skirts and dashed across the dance floor straight for him, knocking the cup out of his hand so it clattered to the floor. "How many drinks have you had?"

"Clearly less than you," he teased, shooting nervous glances around us. "Kea, are you okay?"

"Answer the question!"

"Jeez, just a few, I swear."

"This was the same drink you had at the bar?"

"Of course! How much do you think I can drink in the span of ten minutes? What are you—?" Basilio was cut off as he suddenly choked.

I was too late. My fingers went immediately to his throat, which I could feel tense under my touch. His mana pulsed under my hands, but it was dampened by the layers of clothes. Thinking quickly, I tugged at his bow tie and began unbuttoning his shirt. He tried to push my hands away.

"Stop that if you want to live!" I snapped.

The fabric ripped under my hands, and I shoved my palm onto his stomach, his belly button right at the center. I knew what to do this time to get his lungs to open, but pulling that amount of mana into myself again was going to hurt both of us. My headache thwacked against my temple, and I felt nauseous. This was a bad idea. A really bad idea. But I couldn't see another choice.

"Relax," I said, feigning calm. My bedside manner had never been great, though, and I was sure the sound of my voice was more grating than soothing. "This might . . . tickle."

Basilio's eyes went wide, and he mouthed a single word to me that I pretended not to understand. *Liar.*

I released my mana into him. "Hā!" The spell burst outward with the force of a torrential stream, pumping through Basilio's stomach and up his throat. He opened his mouth and let out a yelp as mana exploded forth in a rush of wind. Basilio gasped and sucked in a deep swallow of air, his hands flying to his throat.

"That . . . did not . . . *tickle*!" he croaked, voice hoarse.

"Sorry," I said retroactively, standing and trying to hide that the world had started tilting sidewise. I took a few missteps, then regained control of my limbs. The crowd had grown thicker around us. Nosy onlookers wanting to witness the drama up close. "Someone take care of him," I demanded, trying to emulate Sora's authoritative tone.

"Kea," Basilio rasped, pulling at the edge of my dress. "Wait—"

"Sora went after the bartender," I said. Of course, he'd chased after an assassin all on his own without a second thought.

"He can take care of himself."

I hesitated and licked my lips. Basilio was probably right. Sora was the head of his clan. The youngest Board member in history. Still, Sora

Kaiser was a person. I glanced at the hallway he'd disappeared down and decided then that no one could win a war alone.

I ran from the dance floor after Sora's shadow.

I sprinted down the hall and nearly ran straight into his back as I turned a sharp corner. Recoiling, I stepped back several paces, panting as I tried to gather my breath. "Are you okay?"

"Fine," he answered shortly, glancing over his shoulder at me. Sora was rigidly standing over the unmoving figure of the man he'd chased, a thin trail of blood trickling down from his ear. He wiped a hand across his sweaty brow and cursed.

"He's dead?" I asked.

He spun on me, his expression furious. "Poison." Sora's red eyes scanned me, and he frowned. "Why on earth did you follow me?"

"I wouldn't just leave you on your own," I stammered.

"I'm fine," Sora growled.

"Clearly," I said, glancing at his feet.

His expression went flat, and he turned sharply back to the body. "He killed *himself*. Swallowed that same stupid smithing that you did." He bent over and began searching through the pockets of the man but found them all empty. "You should've stayed at the hall."

"I came to help," I protested.

"How?" he snapped and straightened to round on me, eyes aflame. His tone had taken on that shaky-angry quality that Nana scolded me in when I did something particularly reckless. "You almost had a mana overload earlier, or did you think I didn't notice? You're no good to anyone for a few hours."

Mana overloads, or even the threat of one, completely drained people of power temporarily, and I'd just triggered one *twice*.

I tried to defend myself. "I was just trying—"

"I don't care what you were trying to do! You almost *died*, Kea!"

"So, you can risk your life chasing murderers, but I can't?" I leveled back, chest out and voice pitching. He was really starting to irritate me.

"You . . ." He sucked in a sharp burst of air and buried his face in his hands. "You shouldn't be taking cues from me."

"I can do whatever the hell I want." I closed my eyes, struggling to stay standing.

"Why are you so damn stubborn?" He stopped shouting, and I suddenly felt his hands on either side of my shoulders.

I opened my eyes to see Sora's eyebrows knitted together with worry. His voice lowered unexpectedly, and I felt his cool fingers against my face. "Are you okay? You look a little—"

"I'm *fine*!" I snapped, throwing his own words back at him and shaking him off. If this was what I got for worrying about the great and terrible Sora Kaiser, then I promised to never do it again.

As I turned to leave, my foot slipped, which was strange because I was no longer wearing heels. My head went light as the room started to spin. I looked down to see that the tiles under me had disappeared, and when I tried to scream, I found that I couldn't.

Sora could, though, and I heard him shout my name and rush to catch me. The floor came up toward my face, and I realized something a split second before I hit the ground. One, I was fainting. And two, Sora was right. I'd overextended myself.

That one hurt worse than the actual fall.

CHAPTER 10

I blinked awake.
Not my room.

My body tensed as I snatched the covers around myself and shot up arrow straight. The wall behind me was a dark gray, but every other surface was some shade of white or beige. A TV droned on in a corner, but other than that, it was surprisingly bare. I'd only seen this kind of ridiculous minimalism in one place before. Sora's house.

I leaned into the single squashed pillow behind my back, trying to think about how I'd gotten here. Unwanted flashbacks from the gala appeared when I closed my eyes. Instinctively, I reached for my head and found a small raised bump at the side of my forehead when I realized—

I hadn't gone home.

In a panic, I grabbed my phone off the side table to my left and flipped it open. Twenty-eight missed calls. All from family. The last message was from my Papa, telling me that Sora had gotten in touch with them and that if I didn't call them back soon, I'd be sorry. *Shit.*

"You're awake," Sora said, sitting up straight in a chair next to the door. His voice was scratchy. I hadn't seen him come into the room and wondered if he had just been waiting there, with his eyes closed and head tilted back, pressed against the wall. Dark half-moons hung under his eyes, and his hair was fraying out of the bun he'd tied it up in.

"Where's Basilio?" I asked.

"Sleeping. Don't bother trying to talk to him. Your wild magic made him lose his voice, but other than that, he's fine." Sora eyed me carefully. "Don't worry."

Relief washed over me, immediately replaced by exhaustion. "I feel terrible," I said, setting down my phone. My head hurt, of course, but so did my ego.

In a way, Basilio's prediction had come true. Sora *had* carried me from the ballroom gala after causing a scene, and that wasn't even the worst of it. I had to give Sora some credit—I was sure it hadn't been fun to break the news that I had been almost murdered to my grandparents. Especially Papa. I grasped my elbows instinctively at the terrifying thought.

"I brought you here to rest," Sora said. "But I didn't undress you, so you slept . . . like that."

He stared at me for a beat, and a tickle of heat crawled up my neck. Still decked in the ridiculous lavender monstrosity that was my gown with my hair a wild mane, I was sure that I looked about as good as I felt. Sora had likely seen me worse off, but I ached for his eyes to slide past me the way they used to. They refused.

"We tested every bottle but couldn't figure out what poisoned you," he said finally.

"The leaves in my drink," I said. "There was a smithing etched on them."

"I should've thought of that." He rubbed his eyes and frowned. "I've seen it before. The poison spreads from the plant into the liquid over time. Strange that it happened so quickly. Usually, it takes a few hours to have an effect."

"Well," I said sheepishly. "I might've sped up the process a bit by swallowing it. Basilio did the same."

His mouth parted slightly in surprise. "You know garnishes aren't really meant to be eaten, right?"

"What's the point of a plant you can't eat?" I asked. I always nibbled at the herbs and fruits restaurants and bars put on top of their food or drinks.

He leaned back, crossing his arms. "You're a very unusual person."

"Thanks?" I grumbled, mirroring his movements.

Sora sighed. "The unfortunate thing is that you've digested most of the evidence. I may have something, but it's not much." He held up what was left, a corner of a leaf no bigger than a pin top in a sealed plastic bag. A single mark remained, but it just looked like a curved line. He crossed the room to give me the bag. "I don't suppose you recognize the smithing's alphabet?"

"No," I admitted, squinting at the squiggle etched on the plant.

"Shame," Sora muttered, scowling at the useless thing before putting it back into his pocket.

I shook my head. "I've never seen any magic like that before."

"Speaking of magic," he began, his voice low even though his pupils had widened. "That spell you used was *one word*. A smithing like that shouldn't be possible, yet you managed it." He looked at me like I was an entity put on this earth with the express intention to confound him.

"My mana's always been strange," I said, not sure if my explanation would make sense to anyone other than me. "It never does what I want unless I write the smithings myself."

"You created that counterspell?" he asked.

I ran my tongue on the underside of my teeth. "Not exactly. Usually when I create a new smithing, I have more time to think, so it follows the proper conventions. Last night, I had no time and very few options, so I went with the first word that fit. I'm lucky it worked. In the past, things have gone awry when I'm not careful."

He raised an eyebrow. "Meaning?"

"Meaning they backfire." I paused. "This time, it did what I wanted, but I could've just as easily blown myself up." The memory of me pulling in that giant flood of mana gave me a bout of chicken skin, the hairs on my arm raising. That had been *very* close.

I had seen a mana overload only once before, in a past raid. It was like an internal bomb; the person had been fine one minute, then dead the next, their insides destroyed by the sudden burst of power.

His eyes widened a fraction of a millimeter as he took a step closer. "You don't feel . . . ?" He trailed off, his gaze landing on my mouth.

"I'm fine, really."

"Are you sure?" he asked sternly, using his finger to lift my chin so I was looking at him.

Forced to stare at his face, my throat dried up. The sudden closeness made me remember how his mana had tasted, sharp and sweet like candied ginger. I glanced down at his lips and wondered if his tongue would taste the same.

A ringing from Sora's pocket startled me out of my temporary insanity, and I devolved into a coughing mess, my cheeks hot. Sora straightened, answering the phone as he retreated to his corner of the room. "There's been a situation. I was hoping to reschedule." He paused, smoothing down his hair. "You know what happened at the gala, surely we could make an—yes, I understand." He hung up and turned back to me. "Charles insists on keeping our appointment for today. I'm sorry about this."

I blinked. It wasn't like Sora to apologize, especially for something that wasn't his fault.

"You could stay here and rest," he offered.

"Fat chance," I grumbled, getting out of bed and tugging at the layers of frill that still surrounded me like a cage.

The barest of smiles touched the corners of his mouth. "I thought as much. There are some clothes hanging over there." He gestured to the far side of the room. "Pick whatever you'd like."

It took me all of ten minutes flat to pull off the gown and slip on a simple brown dress from the closet. Curiosity had burned inside me as I ran my fingers along the fine fabrics—Sora had a whole wardrobe of expensive women's clothes. Were they someone else's? An old girlfriend, perhaps? Or a current one?

I shoved all my questions out of mind and twisted my hair into a passable updo before stumbling out of the room in bare feet, a pair of slingback heels dangling from my fingers. I was as ready as I was ever going to be. We were speeding away from his estate within minutes.

I looked out the window as we jumped onto the highway. The cityscape flew by, gray and harsh with smog, and an aching for the Homestead filled my stomach. I hated the color gray. The scenery was depressing, so I turned my attention back to Sora, who was focused on the road.

He kept his right hand on the wheel and leaned on his left shoulder with his elbow squared against the window for support. I had expected him to turn on some music, maybe classical, but he never once reached for the radio. Like it wasn't a habit for him to listen to music on the road. The idea of driving in silence like this was so foreign to me that my legs had begun bouncing. Personally, I couldn't make it far at the wheel without blasting cheesy pop songs to sing along to.

His eyes slid to me. "You've taken this attempt on your life rather well."

"People have tried to kill me for less," I said, sighing as I sank deeper into the leather seat of his car. "Not sure if you've noticed, but I have a bad habit of saying whatever I'm thinking out loud."

"Who, you? I haven't noticed a thing," he said with a sly half smile. Then the teasing evaporated from his voice. "Have your guard up today. We know that someone at that party hired that hit man to get rid of you, and Charles is high up on my list."

My first talk with Charles had been disorienting, and the odds of a better second conversation were looking slim. Sora was right about the guy being a piece of work.

"Make it through this interview without getting into trouble," I said. "Easy."

Sora rolled his eyes. "At least *try*. I still have to get you home before your family hunts me down."

Which meant, after Charles, I'd have to face my grandparents. I couldn't decide which was scarier.

Sora took an exit and we hit a smooth road in a quiet, posh neighborhood that led to the Lam Syndicate. "It'll be fine," Sora assured. "Just try not to talk too much."

"Ha, ha," I grumbled dryly.

"And no casting," he warned. "Your magic *is* unusual, and if Charles were to find out you can cast that way, he'd pry you apart to find out how it works."

I snorted. "No need for that. It doesn't even work right—I'm not fluent."

The car jerked forward so suddenly that I was thrown heavily against the belt and my head snapped forward.

"What did you say?" Sora turned to me slowly, his face pale as he leaned across the armrest between us. The light shifted to red, and I realized he had slammed to a stop at a green light.

"That I'm not fluent?" I asked. I didn't think that it was such a shocking thing. Fluency helped with the strength of one's smithing, but it wasn't a requirement. I was living proof of that.

"That doesn't—" Sora's mouth opened and shut, then he pulled back abruptly and pressed urgently on the gas again so we sped away from the light as it changed back. "Never mind."

He said that, but his knuckles turned white from gripping the wheel.

~

The building that housed the Lam Syndicate was glass and shaped like an upright deck of cards. The tower rose over the dense suburbia of Monterey Park, sticking out like a sore thumb. Its impractical design refracted sunlight, sending rainbow prisms onto the sidewalk that blinded passersby with the glare. Charles Lam was as ostentatious as his building, and I knew then that this was going to be a grating few hours.

With each passing minute that we waited in the Lams' lobby, Sora's glower worsened. He'd closed himself up: legs crossed, arms folded over his chest, and every muscle in his body as tense as a bow.

"The man is incorrigible," he seethed. "*He* was the one who insisted on keeping this meeting."

After another five minutes, Sora stood abruptly. "Enough. I won't wait any longer. Let's go in."

We walked toward the elevator and when the doors popped open, Sora pulled me inside with him. An array of buttons climbing into the double digits stared back at us.

"Which floor?" I whispered.

Sora looked over at the choices, rolled his eyes, then pressed the top button. The elevator started with a jerk. A digital pad at the top of the metal box announced each floor we passed with a merry chirp until we reached the highest one. The elevator slid open and we came face to face with a line of broad-shouldered men in black suits with scary-looking guns.

"Mr. Lam isn't expecting anyone," the middle man said, crossing his arms.

"He should be." Sora tried to take a step into the room, but the men blocked his way. "Charles, call off your damn guard dogs!" he shouted in frustration.

"So loud," a voice chided. "But fine. Gentlemen, no need to frighten my guests. They're no threat to me."

The men drew back, and Sora stepped out into an expansive room, looking around with his mouth drawn in a tight line. "Of course you're in the penthouse."

"Where else would I be?" Charles said, sliding into view with a bemused smile on his face. Out of formal wear, he was even more striking. The Lam head was tall and slim with delicate features and dark, blunt bangs that contrasted with the paleness of his skin. An Asian Adonis. I closed my mouth to stop from gawking.

"I was just coming down to get you," Charles said, beckoning for us to follow him to the sitting area beyond the entryway. "My last meeting ran over, but I should've known you'd barge in anyway. How like you, Sora."

The room stretched out impossibly large and covered an entire level. It featured floor-to-ceiling glass windows, marble floors, and sleek metallic furniture accented with futuristic pieces of art that were specially designed for the office. Charles's desk, for example, was a black rectangle that floated above the ground, suspended by wires.

The modular seating we'd been herded onto replicated the same color pattern, like a chessboard come to life. I sat next to Sora, noticing Charles's eyes follow the curves of my waist and hips. "It's lovely to see you again, Kea," he said.

Pretending not to notice his wandering eye, I opened my journal to take notes and kept my legs and mouth tightly shut. While I disliked wearing skirts and high heels, I was glad I'd dressed up. Something told me I might not have been let into the building in my usual jeans.

He sat upright with a hand on either knee. "Go ahead and ask your questions. I have nothing to hide."

"Why were you against Tagalog's advancement?" Sora asked.

Charles wasn't shaken. "For ten years I've fought to build the Lam Syndicate and cement Cantonese and Mandarin as spell-casting languages that can be relied on. I started even before our regulation and worked with my nose to the ground, a process that never stopped. The fact that Angelo waltzed in like he was owed a spot was insulting."

"You resented him, then," I said.

Charles laughed sharply, like a smattering of bullets. "I'm only thirty-five and the head of one of the wealthiest clans in LA. I have no need to resent Angelo Reyes." His eyes found mine. "Except in his choice of partner. If I'd married Vanessa, the Lam Syndicate would've had a monopoly on both luck-based magic and curses. A pity it didn't work out. Society talks as if it's only women who sleep their way to the top, but Angelo's a clear example of the reverse being true."

Having spoken to Vanessa, I believed that she and Angelo had been deeply in love. It didn't seem that Charles had cared in the same way for Vanessa; he assumed Angelo couldn't have either. Not necessarily animosity there, but a lack of understanding.

"I didn't kill him, by the way," he added. "I may have wanted to strangle the man on occasion, but that wasn't out of murderous intent. I despise white knights. They're obsessed with moral duty, with what they see as 'right.' He tried to shame me for spending my fortune on my own clan—the sheer audacity."

Nothing about Charles signaled hidden motivations. If anything, the man was too blunt.

"You also don't have a clear alibi," Sora reminded him.

Charles lifted his palms up to the air. "Neither does most of the Board. There are no cameras in our private offices and that's where I was until eight. You can see me in the security footage from the parking lot after that time but that probably doesn't push me into the clear."

"You have an eye for finding the holes in your own story, Mr. Lam," I said. "How honest of you."

He winked at me. "I've heard women like that."

I ducked my head back into the journal and scribbled down a sentence that was less of an observation than a stream of profanities. Sora's assessment had been correct. I hadn't thought it possible, but Charles was worse than Sora in every measure, except *maybe* appearance.

"We can clear this up quickly," Sora interjected. "A look into your business files should—"

"No," Charles said flatly. "Those contain trade secrets, and I don't feel comfortable with the Board looking into my business affairs. The Lam Syndicate doesn't make death spells. You'll have to take my word for it. Most of the information you need is public, anyway."

Sora frowned. "Sorting through data takes time. If you'd just be a little more flexible—"

Charles smiled viciously. "I don't think I will. I can be flexible in the right circumstances, but with you, Sora? Well, I'm less willing to compromise."

"Then we're done here," Sora said neatly. He stood to leave. "Thank you for your time, Charles. We'll be in touch." The men shook, but the Lam head didn't offer me a hand. For once, that didn't bother me.

Charles, though, hadn't pulled his gaze from my figure. "Next time, just send Kea. Maybe then I'd be more compelled to, well, loosen my belt, so to speak."

I resisted the urge to punch him in the face and smiled, hoping my teeth would make clear the daggers I shot his way. Charles didn't get the message. When we turned to leave, a hand grazed the side of my waist and slid to my bottom. Instinct hit, and I spun, slapping him across the face. He stumbled back, clutching his cheek.

Sora stepped between us, his hands held out in front of him as if to push back Charles, but I was done taking this privileged douchebag's inappropriate comments like some willowy wallflower. We locked eyes.

His smile glinted like the edge of a blade. "I accept."

What?

"Be reasonable, Charles. She didn't know what she was doing," Sora said.

"She'll learn," the man snapped back.

I didn't have time to ask what they were talking about. Two large men materialized on either side of me and lifted me off the ground. One placed a gag over my mouth while the other hauled me back. The last thing I saw was Sora's stricken expression as he ran after me, but Charles held him back as the elevator doors closed in his face.

CHAPTER 11

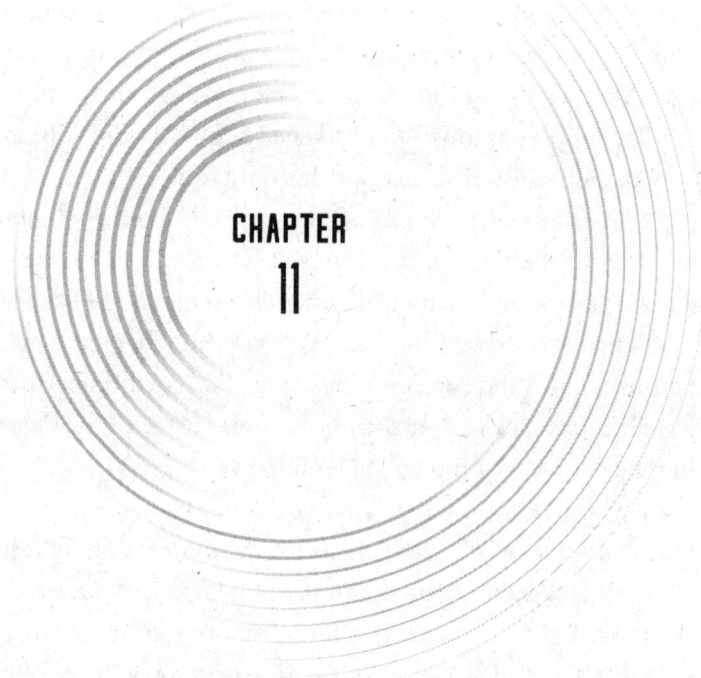

When Charles's security ripped me out of the Lam Syndicate, I was sure that they intended to execute me in some dark back alley. Instead, I'd been checked into a fancy hotel while my captors stood guard at the door. I didn't know how to handle the situation. For the first thirty minutes, I wandered the suite in shock, trying to find a way out, but short of miraculously learning to fly, that wasn't going to happen.

This had to be some kind of sick joke. Did Charles want me wined, dined, and comfortable before he came to slit my throat? Rich people were the worst. Sulkily, I ignored all the luxuries that had been left out for me—a silver platter covered with cheese, fruit, and champagne—and headed to the bathroom.

The only thing I wanted right now was to be clean.

That was why, when Sora broke into the room hours later, he found me soaking in a bubble bath the size of a small pool. He blinked, stared at me like he'd seen the Grim Reaper, and abruptly shut the door. My scream turned into a squeak as I sank into the hot water.

"What are you *doing*?" he shouted through the wall.

"What does it look like?" I yelled back. "Taking a bath!"

An embarrassed silence was his only response.

I rinsed off, stepped out of the tub, and covered myself in a snow-white towel. Something about fresh towels for a single use still felt like a luxury. As kids, when we'd gone for a swim at the beach, Nana and Papa made us dry off on the warm cement, flipping over like frying pancakes until the sun dried our skin. I'd hated doing it when I was little but was guilty of enforcing the same rule with the kids nowadays. In the end, it saved money on laundry.

I wrapped up my hair and exited the bathroom, grateful for the heated marble floors, which warmed the bottoms of my feet. The suite included a bedroom, powder room, and large living area, decorated in the typical neutral tones of a hotel. A stone-colored carpet stretched from each end of the room as a backdrop for a gray couch and two cream-colored armchairs. Sora was waiting for me in the living room, standing with his back to the hall.

He turned around, spied the towel around my figure, and spun right back. "For the love of god, can you please get dressed?" he stammered, and even though I couldn't see his face, the tips of his ears were lit up as red as the end of a cigarette.

"Someone took my clothes," I explained.

He extended an arm, pointing at the far wall, and I followed his direction to a closet. When I opened the door, I was greeted with a full department store collection's worth of clothes in different sizes, cuts, and styles. Not sure what to wear, I slid on a French blue nightdress. My hair was still wet and left damp spots on the front and back of the cloth when I pulled off the towel, but at least I was freshly bathed.

We settled into the plush chairs near the fireplace. Finally satisfied with my state of dress, Sora relaxed and was able to look directly at me again. Though his reaction had surprised me, I'd be lying if I said I didn't enjoy making him squirm. It was nice to know that even Sora Kaiser was ruffled by something.

"Do you have any idea what you've started, Kea? Have you done anything other than lounge around since getting locked up here?" he asked.

"Was I supposed to?" I asked, squeezing my toes so they dug down into the soft carpet.

"I'm assuming you didn't go through the arsenal to select your weapon." Sora gestured to the wall of artillery that hung next to the mantle on the other side of the room. Each piece was identified with a little silver plaque that also documented its most famous owner. I'd assumed it was all decorative.

"My what?"

"Your weapon. For your duel with Charles," he said. "You challenged, and he accepted. You get to select the weapon both of you will wield, since you're the initiator."

My mouth hung open. We squabbled on the Homestead, of course, but that had never amounted to more than your average street brawl. Duels were a city thing. LA had legalized the practice decades ago as a way to curb raids and keep peace between clans. Modern ones, however, were usually more sport than politics and often televised. Private challenges without an audience were more like a game of cards; the parties could wager anything, even their lives.

My jaw unclenched. "I *didn't*."

"You did," Sora confirmed. "Striking someone in the face is an invitation. Old rules still have teeth."

My five-star prison made sense now. Charles didn't want me running before our fight. Maybe Sora had come here to break me out? "If we leave now, we can be back at the Homestead in less than an hour."

"You're not going anywhere," he said. "Once a challenge is issued, it must be completed. Running from a duel means that anything of yours that Charles wants is forfeit. He'd have the right to come after your whole clan."

I wasn't an idiot. My clan wouldn't stand a chance against the Lams, especially not without the rest of the Homestead to back us. "I can't let that happen."

"Then you have to fight," Sora said. He opened a briefcase that sat at the foot of the couch and pulled out a stack of papers that was half an inch thick. "Here's the contract—it's not signed yet, so we can still change the terms."

I took the documents and scanned over the text. The wager was simple: If I won, we got the records we needed from Charles. If he did, he got a night with me. I fought off a shudder. I supposed I didn't have much to put on the line besides my own time. "So how can I beat him?"

"You won't," he declared. "Charles is an expert sharpshooter and a trained swordsman. He's also more than proficient as a Caster."

I pressed my forehead into my knees and groaned.

Sora reached across the table and tapped me between the eyes. "Exactly. Any weapon you choose, Charles will cut you down with. He *loves* the pomp of duels."

I scanned the wall again but didn't see anything I knew how to handle. On the Homestead, I primarily wielded combat paddles, spears, or shark-tooth-studded leiomano, but the closest things to that on the wall were a mace and club. Both looked too heavy to lift.

"Can I pick something that isn't displayed here?" I asked.

Sora stroked his chin. "Probably. Write down what it's called, and I'll make sure you get it."

I scribbled my choice down on a hotel notepad and handed Sora the paper. "If Charles can use magic, then I can, too."

He rubbed at his eyes. "I wouldn't advise it."

Doubt sloshed in my stomach; I wondered if he, too, doubted my abilities. I ran a hand over my damp hair, separating it into sections. I thought that I'd managed to impress Sora over the few weeks we'd worked together. We weren't friends, not by a mile, but things had been less antagonistic lately.

He didn't trust in me or my mana, then. Sora attributed my recent success to luck, or maybe just resolve, rather than skill. The epiphany grabbed my heart and squeezed too tightly.

Sora walked over to my armchair. He placed a heavy hand on my shoulder, where it lay like a dead fish. When he didn't move it, I raised my head to look at his face. Was this his poor attempt at *comforting* me?

"Don't cast," he warned. "Your magic is too unpredictable. Use your sympathetic ability to dodge Charles's magic and outrun the clock, but that's it. If you can survive to the end, he'll have to let you go."

My defensiveness hardened into a diamond. "If I don't fight back, I'll lose for sure."

His voice raised and his hand on me became a vice. "That's the point!" Sora released me and glared. "Your goal isn't to win, Kea. It's *not to die.*"

His proclamation complete, Sora marched to the exit and left me in the posh hotel room to contemplate the next day's duel by myself. Heat bloomed like an ʻōhiʻa blossom in my chest, and I grabbed a pen to add an extra clause to the contract, just in case.

~

The arena for the fight looked like any standard dueling arena: a flat, circular area covered with red dirt. Unlike other countries' stadiums, which featured obstacle courses and different terrains, Americans stuck to dust as their dance floor—the minimalist design ensured no one had an unfair advantage.

Approaching the armory table, I took my time selecting my weapon. Sora had managed to curate a variety of shapes, sizes, and materials. I hoisted each piece until I found one that felt most similar to my own. Unlike what was used for canoes, the blade of a fighting paddle stretched out in a long oval, and the shaft ended without a grip. It was sturdy but not sharp. I was betting that Charles's lack of familiarity with the weapon translated into him being less efficient with it. In fact, every detail of my plan relied on putting the man in a position where he felt less in control.

I just hoped my gamble would pay off.

A warning beep sounded and I moved toward the starting pads with my heart buzzing in my chest. The duel was fifteen minutes long. That was it. I scanned over the particles of dirt glimmering in the air, chewing on my lower lip. I'd spent my whole life surviving. I ought to be able to last a few minutes more.

Sora's advice wrapped through my head on repeat: *Outrun the clock*.

My feet hit the hard rubber platform, and I pivoted to face my opponent, light on my toes. Charles was as carefree as ever, smiling as his chest rose and fell in a steady rhythm. His dark eyes locked onto mine, and he tightened his grip on the paddle. "Ready?" he asked.

The buzzer rang, and he charged.

Charles Lam sprinted forward with a single powerful swing, clutching the paddle with both hands like a baseball bat. The force of his blow sent me skidding. He was stronger than I'd expected. Our faces were inches apart, and when he caught my gaze, he winked. Asshole.

Locked in a parry, my eyes dropped to his stance. All wrong. The majority of Charles's weight was balanced on one foot unsteadily. If he hadn't been so muscular, that first blow would've done nothing at all. A lot of men saw brute force as an advantage, but then again, a lot of men were stupid. He kept readjusting his grip on the staff, and I could see the damp sweat from his palms.

"Looks a little heavy for you," I taunted through gritted teeth. "Having trouble holding on to your stick?"

Charles grimaced. "Not at all."

He wielded the weapon like he expected it to scramble brains in a single hit, which meant he'd probably selected the heaviest one he could find. In actuality, a paddle was most effective when it was light. Its true power came not from big, powerful swings, but in smaller adjustments as its user twisted the handle to strike. I diverted my swing upward and came back down with a hard drive that smashed into Charles's shoulder. He howled and leapt back, a hand moving to massage the area.

"You're going to pay for that," he growled.

Charles jabbed forward, and his paddle grazed against the side of my stomach. Grunting, I twisted my torso so the rest of the weapon slid past me. But instead of instinctively pulling back, he leaned into the sudden release, tumbling forward. As he fell past, one of his hands smacked me at the small of my back and then he was gone.

The hairs on my arm raised.

What was that?

I couldn't feel anything different, but Charles had regained his smug expression, which made my stomach flip. Something was wrong. I reached behind me with a free hand until my fingers found a thin piece of paper stuck to my spine. I yanked it off and tried to read what was written on the red ribbon. 倒霉. Likely Cantonese, knowing the Lam Syndicate, but it wasn't like I could read the spell.

I didn't have to know Chinese to know that this was bad news. I swore, attempting to rip the thing in half, but the paper was sturdier than it appeared. When I looked closer, it wasn't even paper, per se, but some kind of woven material. I tried to throw it to the ground, but it stuck flat against my palm. I peeled the fabric off my hand, but then it clung to the other as if it had been glued to my skin. Then it moved, ribboning up my arm until it returned to the spot on my back. What the hell *was* this thing?

Across from me, Charles's smile widened. "Good luck with that. You'll need it."

Charles didn't give me room to breathe, though, let alone think. He ran at me until our paddles connected with a loud *crack*. In hand-to-hand combat, his strength was impossible to hold out against. My grip on the staff was faltering, and I knew that if he gave me a hard push, I'd topple over.

Beginning to panic, I searched for an opening, but there was none. He kicked me away and I stumbled back, his paddle swinging overhead. *Shit.* I dove, falling to the ground on my side as his blow smashed into the red dirt, shattering the weapon's flat blade.

Charles roared, kicking aside the splintered wood as he inhaled a stomachful of mana and rushed forward to charge, the lengths of our paddles thwacking together. This was bad. If Charles added magic to this equation, I'd be completely overwhelmed. He was so close that I could feel his breath on my nose and the mana in his core expanding. I opened my mouth to preempt him with a smithing of my own but flinched at the last second. A haywire spell right now would be the last nail in my coffin.

"Daa se ceoi gwan soeng," Charles recited, unleashing his magic.

The handle of my paddle hissed, warping into a snake. Yellow with black markings down its back, the noxious beast raised its head and lunged for my throat.

I screamed, throwing the weapon as far as I could before falling on my behind. The snake hit the ground with a light clatter, and I froze, confused. This was impossible. Magic didn't let you transform things that way, especially not from an inanimate object to a living creature. I glared at the animal, reaching out with my sympathetic talent, and a haze of mana filled the area like a cloud where it lay writhing. I blinked, and the animal disappeared. A hallucination.

Charles had gotten the better of me with that trick, and now I was stuck. Unarmed, flat on my ass, and with Charles's smithing stuck to my back. There was nowhere to run. No way to counter. And there were still eight minutes left on the clock.

Charles strolled forward, moving slowly as he reached to pick up my paddle from the ground. Both weapons in hand, he let the tips trail behind him, drawing parallel lines in the dirt. I scrambled backward like a crab, maintaining eye contact. Charles was a shark—the moment I tried to run, he'd ambush me from behind.

My eyes flitted to the side of the arena and found Sora. He was on his feet, hands shoved in his pockets as he observed our match. When he saw me looking, he shook his head in a single decisive motion. Our conversation from yesterday returned to me.

Don't cast.

So, I was supposed to just let Charles kick me around but not *too* much, because I wasn't allowed to actually die. Next time, Sora could duel with no magic. See how he liked it.

Charles swung the two weapons at once, raising them overhead.

I curled my legs up to my chin and kicked hard, the soles of my feet connecting with wood and sending both weapons flying. Charles cursed and reached into his pocket, pulling out another red paper. He threw it, and the spell flew straight for me. I ducked but wasn't fast enough. As its paper arms wrapped around mine, I saw the smithing scrawled on it in black ink: 仆街.

The second the spell touched my skin, a stupid misstep brought me back to my knees. Charles watched me fall and laughed, which sent a river of heat through my entire body. Each error, each stumble, each hesitation—caused my chances of surviving this to plummet. And they were beginning to add up.

I wiped the sweat off my brow with a scowl. I couldn't understand what was wrong with me—I'd never been so clumsy in my life. It was rotten luck. A shiver ran down my spine then, and I became acutely aware of the ribbon on my back.

Maybe that's exactly it.

The thought brought me to a full stop as I remembered what Charles had said yesterday in his office when lamenting Vanessa's rejection. He'd always wanted to be able to curse people, but that wasn't what his magic did. The Lams granted good omens. However, *removing* a person's luck was likely as close as they could get to inflicting real harm.

In another context, I'd have been impressed, but at the moment, my own brand of magic was a particularly poor shield. Languages had natural counterweights. While one might excel in a certain area, aided by the structure of its grammar, form, history, and vocabulary, it would struggle in another. Hawaiian, for example, had no natural word for *luck* at all. While in theory, any language could be twisted to do what a Smith wanted with the correct approach, some things would always be easier or harder to express.

Casters were like this, too. For example, Sora's use of physical movement and simple commands reflected who he was at his core and how he saw his own magic: straightforward and strong. I'd bet the same was true of Charles. His spells were pragmatic, authoritative, and proud. Charles was able to use every situation to his benefit, blessed by a wind of fair-weather luck. Some of it was undoubtedly manufactured, but that was beside the point. For a distinguished language like Cantonese, the counterbalance would need to be simple and playful. Something malleable, with enough blurry rules that it'd oust him from his ivory tower.

Like English.

But Sora had said no magic.

Across the field, Charles focused in on me, rolling his shoulders back as he strolled toward the fallen weapons. He picked up the broken paddle, letting it hang casually from his side. "You're funny," Charles said, wrapping a pair of red cards around the tip of the incomplete paddle handle. "But annoying."

"You know, I hear that a lot," I said, trying to keep him talking so I could formulate a plan. I'd failed on all fronts, and it was clear that Charles was past the point of being entertained.

He smiled. "Then I guess I'll have the privilege of being the last person to ever say that to you."

Charles launched the weapon through the air at me, but before I had time to scream, the pole lodged into the ground at my side.

He'd narrowly missed, but my elation was short-lived as the red paper unwrapped itself, reaching for me. I screamed, kicking it away like a flying cockroach, but the ribbon found its mark, settling around the curve of my ankle, its text a poisonous promise. 大石笮死蟹.

Above us, the beams of the ceiling creaked. The slow snapping noise drew my attention upward, and I watched in horror as one of the mounted cameras groaned and tilted, ready to fall right onto my head. I got up to run, but the red smithing on my back pulled against my clothes, sending me back onto my butt.

If I didn't cast now, I'd die.

I needed a Hail Mary of a spell. Something ridiculous that would somehow hinder his spell-writing ability, counteracting the seriousness of Charles's carefully constructed smithings that were sticking to me like sap. Something silly, something powerful, something that would undermine everything that Charles and his brand of magic believed about the world. A wild idea struck me, and I nearly laughed aloud at how perfectly it fit the situation. It was so stupid that it just might work.

"I'm rubber, you're glue," I said, pointing a finger at Charles. "Whatever you say *sticks back to you!*"

The papers fluttered off me and shot toward Charles as his smirk melted off, leaving his jaw hanging open.

He swung my paddle out in front of him, trying to swat the smithings away, but they crept up the weapon and cemented themselves to his body. Charles scrambled to yank them off but was interrupted as another crack brought our attention back up to the ceiling. The heavy camera dislodged from its stand, plummeting to the ground. It hit a hanging pole, shifting its fall his way instead of mine. A fatal stroke of bad luck.

His eyes filled with panic as the ribbon at his neck pulled taut.

I frantically drew mana into me and pointed at his chest. "E kula 'ina!" *Push over.* Charles was a jerk, but he didn't deserve to get crushed to death.

My magic went off like a bullet and Charles flew back. He crashed into the wall behind him and slid to the ground seconds before the heavy camera smashed in the spot where he'd just been standing. Unfortunately, my messy search for a spell on the fly cut both ways. Mana pushed back and slammed against *my* chest in retribution, ripping the air from my lungs.

The Lam Syndicate head was down. Legs spread before him, he weakly leaned himself against the wall. He tried to prop himself up, but the blunt force of the impact had been too much, and he slumped back down to the floor.

I gasped, trying to catch my breath. My knees and palms stung, and when I looked down, I realized they were scratched and bloody.

Ignoring the dull pain, I clenched my fists together and walked toward Charles, pulling his ruined paddle from the ground. The endorphins had chased away any fatigue and I felt numb, but this duel would end on my terms.

Charles watched me approach warily, but the fight in him had dissolved. His breathing was sharp, and he moved a hand to the back of his head. When he pulled it back, it was stained rust red. My spell must've been stronger than I realized, but it had still saved his life, so I wasn't about to apologize. Everything burned. My skin felt too tight, still buzzing with adrenaline. I was breathing hard, too, but in measured, careful breaths.

I positioned the tip of the splintered paddle at his neck. "Yield."

As the jagged end touched his throat, Charles gulped, his Adam's apple bobbing furiously. There were three minutes left, which meant Charles had no chance of running out the clock. There was only one rational move left, and I needed him to say it.

Charles's eyes shot down to the weapon at his neck, and his mouth hardened to a line. Slowly, he reached for the smithing on his chest. He ran his fingers over the peony-colored ribbon, the characters briefly glowing under his touch. It loosened and fluttered to the ground harmlessly. The rest of his identical bad-luck charms trembled with a final exertion of mana before lying still.

"I yield," he said gruffly.

I dropped the staff of the paddle, every muscle in my body going weak now that the danger was gone. Relief swept over me in waves—it was finished.

Charles's lips slanted into a grimace and he groaned as he slowly got back up, dusting off the front of his pants. "All this over a fucking misunderstanding," he complained, face red. He begrudgingly stuck out his hand.

I hesitated just a moment before extending my own hand in return. We shook, and a buzzer sounded around the arena, announcing the duel's end. He held my hand slightly longer than was necessary, his lips tweaking back into a practiced half smile that was meant to be endearing.

"You're full of surprises, Miss Petrova," Charles said.

I jerked my hand away. "It's easy to surprise people when their expectations are low."

He wiped a cut on his lower lip with his thumb without breaking eye contact, his mouth dipping into a grimace. "I promise that won't happen again."

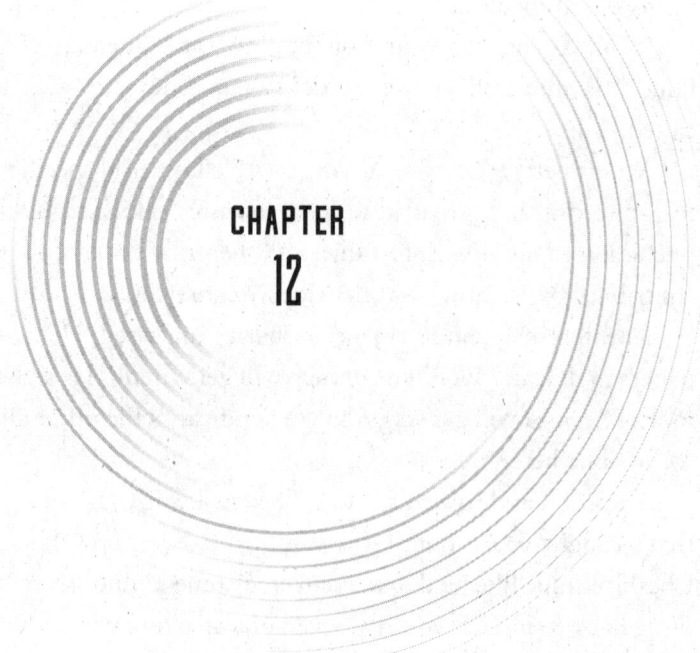

CHAPTER 12

"You can expect those business records in your inbox by the end of the week," Charles said with a casual smile. It was hard to imagine that the angel in front of me had tried crushing me to death an hour earlier. He had the kind of face that made you forget things like that.

We were sitting in a holding area near the lockers, discussing how the final terms would be executed before leaving the arena. The cramped quarters housed a single table with a wobbly leg and three chairs that reminded me of the plastic ones in school.

"Good," I said, tapping my fingers against my forearm. "And as for that hefty lump sum, we'll hold you to the end of the week for the transfer as well. I hope you read the changes before signing?"

Charles's smile dropped. He grabbed the contract from the center of the table, flipping furiously through the pages until he found the clause I'd slipped in before the duel. His dark eyes scanned the page and he swallowed. After a few seconds, he let out a huff of air through his nose. "Ridiculous."

"Thank you for your donation to the Language Advancement Fund," Basilio said with a smirk. "Your generosity is greatly appreciated."

Was it petty? Yes. Was it worth it? Hell, yes. I'd specifically chosen the nonprofit that provided support to clans seeking regulation. Everyone deserved a voice at the table, and the irony of having Charles Lam contribute to the cause was deliciously satisfying.

"Beaten by a child's rhyme," Charles muttered. He laid down the papers in defeat. "Fine. The money will get wired." He sighed. "And it looks like Sora will get access to my Syndicate's files after all. I suppose we're done here?"

He stood and turned to Sora. "Seems I was right after all. Anyone that's caught your attention is sure to be diverting." He gave Sora a Cheshire smile like he'd just uncovered some kind of secret before pivoting back to me. "If you're in need of a sparring partner in the future, call on me."

"I'm not much of a fighter," I said.

The look he gave me sent a swarm of butterflies to my stomach and I was unable to respond with something witty. If only he had a scar or something to dampen his good looks. I stared at his face, imagining the imperfection striped down his cheek, and frowned. Scratch that. A scar would be too dashing.

Charles caught me looking and winked. "Could've fooled me."

He left the room, the door swinging shut behind him, and I collapsed across the tabletop, setting my forehead against the chilly metal. Behind me Basilio gave a low whistle. "I know he's awful, but he's hot, right?"

I punched Basilio in the arm. "He's trouble."

"More like bad luck," Basilio said. "Which makes you, Kea, my lucky charm." He bear-hugged me and I let myself get squished.

I'd won. Actually *won*.

"You're right about one thing: That duel was pure luck," Sora said out loud as if reading my mind as Basilio released me. "Be grateful that last spell didn't squeeze Kea's lungs shut permanently."

My forehead wrinkled. "It worked."

"Barely," he said. "Your magic is strong, but your smithings are wild. Without control, they're just as dangerous for yourself as for others."

"The two you saw were cobbled together. When I have time to think, they're more stable. Right, Basilio?"

The man avoided looking at me and started whistling. Traitor.

"As a Caster, there often isn't time to think," Sora lectured. "Better to say nothing than to speak and accidentally incinerate yourself."

He rose and I followed him from the room, seething. I shouldn't have felt like this. I'd just won a duel against a prominent Board member *and* helped get us access to the Lam Syndicate's files. The least Sora could do was say something nice.

Being near him all the time was throwing off my equilibrium. I liked having people around me and had become so desperate for a friendly voice that I was starting to lean on him for feedback. As if his concealed compliments could even pass for genuine affection. As if he had at all warmed to me. As if I cared about what he thought of me.

At the entrance of the stadium, Sora's feet stopped moving and I nearly ran into his back but stopped just short. He looked over his shoulder to make eye contact. "Forcing Charles to give his money to charity was . . . clever. Though you were right—you're not the best fighter. We should work on that."

I must've done some real damage to myself with my last reckless spell, because for some reason my chest felt tight.

"Later, though," he said and went back to walking. "I have to get you home."

Basilio gave Sora a knowing look. "Oh, did her grandparents threaten you, too?"

"*Too?*"

"Papa Ivan is a lot," Basilio said, placing an arm around Sora's shoulder. "Have fun."

The expression on Sora's face was priceless.

~

We took Basilio home while Sora explained what had happened overnight. Apparently, Papa had threatened to break Sora's legs if I wasn't back by eight. Failing to come home once again had been the final straw. I called them immediately, trying to explain things, but Nana and Papa wouldn't hear it. They even went so far as to accuse Sora of trying to "take advantage of me." When I reminded them that I'd spent the previous night in a hotel bed rather than in Sora's, Papa threatened to break my legs, too.

The lot came into view as the road ended, and Sora was forced to drive his fancy black car on the rugged terrain that marked the start of our property. He pulled to a stop on the lawn, near the wide stairs that led to our wraparound porch. As we exited, the squeak of the screen door sounded, and I turned up to the house.

Makani stood in the doorway, his sleep shirt tilted off one shoulder, and a once-white stuffed animal trailing behind him. He called it "puppy," but the thing resembled no animal I could think of. He rubbed his face as he tried to make sense of me in the yard. Then, he sprinted down the steps, grabbing my waist.

His face was buried into my shirt as he spoke. "I've been watching the chickens for you. Well, Fiona anyway."

"I thought you didn't like eggs," I said.

Makani broke away and looked down at his feet. "I don't, but you do."

This kid. My heart swelled in my throat, and I reached for him again, giving him one last hug so that I could kiss his head. "Thanks," I said, finally releasing him. "Is there food? I'm starving."

"Yeah, Papa made curry."

Makani and I walked up the steps, until I realized that Sora wasn't with us. I turned back to see him frozen at the car. "You, too," I said, waving a hand so he'd come closer.

Sora's shoes squelched in the muddy grass as he ascended the porch. He stopped just outside the threshold, placing a hand against the frame of the door. "I'm not sure that I should."

"Scared your legs will be forfeit?" I teased and pushed open the door. "Relax. I'll protect you." I tugged on the end of his sleeve until he followed me inside.

The second that we entered, the household erupted. Nana took one look at me and made an ungodly shriek as she launched off the couch faster than I'd seen her move in years.

She stood on her toes to hug me, her bare feet sticking to the tiles of the floor. "*Two days*, Kealaokaleo Petrova! And then I get a phone call telling me you've been poisoned—and kidnapped? I'm the reckless one, huh? And *you*, young man. How could you put her in all that danger?"

Sora started to say something, then stopped himself, changing mid-word. "It won't happen again."

"It won't happen because she's done doing whatever this is," Papa interjected. He was, for no reason at all, sharpening all our kitchen knives.

Sora swallowed. "I'm afraid that I need Kea close."

The scraping sound of blade against steel intensified, and I could see Papa's knife moving swiftly back and forth in a rhythmic pattern out of the corner of my eye. "And who are you to insist on that?"

"I'm . . ." Sora ran out of words, hovering awkwardly between the kitchen and living room.

"He's hungry," I declared. "I invited Sora to eat with us."

My grandfather's frown deepened the lines near his mouth. His hands clenched around the handle of his blade, then he sighed and slid it back in the wooden block. "He goes after he eats."

"Nonsense, Ivan," Nana Kūlia scolded Papa and turned to Sora. "You're welcome to stay the night. There aren't many streetlights out here, and the potholes are big enough to fall into, I swear!"

As Nana went on about the dangers of poorly maintained roads, she gave me a conspiratorial look behind Papa's back. Oh, no. The last thing I needed was for my grandma to try to play matchmaker between me and Mr. I-Can-Open-Your-Head-with-My-Mana. Hard pass. I pretended not to notice her waggling eyebrows.

"Should I stay?" he asked me. "It would simplify things . . ."

I shrugged. "You can have my bed."

His ears reddened. "That's your room. I don't think I should—"

My grandfather coughed like he was hacking up a lung. "Mr. Kaiser, I think, will be more than comfortable on our couch."

Sora nodded quickly. "The couch is fine."

"Glad that's all settled," Nana said. "Now, Kea, go fetch your sister and cousin from the beach. It's time to eat."

I kissed my grandmother on the cheek and pulled Sora back out the door before Papa could grab another sharp object to wave around. We shouldn't have been arguing anyway. Everything was going to be fine.

I was home.

~

Out back, the drop down to the beach was a gradual slope that started in thick blankets of grass that slowly faded to patches then nothing at all, until powdery white sand and crisp blue water was all you could see. A thousand years ago, my ancestors had likely stood on a beach much like this one and stared out at the same sea. Though we were in different times, in different lands, and speaking different tongues, some things never faded: the might of the ocean, the richness of soil, the everyday magic that this universe offered us.

I exhaled deeply, letting out the last of LA's pressure upon me, then looked around and bellowed out a *hui* to the water beyond where I could see Sisi and Newt searching for limu. When the pair saw me, they tossed their baskets ashore and ran toward us. Cold water splashed wildly around their ankles as they approached.

Newt was the first to reach us, and he embraced me so tightly that he lifted me off the ground. Sisi joined in after, smashing Newt between us as she hung on to us both. They spoke at the same time, filling me in on everything that had happened while I was away. In my absence, Sora had sent men to our home to protect my clan. Apparently, the place had been flush with guards round the clock. Since the men on watch hadn't had much work to do, they'd spent most of their days running errands off-property or eating the moon-shaped cookies Nana insisted on buying from the Lins. A minor scuffle with some of Keanu's clan down at Bobby's had been the only source of excitement.

The sky turned purple as we talked on the beach and the lights from the house began to glow a hazy yellow, inviting us home. I ushered the kids back up the path but insisted on staying awhile longer when I realized that I hadn't swum in ages. Sicilia and Newt left without question, understanding that internal tug toward the water, but Sora didn't. And he made his displeasure clear.

"It's dark," he said as I began to tug off my jeans.

He looked away, but I had no qualms about wearing underwear as a swimsuit. It wasn't like the parts it covered were any different.

I snapped my fingers. "I have to check first."

"Check what?"

"For magi," I said and pulled off my shirt.

He stumbled back. "You're joking."

I ignored him and searched the plants at the edge of the grass for ti leaf.

"*Kea*," he repeated. "You are joking, right?" When I didn't respond, Sora started rambling. "I'm sure you didn't forget that those things are more active at night."

"I've only lived here my whole life," I said sharply.

"Then why risk it?" he asked.

I pretended not to hear his question as I found what I was looking for. Holding the inner stem firmly, I used my free hand to pull downward until the leaf came cleanly off. Armed, I approached the edge of the water, waves curling around my toes. It was a calm night, and the ocean was the same blue-black as the heavens.

Sicilia and Newt hadn't tried to stop me because they understood.

The city was exciting, bright, and bustling, but it lacked soul. Whenever I returned from LA, the first thing I wanted to do was jump into the ocean. It felt like the salt water cleansed me of all the glitz and gray.

I tossed the leaf onto the water, watching as it floated along the surface. It bobbed across the waves, then tumbled into a spiral of foam, barreling back to shore, where it was once again swept out. No magi had lurched to the surface to swallow the leaf, which meant it was safe to swim. Relatively.

I waded out until the water kissed my waist and watched as a wave approached. It crested overhead, a fast-moving wall of glittering navy. As the edge of the wave dipped, the crash impending, I took my final gulp of air and dove under.

I was instantly buried under the pressing weight of the ocean, the only sound a distant rhythmic roar as each new wave fought and died above. If I ever had to explain the word *peace*, this would be what I thought of.

I kicked down to the ocean floor and released a bubble as I settled with my legs crossed, holding my breath and staring up at the barest glimmer of moonlight. By the time I counted to a hundred, I'd run out of air. So, I unfurled my legs and propelled myself upward in a single powerful motion. When I broke to the surface with a gasp, I found Sora up to his knees in the break with a panicked look in his eyes.

"Did you want to swim, too?" I asked dumbly, unable to process the picture of a soaking wet Sora in front of me.

He splashed me in the face, cheeks red. "No!"

I swam closer. "Then what are you doing?"

Sora's face had taken on a mix of irritation, embarrassment, and fear. His pants were soaked past his crotch, and his white shirt had turned transparent, sticking to his chest. Behind him, the matching blazer was abandoned on the shore, where waves lapped at the edges, likely ruining the wool.

His mouth twisted, and he turned his back to me abruptly, walking back to shore. I followed, shivering as the cold night air hit my body. Sora, on the other hand, was less graceful. Weighed down by clothes now heavy with seawater, his motions were sluggish. I had to wait for him to unstick himself as he sunk into the wet sand. When he finally got out, I noticed that he was still wearing his shoes.

Dripping and shivering, Sora and I walked back to the house, where I hoped Papa could supply a change of clothes for Sora to borrow. The warmth of the entryway was enticing, and I was already thinking about fluffy towels and steaming plates of food, but the squelching sound of Sora's sopping leather shoes against the steps brought me back to reality.

"People generally take their shoes off *before* getting in the water," I teased.

He sighed, pressing his thumb and forefinger against his head. "I wasn't going for a swim."

I laughed. "Diving then?"

"You didn't come up," he mumbled. "I thought . . ."

The humor was knocked out of me as his words hung between us. Sora dropped his hand so that his eyes were uncovered, the flame of them becoming maroon in the moonlight. He was the ocean's rage and peace, bottled up and coated in red paint. If I leaned closer, he'd sweep me away. And if I kissed him, I'd surely drown.

I took a step forward, and Sora extended his arm out like a hook. My eyes trailed over his figure. This unpleasant, moody man who teased too much and smiled too little. He knew just what to say to raise my hackles, and he pushed me to every limit I had. But sometimes, it almost felt like he actually cared.

"Why did you jump in after me?" I asked, finally managing to squeeze the question out, though it was breathless and shaky.

Sora took my hand in his, static electricity jumping between us. This close, he smelled of citrus, and I resisted the desire to reach out, letting Sora lead. Every inch toward him felt like a million years as he lifted my hand to his chest. He paused a centimeter away and inhaled, like sucking in a large breath of air before diving underwater, then pressed my palm against his skin.

The live wire between us jolted to life.

I opened myself up to the connection and focused on the current of thoughts, but there was no thread of consciousness that I could find. Unlike before, there was only one thing in his head, running like a loop.

Kealaokaleo.

My full name.

He let go, and silence stretched between us as I stared at the worn planks of the lānai, unable to meet his eyes. Our magic wasn't intertwined any longer, but the sensation of it came back. Ginger bit into my tongue, and I resisted the urge to place my mouth on his. I'd never met anyone whose sympathetic abilities meshed with mine the way his did. Perhaps I was the only one of us affected, but the look in his eyes told me that if I pulled him close right then, he wouldn't resist.

Sora's eyes followed my hands as they hesitantly crept up the side of his shirt. His breath hitched as I grasped the edge of the cloth, tugging him a little closer, but at that moment the door swung open, saving me from myself and casting an orange glow over the back porch. Sora turned his face back to the ground, and I blinked like I'd just woken up.

Nana stood in the open doorway, her mouth a round O as she saw us standing there soaked. Sora sneezed, and her last bit of apprehension toward him dropped. She didn't see Sora Kaiser anymore; she just saw a shivering man on her back porch in need of help. Nana shouted for Papa to bring us towels and make sure the water heater was on, then ushered us inside.

As we showered and changed, getting ready for the evening meal, all I could think of was his ruined suit, his shoes sinking into sand and seawater, and of how he thought of me so intensely that he'd memorized my full name: Kealaokaleo. The way of the voice.

CHAPTER 13

Elated with the previous day's success, I'd slept well even with Sora Kaiser on my couch. By morning, I'd even managed to convince myself that my present situation was a minor inconvenience. I'd figure out the key smithing, rub it in their dumb, beautiful Board faces, and then traipse home to live my inconsequential life raising chickens and children by the seaside. Damn them if they thought I was going to be pleasant while doing it.

I stared at the translation provided by Ivy, my vision blurring as I reviewed the smithing in the boardroom. Charles was planning on emailing me the Lam records soon, since Sora didn't have a computer with internet access. I'd been here for hours, hunched over the laptop at the foot of my bed, and yet was no closer to cracking the spell. I hit the return button on my keyboard a little too forcefully as I separated the lines out like a poem.

> *When a blade tastes blood from one of its own, it cries*
> *Misfortune has brought death, arriving in twos*
> *The death of a hero, and the death of a dream*
> *Wings broken, the angel falls to the forest floor, returning like a stone*
> *And the raven-haired king who shot him from the sky, weeps.*

Translations were always poor mimics of the original, but that couldn't be helped. My Latin teacher in school had described its limits as being like kissing a bride through a veil. But difficult or not, I'd scrape together some greater understanding out of this jumble of words. I replayed the audio of the death spell and readied the journal and pen at my side.

There was an H-sounding word at the start of the smithing. I read the translation aloud again, running my finger under the lines as I spoke, leaving a smudge on my laptop screen. My voice halted on the word *returning*. I blinked and rewound the audio, playing it again. Having an idea in mind crystalized the sound, and a clear glottal stop between vowels surfaced.

"Ho'iho'i," I said. *Return.*

Maybe the text was more direct than I'd realized.

Excitedly, I translated each word of Ivy's spell individually, ending up with a list of over fifty. Biting the tip of my pen, I contemplated how to narrow it down. There were a few words that didn't translate well into Hawaiian. Words like *king*, *hero*, and *raven-haired* were unlikely to appear since the concepts for these things didn't exist naturally in the language, so I crossed them out. That got my list down to around thirty. Progress, if still unwieldy.

Because of Hawaiian's structure, I was positive that the *au* I'd first heard came after ho'iho'i, making it ho'iho'i au. *I return.* The rest still wasn't clear, but I'd figured out the meat of it. In accordance with Hawaiian grammar rules, the remainder of the sentence would be connected by a preposition, in easily digested parts. It would take time to explore different variations, but I'd bet that I had at least one object in the vocabulary soup I'd written.

I copied down the words I'd sifted via elimination onto a separate sheet, switching them back to English. Even though they wouldn't be present in the Hawaiian spell, it didn't mean they weren't useful. *Angel*, for example, was a clear reference to Angelo, and I was almost certain that the weeping king was his murderer. I rewound the audio and texted Charles.

Send. Me. The. Files.

Three bubbles danced at the bottom of my screen as he typed his response.

Say please.

I frowned and sent him a single word, though not the one he wanted.

Now.

If he continued to push the issue, I had a few more colorful ones just for him. Single-word curses happened to be my specialty.

My door cracked open, and Newt appeared in the frame. He yawned pointedly at me as he plopped onto the edge of the bed, jostling the laptop. My sister and cousins had no idea what personal space meant and came in and out of my room as they pleased. I'd given up trying to lecture them about it.

"Sora told us you weren't taking the smithing exam," he said.

That was the lie I'd used to explain why I'd been going to LA so frequently.

"What's the point?" I said noncommittally. "I've already failed more times than I can count."

"I could always just hack into the Guild and change your results," he offered. He was joking—probably.

I rolled my eyes, ignored him, and began crossing out any words that were prepositions, articles, or other fillers that I could confidently take out from the next part of the audio. While I was deep into my work, my computer pinged, and a pop-up stretched across the screen announcing that I had mail.

I set the notebook down and opened my inbox in a rush. A new message waited for me with no subject line. The body was blank, other than the forwarding notice at the top from Charles and two attachments. One labeled "Smithing Records Lam Syndicate" and the other called "SPECIAL-FOR-YOU.TXT." The ass. This was truly some next-level passive-aggressiveness.

I clicked on the text file first, and a jolt of electricity ran through my fingertips and up to the top of my head. The sensation rushed up my nose like wasabi, and I sneezed.

Newt glanced at the screen and cackled. "What kind of dickhead sends a text file?"

A sore loser, that was who. The document opened, and I gritted my teeth, staring at the mess of letters and numbers. It made no sense. "Just help me read it," I begged. My head was already starting to hurt.

Newt peered over my shoulder. "I can't. That's not code. It's not even a language, as far as I can tell." He closed the file, but it reopened on its own. Frowning, Newt moved the tab to the side to examine my inbox, going pale as he read the sender's name. "Kea, why the *hell* would Charles Lam forward you an email called 'special for you'?"

"Don't snoop," I admonished, snatching the computer out of his hands. I tried to minimize the screen, but it popped back up. I swore and twisted my head to face my cousin. "Because he's a dickhead, like you said. And stop swearing."

"That's not what I meant." Newt's expression morphed into concern as the computer started beeping. "That shouldn't be happening." He curled his hands at me until I passed him the laptop. "Were you expecting an email from him?"

"I was," I admitted reluctantly.

Newt's eyebrows raised at the attachment name, but he didn't pry. "Was it supposed to be something 'special for you'?"

"No," I snapped. "Just some documents."

He groaned. "So, you opened this without thinking?"

My forehead felt like it was about to explode. I hated computers. "I thought he was just being a jerk with the name."

Newt sighed. He pressed his thumb and forefinger onto the lids of his closed eyes like he was a tired parent dealing with their idiot kid. He opened them, and his fingers dropped to fly over the keyboard. "Call him. We need to verify that Charles Lam actually sent this attachment to you, because from here, it looks like a virus. A malicious smithing."

I frantically phoned Charles, dialing his number three times in a row until he picked up.

"Did you send me the records yet?" I asked before he could say anything, putting the phone down face up on the bed on speakerphone.

"My god, Kea. Can you please relax? I told you I'd get them to you."

"You didn't already send them?"

"Not yet."

"That doesn't make sense! I just got your stupid email."

At my side, Newt made a face. "Tell him to check his sent items."

I gave the info to Charles, who must've searched his email, based on the clacking of his keys audible from my end. "Hmm. It looks like I did send something. I don't remember doing that . . ."

"Did you receive an email with an empty attachment recently?" Newt asked, cutting in.

The other end of the line went quiet. Finally, Charles's voice floated back through the speaker. "Shit."

Newt jumped up and ran for the door, calling for Sora. The Kaiser head came to my room, uncomfortably staring at the rumpled bedding and abandoned half-drunk cups of tea. When he heard Charles's voice on the phone, he tensed. "What did you do?" he accused.

"Nothing!" Charles protested. "Not on purpose, anyway."

"He gave me some kind of virus," I explained.

"Figures." Sora rolled his eyes.

"A computer virus," Charles clarified. "Although if she would like—"

"*Shut up*, Charles!" Sora said.

I'd never heard him snap before. It was oddly refreshing.

Newt sat back at the laptop, all business, and a frown creased the center of his forehead. "It's not a virus. It's a worm."

His fingers flew across the keyboard as he typed, letters and numbers appearing on the knuckles of his fingers as he worked. The same figures were reflected in the center of his irises. His eyes glowed a faint green, the color reminiscent of the glow of a server room. He hissed as the worm's Technic magic zapped him and pulled back. He sucked on the edge of his fingers as the light faded from his eyes.

"So?" I prodded.

He looked up at me. "It's bad."

Newt spoke so quickly that I had a hard time following, but I generally understood what had happened. He explained that the email Charles had accidentally sent me was embedded with a scripting system setting that was enabled to hide file extensions. It made dangerous attachments look innocuous so someone would click on them. Once opened, the worm would discreetly copy and paste itself into any messages the user sent.

"It looks like this spell's purpose is to keep your email forcibly open until you send something that qualifies as 'confidential' to another user," Newt concluded. "In reality, that information is getting forwarded back to a dedicated server. The intended receiver gets a worm instead of the original file, and the process repeats itself."

Sora groaned. "I've already sent Charles a list of what we're looking for in his files."

Newt sucked in air through his teeth. "Then that information's been compromised. I'm going to disconnect our computer from the internet so we can isolate the spell."

"Shit," Sora said.

I giggled. "It's cute when you curse." *Where did that come from?*

Newt's eyebrows knitted together at my outburst, but he didn't comment on it. "A Technic breathed life into this thing. With some adaptive coding baked into the spell, the worm's learned to adapt, changing in each iteration so it's uniquely suited to each receiver. Social engineering." He pressed a key, his eyes flitting over the script. "Strange. I thought for sure it would search for and flag encrypted files. Your email tab won't close until you send something protected, but without scanning the drive, it shouldn't be able to determine what's what. It must be sorting it somehow."

"Maybe you don't have any confidential files on that computer," Sora suggested. He went quiet. "Sorry. I feel like I just heard wrong. Did Kea just call me *cute*?"

My head felt funny, like it was being slowly inflated with helium. I tried to refocus. "We've got tons of confidential stuff here," I interrupted. "Financial documents. All our login information. Newt keeps his stash of explicit videos here that he thinks I don't know about. Oh, and our social security numbers, too. Mine is 583—"

My cousin's eyes went wide, and Sora shouted to cut me off before I finished. Newt abandoned the computer on my dresser and jumped for me. He pulled down the skin under my eyes to better look at my pupils.

"Social engineering was more accurate than I realized," Newt said. "I think the worm's already spread."

"By jumping *into* her?" Sora asked, his voice raising a decibel.

The idea that a computer worm-virus-thing had hopped into my body like a flea onto a dog was hilarious. I cracked up and fell onto my side, rolling back and forth on the sheets. Newt scooted off the bed. His face was so ridiculous, all twisted like that, that it made me laugh even harder. Tears streamed down my face.

Meanwhile, he hadn't stopped talking. "Kea's sympathetic ability allows her to sense mana better than most. It also means she can feel it in smithings, people, whatever." Newt balanced the phone under his chin, while continuing to type on the computer. "I think the worm lowers your guard and compels you to send or release information. Because of her magic, Kea would be more affected than others."

"She sounds drunk," Sora said.

I pouted. "I'm not drunk. Just . . . lightheaded and fuzzy around the edges." Cotton balls clouded my thoughts. I felt nauseous.

"Until she completes the intended task, the worm's running everything in her system on overdrive," Newt explained. He reached for me and placed a cool palm against my forehead. "She has a fever. If she sends a message out, that should send the worm along."

"Yes, but we don't want this to spread further. It's too dangerous to just let loose," Sora countered. "I could see it burning its way through all of LA." He paused. "We'll have to break it some other way."

Newt grimaced. "I'm decent in Hawaiian, but that won't have any effect here. It doesn't have the range to deal with computers." His hand was still planted against my face. "Her fever's climbing."

Chills rocked up and down my spine, and I pushed Newt away to climb under the covers, freezing. "I'm going to throw up," I whimpered.

Sora let loose a paragraph of curses. "If she's nauseous, that's a bad sign. We have to cool her down."

He yanked the blanket off and let me lie in the cold. My skin prickled in the bare air and I fought to get my sheets back, but he threw them on the floor and out of reach. Too tired to complain, I lay back in the pillows.

"You have to do something!" my cousin exclaimed.

"Even if we left for the hospital now, we wouldn't make it," Sora said. His voice was subdued, like he was wrestling with the concept of being helpless for the first time.

Newt inhaled sharply. "I'll give you three minutes to think of something, or I'm going to reconnect the internet and let Kea complete the worm's task. If it saves her life, I don't give a *damn* that LA burns."

A tense moment of silence passed between them that I barely registered. Newt was upset, his brows slanted downward over his eyes. I didn't want him to be worried about me. I found my cousin's palm and squeezed his fingers. He held tight, using his free hand to brush away the hair that was sticking to my sweaty forehead.

"Just turn off the computer," I said weakly, grasping at the last threads of lucidity I had.

"You can't," Newt explained, soothingly. "You have to contain the worm first."

Thoughts clouded, I struggled to think around the limits of the spell that Newt had described. My typical strategy involved beating puzzles with a bat until the pieces forced themselves together. But coding was more delicate, like chess. One needed to isolate the threat and trap it, limiting the wiggle room an opponent had. Like capturing a butterfly in a glass jar.

I hiccuped. "Worms are tiny. Let's just put it in a cup and leave it alone."

"Delirium," Sora stated. "The inflammation has reached her brain." His voice was hoarse and his cool hands gently stroked the sides of my head. "If she gets the worm out, will she recover her health immediately?"

Newt had run back to the computer and was typing furiously. "Yes. But no. Or, wait. I think Kea's onto something. Do you have a phone? One without a lot of information on it. A new device, or one you've wiped but that still has a live connection."

Sora confirmed he had an old one; he deleted all its contacts and gave Newt the number. My cousin went back to the beeping message on my laptop and inserted the new receiver address. He left the computer on the bed and helped me sit up. "Kea, I need you to find one of those files you mentioned and send them to Sora. It'll make you feel better."

My hands were heavy as I used the trackpad to search our desktop. Neck stiff, I attached the first one I could find. The upload meter crawled along like molasses. I huffed in short, pained breaths as my chest struggled to keep up with my body. Everything was so hot. The bar inched closer to the finish line, a millimeter at a time.

The world blurred and I tipped my head back to stare at the popcorn ceiling of my room. I blinked slowly, wondering if this was how I'd die—as worm food. Newt shook my shoulders and snapped his fingers in front of my face. The sound echoed in my head, and I refocused back on the computer screen.

File uploaded.

Send.

There was a whooshing noise as the message zipped off, and I hissed in relief as the throbbing pressure in my chest, head, and stomach lifted all at once. The edges of my vision regained their sharpness.

"Once you get the message, kill the service," Newt said.

Sora confirmed when the phone disconnected. He inhaled shakily.

"Is she okay?" Charles asked, his voice cutting out on the call.

"I'm fine," I said. "Just tired. I'll look over those records, Charles." I hung up.

My cousin dove for me, squishing me into a hug under his wiry frame. My headache pounded in his grip, but I didn't have the energy to fend him off.

Sora let out a whistle. "I'm glad." He looked over at Newt. "Hey, Kea's cousin. How old are you?"

"Eighteen," Newt replied tensely.

"Then I'm guessing the top-secret file I just got titled 'FishingVids.mov' is not, in fact, a video of anyone fishing," he said.

Newt flushed. "It is not."

An incredible sound erupted from Sora, and it took me a second to register it as laughter. Sora Kaiser was laughing. Actually *laughing*. In an uncharacteristic, full-bellied, bent-over-a-desk kind of way. I was too stunned to do anything but listen to his messy gasps.

Eventually, Sora managed to contain himself, and his voice returned to a crisp professional note. "Well. Let me know if you find anything else." And he left the room.

The moment he was gone, a pillow slammed into the side of my head.

"I hate you," Newt whined. "You just sent Sora Kaiser my . . ." He trailed off, blubbering. "I should've let that worm eat your brain."

I stuck my tongue out at him. "I made a calculated decision. That was the least damaging thing on there."

"At the cost of my soul," he complained. "My reputation, my future prospects."

"You're not a lady in the English countryside," I snapped. "And no one's trying to blackmail you."

Newt huffed and exited the room, standing in the hallway with his arms stretched upward to grab on to the top of the door. "Well, I'm going to let Nana and Papa know about the near-death experience you just had."

My teasing stopped dead. "You can't."

Newt's mouth tweaked up at one corner. He turned and sprinted out the front door, and I ran after him, screaming for him to stop. Head of my clan or not, I was still terrified of my grandparents' wrath. Even the great and terrible Sora Kaiser paled in comparison.

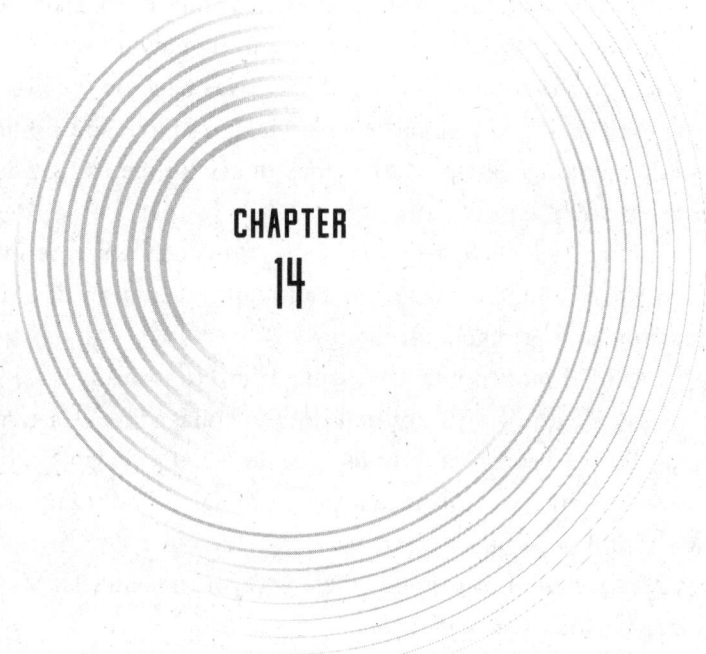

CHAPTER 14

After I was strong-armed by Newt into telling my family everything about the investigation, Papa "encouraged" Sora to leave. We were left alone, mulling over the information we had at the kitchen table while Makani watched TV in the living room. The noise of his cartoons and the sight of his curly black hair peeking above the beige couch cushions was a thread of normalcy that I was grateful for.

Papa's face was grim. "This is exactly what destroyed the Palakikos."

In truth, I'd been trying to avoid any family meetings at all. The questions and the concern. The long glances filled with worry that I was failing in my role. As the head, I should have been able to take care of all of it myself without crying to Papa and Nana. The fact that I couldn't, even when I'd pushed myself to the brink, was crushing.

"Everything is fine. We don't need to discuss this," I said.

"If the Board is involved, there is definitely a need. You almost died, Kea. We need a plan to keep the city away from us," Papa said.

My family looked at me expectantly, but under their steady gazes I was flooded with doubt. Panic ran through my nerves as I tapped my fingers on the table. All of a sudden, I was back on the highway rushing to the Palakikos' home to save Makani's mom and coming too late to do anything. The phantom smell of ash hit me like a wall, choking off my other senses.

Nana spoke before I was able to. "Let's deal with the smaller issue and worry about LA later. We can launch a raid on the Mahiʻais tomorrow and get back our money.

"No," I interrupted. "We can't afford to lose anyone."

The death of my aunt had deeply damaged us as a family. Every clan buried people from raids, but the Palakiko clan's end had been so sudden and so violent that the Homestead had no time to recover. Grief still coiled in my gut, ugly and unmoving. All of our eyes shot to Makani, who was quietly flicking through channels. My silent plea hung between us: *Not again.*

Papa patted Nana's hand. "Kea has a point, love. We're much older now than the last time we had a raid against any large clan. If you were hit, your body might not be able to take it."

Nana's hands clenched the top of her cane. "They stole from us."

"We owed the Mahiʻais the mortgage anyway," I reminded her. Keanu was a thief, but not a cheat. He really would just take it out of our debt.

"Yes, but on our terms." Nana's lips curled.

Here we go again.

"By doing nothing, we make ourselves look vulnerable. That will only lead to future attacks from other clans and weakness in the eyes of the Board. We're stronger than they know." Nana accented her speech by slapping her hand on the smooth wood of our dining table.

She was both right and wrong.

It was true that Keanu probably saw my lack of retaliation as a fragility he could use to his advantage. My hesitation had been the fuel that emboldened Haʻaheo to approach me with a trap of his own. But the solution wasn't a raid. We had neither the numbers nor the strength to pull one off.

"I'm with Nana," Newt agreed. "We might stand a chance, especially with her magic."

"I'm not willing to take the risk that someone might not come back," I said.

"So, we just do nothing?" Sicilia said, crossing her arms.

The table erupted with smaller arguments as I rubbed the side of my head to chase away a growing headache. I needed to rein everyone back in. We couldn't fight the Homestead Council *and* the Board. It was better to stall for time by leaving Keanu alone and focusing instead on the investigation into Angelo's death. LA was the bigger threat and took priority. And no matter how much I hated it, we wouldn't win in a battle against them.

I held up my hand to quiet everyone. "We'll have to go on the defensive for now while I finish the Board's task," I said. "If I succeed, we'll get paid, which will give us more leverage with the council. We don't really have a choice."

Nana pounded her fist to the table's surface, shaking it. "There is always a choice, Kea! You are a head from the Hawaiian Homelands. We do *not* kneel to LA."

I stood abruptly, my chair scraping against the tile floor as I moved. "Your ego puts all of us at risk! If we really were as powerful as you claimed, we'd be on the council, we'd still have our mana o ka moʻokūʻauhau, and the Board would never have forced me into this. But we aren't, we don't, and they *did*."

Nana's face fell. "I'm just trying to advise you with what I would've done."

"I'm not you," I said sourly. "I can't do what you did when you were head, just throwing around wild spells without worrying about the consequences!"

I stared at the dark skin on my grandmother's arms. Her strong jaw. Her calloused hands. She didn't understand what it was like to not be good at everything. In her eyes, I was a faint outline of who she'd been at my age—a young head with limitless power at her fingertips. Tears prickled at the edge of my vision, and I turned away from everyone to stare out the window at the spot where the Palakiko house used to stand.

The room quieted. Even Makani had stopped watching his show and was staring at me from behind the couch. I knew it wasn't entirely fair of me to blame everything on Nana's past successes. Fate had cast me as the eldest daughter and the next head, claiming for itself all the other adults who could've instructed me in my role. All I had left was my grandmother. But I was the one leading us now.

"We wait," I said decisively. "Everyone is to stay on the defensive and together at all times. I will continue assisting the Board."

Nana paused, clenched and unclenched her hand on the wood of her cane, then finally gave me a short nod.

"Meanwhile, the rest of you should be ready for an attack," I said. "Keep off-property trips to a minimum, stock up on supplies, and reinforce our wards. Newt, I'm sorry but you'll have to choose to stay here or with your dad in the city until this is over."

"That sounds a little extreme," he said.

I grimaced. "We have to plan for the worst."

For a second, I thought I caught a whiff of the fire and smoke that had taken the Palakikos from us. Maybe everyone else could smell it, too, because none of them argued back.

~

I woke up at the crack of dawn with a jerk. Makani had fallen asleep next to me on the couch. His head was pressed against my arm, and a thin line of drool fell from his open mouth. The TV was still blaring. It had probably been left on all night. On the other couch, a faded beige thing spotted with stains, Newt was sprawled out on his back, snoring. Meanwhile, Sisi was sleeping sitting up on the large armchair opposite from me, her face pinched like she was having a bad dream.

I rubbed my own swollen eyes and gently pushed Makani's head off me, basking in the normalcy of this morning. Two weeks ago, I would've already been up to feed the chickens and weed the yard before noon. Now, I had a killer to track down. Groaning at the reminder, I tried not to think too hard about it as I shuffled over to the bathroom and brushed my teeth.

It wasn't just my neck on the line, but those of all the clans residing on the Homestead. If I wasn't able to seek out the traitor, then the Board had arguable cause to interrogate and even imprison members of our clans, which wouldn't go well. Our people were proud and wouldn't stand by as the city came to snatch their own away. They'd fight back, which meant a lot of us would die.

After the worm incident, Charles had sent his business records over via courier, and we'd spent most of the evening reviewing them. I could find no mention of anything like the spell that had killed Angelo. The Lams primarily dealt in luck, both good and bad, but I'd never heard of their spells fatally wounding someone, let alone disintegrating a body down to dust.

I checked the clock on the wall. It was almost ten, and Sora would be here soon. Papa might not have ended up breaking his legs, but he also was firm about me spending the night at home. We had a whole argument that ended with me getting the old *you may be my head but you're still my granddaughter* speech. I didn't put up much of a fight after that. I'd made them worry enough. Still, Sora promised to appear first thing in the morning so that we could investigate two of the most suspect Board members: Reagol Stone and Matthew Greyson.

I pulled on a pair of jeans and a white button-down that was a little too big. Sora would hate how wrinkled the shirt was, which made me smile. As if he'd read my mind, my phone rang, and his name popped up on the screen.

"Can you be ready to go when I get there?" Sora asked, his voice smooth and unblemished. He clearly had not just woken up, unlike myself. "I'm driving over now."

I yawned, my voice breaking as I shuffled out to the kitchen and filled up the kettle. "Making tea as we speak. Want a cup to go?"

From the window, I heard a strange sound. Like the rumble of an earthquake or a chorus of voices in disharmony. I glanced toward our wobbly, unmounted bookshelves, expecting to see a slight sway, but they were still.

Must be my imagination.

"I'm not a tea person," he said.

I lifted the kettle onto the stove, but the sound persisted. There was also a faint scent, like dirt and incoming rain. I stared at the glare of light reflecting off the surface of the steel teapot and caught the scent of medicinal herbs. That specific smell bothered me . . . had I come across it recently? I felt intuitively that it meant danger but couldn't remember why.

Instead, I refocused on Sora's phone rant about how he hated tea, my hand reaching for the faucet. "What kind of monster are you?" I joked.

When I looked up, a gigantic eye peered back at me from outside our kitchen window. The vague scent from outside had become a sour herbal mess. Just like my drink at the gala, the smell of the wet earth I'd fallen into. Damp and pungent, like fermenting plants.

An enormous pupil met mine, and the final pieces settled into place. We were being attacked—and our wards didn't work against magi.

In shock, I dropped the phone. As it clattered to the ground, the creature outside roared and a clawed hand lunged through the window, tearing through the netted screen like tissue paper. I leapt back, but not before a single talon tore through the shoulder of my shirt, leaving a shallow gash. My scream woke the house.

I could hear Sora yelling my name from the phone, but I couldn't stop to answer. Adrenaline coursed through me as I threw myself into the living room and quickly counted the heads. I reached for Makani first, grabbing him in my arms, then whacked the back of Sisi's chair with my leg so she jumped up.

The magi roared as it tore at the kitchen window, trying to press itself through the wooden frame and splintering the whole windowsill in the process. This was wrong. All wrong. The Petrova clan had lived on this land for more than a century, our mana drawing all kinds of magi.

From when we were very little, Nana had made sure that we studied every possible creature that could crawl out of the ocean so that we'd be able to defend ourselves, but this magi was unlike anything I'd ever seen. Magi followed cultures, and ours were always of the Hawaiian or Russian variety.

It was huge, almost humanoid, with a single bulging eye the size of a basketball and a thick body filled with grotesque muscles and flaps of skin that jiggled with every move. Spiky, unruly hair lay greased flat against its back in a tangled mess, and its unhinged jaw revealed a set of spiked teeth and a pair of yellowed tusks. It gnawed viciously on the cracked wood, making mewling sounds as it attempted to enter the house. The arm of the creature, which was ripping back planks to enlarge the window, ended in three large fingers with sharp claws.

The monster stopped moving as its pupils shrunk to pinpoints, focused directly on me. A flash of glowing mana drew my eyes to its neck, where the beast had been fitted with a stone collar inlaid with a spell. Fear gripped me by the throat and glued the soles of my feet to the ground. This magi was being controlled by someone. Its gaze was the trained eye of a hunting dog who had been sent to catch its prey.

And it had just found its target.

"Get everyone. Get them all out *now*!" I yelled.

Sisi screamed. Her face was torn between half sleep and terror as she yanked Newt out of his slumber. Papa and Nana appeared in the hall, having just woken up. Papa's bare chest was covered by a too-short gray cotton robe, and Nana's lacy nightgown looked mismatched with her grim expression.

"Newt, Sisi—hurry!" Papa commanded.

Newt had sprung up much faster than Sisi and was already bolting toward the back exit.

"Run!" I urged, pushing at Sicilia's back as she stumbled down the hall. I was right behind her, Makani crying in my arms.

We can't leave them. I turned back to my grandparents, but my grandmother didn't miss a beat.

"Go, Kea!" she yelled. "Papa and I will take care of this. Keep them safe!"

I held back my protest and kept sprinting for the back door. Nana was right. The kids came first. We shot out of the exit and descended the steps of the porch, circling around to the open garage. The key would be hanging on the wall near the opening. I would load them up, make sure Sisi drove away safely, and then go back to help Nana and Papa.

Almost there.

I was so focused on the next step of the plan that I almost ran straight into a second monster. This one was standing in front of the garage, grinning from ear to ear. It looked similar to the one at the window, but its skin was a sickly brown-green, its lower body balanced on spindly legs with feet like a bird of prey.

Makani let out a high-pitched scream as it jumped at us, mouth agape, ready to snap.

I cast on instinct, flinging out my left arm and letting the mana explode outward from my core. "E pahū i hope!" *Force back.*

My spell caught the beast in its mouth. It went flying backward, but so did we. The force sent us sliding on our toes across the grass. Unharmed but still farther away from the car.

The creature howled and scrambled to its feet, unbalanced and angry. It gnashed its teeth. I handed Makani to Newt and ran head-on at the thing. Grabbing a hammer from off the wall of the garage, I slammed it hard into the beast's deformed face.

It went down, crawling out and away from the house. But then the first one exploded out the back door. Not good—it had gotten past Nana and Papa? I dodged out of the way of the beast, then started ripping tools from Papa's workstation and hurling them at the magi, pushing it farther and farther from the garage.

I turned back to my family. "Get in the car!"

My right arm began to throb as my adrenaline dropped. I ignored the pain and used my other hand to yank a shovel off the wall. It was Papa's favorite, mostly used for setting potatoes or, more recently, threatening Sora.

"Everyone's in!" Newt called from the passenger seat.

"Drive!" I called back.

Sisi turned on the ignition and put the car in reverse. The monster in front of me roared and charged at the car, knocking my shovel aside.

They weren't fast enough.

I saw it in slow motion. The monster leapt onto the hood of the car, causing Sisi to swerve and crash into the garage wall. I could hear Sisi, Newt, and Makani shrieking. Their panic crashed over me like an ice bucket. The beast peered in through the windshield, its breath fogging the window, and raised its fist to smash the glass. If it shattered the windshield, everyone inside that car would be dead in ten seconds.

The spell came from my gut. "E hoʻihoʻi." A part of the same smithing that had killed Angelo.

The word felt heavy as it ripped its way out of my throat. My magic gushed from the tips of my fingers: white, toxic waste that sputtered, thick and gelatinous, settling into the land around us. It hit the second monster, which was still trying to crawl away, and in a gust of wind it disappeared, turning to dust. My spell mostly missed the creature on the car, barely brushing it on the side.

I almost didn't realize that the spell had hit its mark. But then the arm of the magi fell. It was like the joint of its shoulder had just melted off from the rest of its torso. Blood poured from the wound, clotting in thick blobs as the creature cried out and fell over, flailing with its free arm. It filled the air with a terrible wailing. I had killed my fair share of animals: chickens, fish, and even the occasional calf, but this was different. It was the cry of a slow, painful death. Before my eyes, its severed arm wasted away to dust.

The creature continued to shriek as I fell to my knees, the wind deflating out of me. My arm throbbed, and I could feel the blood running down to the wrinkles of my elbow. My spell had cut into half the lawn, destroying the green grass and garden in its wake—all our produce, our herbs, dissolved down to fresh mulch. What had I done?

Another wail drew my attention back to the creature. The beast looked straight at me and opened its jaws wide. A strange mewling coming from its throat, like it was asking me to end its misery.

I raised the shovel to strike.

Just then, it roared and pushed down on its good arm to launch itself up. Its mouth clamped down on my calf and I yelped, falling to the ground as it bit hard, piercing my skin. The shovel fell from my hands and tears stung my eyes as it opened and bit down again on my calf. I resisted the urge to swat at its head—the gleam in its eyes told me it would bite off my hand if I tried.

Suddenly, the edge of a sharp blade cut through the beast's head. Its eyes went slack. Sora was there, as if he'd just materialized out of the chaos, sword in hand and eyes all fire. I sat, too stunned to move or speak, a searing pain crashing through me in waves; yet, in that moment, I felt such a great sense of relief that it stole my breath away.

Sora's strong hands gripped me on my side and tilted me to the left until I could see his face, his brow furrowed in worry.

"Kea?" he said.

I opened my mouth but couldn't answer.

He slapped my face lightly, and blood rushed to my cheeks. "Kea?" He spoke lowly to himself when I didn't respond. "She's in shock. I need to cut this thing off her before its rigor mortis sets in."

I watched everything as if from a distance as Sora leaned over my leg and sliced through the creature's jaw joint. He pushed the dead monster over and crawled back up to face me, holding me up. "It's okay. Everyone's safe."

The creature's blood soaked the dirt around the house, and a few yards away, smoke poured from the destroyed hood of our car as Sisi helped Makani out of it, his face tearstained.

I blinked slowly and felt my chest start to rise and fall in rapid breaths as I surveyed the mess. "Don't let anyone touch that," I said as I watched the white liquid of my spell crawl up the remnants of the creature's body, disintegrating it.

The roots of my casting had sunk deep into the soil, and now anything that had been touched by the spell lay shriveled, turning to dirt. The scent was all around me, and I recognized it for what it was: death. It was the same layered scent that one encountered when wading knee-deep in a stagnant taro patch, the mud bubbling around one's legs as gas from the fermenting greenery under the loʻi escapes. From that decay comes new offshoots, fresh water that pools on the surface: life.

"I figured it out," I whispered.

Sora ignored the comment, pressing me to his chest. The weight of him against me settled my breathing. "We need to get help," Sora grunted, lifting me up princess-style. "My car's just over there."

"*Wait!*" I gasped, realizing he was trying to take me away. "My grandparents are still in the house."

Sora cursed. "Reach into my pocket and throw the keys to your cousin," he told me. I obliged and tossed the car keys to Newt, who took off with the rest of the kids.

Sora walked toward the front of the house with me still in his arms. Before we made it to the front door, the wails of sirens rounded the corner of the street above us and blared down our hill toward the house at full speed.

Had Sora called them?

With me still in his arms, Sora walked through the frame of our house. In the living room, our front door had been ripped off its hinges, tossed to the side like a piece of discarded trash. Long, deep claw marks had torn into the drywall, and feathers from the couch were scattered on the floor.

"Nana? Papa?" I called out, my voice rising in panic, getting Sora to set me down. They weren't answering, and the house wasn't that big. Another stone dropped to the pit of my stomach.

"Deep breaths," a small voice said from the hall and Sora gripped me tighter, following the noise. "They're on their way."

As Sora and I stepped into the hallway, I saw the monster face down and Papa lying on his back. Nana crouched over him, her cell phone on the floor. Papa's robe was completely ripped open to reveal three large, deep gashes down his chest. His left arm had been bound, but the rags were stained scarlet. Blood oozed out of the wounds.

My entire world shrank to a single room. My Nana's clever, wild eyes softened to those of a crying child. Sora's arms were around my shoulders, keeping me from falling into the ether beyond. The sirens from outside became deafening and the sounds of boots on hardwood and metal wheels scraping against old laminate echoed from the front door.

"We're in the hall!" Nana called out, her voice breaking. "Please hurry! He needs help!" Sora stepped aside to make way for the paramedics. I could do nothing but watch, numb, while Papa was lifted onto a stretcher and carried away.

"Is he going to—?" I asked, reaching weakly for his hand as he passed by. It was warm, but barely.

"Don't," Nana warned as she passed me, clutching my arm. "Words have power, Kea. Don't speak it and make it true. He'll be okay. He *will*."

"He will," I whispered back.

My Nana leaned over and gave me a peck on my forehead, which broke the dam inside me. I sobbed as they took him away, as the sirens faded, as Sora buckled me into his car next to the kids and drove away. I didn't stop until the ocean in me had dried to fields of salt. And even then, I cried without tears until, at some point, I drifted off into a corner of the universe where I was just a speck of dust.

CHAPTER 15

I'd woken up to Sora trying to kidnap me, which hadn't ended well for him.

In the aftermath of the attack on our clan, he'd taken the kids to his estate, where they'd be safe. Then he'd tried to trick me into seeing a doctor when I'd passed out in his car. I, however, had been shaken awake by sheer pettiness. When I'd realized what was happening, I'd outright refused. I hated hospitals, and it was only a flesh wound.

Sora disagreed. Loudly.

Then we spent thirty minutes arguing and driving in circles until Sora compromised, agreeing to take me to the closest "medical facility." I'd happily directed him to my old high school, which I knew from experience had crap security and a bad habit of leaving doors unlocked. When I'd waltzed in through a side door by the principal's office and helped myself to a first aid kit, Sora was pissed.

"Stop squirming!" he growled at me, a bandage roll in his mouth. We were seated on the floor of one of the empty classrooms, a few doors down from the old nurse station that I'd raided for supplies.

"That stings," I complained. The tiles of the classroom floors were freshly waxed, and every time I moved, I slid farther away from him. I was trying not to look at Sora's hands on my calf, trying to pull me closer, but that only made me focus on the smell of his skin—sweat and bergamot. He was so close that I could feel his warmth like a furnace.

He finally got ahold of my uninjured leg and drew me back. "It'll sting less if you stay still."

I stopped fidgeting, and in that second of peace, Sora rushed to pour some clear liquid over the bite marks on my calf, creating a hellish foam. It felt like a thousand ants had suddenly started to salsa in my open wound. Tears brimmed at my eyes, and I let loose a flood of cusses in both Russian and Hawaiian to keep from screaming.

When the pain finally subsided and Sora was wrapping up the bite, I squeezed out an airless accusation. "You *lied*."

"I did. That stuff burns like hell but it works," he admitted. Sora finished up the bandage and slumped next to me. "Nothing's broken, by the way. You should be fine in a few minutes." He looked over at me. "I'll cover the cost of the injuries to you and your family, Kea."

I rolled my eyes. "You don't need to do that. Just try being less of an ass."

"What would you call me then?" he teased, scooting an inch closer.

The edges of our pinkies touched, and I realized that Sora was starting to say my name more. It was usually when I did something wrong, sure, but he still hadn't called me *girl* or *idiot* in a while, and I couldn't say the same. Was I afraid of what might happen if I did?

My words were as sharp as ever, but the tremor hadn't left my hands. "I'd still call you the same thing. I'd just mean it less."

We sat in silence, completely drained of energy, while I avoided looking at the magi's bite mark on my leg. The problem was, I could still *feel* it: the thing's teeth sinking into my flesh as it bit to inflict pain rather than to feed, as if it was being controlled somehow by that stone collar. My shaking worsened. Sora's fingers brushed against mine again, bringing me back to my senses.

The classroom smelled like pencil shavings and chalk dust, and the floors were a Pepto-Bismol pink that clashed horrendously with the chipped teal walls. Maps of LA, the Homestead, and the lost islands of Hawaiʻi were pinned to corkboards alongside exemplary papers from five years ago. After the Flood, our homelands had just . . . disappeared, like the legendary city of Atlantis. It wasn't the only place to suddenly go missing, but we would never forget. How could we? For what were Hawaiians without Hawaiʻi?

The thought hurt far worse than the medicine Sora had given me. An ache like a hole through my gut. I took a deep breath, and the hole closed a fraction of an inch. We were family. We were land. And most importantly: *We were still here.*

"Do you know what those monsters were?" Sora asked.

I clenched my hands together and shook my head. "Those aren't ones I've seen before, and I've seen a lot."

Sora raised a brow. "If you know creatures that dangerous are present, then why would you insist on living there?" he asked.

"Mana," I explained. "It may not mean much to you, but a small clan like ours needs the extra boost." Magic flowed like water over the land and pooled in deep forests and navy ocean depths. It was intrinsically linked with magi; the two were a package deal.

Sora leaned in closer, an uncomfortable habit of his that made all the blood rush to my face. "You seem strong enough on your own."

I laughed. "I've seen your clan, Sora Kaiser. Hundreds of people to fuel your wards and boost your family spell. *That's* power. My clan is composed of two senior citizens and children. What we lack in numbers, we have to make up for in other ways."

"Meaning?"

"Land," I said, giving him a puzzled look. "Obviously."

"Obviously," he echoed, though he frowned as if he didn't quite understand.

I scanned the walls of my old classroom, which tracked the thousands and thousands of years of human history that revolved around the same core idea. Sure, the wars were different, but the sentiment behind them was the same. Tribes fighting over resources, people, and land. Colonization and oppression that twisted in new ways with each century.

The tips of my toes tingled. "When they talk about magic in LA, where do they say it comes from?" I asked.

Sora sat up, confused by the change in topic. "No one is totally certain, but the most common theory involves ley lines."

The ley line theory had been hypothesized by a scientist in New Mexico who'd documented the frequency of magi sightings in different areas. When they'd discovered that magi avoided large groups of people, it was theorized that magic flowed toward natural areas like oceans, deep forests, and deserts as a kind of reserve. Magi, in turn, were attracted to those flows like animals to a water source. According to this theory, people existed outside this cycle. We were free-floating radicals of magic that didn't fit into the natural order of things, neatly explaining why we didn't lose our abilities when far from a ley line. Our power was a superior, evolved form of magic that we'd inherited at birth, and our limits a predetermined trait.

The Homestead didn't subscribe to the same train of thought.

While we did learn about the Western theories, we held our own claims closer to heart. Like the ley line theory, we believed that mana flowed and collected in sacred places, but we also believed that it was *everywhere*. Housed in every rock, tree, and leaf. Mana existed at all times innately, and humans weren't so all-powerful as to float independent of the world, but rather as an essential part of it. The land, after all, was our closest sibling.

"On the Homestead, we think that living in certain areas can give people a little more power," I said. "You might think that magic in humans is this anomaly, but what if it wasn't? What if we got mana by sort of . . . borrowing it from the world around us? And there are certain areas where you can more easily tap into those 'ley lines.'" To use his own term.

"Humans can't access ley line magic," he said.

I scowled. "I'm just using vocabulary you're familiar with. Our beliefs run counter to that theory."

"You're saying that people draw magic—mana—from the land?"

I nodded. "Kind of. But it's more than that, because everyone, everything is mana."

"That sounds pretty superstitious," he dismissed.

"It's not superstitious, it's *true*."

I sat straight up as I stumbled upon the answer. Just like the legend of Hāloa had taught us: There was no distinction between the land and the people. The earth was mana. Its people were mana. One and the same.

"It's how I figured out the smithing used to kill Angelo," I said, surprised once more that it had been so simple.

Sora sucked in a breath as he connected the dots. "The spell you used on the monster." He reached for my hand and squeezed. "If the smithing you used earlier was a killing spell, why didn't it look like one?" Death spells, regardless of language, all looked the same, distinctive purple sparks of lightning that sought out a person's core.

"Because it technically wasn't," I said, struggling to explain the concept. "It's not specifically intended to hurt someone, even though it was wielded that way. In many ways, it's not a death spell at all, but one made for life."

"We should tell the Board now," he said. "At least about the spell. Although if one of them is involved with the attempts on your life . . ."

"Those magi had stone collars inlaid with Latin," I said. "It could've been written by anyone." Since it still functioned as the primary academic language, most magic users knew it.

"Magi are extremely difficult to control. Don't you know that, Smith?" he asked jokingly.

I lowered my eyes. "I don't like written spells."

"Ah," Sora said. "That's too bad—it's very efficient. Latin works best when etched into rock, metal, or another hard material. Could you read what the collar said?"

I shook my head. Not only had I not looked closely enough at the stones, but I'd accidentally destroyed them with my spell. They'd turned to dust along with their wearers as my spell spread across the property.

"No matter," he said quickly. "We already know plenty. We're looking at someone with an exceptional amount of power. In addition, whoever sent those monsters was specifically going after you. It's not a wild guess to say it's related to our investigation. Knowing that you've been attacked twice now makes me think we're making someone nervous."

"We're getting close," I agreed. Then I realized something.

"Kea?" Sora asked, noticing my eyes widen.

"This isn't about Angelo," I said, shooting to my feet and circling the room until I found a map of the city. I placed a palm across the crisscrossing lines of roads and bridges, dragging my hand down to the coast where the Homestead lay. "It's about *expansion*."

"Where?"

"Where else?" I asked bitterly.

The Board had talked about how raiding the Palakiko land had bolstered the city's power. Now that the Filipino clans were preparing to leave in droves, LA would need a replacement for their collective mana. Better to find another group that would more willingly assimilate, one that wouldn't have a choice.

They'd even done a test run already with Basilio's Homestead clan, and the decimation of the Palakikos.

Everything made sense. It was why the Board had so readily blamed the Homestead and ventured into our land; they *knew* it would lead to retaliation. My hand curled into a fist. The Board wanted more than just power; it wanted total control, and it would pay in blood to get it.

The only one standing in their way was me.

The head of a small clan on the Homestead who had forcibly inserted herself into this investigation to save a friend. They thought me so bold, so persistent, so *annoying*. More than that, they'd never thought I'd actually complete their task. But I had the spell they used to kill Angelo now, and it would be the nail in the coffin for the true culprit—unless someone silenced me before then.

"You're right," I said, getting to my feet and wincing at the burning running through my leg. "We need to go see the Board. Right *now*."

~

The first time I'd entered the Board's meeting room, I'd been plucked off the side of the street and dumped there with no explanation. This time, Sora briefed me on what to do. The rules of engagement were simple: Hand over the smithing and only speak when spoken to. Easy.

The room was ice-cold, and I wished I'd brought a jacket as I sat uncomfortably in the same bloodied T-shirt and torn shorts that I'd been wearing when we were attacked. My leg throbbed, still bandaged, and my hair was a matted tangle of waves. Sora was apparently on trial, too, as he had been seated next to me at the tip of their teardrop table, its onyx-black surface reflecting the Board's faces like a still pond. Instead of watching them directly as they discussed my fate, I just stared at the polished top.

"Completely irresponsible!" Reagol Stone's floating head on the table argued. "How could you have allowed her to use *unregulated* magic, Sora?"

"What would you have recommended?" Sora countered. "The lives of Kea, myself, and her entire clan were in mortal danger."

"I can hardly think a few roaming magi would be a problem," Matthew said.

"These weren't ordinary magi," Sora said coldly. "They were hunting dogs. They had stone collars with smithings etched into them. Latin."

Matthew frowned. His eyes found Sora's once again. "What are you suggesting?"

"That someone in this room is responsible for both the attacks on Kea and the death of Angelo Reyes," Sora said.

Matthew leaned back slightly. "That's a dangerous accusation, Sora. Latin is the most common language for Smiths to work in."

"But controlling magi requires an incredible deal of mana," I said. So much for Sora's second rule. "As does the spell I resmithed, the one that killed Angelo. The only people with enough power in LA to accomplish something like this are the people in this room."

There was a silence as the Board looked around at each other.

"Recite in lingua veritas and put Sora's fears to rest," I said simply.

A twitter of apprehension went around the room, though Charles Lam caught my eye and grinned.

"That is an unorthodox demand, Miss Petrova," said Matthew Greyson.

"This is an unorthodox situation," I shot back. "Surely if the Board has nothing to hide, it shouldn't be a problem."

"I agree," Ivy said in support. "I have no issue with Miss Petrova's request."

"Neither do I," Vanessa said. "Tell us the spell, and we shall recite it."

I reached into the purse I'd brought and pulled out a shiny red apple, setting it out on the tabletop.

In the assassin's spell, I'd known that they'd said hoʻihoʻi—return—but *what* was being returned and *to where* were questions that had been spinning in my head. The second that magi had disintegrated, I'd realized the answer. The smithing wasn't a riddle, it was a *cycle*. We were born of the land, and when we died, we returned.

A promise—and a curse.

"E hoʻihoʻi ana wau iā ia i ka ʻāina," I said, directing my mana directly at the apple. *Return to the land.*

The fruit rotted before our eyes, skin peeling and dropping off as it crumbled to a decomposed pile of dirt. Instead of the elation I usually felt when a smithing worked, my core filled with dread.

Vanessa gasped. "That—I've never seen it. It shouldn't look like that."

"It's not exactly meant to kill," I explained. "Death isn't always a malicious occurrence, just a natural progression. I imagine that's why there's no purple flash." It still pained me that something so fundamental to Hawaiian identity had been corrupted into a death spell. Only someone with roots in my culture could've known the kaona, the deeper meaning, behind these specific words.

"It must be destroyed," Matthew said immediately. "It's far too dangerous to be kept around."

"Have her write it down," Reagol suggested. "Basilio mentioned that doing so would drain the spell of its power."

I stilled, shocked at the order. "That wasn't part of the deal."

If I wrote it down and gave it to the Board, it wouldn't only cause the mana of those words to fade forever. It might be a dark magic, but it was still *power* that belonged to me and my people, and I would be surrendering it to the city we'd been at odds with for over a century. It wasn't right, not when such a thing could rightfully be wielded as my own mana o ka moʻokūʻauhau. I held the key to everything I'd wanted since I was a child. Respect. A pathway to the Homestead Council. Validation in my title as head of the Petrova clan.

And the Board wanted to take it from me.

"It is now," leveled Charles as he gestured to the door and a small pulse of light pushed through it. A moment later, an attendant entered with a heavy tome. "Do your part to write it down Miss Petrova, and then we shall do ours to recite in lingua veritas."

The book slid across the table toward me and I stared at the solid black cover. Thick, full-grain leather covered the entire thing. A spell book. *The* spell book, to be exact; the one that recorded all the family spells from the Board and those who wanted to demonstrate their loyalty to the city government.

I hesitated, but Sora's hand found mine under the table and our fingers touched briefly. It was the reminder I needed. LA wasn't just made up of Reagols or Matthews. It had people like Ivy and Vanessa— like Sora. Together, we'd protect each other, and this smithing wasn't really mine. Though it was tempting, I wouldn't steal a mana o ka moʻokūʻauhau that I hadn't invented. I would find my own.

My nerves steadied as I opened the book and flipped through its contents. It was old, recording generations of leaders in the city. The earliest records were mainly in Latin, but more recent entries housed other alphabets. I flipped to the first blank page, turning back briefly to make sure I was in the right spot when familiar words caught my eye. *Hawaiian.* It was Basilio's family spell.

I shouldn't have looked. It was a sacred thing to know a mana o ka moʻokūʻauhau; but this one was already dead, or it should've been, anyway. As I scanned the page, I smothered a smile.

It was nonsense.

Basilio had written down words in Hawaiian, sure, but they made no sense. It was a random assortment of real words and fake ones all with the appearance of actually being ʻŌlelo Hawaiʻi. What a risky move.

Basilio had probably thought the Board would be too damn high-makamaka to even check that what he was writing was real, and he'd been right. The clever bastard. He'd gotten one out from under them.

Relieved, I carefully wrote down the smithing. My fingers traced over the words once I'd finished, feeling the magic in them click together like links in a chain, and then the glowing in the letters faded away to nothing more than dull charcoal.

The Board might be taking this spell from us, but at least it didn't have Basilio's; it wouldn't be able to take all our magic no matter how hard it tried.

I handed the book to Sora, who then stood, delivering it to Matthew on the other end of the table, who raked over the single sentence once, twice, three times, before closing it tightly and setting it back on the table.

"E hoʻihoʻi au iā ʻoe i ka ʻāina," Matthew recited. "In lingua veritas." Though the spell's magic was gone, in lingua veritas would still reveal the Smith who'd used it by marking their mouths in silver. However, when Matthew opened his mouth to reveal his tongue, it was still a fleshy pink.

The rest of the Board repeated the ceremony until none were left; no culprit found. The color drained from my face.

"Well," Charles said blandly, "that was a waste of time."

"It just means no one here spoke that spell," I argued. "But it doesn't mean that they couldn't have hired someone else to do their dirty work."

"You said yourself," Matthew retorted, "that no one smiths in Hawaiian anymore."

"I—I did," I stammered. "But many clans have old spells that—"

Charles sighed, cutting me off. "We're back to square one. We should follow our initial plan: Invade the Homestead, capture their heads, and force them to surrender their family spells."

"You can't—" I exclaimed, but they were already all talking over me.

"It would be easier to simply raid them like we did with that small clan a few years ago," Matthew proposed.

They were talking about whether to start a war with the Homestead as casually as one might discuss a coffee order, as if I wasn't right there. Anger burst in my core, burning its way out to the tips of my fingers.

This wasn't right. They couldn't just do whatever they wanted.

"*E ho'olohe!*" I shouted, slamming my hand against the table and standing. The mana burst out of me, and everyone's mouths shut against their will, their attention forced back to me. "You will *listen* to what I have to say."

I knew I'd messed up when I heard Sora curse at my side. Cautiously, I released the flow of magic from my unintentional spell, and the restraints on the Board members loosened. Charles, wide-eyed, rubbed his jaw, while Reagol, Matthew, and Celine were on their feet, hands outstretched in my direction and mana glowing faintly around their cores. Reagol and Matthew looked furious.

"Her spell was completely harmless," Sora soothed, quickly shoving me behind him. "Don't be so reckless."

"She just *attacked* us!" Celine protested.

"Hardly," Sora said. "It was just a diversion. Plus, you can't really expect someone to remain calm while you're discussing the annihilation of their home."

"I . . . suppose not," Celine agreed reluctantly. She settled back into her seat, arms crossed over her chest. "Well, Miss Petrova, you certainly have our attention now. What is it?"

I leapt on the chance to speak, not certain I'd get another. "You said you'd rather use a scalpel than a sledgehammer, and it *worked*. I have the assassin's spell. Allow me to finish this investigation and to find the Smith responsible. The Homestead clans will be far more amenable to talking to one of their own than having their leaders kidnapped. That will only lead to violence."

"We can't possibly trust her," Reagol argued.

"Haven't I just proven myself trustworthy?" I asked, gesturing to the spell book. "And believe me, I have no desire to go to war with LA."

"There's also the matter of your 'magic,'" Reagol protested, spitting out the last word with enough force to make it clear exactly what he thought of it. "Whatever show Miss Petrova just demonstrated has proved that she, herself, poses a threat. You all saw that spell just now, felt it control our movements. It was a *single word*. It never should've worked!"

The fundamentals of casting determined that three requirements were always met: intention, that a Caster knows what they want their spell to do; utteration, that they vocalize their spell; and finally, incantation, that their spell be encapsulated in a series of words meant to fit together. The last part is where I was usually left flummoxed. Without great fluency, I tended to throw together shorter, less perfect spells on the fly.

"You're wrong," I said. The room turned their attention to me, and I cleared my throat. "It *didn't* work. I cast that spell trying to get you to listen, for once, but instead it closed your mouths. I'm not nearly as powerful as you're implying."

Charles leaned forward in his chair, the leather squeaking under him. "Does this happen often with your spells?"

"Unless I'm very specific," I explained. "But I cast that without thinking, which meant shoddy craftsmanship. I don't typically cast single-word spells." A lie, but they didn't need to know that.

"Fascinating," Charles said. "And these one-word spells of yours, they usually work?"

I hesitated, souring on my deepening lie. "I don't know. This was a one-time thing. I apologize."

Charles smiled like I'd just given him a piece of candy. "Now, I hate to question your truthfulness, but I must. Is there a way for us to validate what you're saying?"

I squirmed. "No."

Charles turned to the Board. "I maintain that Miss Petrova should be detained until we assess whether she is a potential danger."

"She's not," Sora said quickly. "I can vouch for her."

Across the room, Charles's smile grew fangs, and he stretched out his response into a drawl. "Oh, no, Sora. You *didn't*." The man chuckled. "Now things make so much more sense."

Sora stiffened. "That's not—it hasn't affected me."

"Hasn't it?" Charles dug.

"Hold on," Matthew, the Board's leader, said. "Sora takes his position seriously. If he used his sympathetic ability, then I trust it was necessary. LA has weathered worse, and Sora has always moved in our best interest."

Was there something about Sora's sympathetic talent that he hadn't told me? I thought of the electric current of our magics and shivered. I wanted to prod further, but this wasn't the time.

"Regardless," Matthew continued. "There is truth to what Reagol is saying, but Miss Petrova has also made a clear case for the merits of her investigation. That said, I can't see letting her remain unattended." He cleared his throat. "You may continue but only if you agree to three conditions. One, Sora must consent to continue monitoring you."

Sora nodded.

"Two, you will subject yourself to a physical under Charles's care. And three, you are not to cast *any* magic whatsoever until the conclusion of this case as an additional precaution. Any violation of these three rules will result in your immediate confinement and removal from the case," Matthew said.

His eyes swept through the room to confirm with each Board member that the terms were acceptable, then he had them cast their votes.

I won by a greater margin than the first time. Though Matthew and Charles were swayed to my side for now, I didn't trust either of them. One had placed me on a very tight leash, and the other was Charles Lam.

CHAPTER 16

"Strip," Charles commanded.

"Like hell," I shot back.

Charles pulled an innocent face. "I need bare skin to attach these to." He wiggled some wires that ended in sticky pads up to my face. "If you don't take off your shirt, I'll have to reach underneath it, and there's no saying what I might grab by accident."

I scowled but complied, pulling off my stained shirt and shorts until I was standing in only a lacy black bra and mismatched pink underwear. I didn't have a perfect body by any means; my hips and thighs were too wide, and my stomach was soft rather than firm, but living near the ocean meant I'd grown up wearing swimsuits as daily attire. Over time, I'd become accustomed to seminakedness, so I wasn't flustered by a bit of bare skin.

The same couldn't be said for Sora. He made a startled noise when I suddenly dropped my clothes, the tips of his ears turning pink as he glanced away. Charles, on the other hand, was unbothered. He had me raise my arms and began to attach electromagnetic pads and wires onto the skin of my stomach, my piko, or belly button. It was equal parts ticklish, cold, and uncomfortable. The room was chilled by a high-powered air conditioner that buzzed in the background like a mosquito overhead, making me shiver.

"Black is a good color on you," Charles commented as he finished attaching a pad to my sternum and I rewarded his lewdness with a scowl. He held out his hand and gestured for the ring that the Board had given me, which I slipped off my finger and handed to him.

"We came all the way down to your lab for this. The least you can do is be polite," Sora snapped.

"It was just a compliment," Charles protested.

"No, it wasn't," Sora and I said in unison.

I had expected a minimalist laboratory with white walls and spotless floors, but Charles's lab disappointed. The floors were an off-beige, with every other tile cracked like something heavy had been dropped against it, and the walls were a dull green reminiscent of cow cud. Cream-colored bookshelves lined the walls, overflowing with boxes of medical gear, binders, and loose papers. Each corner was stacked with utility carts of cardboard boxes and junk, yet the lab tabletops were clear of any clutter.

Charles dragged out a rubber pad attached to more wires that he set on the giant metal contraption that looked similar to a scale. He guided me onto the pad, then escorted Sora into a corner office hidden behind a wall of plexiglass. The two men stared, a wall of computer equipment behind them.

Charles tapped a bunch of buttons from behind his station and leaned down into a microphone to speak. His voice cracked from a speaker overhead. "Don't worry. This shouldn't hurt."

That wasn't comforting at all.

"All you need to do is cast something, and I'll measure your output," Charles explained. "Make sure it's a single-word spell."

"I was told not to cast," I warned.

"This will be fine. The machine converts magic to energy, so your spell shouldn't actually activate," Charles said. He adjusted a few more dials, then looked back over to me. "Just say the first thing you think of."

My mind immediately went blank. As usual, whenever I needed to reach for my magic in a pinch, the well of words in my head dried up. Sora and Charles stared at me as I stood there half clothed, doing absolutely nothing. I wiggled my toes on the top of the pad, straining for a single word. Charles had said nothing would cast, but I didn't trust him as far as I could throw him. He'd never seen how bad my spells could turn. It was better to stick to something that couldn't be misinterpreted.

I took a deep breath and raised my hand, concentrating on my gut and said the only one that was likely to produce a result. "E hoʻomālamalama." *Illuminate.*

Light poured out of me, bright and penetrating. It washed the room in a golden glow, and the pad beneath my feet heated like concrete that had been baking in a summer sun. After a few minutes, the electricity in the lights overhead began to zap. A bulb burst in the far corner of the room.

"Pull it back!" Charles shouted from behind the station.

Usually, my magic felt wild, but this time was different. It was as if a plug had been pulled inside me and all my mana was just rushing through it like a geyser. Sora shouted through the white noise, and I focused on the sound of his voice to keep me tethered. The power in me faded, and I swayed from side to side until Sora ran out of the office and toward me.

"You okay?" Sora asked, pressing his hands to my head. His palm was cool against the burning fever in my temples.

Charles came back into the room, muttering while he examined the machine around me, with a grin splitting his face in two. "It's not supposed to break." Charles met my gaze and laughed. As I got dressed, he continued talking. "I don't know what that was, but it couldn't have been a real spell."

"Of course it was," I said, grabbing my clothes off the floor and getting dressed. "I'm a Smith. I know how to use a spell." Mostly.

"If it wasn't a spell, then it wouldn't have worked on your machine," Sora said defensively.

Charles smiled and raised his eyebrows at me. A cat who had found a particularly interesting mouse. "What I mean is that it *shouldn't've* worked. Like Reagol said. A single word isn't an incantation. By our standards, your spell should've had no effect whatsoever."

"Who came up with those stupid rules, anyway?" I grumbled.

I was so sick of people telling me what I could and couldn't do. Sick of limiting myself. My gaze drifted toward Sora, but I forced myself to look away.

Charles walked in small circles, talking more to himself than to me. "This would be an upheaval of everything the world knows to be true about magic. If one can cast without a true incantation, then there may be other self-imposed boundaries to magic that don't truly apply."

"I wonder if it's Kea's belief that frees her." Sora looked over at me. "The fact she doesn't see it as an impossibility might be why she can harness magic in this way." He twisted in my direction. "Have you ever imagined that a spell wouldn't work?"

"No," I said. "Although I often think about how they might go wrong."

"And?" he prodded.

"They often go wrong," I admitted.

"A self-fulfilling prophecy," Charles said and handed me the ring I was supposed to wear until this business was done.

The weight of his statement was crushing as I slipped the band on my finger. "That's not fair."

The reason my casting didn't do what I wanted it to half the time was that I had to use it in rushed situations. With time to *think*, I could cajole the mana into doing what I wanted, rather than throwing around single-word spells and hoping for good results. Which was exactly why I'd committed to becoming a Smith rather than a Caster.

I looked down at the stupid, gaudy ring on my hand, courtesy of the Board. The jewelry was just a fancy monitor in disguise, meant to alert them the second I used magic outside of Charles's exams.

"Let me guess," Charles said. "If you don't create a very, *very* specific smithing, something goes wrong?"

"Yes," I sighed, relieved someone understood.

"Yet your spells always *do* something, right?" Charles prodded. "It's not like they just fizzle out or fall flat."

That was . . . true.

"Your core holds your magic," Charles explained, pointing at my navel. "Each person's capacity is different, but imagine that yours is large, enormous even. Now imagine trying to funnel that immense power through the smallest sieve. All that excess power leaks through, erupting in unpredictable ways.

"The only way to control it would require you to be incredibly specific with your intention. It would only probably work with spells you've crafted yourself. If you aimed larger, higher, bigger, there's no saying what you could do."

I reflected on my high school days. The explosions I had caused. The way my spells always seemed to take on a mind of their own. *That* was a sign of power?

There was no way that could be true. I'd lived my whole life knowing I wasn't nearly as strong as my Nana. It was what made things hard for me as head. If Charles's test showed I actually possessed greater power, then I had no excuses left. I was just a bad leader.

"I know you aren't allowed to use magic now, Kea, but when all this is over, there will be countless opportunities available to you," Charles said, his eyes stuck to me like sap to a tree.

I began to get dressed. "Meaning?"

"Jobs. Or potential matches," Charles explained matter-of-factly. "Marriage is a legal contract, above all else."

I laughed shortly. "Excuse me?" I said. "Are you throwing your hat in the ring?"

He chuckled. "Maybe."

I couldn't take his proposal seriously.

"Please, shut up," Sora said tensely.

Which only served to egg Charles on. "Why? I've been told that I have much to offer. I can guarantee Kea protection, money, power."

"I believe you mean *her* power," Sora interrupted, growing increasingly agitated. "Such a union would give the Lam Syndicate access to Kea as their own personal geyser of magic."

"I won't pretend that isn't a very attractive asset," Charles said, shrugging. "I'm a businessman at heart."

Sora clenched his fists at his sides. "Is this why you asked to conduct a physical? For *business*?"

Charles leaned back against the glass wall of his control station, his lab coat open to reveal a crisp, blue button-down and slacks. "No." His smile came slowly, like honey from a jar. "I just wanted to see her with less clothing."

Sora's face went red. "Hurry up, Kea. We're leaving." He exited abruptly, while I hopped on one foot, struggling to get my shoes on.

Charles laughed again, a single sharp bray, then stepped close until we were two hands' width apart. His voice was low, a gentle note meant to ply me with sweets. "Tell me, Kea, was I right the other day in suspecting that Sora used his sympathetic ability on you?"

I recalled Charles's taunts from the meeting and immediately went on the defensive. "Not on purpose. He was just humoring me, most of the time."

It was exactly the wrong thing to say. Charles's eyelashes fluttered and his hands froze, his forefinger an inch away from my nearest strand of hair. He regained control and brushed the piece of hair behind my ear. "Ah, so he's triggered it more than once. How many times?"

I felt like I'd been tricked and wasn't about to offer anything more. "I don't know, exactly."

He smiled. "I see. Well, until next time, then." He waved me off as I left to join Sora by the door.

When I got close enough, he reached for my hand. An electric current of mana sparked between us, making the breath in my throat catch. I was completely swept up in the sensation of his skin on mine. Though Sora's expression didn't change, he ran his shaking middle finger down the back of my hand until it landed on the Board's ring.

"You'll need to train. Your ban on casting makes you vulnerable," Sora finally mumbled. "Magic geyser or not, you can't keep relying on luck to not die." He let go of me.

"It's not like I'm getting into any fistfights," I protested half-jokingly. We walked to his car, and he held the door open for me to climb in. When I buckled in, he peered at me before shutting it.

"Not yet," he said.

I knew then that I was doomed in more ways than one.

~

"Can't I take it off while we practice?" I asked, toying with the gaudy, heavy gold signet ring that was now apparently a permanent fixture on my hand.

"No," Basilio said as he wiped beads of sweat off his face. "Removing that tracker is as good as committing a felony in broad daylight. The Board will immediately be alerted and come for you." He helped me off the ground and tapped a couple spots to correct my stance. "Next time Sora attacks, dodge. Don't just stand there and get hit."

"He's too fast," I complained.

"Then be faster."

We were on a lower level of the Kaiser home in a training room with padded black floors and bare cement walls. A collection of swords sat stacked on a rack on the far left, and three punching bags hung from heavy metal chains at the back of the room. I hadn't had time to explore this level of the estate, but on our way in, I'd spotted an additional weight room and what looked like a ballet studio.

Since I was temporarily unable to use my magic, Sora had insisted that I start a strength and agility program. Basilio had decided to get in on my practice sessions, apparently just so the two of them could knock me flat on my back. My ears were ringing, and I felt no more equipped than earlier to defend myself.

"So, I just have to let them throw a leash on my magic?" I asked as I crawled back up. Every inch of me ached.

"Yes," Sora said. "Unless you're interested in being confined."

I turned to Basilio. "And you," I said. "Go home. Don't you have anything better to do?"

The two of them only laughed. Their burgeoning friendship was becoming a pain in my ass—Basilio's sass was even beginning to wear off on Sora.

"I'm having fun," Basilio said. "There's so much to do here."

Sora stretched, pulling the thin fabric of his tank top across his chest and flexing the muscles on his bare arms. I looked down, trying not to stare. Sora was usually a modest dresser, so this version of him was distracting. Sweaty. A quarter naked. Panting. When we sparred up close, I had a difficult time maintaining my composure.

I snuck another glance at him as he lifted the bottom of his shirt to wipe his face, briefly flashing his toned core. Heat spread from my neck to my ears, and I hid the flush by pretending to retie my hair. I needed a break. And some cold water.

Basilio noticed my squirming and laughed. "Lots to look at, too."

I flipped him off, fighting off a creeping burn in my cheeks.

Sora, oblivious, dropped his shirt and placed his hands on his hips while he looked up at the ceiling. "Instead of fussing over your ring, why don't you plan how you'll be approaching the Homestead Council?"

I frowned. "Accusing the Homestead heads of any sort of involvement with Angelo's death will be considered an offense. It will risk them raiding my clan."

Not that we had much to defend now. The house was in shambles, and Papa was still at the hospital. Nana stayed with him most days, charming the staff into letting her spend nights at his side. Which meant that presently, the Petrova household consisted of two teenagers and a ten-year-old.

"Then we'd better be right before we approach them," Sora insisted.

"I'm just saying that I don't see why *anyone* on the Homestead would cooperate with the Board to kill a city politician," I argued, still unconvinced. "Someone on the Board got around in lingua veritas."

"Impossible," Sora dismissed. "That spell is foolproof."

I bit my lip, knowing he was right. In lingua veritas was essentially a fail-safe plagiarism detector. Still, only the Board and their guests had access to the back rooms of Griffith Hall, and security cameras hadn't picked up any outsiders in the building on the day of Angelo's murder. Yet, the spell was undeniably in Hawaiian, which led us right back to my own backyard.

Something was off.

My phone pinged, and I marched to a bench that was flush against the wall. I grabbed my bag and unzipped it, rooting through for my phone. I sat on the bench, knees spread, to read the message.

Dinner tonight?

I didn't even need to read who'd sent it.

Busy.

Charles typed back: *What about next week?*

Still busy.

"Your other beau?" Basilio asked, peeking over my shoulder.

I shoved the phone back in my bag before he could see anything. "Yes."

"Sorry," Sora interrupted. "*Other*? Who's the first?"

Basilio winked at me. "Ah, just some guy. Kea's got a long list of admirers, you know."

Sometimes, I truly hated Basilio.

Sora stepped up to me, placing his thumb under my chin to tilt my head upward and looking straight into my eyes. "You know, just because we've ruled Charles out, doesn't mean that he's harmless."

My throat thrummed with a quickened pulse as I tried to ignore the heat from his fingers against my jawline. "I know that."

He let go and told me to take a break, then asked if Basilio would spar with him instead. Basilio agreed, though he complained as he pulled out his long, curved ginunting from a duffel. The casualness in his movements was a farce. Basilio was an excellent swordsman. The two launched at each other, and I observed their match with half-hearted interest while mulling over the investigation.

Sora was right to be concerned, but everything I knew about Charles pointed to a man driven by rationality alone. I'd proven to him that I was powerful. He'd casually lobbed marriage at me in a transparent play for that power. Even when he challenged me in Board meetings, his reasons were easy to understand. The only nonsensical thing about Charles was his distaste for Sora.

Maybe I should take a cue from the Lam head and find a motive here that ran beyond simple prejudice. Angelo's death was undoubtedly about maintaining a specific balance of influence on the Board, but there were easier ways to do that than through unregulated Hawaiian magic. How did the Homestead fit into things? Who on the council would've betrayed us, and why target an up-and-coming political leader in LA?

An old saying came to mind. Nānā i ke kumu. *Look to the source.* When in doubt, experts ought to be consulted. I needed an expert on the Homestead. I knew exactly where to go; I just didn't like it.

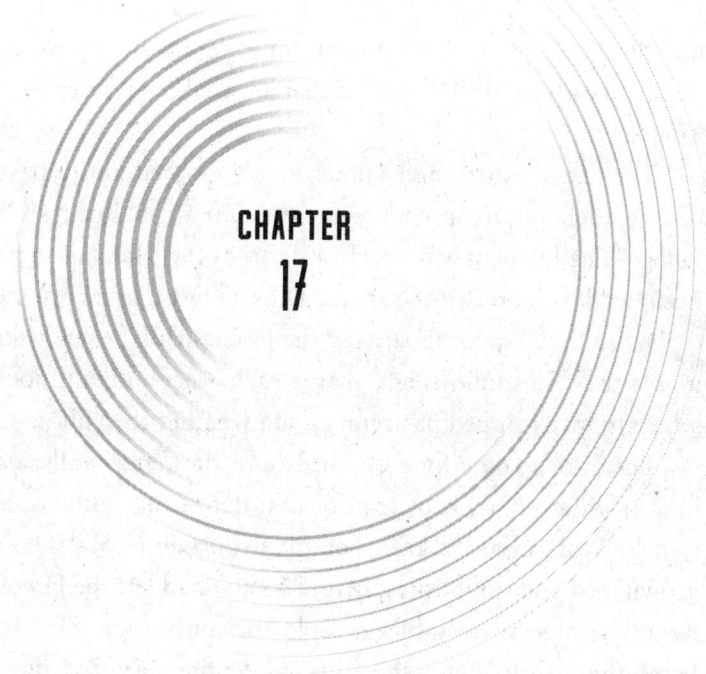

CHAPTER 17

The Lin clan had built themselves a terra-cotta-shaded compound in the hilly area of the Homestead. Surrounded by green fields, stone walls, and excellent archers, their property was effectively shielded from most raids. Their residence housed the best bakeries in the Homestead, specializing in almond cookies that melted on the tongue, and the archive.

Sora and I walked through the wrought-iron gates to the main courtyard, where their merchants hawked their wares to Homesteaders and city folk alike. Predominantly Makers, the Lins could weave their magic into objects. Everything from taro-filled mooncakes stamped with a spell guaranteed to add a day to your life to spears inlaid with magic to ensure your throw was true.

Weaving through the market amid colorful scarves, lauhala mats, and baked goods in labeled paper bags with greasy bottoms, it wasn't hard to see why Haʻaheo wanted to stay on the city's good side. Under his leadership, the clan attracted their fair share of business, primarily middlemen from the city looking for exotic wares. Losing LA's trust would dry up the well of wealth that allowed the Lins to live in relative safety.

The uneven stone paths underfoot smoothed out to paved asphalt once we left the main square for the narrow walkways of the inner village. The Lin clan was nearly as large as the Mahiʻais in number but occupied less than half the space. Thus, their quarters resembled a real city more than any other area in the Homestead: beige concrete buildings with small studios stacked atop each other and rain-pocked streets where mopeds zipped past, not caring whether they hit you.

Local kids sometimes climbed onto the outer walls, daring each other to jump from roof to roof in a dangerous game of aerial hopscotch. Years ago, I'd been one of them. Before Haʻaheo and I had grown into polar opposites, before Basilio had left the Homestead and Keanu became an even bigger tool. Ancient history. Yet I still remembered the way to the archive by muscle memory, twisting down the lanes until we came to its entrance.

An outsider would never know that the plain wooden door led anywhere other than another minuscule apartment. There was no sign or placard that identified it as an archive, just a rusted handle that needed a good jiggle to open right. The door swung open, and I ducked into the cramped room with Sora at my back.

The air inside smelled of paper and dust. The walls around us were painstakingly organized, with handmade tags on every item in sight. I'd bet anything that there were even rarer oddities tucked away in drawers to keep them safe from sunlight. Not that this was much of an issue. The windows had been blocked up with black contact paper, and the only light came from an old chandelier hung so low that it brushed the top of Sora's head.

The archivist, an older woman who was all angles, with sharp cheekbones, elbows, and shoulders jutting out from under a lime green muʻumuʻu with a high neck, lifted her head toward the door. "What do you need?" she asked curtly.

"Anything about interactions between LA and heads from the Homestead over the past few years," I said. She wasn't the same woman I remembered from childhood, which meant my plan to sweet-talk my way in needed some tweaks.

She frowned, her thin lips nearly disappearing. "Legal documents require proper certification before I can release them. Form B52." She gestured to a wall behind us near the door with the nooks labeled in alphanumerics. "Get it filled out, then come back."

By the book, just like her clan's head.

I took a step to the wall, scanning the documents. Haʻaheo certainly wasn't going to sign anything I put in front of him. Even if I wanted to try that route, explaining things to him would take hours we didn't have. Feeling Sora on my right, I leaned into him and whispered, "Give me a minute. I need to come up with another way in."

Sora tapped his foot. "I'm going to talk to her."

"By talk, you mean threaten," I said. "*Don't*. It's not going to work."

He huffed. "She hardly looks intimidating."

I glanced back over my shoulder, taking in the woman's frail frame and stark white hair braided down her back. Compared to the previous archivist, a broad, tan woman who must've stood at near three hundred pounds, his assessment was true. But I wasn't convinced. Haʻaheo was too clever to leave his documents unguarded.

"Just give me a second to think," I insisted.

Sora disregarded my advice and marched back up to the woman. "I have to insist on entrance," he said, raising his voice. "It's very important."

"I'm sure," the archivist said calmly, folding her fingers into her lap. "B52 would make this all much easier on you." Her eyes were unfocused, staring past him.

"Did you not hear me? I don't have time," he pushed, his gaze flitting to the plain white door behind her.

"I understand, son, but wasting it here won't help your cause," the woman said dryly.

We stood awkwardly in front of her until Sora said, a little too loudly, "I'll get on that paperwork." He purposefully walked around the room with heavy steps, then ducked behind a tall bookshelf, pulling me with him. "We may just look around for a few minutes more."

The woman sighed at the inconvenience. "Just don't touch anything."

Hidden behind the bookshelf, Sora stared at me meaningfully and jerked his head toward the door. I pulled on his sleeve with a firm shake of my head. This was a bad idea. I could feel it in my bones. I peeked at the woman from behind a case, noticing she'd left the desk and was now wandering the aisles.

"We have to go now," he whispered. "This is our chance."

"*Wait*," I hissed, but he shrugged me off and tiptoed out and around the desk, checking to make sure the woman was out of sight.

My feet itched as I hesitated, torn between keeping an eye on the woman and following Sora. The archivist had stopped in front of a curio cabinet and had pulled open the drawer, rummaging for something inside. Pulling up a wooden bowl, she ran her hands over the smooth surface before pushing the drawer shut with her hip. It was so dark, I wasn't sure how she'd found what she needed, but every move she made was confident. While I spied on her, the archivist lifted a tag that had been taped to the bowl, but instead of holding it up to the dim light to read, she rubbed the brown paper between her fingers. As she set the bowl back down, the wood gleamed, magic wrapping around its surface.

Oh, crap.

This wasn't some helpless old lady, she was a Smith. My gut twisted and I held my breath, turning to Sora's back as he reached for the doorknob. I'd been right. I held out a hand in silent warning, but it was too late. The instant Sora's fingers touched the knob, his body went arrow straight like he'd been electrocuted. Was he stuck there?

Feeling her spell triggered, the woman clucked her tongue. "I knew that boy was trouble the second I heard the squeak of those shoes," she said to herself. She lifted her head and sniffed. "Girl! Get out here."

"Yes, Aunty," I said, coming back into sight with my head hung.

"Answer me truthfully, or I swear your friend won't leave this place. Did he ask you to bring him?" she asked, pointing at Sora without looking at him.

I shook my head. "No. I'm the one who needs the information."

"The only people who ever ask for records are people from the city," she said. Her hands trailed along the drawer in front of her, and I noticed the small bumps pressed below each label, nearly invisible. Braille. "So why are you, girl from the Homestead, here asking about LA?"

I started to speak but trailed off as I realized she'd clocked us both in such a short time. "How do you know I'm from the Homestead?"

She shrugged. "You walk to take up space. People only walk like that when they're home."

"I'm not a Lin," I said.

The woman went back to organizing the cabinet to her left. "Home is where the land meets the sea, regardless of clan. When you deal in history, things take on a broader perspective. Get your paperwork done, and you'll see what I mean."

"What if I can't?" I asked. "We don't have much time, and what we're looking for is important."

"*All* information is important," she said. "That's why you give me the form. It's not just bureaucracy. There's a hidden seal on the door."

Ah. It must have been placed on the doorknob. Seals were a specialized form of Making that inlaid a magical lock on an item, regardless of what it was. Most were deadly without the right key, and Braille was an excellent weapon for making such items, as the text was near invisible.

The key could be anything. Simple seals required a secret passcode, but nothing about this door screamed simple. More likely, it was a trade. Something that I could give the woman of value equal to what I was seeking. That was what the forms represented. It wasn't the documents themselves, but rather their significance.

I thought over the woman's cryptic response, twisting the hem of my shirt until wrinkles formed. "Can I give you something of similar value to Haʻaheo's approval?" I asked tentatively.

The woman closed another drawer with a clack. "Perhaps. But without those signed forms, even if I tell you how to get past the first seal, you won't make it past the rest. You'll be on your own. Is what you need worth that danger?"

"It's worth it," I said, my mind spinning with images of the Homestead. Separate clans but still connected.

The woman smoothed out her dress. "Then tell me who you are."

"That's all?" I asked, confused.

She laughed, the sound like a rusted bell. "It's everything."

I hesitated, wondering if I should question her price, then decided that I better not dwell on my good fortune lest it disappear. "Kea Petrova."

She laughed. "Not just that, silly girl. I need to know all of you."

I flinched. If I didn't do this right, the mana in the seal would know, and I'd be laid out right alongside Sora. Magic required clear intent.

But who *was* I?

My family came to mind. My home. Funny that when I tried to define myself, I only managed to think of others, but maybe that was the whole point. I'd been so concerned that I, alone, wasn't good enough to lead my clan—but I'd never really been alone.

There were the generations before me who had planted seeds for our success, the family and friends who surrounded me now, and even the souls that had brushed into mine, no matter how briefly, and left a mark. Who were we but reflections of the world around us?

"Kealaokaleo Petrova," I said, though my cheeks burned as I spoke. "The way of the voice and the leader of my clan."

"Ah," she said. "The young head of the Petrova clan. What a lovely story you'll make."

"I thought you dealt in history," I questioned. "Not stories."

The archivist twisted her braid into a low bun, pinning it in place with a chopstick, and wandered back to her desk. "Aren't they the same? Now, go pry his hand off the door before his muscles start to atrophy."

I rushed to Sora's side and pulled his fingers from the knob one by one. The second he was released, the color rushed back into his face. He gasped and grabbed at his sides, gulping down air like he'd been drowning.

"Reach under the handle and be careful to avoid the seal," the woman called as she pulled out a black keyboard across her desk and began to type. "And touch the smithing in the door frame instead."

I did as instructed, feeling her magic spark to life below my fingers as I traced the sentence carved into the wood with small raised bumps. The door cracked open. Beyond was darkness, the smell of stagnant water and must. A step into that was a step into the unknown.

I paused at the threshold, hearing the archivist behind us as she clacked something on her keyboard, maybe our slice of history in action. It felt so small, so insignificant that I doubted that anyone would read about Kea Petrova taking a trip to the Lin archive.

I realized with a start that I was right. If I failed and the Homestead disappeared, no one would be left to care. We learned only the histories of people society deemed important, the ones that mattered. LA thought the Homestead didn't matter, and if they had their way, that would be true—we'd become a blip violently erased from their history.

The only way our history would survive was if our people continued to live. If we took up space unapologetically. I took a deep breath, squared my shoulders, and pushed the door wide open.

~

The door led into a cave that tunneled underground. Black lava rock covered the walls, rough to the touch and dotted with patches of moss that squished under our fingertips. We walked forward, guided by a glowing orange light ahead, until we came to a small room. An office at the heart of the cave system.

The walls were still black rock, but underfoot, the floor turned from stone to wooden planks, occupied only by a single heavy desk in the center of the room. On the table, a bronze scale was lighted by a banker's lamp on each end, and a stack of crisp paper and a pen were set to its right. Electric torches brightened as we entered, and an audio crackled to life around us.

"Please have your paperwork ready," a pleasant robotic voice demanded. "Request your documentation."

Sora and I split up, each of us walking around the room's perimeter to try and find something useful. The walls were craggy, but unbroken. The office bare other than the desk. When we met back in the middle, I held my open palms out and shrugged.

"Nothing," Sora concluded. "We must have to use the scale to get what we need."

"Request your documentation," the room repeated.

Squinting at the scale, I noticed fine lettering engraved into the metal and groaned. Latin.

Sora was already translating, his face pinched. "It's a seal, all right," he said. "An etymological lock, if I had to guess." He recited some of the text under his breath, then picked up the pen and wrote *records between the Homestead and LA* and placed the paper on one side of the scale.

We both stepped back.

"Your request has been received," the room said. "Please place your authentication paperwork on the pan."

I sucked in a breath. "Now what?"

"Please place your authentication paperwork on the pan," the audio said again.

Sora held his breath and slipped a blank sheet onto the other side of the scale.

The scale creaked dramatically, and the side where we'd placed our request dipped down until the metal pan banged against the table.

The scale and the entire middle section of the desk dropped down like a shelf had been removed from under it. A smooth piece of wood took its place, with a carved image of a map drawn into its face.

"Request denied," the room stated. "Unable to verify. Please enter the security codes located on page three of your form."

Sora grabbed a pen and began scratching down a long line of Latin. He repeated the smithing under his breath. "This is all I remember from the scale. It's worse than I thought. This isn't just a lock; it's a puzzle."

"And?" I pressed, peering over his shoulder. My shoddy Latin kicked in with the strength of a drowsy infant. I was only able to understand a single word: Libra. *Balance*.

Sora dropped the pen as what he'd written faded back into the page, replaced by a single word in dark black letters: CONTRACT.

"I have no idea what we're supposed to do," he admitted.

"I'm good at puzzles," I offered.

"But bad at languages," he countered, his hands trailing over the wooden map that had taken the place of the scale. "And I'd bet my left arm this has something to do with Latin."

Sora was probably right. Ha'aheo was unique as a Homestead leader, far more adept at learning the ways of LA, and thus more inclined to put his trust in the modern magics of the city. He loved order, bureaucracy, and paperwork. To his credit, legal language, even without a smithing or a seal, was its own kind of magic, and Ha'aheo had always been a wizard when it came to deals.

I bent closer to the table, my hair falling over the wooden map as I peered at the flat globe. Decorative letters—a smithing, no doubt—had been carved over each landmass and ocean. Sora brushed aside my hair and leaned against the map, his hands pressing on an area that covered Russia. The country dipped down until it was flush with the rest of the table. It clicked.

"Incorrect," the room chimed. "Two attempts remaining. Please enter the security codes located on page three."

I bent down and looked even closer at the desk. "They're buttons."

I straightened up and stared at it from a bird's eye. "But the map is wrong. None of the borders are in the right place."

Sora whistled. "*Contract* is likely just a password clue. If this has to do with etymology, then maybe we need to find the word's origin." He pondered the image, his fingers hovering over Europe before landing on one country. "This is the Holy Roman Empire, so I'm going to guess this map is from the 12th century." His finger moved upward across the English Channel. "Which means this is Britain. Though *contract* has Latin roots, it comes from Middle English." He took a breath, then pressed down.

"Incorrect," the room corrected. "One attempt remaining."

Sora frowned. "That's *not* incorrect."

"Don't make her angry," I chided.

He shot me a withering look.

"What do you think happens if we get the last one wrong?" I asked, taking another turn around the room. "Booby trap? Sudden death?"

"Well, the room's operating a bit like a computer system's security, so it'd probably just lock us out," he guessed.

"We'd just get stuck here?" I said. "Doesn't sound too bad."

Sora didn't look up from the map, wrinkles creased into his forehead as he frowned and considered the lamp. "Until we run out of food."

Yikes. Then this fun guessing game was a three-strikes-then-starve-slowly game of wits. I walked to the map, thinking I could be of some help, but that self-confidence withered as I counted all the countries that no longer existed.

"Don't worry, we won't starve to death. We'll die from lack of water first," I remarked.

"Comforting," Sora said dryly.

"Maybe it's that one instead," I said, pointing to the blob he'd identified as the Holy Roman Empire. "Since *contract* comes from Latin." I wasn't great at history, but it didn't take a genius to figure that the Romans spoke a language that was as dead as they were.

"It started with Latin, but I'm positive that *contract* as we use it is based more in Middle English," he assured me, gesturing to the isles. "Hence, Britain."

I pointed to the map, drawing my finger upward. "And what? It just jumped over this big piece of land and hopped a ferry all the way over there?" I asked. "That doesn't make sense."

"That's modern-day France," he corrected. "It didn't hop. It traveled *through* it."

"So maybe it's French, then," I said, exasperated with the linguistics lesson. "Why do words have to shift around so much?"

"That's quite literally what etymology is," Sora responded.

I pushed his arm away, staring at the map. It reminded me of LA, in a way. The way people migrated in and out of the city was no different than in medieval Europe. If that was true, then the origin of anything wasn't a fixed point in time, but a process.

My fingers skirted the edge of the map. "I have an idea."

Sora hesitated, acutely aware of my lack of European history knowledge, then gave up, lifting his hands off the board. "Fine, but if we get trapped here, I'm eating you first."

"I'm not tasty. Too much gristle," I snapped.

"Give yourself some credit," he said. "I'm sure you'd taste delicious."

I flipped him the bird, ignoring the heat that crept up my neck.

Here goes nothing.

I pressed down on the Holy Roman Empire until it clicked. The room held its breath, but didn't scold me for being incorrect. Next I clicked on France and Britain in quick succession. Hidden gears ground within the table and the wooden map lowered back out of sight, replaced by the scale once again.

Our original request was gone, leaving behind a stack of papers that weighed down one end.

"Clever," Sora said with a smile, patting me on the shoulder.

Under his touch, my back went straight, and my heart leapt to my throat. I wanted to say something sassy and shove him away, but I also didn't want his fingers to leave my skin.

Sora took the papers from the scale and scanned the pages, his eyebrows knitting together. "It's all nonsense."

Each word was written in a different language, indecipherable to even the most well-versed polyglot. To make it even more ridiculous, the text shifted as you read, so even if you could decode a few words, they'd flip into another script before you could translate a full sentence.

I took the stack from him, then held the first sheet to the light. A slight embossing, nearly invisible, appeared below the changing text. Another seal.

"Quid pro quo," the room chanted.

"An equal exchange," Sora translated.

The woman guarding the archive had warned us about this. In order to receive the correct documents, paperwork equal in value must be given in return. Ha'aheo's signature on the correct form was the obvious answer but we didn't have that. Something else would have to do.

Sora took the papers off to the right, quickly writing down a description of why we needed the files. He set the papers on the scale. It barely moved.

"Two attempts remaining," the room said.

"Maybe it needs to be more robust," Sora mused. He took a stack of papers and began writing down an account of what we needed and why. He pushed another stack at me. "Write," he directed. "You can explain the beginning of all of this, and I'll jot down a more recent history."

I sat on the floor next to him, picked up a pen and placed the tip against a blank sheet of paper. This was like schoolwork, and just like when I was a student, my mind ground to a halt. Writing down a play-by-play of why we needed these documents felt so sterile. It didn't capture what we needed, not really.

In the Amin clan, their family spell recorded their family's history with flourishes. I'd thought it a frustrating obstacle at the time, but there was a reason people would read books a thousand times over, losing themselves in a world of letters—the same people who would fall asleep trying to read a legal contract. My assumption that one was more important was the same as Reagol putting the classics on a pedestal. Who was to say that any one way of thinking, writing, or smithing was wrong?

The bronze scale gleamed in the torch light, and my eye returned to the single word I'd decoded from Sora's translation. Libra. *Balance.*

The fog in my head cleared and I knew where this story really began. This time, the words flowed out of me easily, without judgment or worry, fitting together in the way that my smithings did. We all had a history, a place of origin, and this was mine. Ka moʻolelo o Hāloa, the legend of the first man, from which all Hawaiians are descended and the source of our connection to both mana and the land.

When the earth was new and the gods young, Wākea and Papa conceived a stillborn child. The couple wept with grief and buried his body in the warmth of the land he would never walk.

In time, a plant grew from the grave. It was tender and bright green with a fluttering heart-shaped leaf that turned its face to the sun. The first taro plant. Thus, it was named Hāloanakalaukapalili. Papa watched the plant grow strong and was content.

Soon, the goddess was with child again, and this time, Papa gave birth to a healthy baby boy.

The elated pair named their son Hāloa, after their eldest son, and the gods instructed their children to care for each other—for neither could survive without his sibling.

Hānau ka ʻāina, hānau ke kanaka.

Born was the land, born were the people.

Sora finished first and set his papers on the scale. It creaked down another few centimeters. He swore and grabbed another stack, sitting down to write more while I took my single sheet to the desk. It wasn't much, but I couldn't write any better than the legend I held in my hands.

Story. History. Same thing.

Sora looked over my shoulder and his eyebrows knitted together. "Kea, that's not what I asked for." His eyes scanned over the first page. "That's a fairy tale."

"It's not," I insisted. "I mean it *is*, but it's not just a moʻolelo. It's the tale of our beginning, and it's the main reason why I'm doing this. Our home is more than just land; it's our kin."

In English, people spoke about facing the future head-on, but Hawaiians viewed things differently. The future was at our backs, and we stepped into it unseeing. No one could know what would happen next. But you *could* see the past, the stories that were at the heart of our culture, the generations that came before. These were our guides and as long as we didn't lose sight of those north stars, we would survive.

His mouth twitched. "You can't really believe that."

Doubt flooded my system like fear, an immediate wash of icy cold ocean spray that shut down all my muscles. It sounded crazy now that I'd said it out loud. Like some hippy-dippy, New Age bullshit with crystals and moonlight. I steeled myself as a small bit of mana coiled like a snake at my core, guarding the wary light of certainty I felt from within.

Moʻolelo might be shrouded in metaphors, but there was always truth to those stories. Academia taught us that there was no value to these unscientific beliefs, but I disagreed. The two could coexist happily because the conclusion was always the same. People needed land—and the land needed us.

"I believe it," I said.

Before Sora could stop me, I set my paper on the plate with little more than a squeak. We both drew back as the weighing mechanism groaned. It plummeted to the desk, the metal pan crashing against the surface with a *clang*. The sound made Sora jump, his papers scattering. The documents from the archive shivered as the words on the page began to settle.

"Look!" I exclaimed, picking up a page. The words had righted themselves into English.

The city of Los Angeles and the remaining Hawaiian clans declare that the policy of this Act is to relocate native Hawaiians to maintain their self-determination and governance . . .

Sora picked the papers up and began scanning through them, doing another kind of translation as he converted the legalese into something digestible.

"The first section is the original agreement between the Homestead and LA, but later on, these are amendments," he said, flipping through some pages and setting others aside. He paused then his eyes widened. "The Homestead is shrinking. The last sale Basilio made to LA took a large chunk, and the smaller clans have started selling out to larger ones.

"In the original document," he added, "it states that if LA were to reclaim more than half of the Homestead, it would get a right to intervene in the self-governance of your council."

"Basilio's clan didn't own more than half," I said.

Sora set down the documents, pointing to a section. "But Keanu Mahiʻai's does. He's been consolidating land for years."

I had known that, too, but had always considered it more of an irritation than an actual problem. Keanu's property holdings were like his ego: large and mostly empty of actual substance. Hell, he technically owned *our* land until we finished paying off our mortgage.

"Do you think he could've been purchasing land as a proxy for LA?" Sora asked.

It wasn't out of the question. Keanu was resource-hungry, and LA had deeper pockets than anyone in the Homestead. Maybe Keanu had gotten tired of chasing down small fries like me for our monthly payments and decided to hunt down a whale.

"I'm not sure," I said, a shiver running down my back like ice water. "But we should find out." It was time for a council meeting.

CHAPTER 18

My heart was thumping loudly enough to start its own marching band as I stared at my reflection. Dark bags lined my eyes, and my skin looked sallow. Worse, there was a perpetual sheen of sweat above my upper lip. I kept nervously swiping at it with the back of my hand.

In a million years, I'd never imagined that I'd be getting ready for a council meeting in Sora Kaiser's office. But the humor in it paled as worry struck me through the heart. I felt sick. Weak, nauseous, and ill-equipped to stick my landing, but I'd already leapt into the air.

Either Nana or Papa had accompanied me to all our previous council meetings, but they couldn't this time, not with Papa still recovering. I'd have to lead without their support—and convince the council that one of our own should be given up to LA before the city came to invade our home.

"Hey." Sora's soft voice startled me, and I turned to find him dressed in black robes with a katana at his waist. His hair was tied in a loose ponytail at the top of his head, and his expression was grim. When he saw me, however, his face went slack, then broke into a smile. "You look beautiful."

Since Nana and I were two different sizes, I didn't own anything suitable, so Sisi had swooped in to save the day. She had taken some old fabric printed with scarlet 'opihi shells and sewn it into a strapless dress that grazed the floor. A deep slit ran up either side so I could move easily. To complete the look, one of Papa's decorative fishing nets had become a makeshift cape that hooked around my neck, draping over one shoulder. My hair had been let loose down my back, frizzing at every end.

I fought the urge to protest the compliment and went back to adjusting my outfit in the mirror. "Thank you."

My makeup was spread across his office desk, and the pullout bed I'd been sleeping in was unmade. In the past few days, whenever Sora had entered this room, he'd sighed loudly at my things thrown about, but right now he didn't look at anything but me. I turned back to the mirror and saw him creep closer. He reached out to pull lightly on one of the waves of my hair. The strand uncurled between his fingers, then bounced back into place.

"I have something for you," he said. "Since we're supposed to look like a pair." I had explained the complexities of these kinds of meetings, and he had quickly grasped the importance of showing a united front, especially with someone from outside my clan.

He shuffled through his pockets and pulled out a gold chain with a circular pendant. He stepped up behind me, holding the necklace out overhead so I could look at it. I pinched the pendant between my fingers, a thin disc with an oblong oval gap in the center and two smaller openings on either side. The main face of the disc was decorated with fluttering gingko leaves. "It's beautiful," I said.

Sora motioned for me to look forward and hooked the necklace onto my neck. His fingers lingered around my collarbone, sending an involuntary shiver down my back. "It's the same design as my tsuba; the hilt of every katana is decorated with one of these." He gestured to his sheathed sword to show me its matching end. "A family talisman of sorts."

My hand went to the pendant, which fell just below the divot of my collarbone. The metal was cool against my skin, but that might have been because my neck was burning up. "I didn't realize you were superstitious."

"I'm not but it will be good for others to see us allies," Sora explained. In the past few minutes that we'd been talking, Sora hadn't once looked away from my face. I wanted him to touch me. To bury his hands in my hair instead of gently tugging on a single strand.

He didn't move, but he did mumble, "Kea," my name sounding sweet when he said it.

Something crossed his expression, and his voice fell to a near whisper. "We should go or we'll be late." He offered me his arm, and I accepted, pulling myself back from the brink of a rash decision when there were more important things at stake.

~

Council meetings always took place on the Mahi'ai compound—the last place I ever wanted to be. But as with most of my dealings with Keanu and his clan, I had little choice in the matter. The Mahi'ais had built circular wooden palisades to enclose their village. Thick wooden stumps were used at the gates, spiked at the ends, and at the entrance, two heavy-looking doors barred our path.

I pressed a palm against the wood and felt the resistance of a ward set in place. *I'm here for the meeting,* I assured their protective spell.

Wards were good at repelling human invaders but only worked at repelling magi if they'd been specifically designed to do so. Wards that worked against both magi and humans were too expensive for most, so clans settled for buying smaller ones to protect our coops and gardens. The Mahi'ais, despite their size and land wealth, didn't have as much in liquid assets as the Lins. Therefore, their ward was like ours: a simple barrier to repel people that meant them ill.

That said, Keanu never shied from a fight and ensured his people did the same. As a result, the clan had many skilled warriors who specialized in combat casting. It made them powerful friends—or enemies.

The gates creaked open, and Sora and I drew back as the doors swung outward, revealing a grassy hill that led up to their main building. The open-air hālau was recently thatched and the wood gleamed. As we approached, treading up the hill, I noticed that Keanu and Haʻaheo were already there, side-eyeing me and Sora as we approached. Basilio, too, had promised to be there in support of me and was waiting patiently to their left. I sat at my expected place in the circle, and Sora sank down behind me, tucking his legs under himself.

"We really ought to change the rule about letting anyone call a meeting," Haʻaheo grumbled. He was dressed in a sharp mandarin-collared blazer that buttoned up to the neck, flanked by two others. "I really don't have time to waste on another of Kea's failed attempts to craft a family spell and join the council."

My cheeks reddened. "This isn't for that." A wave of panic splashed me in the face. No one wanted to be the bearer of bad news, and I had truckloads to unload. My mouth was dry. "I have good reason to believe that the whole of the Homestead is in danger from the Board."

Keanu snorted. He was surrounded by four of his men, all dressed identically in traditional malo made from beaten bark. The stiff fabric hugged at the hips and hung down to cover his groin but little else. "None of our clans have done anything to provoke a raid."

"Someone did," I disagreed. "A Hawaiian spell was used to kill one of the city's politicians. I'm here to invoke in lingua veritas on behalf of LA."

Having grabbed their attention, I recounted to the group everything that had happened since Angelo's death. Basilio's face fell, and one of Keanu's men leaned to whisper something in his ear.

The woman with Haʻaheo leapt for me as I finished talking, the glint of metal appearing in her hand. Before I could move, Sora slid in front of me, his hand extended outward. He pressed two fingers to the side of her torso and she stopped moving, her hand frozen in the air with the dagger still visible.

"Move, and I'll make sure your intestines burst," Sora warned.

"Do it," the woman challenged. She turned to me. "You'd really turn in one of our own people to LA?"

"If they murdered Angelo, then yes," I said.

"And *who* exactly do you think is responsible?" she asked icily.

The question lay heavy on the room and Sora allowed her to withdraw back to Haʻaheo's side while I found Keanu's eyes. "Keanu Mahiʻai."

The outroar that followed was palpable as Keanu's attendants discreetly reached for their weapons.

"Kea," Haʻaheo warned. "What you're accusing Keanu of is worse than treason."

"It's the truth," I insisted. "I know for certain that the spell was Hawaiian and I also know that Keanu has been buying up land on the Homestead for years. I believe he intends to sell to LA, giving them control of our territory in exchange for some kind of protection, some false power within the city—"

"How *dare you*," Keanu said, his voice shaking with anger. "I would never!"

"Prove it," I snapped back. "Recite in lingua veritas and let this all be laid to rest."

"No," he growled. "Of all people, you have no right to make such a demand from me. You with no mana o ka moʻokūʻauhau, no power, barely even a clan left. Know your *place*."

"Eat shit, Keanu," I said.

I only had a second to think about my mistake as Keanu hurled his mana straight at me. "Ke ahi o ka lewa!" he shouted. Mana burst outward like a comb, and the sky cracked in two as a bolt of lightning ripped down and struck the ground in front of me. The air reeked of electricity.

I scrambled backward from the show of power while Keanu glared.

"Until your mana can contend with mine, I won't speak a word at your request. If you've messed with LA and its Board, that's your own problem, not ours."

"Then I'll join the council," I said, hands clenched to fists at my side. "If I have a strong enough mana o ka moʻokūʻauhau, you'll have no basis to refuse me."

"Go on, then," Keanu taunted. "Show us this mighty smithing that you've created."

"Kea," Sora warned, reaching for my hand, pressing a finger to the golden face of the Board's ring. "You can't use your magic. You'll be forfeiting your freedom."

"I have no choice," I insisted, brushing him off. "It'll work. I *know* it will."

If I used my magic, it would trigger the Board to collect me, but by the time they arrived, I would be able to identify the assassin. Everything would be resolved peacefully. It was a gamble, but one I was willing to take.

Sora nodded. "Then show them."

I whacked a hand against the floor of the hālau, the smack of my palm like the sound of a hollow gourd as I found a rhythm. Before when I'd tried to craft my mana o ka moʻokūʻauhau, I'd been so focused on the words themselves that I'd stopped seeing the bigger picture. I knew better now. The stories we told each other were so much more than myths; they were the pathway to our own survival.

I opened my mouth and let the chant flow out of me.

Ola i ka hā
Ola i ka wai
E ola ka ʻāina ʻōiwi

Life from Hāloa, the child of heaven and earth
Life from water, the creator of man, which feeds all
May this land flourish.

The power of the spell ripped through me, reaching down deep as it buried into the earth. My piko opened, overflowing with the mana I'd called into myself, gushing up from the earth like a raging river. But even as I spoke, I felt the absence of that little *click* in my head; the smithing was imperfect.

It's not working.

I couldn't allow that to be true. Instead, I dug deeper into myself and looked for the source of my mana, ripping it wider. I couldn't control it as it rushed to fill me, frying my nerves. I screamed in frustration, not knowing what else to do as power sizzled in my gut, making me feel like a balloon about to pop.

I began to realize exactly how much mana I had just filled myself with. *Too* much. If I didn't release it soon, I'd end up killing myself in the process. Worse, if I cast something thoughtlessly, it could rebound on everyone. Panic pressed outward from my chest as I realized how screwed I was.

Who do you think you are, Kea? Did you really believe you could force your half-baked magic to work?

"Kea!" Sora shouted. His arms were around me, pressing me tightly to his chest. "She's burning up!"

"A mana overload," Ha'aheo said evenly. "She pushed herself too far."

Sora was frantic now. "Can't you do something?"

"She brought it on herself," Keanu sneered.

I was going to die. Because I wasn't strong enough, wasn't smart enough. A fitting end.

"Move," Basilio yelled and shoved Sora out of the way. His hands pried open my jaw, and the strong flavor of medicinal herbs filled by mouth. "Swallow this."

I obeyed and let the wad of plants slide down my throat. All at once, the simmering power in my stomach began to fizzle out. The open flame became a mere smolder, but I couldn't focus on that. All I could think about was the glowing ring on my finger, the bright orange color of hau. I'd broken the rules and used magic. The Board would not be lenient twice.

Sora released a breath and slumped over. "Is she okay?"

Basilio grimaced. "She needs time to recover."

"She told us the Board would come for her if she used her magic," Keanu said. "They can have her. Keep Kea and her guest somewhere until they arrive. This is exactly what I meant about learning your limits. It's for your own good."

As I glanced down at the glowing ring on my finger, I couldn't even argue.

~

The house Sora and I were confined in for the night was empty for a reason. The walls were planked wood, each panel a different color, and the floors were more of the same. The effect of wood on mismatched wood reminded me of being in a matchbox. Everything squeaked. The red couch that bent too low in the middle squeaked when you sat, the floor squeaked when you walked, and I swore that the rats in the walls squeaked every time I breathed. That said, this holding room was more comfortable than a prison cell, so I couldn't complain.

Basilio crouched in front of me, face drawn as he examined me for injury while Sora took a cold shower. "Why do you insist on doing this to yourself?"

Basilio pulled from his backpack a mortar and pestle and a handful of fresh green leaves. He placed the wooden instruments on the coffee table and began plucking leaves to drop into the bowl. The face of the leaves had been scratched with characters in a language I didn't recognize.

"Pull more mana than I could handle into my body?" I asked.

"Insist on punching above your weight class," Basilio amended. "I hate that you make me worry about you. I just wish I didn't . . ." He trailed off and shook his head. "You could've let things be."

"If I was known for letting things be, I probably wouldn't have even helped you at all," I argued.

"You're right," he said quietly. Basilio didn't push the issue and began to pound the leaves into a paste, aided with a little bit of water. The noise the pestle made was comforting, and he continued to work until the leaves were completely crushed.

"What is it?" I asked, scanning the contents of his bowl.

"Sambong. It's a good astringent for cuts, which luckily seem to be the only harm you sustained," he explained pointing to a small scratch on my left ankle from when I'd leapt back from Keanu's lightning bolt.

Basilio slathered the poultice over my wound, then bound it with a dry cloth from the kitchen. Maybe it was just a placebo, but my leg already felt better. "Stay out of trouble so you can heal properly." His hands stopped moving, and Basilio's eyes found mine. Round, warm, and a deep brown, like the color of rich soil. "I'm sorry."

I waved off the apology. "It's my own fault for jumping into the fire again."

He gave a wry smile. "You could do with being a bit more selfish."

I snorted. "I'll try."

He hesitated, then grabbed my hand. "Why don't you just leave?"

"I'm confined, remember?"

He shook his head. "I mean leave here. You could join our clan. There's space for you and your family."

"We don't know Tagalog," I said. "It would be a hard transition."

"It's safer," he insisted. "Plus, who knows how long we'll even be using Tagalog? It's only a matter of time before another larger clan absorbs us. Spanish, maybe? Or even Latin. It may not even be that bad. We'd be under their protection, at least."

I pulled away from him. "Stop that. That's not going to happen."

Basilio gave me a once-over, and I understood how I must've looked then. Alone in a dark room with a busted-up leg, making promises I knew I couldn't keep. He sighed and leaned over to kiss my cheek. "I just want to make it through this alive."

"We will," I said.

Basilio gave me a tight smile, his lips trembling. He reached for my hand and squeezed. "Okay."

He left, and I got ready for bed. I had taken the living room couch while Sora had camped on a sofa bed in another room, but the air was hot and humid, even with the windows open. I couldn't sleep. I sighed, watching the ceiling fan spin in lazy circles for hours before deciding to finally use the bathroom.

I stood up and walked to the door, pushing it in so that it swung open soundlessly. I let my eyes adjust to the darkness until I could make out something directly in front of me. An occupied sofa bed.

Sora slept like the dead. He didn't snore or fidget. He was lying face up, breathing soundly with the blankets sat upon him like some kind of mannequin. I laughed, and the sound must have woken him, since he sat straight up.

"Kea," he said, rubbing his eyes. They were cast down, sleep hanging on them heavily like he had one foot in reality and the other in a dream. He got out of bed and closed the distance between us in two seconds. He stroked the side of my face, pushing my chin up with his thumb. "Are you having trouble sleeping?"

"Yes," I said quietly, my heart pulsing in my chest as quickly as the wings of a hummingbird. His fingers didn't leave my skin, tracing the outline of my face and ears and neck. Under his touch, I couldn't think.

Sora let go of my face and ran his hands down the sides of my arms. "I could help you sleep."

"How?" I asked cautiously.

He pulled off his T-shirt, and every remaining thought in my head fled. Sora smelled of bergamot and clean sheets and anything smart I had stored as a comeback shriveled and died at the sight of him.

He took my hand in his and spread my fingers out into a fan, his hand against mine. Slowly, he lifted my palm to his abdomen. My fingers pressed against the warmth of his skin, and my sympathetic magic sunk its teeth into him. The taste of ginger hit me hard as his mana melded with mine, soft, warm, and welcoming.

I wasn't sure what he was attempting, but whatever it was, I was definitely *not* tired anymore. Not even a little.

"How do you feel?" he asked, words slurring together.

It was like I had swallowed a whole barrel of champagne, the bubbles popping in my stomach all at once. "Like I want to kiss you."

Sora's eyes went red-hot. Slowly, deliberately, he placed a hand underneath my chin and tilted my face up toward his. I already knew what his mana felt like and imagined that his tongue would taste the same, sweet and spicy all at once. I leaned into his touch, and his mouth was on mine in an instant, rough and hungry. My lips parted as his tongue explored mine. I molded myself to his body, and his hands moved up from my back to tangle themselves in my hair as he deepened the kiss.

His power flowed through me again but all I could feel reflected there was an intense desire. My name ran through his mind on a loop again—my full name, my *real* name. *Kealaokaleo.*

I lost control.

Sora pushed forward until I was pressed against the wall, placing himself against me, his hips flush against mine. Butterfly wings of pleasure rippled through my core. Sora growled against my collarbone, then went for my neck, exploring every part of me he could get to. His hands ran up my bare legs, from my thighs, then higher, lifting up the large T-shirt I had worn to bed as he wrapped an arm around my waist, pulling me closer to his body.

Abruptly, Sora stopped and backed away from me. His expression was raw. "I'm . . . I'm sorry that I did that."

My stomach fell, chasing away the current of jitters that he'd left me with. "Did you not want to?"

"It's not that. It doesn't matter what I wanted—I shouldn't have," he said. He flexed his fingers in front of his face. "I shouldn't have used my ability on you more than once. I knew the risks." He placed his hand over his face. "We're too enmeshed."

So that was why Charles had told me to be wary of Sora's ability.

I could see, from the outside, how useful it was. Sora could not only understand how someone's mind worked, but form a connection with each person he touched—only in my case, it went both ways.

"It's not a bad thing," I said.

"I'm not sure it's *real*," he said, his voice strained. "I've never used my abilities so frequently on a single person, but with you . . . I couldn't help myself."

"Who says it isn't?" I argued. Sure, maybe the attraction between us had begun artificially, but what I felt now wasn't manufactured. "Kiss me again. Please."

Sora's expression tore down the middle between concern and desire, but he obliged. He pressed his lips to mine, and all at once, the tension left his body. Instead of pulling away, he held my head to his chest. "Before I met you, I knew exactly what my life would be. Now, the world is quicksand."

"That's my fault?" I asked quietly, face pressed against his neck.

"Yes," Sora said, raising a hand to my cheek. "You cloud my judgment." His voice was hard, but his fingers against my jaw were gentle. "You scare me, Kea."

"Scare *you*?" I teased. "I should leave, then."

"No," he said so quickly that it chased the wind from him. Sora reached for me, his hand closing around my wrist. "Stay." He returned to his bed and patted the spot next to him.

In any other circumstance, the gesture would've been a different kind of invitation. But this was Sora.

I settled myself next to his pillow, curling into him, and yawned. "Only if you're nice to me."

He lay down and closed his eyes, sighing as his arms wrapped around me. "I'm never nice, but for you, Kea, I can promise to be kind."

It was enough.

CHAPTER 19

The next morning was bright and extremely warm. Whatever gods existed clearly didn't care if I sweated my ass off while waiting to die or be locked away at some prison in the desert. In fact, they'd probably designed it that way for a laugh.

What assholes.

I was frozen in place on the mat of the Mahi'ai hālau, staring at the space above the council's heads. I'd spent a restless night poking at what had gone wrong with my family spell while Sora slept at my side. Had I used a wrong word somewhere? Been too nervous?

Or maybe you just messed up the smithing.

Ha'aheo, surprisingly, stood in my defense. "Handing her over to the Board is harsh. Kea is still one of us."

Keanu scoffed. "She had no issues with sending me off."

"*If* you were guilty," Ha'aheo said.

"Well, *she* is, of breaking a rule she agreed to," Keanu protested. He turned to me. "Can you explain to me again why you chose to antagonize the Board mere weeks away from our lease negotiations?"

"Just felt like it," I said with a shrug.

Keanu wiped the sweat from his face with the collar of his ratty T-shirt. "You and that mouth."

I smiled viciously in return. "I've been told I have nice lips."

"And a sharp tongue," Ha'aheo butted in. "Though neither seems to have done you any favors." He sighed and tapped his watch. "The Board's late. They said they'd be here for you at eight. It's eight-thirty."

Keanu glanced down the hill. "Don't be so anxious. Basilio went to get their delegation at the ward and is bringing them here now."

I was out of time. The city had come to collect, and I was sure it wouldn't stop with just me. Everyone, everything, would be gone, starting with our leaders, because I had failed. In my pocket, the paper with the death spell I'd resmithed for LA had worn thin. I remembered how it had felt as I'd finished finding the words, the familiar *click* that had resounded in my head.

I had been so confident with my mana o ka mo'okū'auhau, too. It had felt right as I'd thought of it. The spell drew on the legend of Hāloa, of the life-giving waters of Kāne. I'd intended for the smithing to help the land thrive, mentioning the necessary components: earth and water. I'd wanted to craft something that would help keep the Homestead alive. But it hadn't worked—it hadn't been wrong, exactly, just incomplete.

Like this investigation.

I frowned and put my hands to my temples, as if the pressure against my skull would help me think better. At least it muffled the sound of people discussing different versions of my doom.

Maybe this was all like the etymological lock from the Lin archives. I needed to trace things back to the beginning, looking at every clue I'd discovered, one at a time. I tried to recall Ivy's spell in my mind.

When a blade tastes blood from one of its own, it cries
Misfortune has brought death, arriving in twos
The death of a hero, and the death of a dream
Wings broken, the angel falls to the forest floor, returning like a stone
And the raven-haired king who shot him from the sky, weeps.

When we'd first received Ivy's riddle, everything had pointed to someone on the Board casting the spell, but in lingua veritas proved otherwise. I'd been attacked twice, by poison and by magi. But those two attempts on my life had used very different types of magic—meaning two different languages.

The spells on the magi's collars were immediately recognizable as Latin, but the first confrontation had used a powerful spell of unknown origin etched in mint. Its medium meant it wasn't Latin *or* Hawaiian. What magic user, then, could possibly have relative mastery of Latin, Hawaiian, *and* a third language?

My head hurt just thinking about it. Even in method, the attacks felt so disparate from one another: an in-your-face assault by leashed hunting dogs, a silent poisoning, and Angelo's boardroom murder itself. It was hard to believe that all three of these crimes had been carried out by the same person.

My eyes shot open. *Misfortune brought death, arriving in twos.*

There were two killers.

A mastermind and an assassin. Someone on the Board pulling the strings and someone from the Homestead who shared their goals. Whoever of my people had aligned themselves with LA could then guarantee safety for their clan from the city's impending raids, as well as secure power, and the only thing it would cost them was their home. Only one answer made sense: a Hawaiian head, someone who would do anything for their clan, who had no problems abandoning the rest of the Homestead.

Only one person fit that description.

My heart pinched as I thought of the balm he'd spread on my

wound yesterday. Leaves etched with magic meant to heal. It wasn't radical to imagine that they could be used to harm, as well. Like the deadly plant I'd downed in my drink at the gala.

Basilio had ushered me into this mess from the very start, and like an idiot, I'd come running. He'd been the one to secure our tickets to the gala, ensuring that Sora and I were in exactly the right place for the bartender to slip something into my cocktail. He'd been calling me constantly and following us around—not to help, but to make sure I was home before sending those magi after me on my family's property. The weight of his betrayal was a cement block across my shoulders.

"Is everything all right?" Sora asked, noticing my hands, which had balled into fists at my sides.

"No," I said quietly, my voice cracking. I cared about Basilio. Despite the distance that had grown between us, I'd thought that we'd begun healing things. I recalled that first deposition when he'd urged me not to get involved as the Board discussed the fate of the Homestead. Had he wanted to spare me from the pain, or had he been worried that I would derail his plans?

I turned to the entrance of the hālau. "Who is Basilio with right now?" I asked, raising my voice to interrupt Keanu and Haʻaheo.

They stopped arguing and looked out down the hill. "Just one person. A man."

My throat constricted. "Don't let them in!" I shouted, leaping to my feet. "They're going to—"

Just then, Basilio and Reagol Stone stepped through the building entrance. I was up and ready, hands out in front of me and a smithing on the edge of my tongue. Basilio's eyes widened in surprise, but Reagol was calm and, more importantly, fast. He inhaled, and I saw the rush of mana that swam into his gut as he cast a spell.

Though thine heritage hath borne bitter fruit
Be not proud of unearthed and withered roots
Surrender thy power, weak heart and mind
A King forces thy hand, pressure applied

My hands ran over my body as I checked myself for injuries, but it seemed the spell hadn't affected me at all. The same couldn't be said for Sora, who stared blankly ahead. I waved a hand in front of his face but got no response.

Reagol turned to Basilio. "Collect it before the magic wears off."

Basilio obeyed, running forward with a heavy bound book under his arm. I moved to knock him away, but he never got close enough, shooting past me straight for Keanu and Haʻaheo. I jerked my head to glance over my shoulder and saw that the two men stood glassy-eyed and compliant. They, too, had clearly been addled by Reagol's words.

Once Basilio was close enough, he slid a pen into Keanu's hand and flipped the book open to a blank page. It was then I realized exactly what was going on. The smithing hadn't affected me because it only targeted people with mana o ka moʻokūʻauhau—which I technically didn't have. This had been Reagol's plan from the start: to steal our magic.

Before I could think fully, I dove at Basilio and tackled him to the ground. He gasped, the wind knocked out of him, and dropped the book. I scrambled over his body and kicked, sending the spell book sliding across the floor.

Reagol lunged for it, but Sora snapped out of his trance and intercepted it. "What are you doing, Reagol? You should only be here for Kea."

"I'm not waiting for the rest of the Board to make up their minds," Reagol snarled. "We already agreed to take their family spells if the culprit wasn't caught, so I'm doing exactly that."

Sora narrowed his eyes. "On whose authority?"

"My own," Reagol challenged as he stood straighter. "Move."

Sora didn't budge, and the two men silently stared each other down.

Basilio finally managed to shove me off and retreated back to Reagol's side. Keanu and Haʻaheo had also regained consciousness, recognizing the true threat in front of them.

My voice rose at Basilio as my accusation poured forth. "You wanted *me* to identify the spell as Hawaiian, pointing the finger at our home, so the Homestead heads took the fall for what you did. They're trying to drain us of our magic. And all for what? A spot for you on the Board?"

Basilio backed away from me, arms raised. "I understand this is a lot, Kea," he soothed. "But this isn't what it looks like. You didn't fulfill your end of the deal; this was the only option. I'm just trying to help to ensure things wouldn't get violent. It was this or a raid on the Homestead." Basilio looked at the council. "Kea promised to deliver Angelo's killer to the Board. She always knew that failing meant sacrificing our home."

Their attention snapped back to me, and I shrank.

"Of all the irresponsible things!" Haʻaheo shouted.

"It's not like that," I argued. "The Board was already planning on coming here, on taking our heads away; I was trying to stop that from happening."

"You only made things worse," Keanu said. He didn't say *as usual*, but he didn't need to.

"Please, just listen to me," I begged. "He's lying to you! And I did find the killer—it's Basilio. He's the one who—"

"Why would we ever believe you?" Keanu asked.

I fought to keep myself composed. "I may be a fuckup, but I'm not a liar, Keanu. You know that."

"And you're saying that Basilio is?"

"Yes," I said. "He's lied to everyone, even the Board. Basilio never gave up his mana o ka moʻokūʻauhau. I saw it myself the other day when I had to surrender the one I resmithed."

"And you didn't tell me?" Sora asked.

"I didn't think it was relevant."

"Kea—" he started, but I cut him off. He could scold me later.

"He's working with Reagol," I explained. "That's why nothing made sense! The variety of magic they were using had to come from two people."

"Do you have proof?" Keanu asked.

"No," I said and looked at them all pleadingly. "I need you to trust me." Blind faith was not a characteristic of the council, but I wished then, *hoped* it would be, just for a second.

Sora gave a sharp nod. "I believe you."

At that, Basilio went still. If Sora was able to convince the rest of the Board that he'd lied to them about his family spell, the punishment would be severe. It was about time he paid for one of his lies. Instead of cracking, he calmed.

Basilio smiled as if to say *isn't this crazy?* "Kea's just trying to talk her way out of the consequences she agreed to," he said.

Keanu frowned and Ha'aheo crossed his arms over his chest. I needed solid proof.

My eye caught on the abandoned spell book. "Pick that up," I said breathlessly, pointing to it. "And read your family spell."

"What?" he asked.

I turned to the council. "Basilio was supposed to give up his mana o ka moʻokūʻauhau to join LA. He might've been able to fool the city with made-up Hawaiian, but he can't fool us. We know what it's supposed to sound like, and it isn't supposed to cast anymore. *Read* it," I dared him. "Or even better, turn to the last page and read the death spell that was used on Angelo. Recite in lingua veritas."

The blood drained from his face.

As Basilio swept a hand through his jet-black hair, my mind brought forth Ivy's riddle. *A raven-haired killer. A leader. A traitor.* Across the floor of the hālau, Basilio met my gaze. He must've seen my resolve then, because his protests stopped. Instead, his features tightened to a sneer. "Fine."

Basilio marched over to the book and picked it up off the ground. For a second, I wondered if I'd been mistaken. He flipped to a page in the middle and licked his finger, then placed the pad of it on the paper and began to recite—but the second that I heard the words, I knew it was wrong. Or rather, it was right.

His real family spell.

He lepo ka ʻai ʻo ka ʻāina, a māʻona nō i ka lepo
Dirt is the food of the land, and it is satisfied with its earth.

Basilio tossed the book aside and bent to place his palm flat against the ground. Below his hand, the earth groaned, cracking in two as the hālau split down the center and wet mud bubbled to the surface, gushing out of the crevice as it crawled down the hill. An earthy smell filled the air with the scent of decaying plants and stagnant water. I sniffed and held my nose, recognizing the smell from both the gala and my home. It was the scent of an untended taro patch left to rot. Another spell meant to heal the land but wielded to harm.

I'd always thought Basilio's control of plants to be benign, but I realized how foolish that had been. The line between life and death was a blurry one. The same could be said of his mana o ka moʻokūʻauhau. The production of fertile earth ought to be used to grow kalo in a loʻi, but Basilio had left for the city, where such magic would be useless. Now, it could only be used to create a treacherous pit, where anyone trapped inside would be forced into the thick, gelatinous mixture, unable to move except in sloppy strides.

The schism divided us into two parts, with Basilio and me on one side and everyone else on the other.

"We're under attack!" a voice shouted in the distance, "There's people tearing through the ward!" Apparently, Reagol hadn't come alone after all.

Haʻaheo scrambled for the exit, calling for his attendants while Keanu barked sharp orders to those around him. Below the hill, I could hear the sound of feet against soft soil. In the middle of the chaos, Basilio stood calmly. He was a striking sight, his thick black hair a smudge of darkness against the bright blue sky. I stared at my former friend, searching for a single sign of remorse.

What I found was worse. It wasn't logic or cold calculations that had led Basilio down this path—it was fear. Stark terror was as present on his face as the beauty mark above his right eye. I was so startled by the nakedness of his emotions that a pang of understanding cut through me.

"You would really let us be wiped out?" I asked.

"We have to make tough choices," Basilio said, his voice calm. "You should know that—you're a head, too. It's just what life is."

If someone had told me the same thing two months ago, I would've agreed with them. But that was before Sora had bound my wounds, before the Lins' archivist let me pay for entrance with just a name, before Haʻaheo refused to give me up to the Board.

"It doesn't have to be," I said.

The world was a scary place for people like us, people on the fringes. As our languages faded, so did our power. It sometimes felt like being on a sinking ship with only a teaspoon to bail out water. I was sure that LA and everything it offered to Basilio looked like a life raft. But all contracts came with strings, and over time, I was sure that the agreements he'd made had tightened around Basilio's neck like a noose until he felt there were no moves left.

Basilio turned and ran.

I followed, making it to the edge of the hālau, where I barreled into Reagol Stone, who was now flanked by his clan. Behind him, soldiers trailed after their leader, and in the distance, I spotted the hole in the ward where more men poured into the Mahiʻai village. I spun around, searching for an escape.

There was nowhere to run.

I backed away from Reagol, making a sharp left turn so I had my back to the wall. Shit. Shit. Shit. The man came closer, his steps slow and casual, like he knew his success was guaranteed.

"Why haven't you taken care of her yet?" Reagol shouted over his shoulder to Basilio, his streaked white hair like spots of snow on a barren mountain. "Her magic's a wild card I don't need."

Basilio winced. "Surely, we don't need to. Kea has no family spell; she's nothing."

"She has a mouth, doesn't she?" Reagol asked, glancing at his watch. "The rest of the Board will arrive on the hour, and I'd rather she be a corpse when they arrive."

Basilio hesitated, his expression torn.

Reagol rolled his eyes and grabbed me by the shoulders, his strong hands holding me still, and his fingernails digging into my skin. "Looks like if you want something done right, you have to do it yourself," Reagol said.

He pushed me into the muddy pit.

I fell back, landing with a wet slap as the earth wrapped around me and pulled at my hands and clothes. Regular loʻi were at most knee-deep, but this one was massive, and I quickly found myself sinking. The mud grabbed at me like wet tongues trying to consume me whole. Panicking, I flailed around, trying to swim to the edge, but my arms couldn't move through the sludge.

"Basilio!" I shouted, making one last desperate plea to my friend.

He flinched as he heard my call but didn't move. Instead, he stood at the edge of the patch, watching as I sank. I opened my mouth to curse him, but it filled with mud. I choked, pulled under completely as his face disappeared from sight. He was right: Without a mana o ka moʻokūʻauhau, I was nothing.

~

Healthy loʻi smells rich and deep with layered notes of fresh water and greenery but the mud that filled my mouth as I sank into the loʻi patch hid something foul. It was imbalanced, almost sour—something rotted.

If plants could be used to heal or kill, then earth was the same. It brought forth all life and became our final resting place after death. Like many things, it wasn't either-or, but both. A perfect balance. It all depended on the way it was directed, as with mana.

A Smith without her tongue was doomed. I couldn't pull on the levers of magic if I couldn't speak. But even when I'd had my words, I couldn't cajole a spell to work, nor persuade a fellow clan head to listen to me. There was nothing left to do but die.

Alone.

For a moment, I was back at the gala with Basilio, discussing the state of the Homestead, of the world. He'd warned me not to stick my neck out for anyone, and I hadn't listened. Did I even have a right to be angry? He'd only done exactly what he'd always promised to do: survive at all costs. I was just collateral damage.

Yet, there were so many other times it had felt like I was right. When we'd once stood shoulder to shoulder and planned to save our home together, when the Lins' archivist had given me the key to her seal, when Sora had held me close and promised to be kind. I had bet my life that most people were like them, like me—and I was wrong.

Though my tears meant nothing anymore, I shed them anyway. The world might be hard and sharp, but that didn't mean I had to be. There was so much I had carried for so long, chipping away slowly at me, but I had to believe that at our core, people were more alike than we were different. I clawed for the surface, kicking desperately and trying to find something to grab onto. If I kept reaching out, *someone* would reach back.

Something clamped down on my wrist. I grabbed back and held on tightly, and then a second hand found me, pulling me back up.

Muffled shouting sounded overhead, and I felt myself emerging from the loʻi. I broke through the surface and gasped for air. Sora, Haʻaheo, and even Keanu had hauled me out of the pit and were now nearly as dirty as I was, panting in relief.

I choked as I crawled out of the pit on my hands and knees and coughed up mud. Someone rubbed my back and someone else pulled the hair from my face as I shook from my skin droplets of wet dirt so dark they were nearly black.

Before I could fully recover, though, Sora pulled me into a sudden, tight hug. "You're okay," he said, and I wasn't sure if he was reassuring me or himself.

"I'm okay," I promised as I looked up at him. He was dirtier than the others, his silk robes soaked in as much mud as my casual clothes.

"Your clothes," I murmured. One thing I knew about Sora Kaiser was that he hated getting dirty.

"It's fine," he said, refusing to let go.

It was his hand that had pulled me out. He had jumped in after me, just like he'd done that day at the beach.

He had reached back.

I fought the urge to kiss him again—that would have to wait. The Homestead Council looked at me, foreheads wrinkled with concern, and I realized that concern was for me. I fought back unexpected tears, lest rumor go around that the Petrova head had even an ounce of affinity for the council.

Instead, I stood. "Sora and I can't do this on our own. We need your help—*I* need your help. Both of you."

Keanu and Haʻaheo exchanged a glance.

"All right," Keanu said. "We're in."

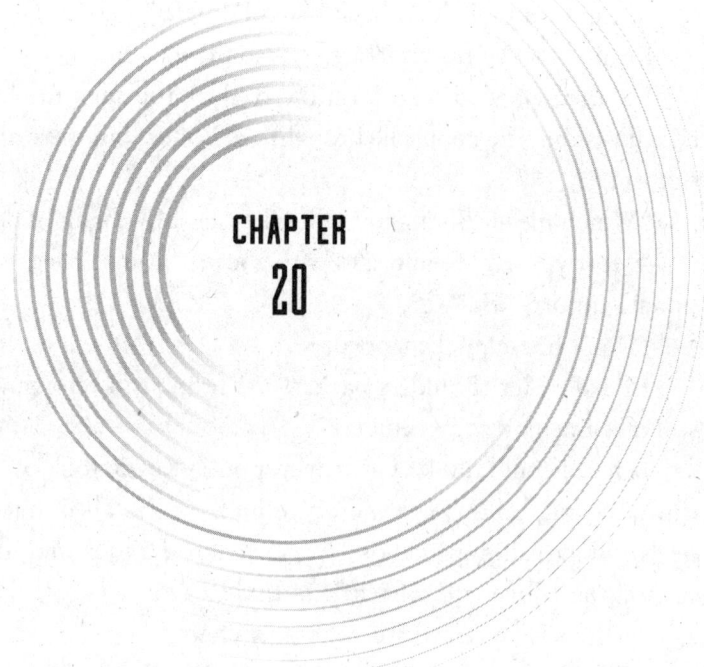

CHAPTER 20

A spell landed a hundred feet away from the hālau, bringing my thoughts to a screeching halt. It was impossible to tell which side it came from; it smashed into the ground, leaving a deep divot and sending dirt flying. Reagol had come as a lone member of the Board, but he certainly hadn't come alone. Below us, the front line of Reagol's troops clashed with the Mahi'ai warriors, spells flying back and forth at a lightning pace.

Beyond the immediate fight, water bubbled up from the earth as Basilio's spell took root, creating a treacherous battlefield of deep pits and patches of thick mud that was impossible to run across. Basilio seemed unconcerned with the ongoing fight, focused instead on shielding Reagol from any outsiders. The new springs brought water to the surface that acted as a barrier as the Board member worked on something just out of sight. Those were our three major problems: the fight below, Basilio's spell, and Reagol. Luckily, there were four of us.

"Keanu, can you hold back Reagol's men?" I asked.

Keanu cracked his knuckles. "Absolutely."

Ha'aheo clapped Keanu on the back. "You take the left and I'll take the right. The people he brought are skilled, but there aren't many of them."

"Which means Sora and I will take care of Reagol," I decided.

"Mostly Sora," Keanu said with a grin. "You're relegated to emotional support, Kea."

"Don't be rude," I snapped.

He rolled his shoulders back. "Just trying to keep you alive. You still owe me money, remember?"

Before I could think of a witty response, Keanu took off in a sprint down the hill, bellowing a war cry as he went. Ha'aheo followed at his heels. Which left me and Sora. We exchanged a look and took a deep breath, then dove into the battle to find Reagol.

There was no strategy in war, only chaos.

All around me fighting raged on, and patches of blood and black smeared the hillside that had until recently been a vivid green. A spell whizzed past me, landing squarely on the Hawaiian woman to my right. She doubled over and started coughing blood as a strange purple tint began to cover her skin. Her screams brought the attention of one of the healers, who rushed over and knelt beside her, chanting. By the time I turned around, Sora was gone. We'd been separated in the mass of bodies.

A crack of lightning to my left deafened me, leaving only a vague ringing in my head. As I turned toward the sound, I spotted Keanu jostling with a man who seemed to have lost his own weapon and was trying to wrest his paddle from him. A sudden force ripped past me and sent me flying. I choked on the air leaving my body as I fell onto my back. In a panic, I ran my hands over my torso but could find no wounds. I must've only caught residual magic.

A figure loomed over me, and I reached out as he extended an arm, expecting Sora to help me up. Instead came the glint of metal, and I snatched my hand back and rolled to the side just as the soldier's blade lodged in the ground. He bent over to pull it from the earth, but I kicked at the sword with the heel of my boot, sending it flying across the dirt. The soldier lunged for it, and I tried to trip him up, managing to wrap my foot around his calf.

He kicked, and it hit me square in the jaw. I saw the glimmer of another blade in his hand, smaller this time, and within a split second, the dagger was lodged in the side of my arm. I screamed in pain, more than aware of the similar screams around me.

Ripping the blade from my arm, I pushed him off. He landed with his back to me, and I didn't stop to think as I plunged the sharp end into his neck. He grasped at the wound, his voice gurgling with blood as he fell headfirst into the dirt. My stomach flipped as I stood, but I couldn't dwell on what I'd just done.

"Look out!" a voice cried as a pair of hands pushed me back to the ground. I rolled over in time to see a purple flash arc down onto the woman who had pushed me out of the way, landing with a crash. I recognized the woman from the Mahiʻai clan. Her body crumpled on impact, and I could tell in an instant that she was gone. Her face was calm, like she was sleeping, her pouf of curly hair spun out like a cloud to cushion her final rest.

Something hard lodged itself in my throat as I looked at her, and I spun on my heels, heading straight for the center of the springs I knew guarded Reagol. My feet flew across the lawn of the Mahiʻai property until the terrain turned to swamp. Without Sora, I had little chance of doing any damage to the warden of LA, but I had to try.

Basilio saw life as a harsh, barren landscape, one we carved out our own survival against, but I rejected that view. If life was difficult, it was by design. The slow, intentional strategy of places like Los Angeles had always been to starve us out, strip away our resources, and wait until the last of us died. No one cared about the stories of fallen societies. Their histories were overwritten with a false, shiny veneer.

They wanted to be a part of the city.

They wouldn't have survived without our intervention.
They were violent and uncivilized before we arrived.
We saved them.
They destroyed themselves.

If we didn't stop the attack, it would continue until we could no longer speak for ourselves—and the only way to truly kill a people was to cut out their tongue.

~

At times I was trudging through muddy swaths of land, and others hopping from firm patches to the occasional rock to get to Reagol. In the distance, I spotted Keanu fighting ardently alongside his clan, pushing a storm onto the uneven land and trying to wash away the pits before they could form. The resulting sheets of rain made it even harder to navigate a terrain of black that I couldn't see the end of. Every inch of me was soaked in mud, and my hair hung in a tangled matted knot down my back. I tried to ignore the cold stinging of the rain on my skin as I made my way forward.

Nearly there.

I stumbled over the final hill, and the wind and rain died away. I realized I was inside a magical bubble that stretched overhead. Its transparent exterior kept the elements at bay; they swirled outside the barrier like a reverse snow globe. Reagol was in the center of the shield, carving something into a piece of stone. He looked up at the sound of my footfalls.

I reacted on instinct, throwing a palm out to knock him back with a spell, but the words fell away on the tip of my tongue. I looked down and realized I'd walked into a trap. The smithing etched on the stone below my feet read vacate et videte. I collapsed, my knees striking the ground so hard that my teeth rattled. My arms and legs went rigid as his spell forced me into total stillness. I struggled to open my mouth, but even that was held tightly shut by magic.

Reagol walked over to me, shaking his head. "You people really don't know when to quit." He squatted down, drawing a finger through the air as if making a point. "You know, I really don't know why you all resist so much. Once LA absorbs your land and power, you'll be *safe*. No more petty raids or having to live in poverty. Your lives will all be much better."

I was reminded of our conversation meeting at the gala. Reagol's fanatic belief in the superiority of regulation, of the classics. He wasn't doing any of this out of a desire to cause pain or suffering. Unlike Basilio, it wasn't out of self-preservation, either—he'd always had the upper hand. Reagol truly thought that this was the path to order and peace. We were just a necessary sacrifice. It was a far scarier justification for evil.

He turned away and ignored me then, returning to the heavy stone he'd lugged onto the Homestead. He was carefully tapping at the rock with a chisel, carving letters into its face. I strained to see the text, internally cursing as the letters became clearer.

Veni, vidi, vici, pro gloria et patria.

Goddamn Latin.

I scrunched my eyes shut. I could figure this out. I started with the easiest words, the ones that sounded almost like English or the Romance languages. This was like the map in the Lin archive, but in reverse. I had to start at the root word and move it forward to find something that made sense.

Veni, *see*, victory, *for glory and the father*.

It wasn't bad, but if I approached his spell like a Smith, I could already see the errors. The structure of the words at the start of the sentence hinted at parallel structure, but *see* was a verb, while *victory* was not. The only options might be something like *win* or *conquer*. I rearranged the lines in my head, taking some creative leeway so the phrase fit better together. The translation clicked in my head, and I knew then that it was correct.

My eyes flew open. I knew the word I'd missed, because I'd seen this phrase before. Everyone had. It was the foundation of our understandings of modern warfare, the very roots of colonization.

I came, I saw, I conquered, for glory and the fatherland.

Reagol's smithing was the promise of death.

A different Smith might see only the victorious shine of the spell, as there was nothing in the text that hinted at violence, but I knew better. From the red wave of the Crusaders to Manifest Destiny and everything in between, those on the ground knew that there was no glory without bloodshed. No conquest without death. This ancient spell had not been crafted as a benign flag planted in the sand. Its intention was to steal—but what was its target?

From the exterior of the barrier came a thud, and Sora tumbled into view, a sword at the ready. His eyes whipped around and focused in on me before finding Reagol. The man hadn't looked up, frantically tapping in an attempt to set the final part of his smithing in stone.

Sora and I made eye contact, and I watched as his gaze moved from me to Reagol and back. I silently pleaded with him.

Please. Help my family. My home.

As if he'd heard me, he went straight for Reagol. Though he gave me one final glance back, I knew then that I loved this man because he charged forward with his sword raised, roaring as he slashed down at Reagol's arm, but it was too late. Reagol had just finished the last letter.

I felt a sudden jolt as the mana around me was pulled toward the stone like it was a giant magnet. As the pressure of it squeezed my organs together, a desperate, wordless wail escaped me. I hadn't realized it, but the words that Reagol had carved into his pallet were no ordinary smithing. They were *his* family spell, handed down generation after generation. A legacy of conquest.

Black, putrid smoke began crawling out of the stone and swam toward everyone I had grown up with. Toward my family and friends. Toward Sora. He was only a yard away from Reagol, and he wasn't turning back, even though I knew he could see Reagol's magic manifest, reaching its dark arms out toward its prey.

Run away, you idiot!

I watched in silent horror as Sora was filled with smoke. His head was thrown back in anguish as the dark power forced itself in through his mouth, his eyes, his nose. Soon, I couldn't even make out his shape in the darkness, only his voice. Sora was shouting my name. Then his cries turned to screams, the sound like a cut to the heart.

It was worse when the screaming stopped.

The darkness cleared, leaving Sora in a heap on the ground. He groaned and rolled to his side, his eyes barely open and finding mine. When our eyes met, my heart dropped to my stomach. Instead of flaming red, I was staring into eyes with a dark-brown color that mirrored my own. Sora reached out a hand but his muscles strained and gave way, and his arm fell back to the ground, where it lay still.

His mana, I realized. *It's being drained away.*

It wasn't just Sora, either. I could feel it within myself as well, or rather the absence of it—a hole in the bottom of a bucket that couldn't be plugged. I attempted to shut it, to hold the mana in, but the hole only grew wider and more gaping with every breath.

The Mahi'ai property had been a cacophony of yells from the start of this mess, but the shrill screams that filled the salty air now were different. Our people doubled over as Reagol's spell brought them to their knees. I didn't see Basilio, but the land below us had stopped shifting, so he, too, must've been affected by the spell. In less than a few minutes, the battlefield had devolved into a mass of writhing bodies.

The Homestead was dying. Reagol's magic had settled into the soil like a fine layer of silt, diverting the flow of mana away from its natural course and toward him.

I stopped struggling, surrendering to my magical restraints. Tears poured out of me in streams, turning the world a watercolor blur as helplessness, anger, and despair washed over me. I had no way of knowing who was impacted or how far the desolation spread. If this was the price of civilization, then I didn't want it.

"Vae victis," Reagol said, standing and surveying his success. "Woe to the conquered." His skin glowed healthy and strong as he fed off of his family spell.

"You're killing them," I accused, tears brimming.

"I know," he said before seeming to notice that the effect of his spell was slower on me. He strode over, a small dagger in his palm. "LA doesn't necessarily need more people—only more *power*. It's more humane to have you go quickly—I'll make sure this doesn't hurt."

On pure instinct, I reached out for the mana that had been a companion to me my whole life, even though I knew Reagol's spell had taken it. I searched for it all the same. I still believed that if I held out a hand, someone would grasp it. I closed my eyes, and there it was, the barest flutter of power behind my piko. There was something beyond that hole in my core, something light and vast: Mana reached back, light as a feather, and brushed against my side.

It was impossible. I'd seen Reagol's family spell settle on us like a suffocating fog and squeeze out the last drops of mana from our people. It had sucked all the color from the world, and yet, I could still feel the flow of mana—larger than ever, just buried deep beneath us. Surviving.

Reagol's blade was already digging into my skin, inching along as if time was slowed down, and I considered throwing the last of my life into the ether and casting something to reverse what he'd done.

He stole your power. There's nothing you can do.

I inhaled that small tingling of mana, letting it fill me to the brim. *But he didn't steal it all.*

The more I let the magic into me, the more words stacked themselves together, snapping into place.

He can't *steal it all.*

Family spell or no, Reagol was just a man, and the force he wanted to control went beyond any legacy. I'd thought the Homestead stood no chance against the Board, but I'd underestimated us. We didn't just have pretty stories and grit on our side; we had actual knowledge. We knew that mana collected in land as much as it did people, that they were one and the same and had always been connected. LA didn't comprehend that. It was why Reagol wouldn't succeed—he thought that he could take our power for himself, but mana wasn't something you could *own*.

That was the missing piece of my own mana o ka moʻokūʻauhau.

I closed my eyes and tapped into the world around me, digging down into the flow of mana in this place, my beloved home. Although I couldn't feel the ebb and flow as clearly anymore, my sympathetic magic had shown me that mana was there, always around us. I dug deeper into the ground until I was blinded by a flood of light so strong it shook my vision.

Power flowed through me, warm and buzzing; it felt like being underwater in the ocean while people laughed and talked above.

I didn't want it to fade away into nothing.

I didn't pull back out of fear of a mana overload. Instead, I widened the hole in my piko and ripped out the plug completely, unafraid of what might happen. The resulting shock sent waves of adrenaline coursing through me. There was so much power here. An ocean. And I knew that in the face of it, Reagol's claim over us was as strong as a sheet of paper.

Instead of agonizing over my word choice, or trying to tame the wave of magic in me, I focused on what I knew to be true: Legacy wasn't something that was handed down to you in a line of succession; it was what you chose to do in the present.

I knew where I came from. And more importantly, I knew *who* I was. I didn't need a particular lineage to tell me that I was worthy of a mana o ka moʻokūʻauhau. I would make one myself, be the writer of my own story. I was, after all, a Smith.

I gave one final push, and Reagol's bindings on my arms and legs shattered. I elbowed him in the gut, and he stumbled back, the dagger dropping from his hand. I knelt down and planted my hands against the earth.

I chanted, pressing so hard into the ground that it cut my palms.

Ola i ka hā
Ola i ka wai
O mākou nō nā moʻo

E ola ka ʻāina ʻōiwi
E ola kākou mau loa e

Life from Hāloa, the child of heaven and earth
Life from water, the creator of man, which feeds all
We, the descendants, are one and the same
May this land survive
May we live on.

Pain shot up my arms as the mana o ka moʻokūʻauhau took over, pouring out of me and back into the surrounding area. It burned as it left me, like each generation was breaking free through the stream of power. Centuries of anger and pain were released so abruptly that it had sharpened to a precise point. It *hurt*.

My teeth clenched, and I dug my fingertips into the dirt, rocks and pebbles digging into the beds of my nails and drawing blood. Through the mana's call, I could feel millennia of war. Battles had been fought and won to wield its power, or collect it, or burn it away. All had eventually failed, for one couldn't control the flow of the universe any more than one could pilot a tornado. But we could borrow some of it.

Mana flowed through me, stronger than ever. Not because the hole that Reagol had punched into me to drain my magic had been closed, but rather I'd opened myself to it completely, allowing magic to come into me of its own accord. There was no need to hoard a power that was an inherent part of all life. It wasn't a limited resource like water or food. It was the very atoms of our being. The fabric that connected us all together.

Reagol stared at me, mouth open, unsure if he could stop the flood that I'd released. I wished he would try, because I knew that the move would be his last. It would be so, so easy. I would crush his life the way he'd attempted to end ours. The world would be a better place without him, but was that how I wanted to spend this chance?

Magic hummed beneath my fingertips, and I knew that I could only hold onto enough for a single one-word spell. Only one opportunity to get this right and repair everything. My palms tingled. Of all the people who could be standing in this spot, tapping into the very core of the Homestead's power, it was me. The girl who was cursed with unbridled one-word castings.

I was a perfect fit.

I smiled. "E ola." *Life. Health. Salvation.*

The power between my fingers sparked and burst into flame, spurting upward until it formed a spear. As mana poured into it, its tip shone with the intensity of a pure white sun. I threw the weapon up into the barrier and watched as Reagol's spell shattered. Pieces of magic scattered across the battlefield in a shower of sparks, like falling stars, covering the Homestead, the outer villages, Los Angeles, everything.

From the battlefield's muddy pits, green kalo plants sprouted and unfurled their green, heart-shaped leaves. The rivers turned clear, and the rain dried up. The land was changed, but it would recover. It would grow even stronger.

The spell reached Sora, and I watched in relief as his irises shimmered, changing from brown back to their recognizable blood-red hue. It didn't take long for him to regain the strength to stand.

Reagol looked at the scene around him, in disbelief, his expression contorting as his eyes landed on me. I braced myself as Reagol raised an arm and recited a death knell.

> *Curse not the messenger who swings the sword*
> *'Tis but the natural order we maintain*
> *Curse the weak line that hath brought you forward*
> *A grasp for false power brings only pain*
>
> *The reaper's great prize: time comes for us all*
> *Those who rise futilely, must also fall.*

As he finished the curse, a purple death spell glimmered in his hands. He aimed straight for Sora, who only had time to look at me and say a single word. "Kea—"

My name.

I rushed forward to block the blow. Magic lashed into my side, tearing through me. My mouth tasted like pennies, and I realized it was blood as I fell to the ground, clutching at my wound. I felt Reagol's curse spreading through my body as it seized up, but I wasn't worried. The other clans would help watch over the kids. Sora, too.

Then, I lay there in Sora's shaking arms. He was crying. Why was he crying? Everything was going to be okay. After all, everyone I loved was safe. Including him. I tried to tell him, but he couldn't seem to hear me.

I was disappointed that I wouldn't get to taste him again, breathe in his ginger scent. I wouldn't see Newt and Sicilia go to college or watch Makani grow up. I wished I'd hugged Papa and Nana one last time, but then I saw my full name on Sora's lips and knew that I'd chosen correctly, even as I closed my eyes. My last conscious thought was of our family crest. Nana's tattoo, a blazing alkonost holding a scroll with the proverb we lived by.

I ka ʻōlelo no ke ola, i ka ʻōlelo no ka make.
In language there is life; in language there is death.

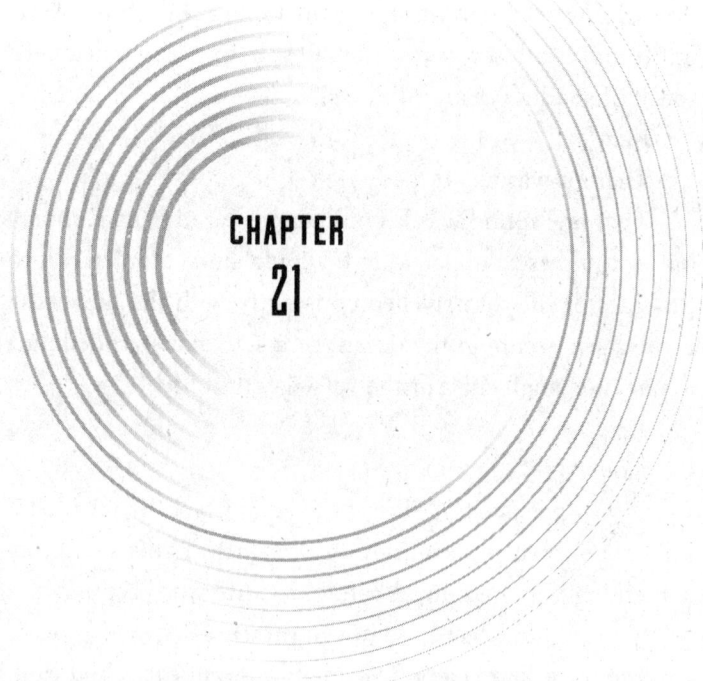

CHAPTER 21

At the time that turned the heat of the earth
At the time when the heavens turned and changed
At the time when the light of the sun was subdued
To cause light to break forth
At the time of the rise of the stars of Pleiades
The slime, the source which established the earth
The source of deepest darkness
The intense darkness
Of the darkness of the sun, in the depth of night
    It is night
    So was night born

—THE KUMULIPO, THE HAWAIIAN CHANT OF CREATION

Mana churned around me, and I felt myself getting pulled along with the riptide of heavens and earth. I was completely enveloped in the flow of power. There was no distinction between myself and this ocean of life and death. I was just a small spot of fire in this universe. A single speck of shadow in an infinite sky.

Kea.

There it was again.

That one sound was keeping me tethered to something far away. If only I could escape that sound, I could sink completely into the world, the tides of life that swelled constantly with the universe. I could become a sea urchin in the ocean, or a star that sparkled and burned, or a part of a small child at the very dawn of its life.

Kea.

Come back.

It was persistent. Below me, I could feel the lava below the earth in constant heat, the rain upon the earth. I was so close to it all, yet something bothered me. A familiar entity was keeping me from letting go. Ignoring the sound, I allowed myself to be swept away.

From the stars came the smell of damp earth and rain and below, fresh water puddled into lo'i that filled with kalo. The heart-faced leaves seemed to multiply in the blink of an eye until lush forests sprung up at my feet.

Remember who you are.

Your name.

My name?

As I searched for it, I could breathe again. I could move. I could *feel*, and my heart ached with a longing for home. In the blackness, I searched for the voice I had heard before. I found the thread and all at once, I remembered.

'O Kealaokaleo ko'u inoa.

The way of the voice.

Head of my clan.

I reached for the tether and pulled.

CHAPTER 22

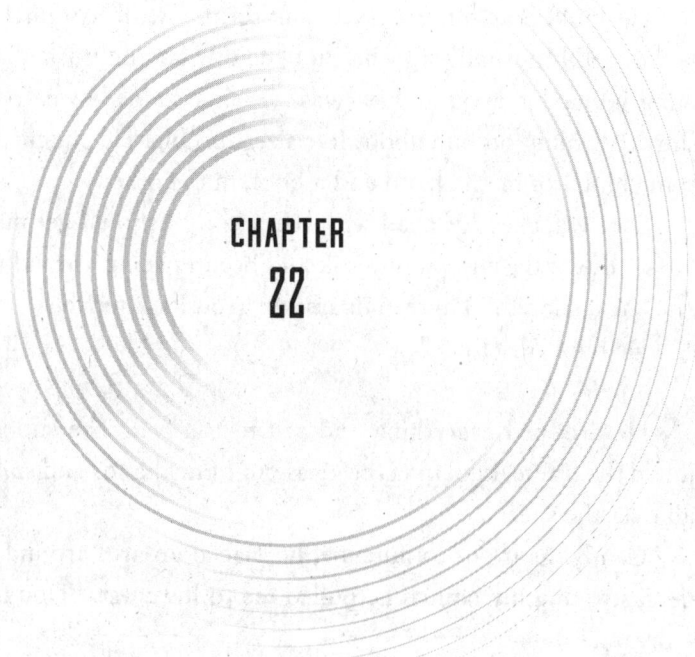

When I woke up, I could barely move. Everything was stiff. It took all my effort to ease myself up onto my arms. I looked around the room and recognized the dark drapery immediately as Sora's bedroom but it wasn't exactly the same.

It was . . . messy.

Sora was always so organized, but there were teacups scattered around the room and books left lying in corners and on windowsills.

It looks like my room.

I tried to speak, but my throat was too dry for my voice to do anything other than crack. Searching around, I found a glass of water near the bed and lifted it to my mouth, using both hands. My stomach cried out for more, but I forced myself to lap at it gently, feeling like I might be sick if I tried to drink too fast.

The door opened, and Sora walked in and froze when he saw me upright.

He looked awful. His face was scruffy with a scratchy, uneven beard, and his usually silky hair looked oily and unbrushed. Dark bags hung under his eyes, and he was wearing stained sweatpants and a shirt that hung on him about five sizes too big. He clutched a mug of something hot in one hand and a book in the other.

Sora whacked his head with the book. "I should get more sleep." He set down the cup on his desk and began pacing around the room.

"You should," I agreed hoarsely. "You look terrible."

He blinked. "Kea?"

"Yes?"

He dropped everything and ran to the bed. The sudden motion jolted the frame, knocking the glass out of my hands and spilling water all over the sheets.

Gently, as if not to hurt me, he placed an arm around my shoulders, stroking my hair as he pulled me to his chest. "Don't let this be a dream."

I was so glad he was alive, and so glad that I was alive with him. I relaxed into his heat. This was exactly where I wanted to be.

"How are you here?" Sora asked, holding my head in his hands like he couldn't believe I was real. "I mean, you were always here but . . . you weren't." A shadow flickered across his face.

"I heard you," I explained. "I was somewhere else, but I heard you and I followed the sound of your voice."

Sora wiped away tears that had run down my cheek. "You came back."

I shrugged, though the effort made me wince. "You asked nicely."

A wave of joy overcame me, and I leaned over, brushing my mouth against his. His lips were chapped, as were mine, but it was the sweetest, softest touch I had ever felt. I finally managed to pull myself away, heat running through my body. My neck and ears burned.

Sora smiled, and I frowned at his triumphant look. He was an unpleasant man. Terribly stubborn and strict. He teased me too much and took pleasure in challenging me on everything. Despite knowing all this, I couldn't stop myself from listening for his voice. Waiting for him to say my name.

I was doomed.

His signature grin cemented itself onto his features, and I knew then that I'd have to deal with that lopsided smile for a long time.

~

The sound of drums grew louder with every step I took up toward the hālau, my feet mirroring their steady rhythm. My family had accompanied me to the Mahi'ai property, but I was supposed to attend the ceremony alone, so I'd left them at the base of the hill. The ascent was slow, so I was left only to my breathing and thoughts. By the time I ascended the hill, my stomach was a knot of anxiety.

At the entrance of the wooden building, I paused and made eye contact with Keanu and Ha'aheo before beginning the chant to ask for entrance. I'd dreamed of this moment a thousand times over, but dread still filled me that maybe, just maybe, they wouldn't respond.

My worries were unfounded though, for at the tail end of my last word, Keanu picked up the beat and called back, inviting me inside.

As a child, I'd always wanted a seat on the council to prove that I belonged. I'd thought that finally earning it would be a slap in the face to everyone who'd thought I couldn't. I'd fantasized about how good it would feel to spite them all, but this was nothing like that.

Neither Keanu nor Ha'aheo looked upset. Their faces were calm and open as they beckoned me inside. I looked down at my bare feet and lifted one onto the cool stones of the hālau floor. It felt no different than the million other times I'd stepped inside this building. Having found our mana 'o mo'okū'auhau hadn't fundamentally changed who I was.

That wasn't to say I wasn't different. I felt more solid, like I was taking up more space in the world. I planted my second foot across the threshold of the hālau.

"E komo mai, Kealaokaleo Petrova, manini head of the Petrova clan," Keanu teased. "Welcome."

"Hurry up, Kea," Ha'aheo said with a gesture to move faster. "We've got work to do."

~

Basilio and every member of his clan who had assisted Reagol in the battle were brought before the council for judgment. Basilio didn't try to dodge his charges, perhaps still stunned at how easily Reagol, even with all his power, had failed.

The Homestead was in rough shape after the battle, so the Reyes clan was tasked with its restoration. Each member was asked to pitch in and, under Vanessa's guidance, the work was tackled one step at a time. It was a slow process, but most were happy to lend a hand. Basilio, however, was extradited to LA, where he was tried for Angelo's murder. I saw him only once after the battle.

In the courtroom, Basilio had sat in the same chair that Angelo had died in, stiffly listening to the Board's decision. Vanessa, though she'd recused herself from the trial, was given special permission to hand out the punishment. She appeared at the end as an angel of death, dressed head to toe in black with a lace mantilla draped over her head and shoulders. Stepping down from the bench, she approached Basilio, bending at the waist to speak directly in his ear. Though I couldn't make out what she'd whispered, all the color drained from his face and for the first time since the start of the trial, Basilio broke down.

Vanessa never did tell me what she'd said to him, but I trusted it was deserved. She was, after all, both a healer and a curse worker. She understood more than anyone that not all justice could be delivered without pain. There were some things that could never be mended. For no matter what language you subscribed to, nothing could bring back the dead.

We buried ours on the last day of summer. The sun was just cresting over the horizon as three boats pulled off from the cement ramp that led them into the water. Their engines purred, zipping quickly into the deeper waters, which darkened to indigo. Two canoes followed in their wake, the paddlers striding together as one until they met up with the waiting cavalry.

Funerals on the Homestead were bittersweet affairs. A celebration of the life led by the deceased, culminating with a return of their flesh to the waters and their bones to the earth. This funeral was no different. There were many dead and few resources left to hold individual ceremonies, so we'd decided as a community to hold one communal procession.

I stood on the shore with my family as we watched the affair from afar. Makani's hands found mine and they squeezed tightly. His eyes were wide, maybe remembering when we had done the same for his own mother. From our clan, only Nana had accompanied the crews out to help while we waited with Papa, freshly released from the hospital, on the shore.

In the distance, a pū sounded a single, long call. The crowd gathered on the shore quieted, and we bowed our heads. Eyes shut, all I heard was the lulling crush of waves against the beach and soft gusts of wind. The conch shell called once again and our moment of silence was over. Out on the water, we watched as people on the boats flung armfuls of fresh flowers into the ocean.

Ha'aheo and Keanu were distinguishable, even from this great distance, the former wearing a navy suit, and the latter in nothing but a malo. The two men held the wooden urns of their fallen members, one at a time, then turned them upside down, scattering the ashes to the wind and the waves. Once the ceremony was complete, the funeral party jumped into the ocean for a final swim with the people they loved. The ocean was a peaceful resting place.

When the boats eventually returned to shore, the funeral on the beach was in full swing. Food was laid out on long, plastic tables: pancit, kalua pig, purple sweet potatoes roasted with coconut milk, and fresh fish sliced raw with a splash of salt and sesame oil. There were even coolers packed full of ice cakes and beer. Most of the people in attendance had begun to eat, talk, and sing.

I went to greet Ha'aheo, Keanu, and Vanessa at the top of the boat ramp.

Vanessa held tightly to her newborn and let me give the baby boy a kiss before wiping her eyes and leaving to join the rest of their clan. She cried off and on throughout the day, but she also laughed and played with her child. I had a feeling she would be okay after enough time had passed.

Ha'aheo was calm. He hugged me when he saw me, then went to join his clan, picking up a ukulele as he left to join the chorus of songs. But Keanu was more reserved. He patted my shoulder but didn't say anything, nor did he join the party. Instead, he walked out on the beach, sinking down onto the sand to stare at the ocean.

I joined him near the shoreline, tucking my legs under me. The water was beautiful. Light reflected off its surface, changing the color of the waves from blue to bright streaks of yellow sunlight. Gently, I elbowed Keanu in the side. He looked up at me.

"Want to grab a drink?" I asked.

He smiled, but it didn't quite touch his eyes. "Sure." While alcohol wasn't the answer to hurt, a drink with friends was a good place to start.

The Mahi'ai head was more stoic now. His clan had taken the brunt of the attack, and losing so many people had hurt him worse than our own physical scars. Only time and continued devotion to home would pave the way to a better future. For some, this came naturally. For others, not so much.

The party lasted all day and into the night. The kūpuna of our clans told stories about their fallen kin. The funny ones left the whole party doubled over with laughter. Whenever they told a raunchier tale, the kids and teens attempted to eavesdrop until their parents caught them and shooed them away. We ate and drank and swam and cried until exhaustion pulled at our limbs like gravity.

Guilty of drinking far too much, I ended up calling Sora to take us home. We were still staying at his place while our house underwent repairs. That evening as a family was quiet, and the Petrova clan drifted off to sleep one by one until only Sora and I were left.

Sora helped me change my clothes and brushed my hair out, then settled me onto his bed, surrounded by cushions and three glasses of water. I sat straight up, waiting for him to finish getting ready and willing myself sober. By the time he strolled into the bedroom wearing only a pair of sweatpants, I had just about managed it.

He slid into bed next to me. "Feeling better?"

"Yes. Sorry," I apologized. "I shouldn't have drunk so much."

"Nothing to apologize for," he said, placing an arm around me. "Oh, I wanted to return this to you," he said, reaching for something in his pocket and sliding it into my palm. The necklace he'd given to me earlier. "I made one minor change."

I lifted the pendant once again to eye level and gasped. There, in a delicate script that curled around the frame of the image, read

I ka ʻōlelo no ke ola, i ka ʻōlelo no ka make.

As a matriarchal clan, the Petrovas had no permanent crest to represent us. We changed our trademark image with each generation, adopting a mix of our partner's culture and our family motto to best represent the pair that led our clan. Our current one had an alkonost with a scroll to reflect Papa's background in Russian mythology. Nana had loved it so much she'd had it tattooed on her shoulder.

"You know, normally only married couples share sigils," I said.

"I know," he said. He smoothed the piece of jewelry out, so it dangled at the front of my outfit. "I won't settle for just a piece of you. I want everything."

I gave a nervous laugh. "You want my rickety house with the hole in the living room? My clan, which is mostly grandparents and children? My chickens?"

"All of it," he agreed solemnly. "I want your grandfather to threaten my legs with a shovel and your grandmother to fawn over my good looks. I want to help your cousins with their magic and hear about your sister's crazy antics. And of course I want the chickens, especially the mean one with a twisted foot."

"Fiona," I said.

"Fiona," he repeated as if committing her name to memory.

His hand spread across my collarbone, and the flicker of magic between us pulsed as his feelings enveloped me. That emotion grew deeper and wider, until it was an ocean before me and I was a ti leaf, floating along its surface.

Then Sora ruined the moment. "Did you read the letter from the Board?"

I scowled. The letter had come just a few days before the funeral, reminding me a little too much of the one that had set this total disaster in motion. I snuggled up to Sora, placing my head against his chest and listening to the rise and fall of his breathing. Well, maybe not a *total* disaster.

"Yes," I mumbled irritably.

Sora had turned Reagol in for his crimes after the battle, and the rest of the Board had immediately taken the man into custody. The legal mess that followed was fueled by a pro-regulation campaign designed to make Reagol look innocent and pin all the blame on the Homestead. The evidence, however, was damning. Reagol had lost the case and been sent to a prison in Death Valley, but relations were still soured between our homes.

Renegotiations on the lease for the Homestead lands were set to start in a few days, which meant we'd need to talk with the Board to secure our home.

I'd rather go back to war.

Unfortunately, as Sora had told me repeatedly, that wasn't a realistic option. So I'd agreed to the summons, and the full Homestead Council was set to appear before the Board in a few days' time. I wasn't looking forward to it. I'd already been warned that the people listening would be more inclined to agree with someone sweet and innocuous.

"They're not your enemies," he warned, reading my mind. "Play nice, Kea."

I was the woman who had united rival Homestead clans, who'd

forged her own mana o ka moʻokūʻauhau, and who'd strong-armed her way onto the council against all odds. The Board should be wise enough to know that I didn't play nice. I played to win.

~

I was in Griffith Hall once again, surrounded by the Amins' beautiful smithing cut into the decorative trim of the room and near invisible in their white-on-white design. However, this was far different than three months ago.

For one, I wasn't alone. Sitting at the tip of their onyx, teardrop-shaped table, I had both Keanu and Haʻaheo at my side. The latter was dressed like me, in a modern suit of gray wool cut close to skin, but Keanu had chosen to come in a malo. We'd tried to warn him that the beige loincloth would draw eyes, but the man didn't care.

Even now, the Board coughed and avoided eye contact with him as he swiveled in a leather-backed chair, rocking back and forth uncomfortably. At one point, he leaned forward to adjust the fabric between his legs and someone gasped.

"I told you, you should've worn something different," Haʻaheo admonished. "Your ass is stuck to the leather."

"I wanted to wear something special," Keanu said with a grin. "To mark the occasion."

He really was a stubborn bastard.

Six Board members remained on the negotiating team after Reagol's imprisonment, but only five were present. Sora had chosen to remove himself from this particular discussion due to his conflict of interest. He was waiting outside, along with the rest of my family.

Matthew Greyson, the head of the Board, spoke first. "We've reviewed your proposal and are a little . . . confused."

"Would you like me to explain things in simpler language?" Haʻaheo offered. He had drafted the agreement and knew every word of the fine print.

"We understood it just fine," Charles shot back. Today he wore a hard expression like armor, none of his trademark charm peeking through. "But the terms you've laid out are unacceptable. You can't simply *buy* the land back. It's a lease. Government-owned."

"And how was this land first acquired by the government to begin with?" I asked. "I believe it was stolen, like the rest of LA's territory."

"We didn't *steal* the land," Charles protested. "We laid legitimate claim to it. There's a difference."

"Yes, and that was centuries ago," Matthew agreed. He folded his arms and crossed his legs, his mouth dipping down to a slight frown.

I was so frustrated with the whole facade—I wished I could scream at everyone that it was the same damn thing, and when it came down to it, no one could truly own the land any more than one could own the ocean. But of course I would say no such thing. I had matured.

I smiled tightly. "Well, we're open to hearing your suggestions."

Charles Lam nodded, smoothed a hand across the vest of his pinstriped suit, and launched into the long list of the different fees they wanted to charge, and Haʻaheo made a show of reading through each page carefully.

Haʻaheo held up a hand to stop Charles from talking. "Right. From what I understand, there's an 800 percent increase in the cost of maintaining our lease with LA. May I ask why?"

Charles mumbled, his hands closing into fists on the shiny surface of the table. "Er, that's because, well . . . recent events have shown us that the land there is actually quite valuable."

"Ah," Haʻaheo concluded. "I see. So before, you didn't mind surrendering the land to the Homestead because you thought it was of poor quality, but now that it might be worth something, you've decided you want it back."

"That's not *exactly* right," Charles said.

"We could just as easily reclaim the land as ours," Keanu said. "It's been stolen before."

"Doing that would plunge the Homestead and LA into war. Is that really what you want?" Matthew asked curtly.

Keanu shrugged. "I think we did that already, actually, and you guys got mopped."

"One of us," Matthew corrected. "Acting as a rogue agent, Reagol was, as you say, *mopped*, but you would stand no chance against all of us."

I cleared my throat and the room quieted. My chair squeaked as I stood up and set my hands against the table, leaning forward. I hadn't noticed before, but the design of this room was as carefully constructed as the rest of LA. It made you feel small in comparison to the Board. But that was only perception.

"I think you're overestimating how many people on the Board would stand on your side on this issue," I said. "If things need to change so that we have true independence from LA, then so be it."

Matthew sat back in his seat, a stunned look on his face. "You can't propose that. You aren't on the Board."

"A week ago, I wasn't on the Homestead Council," I remarked, anger fizzing in my gut. "What are the requirements?"

"For the Board?" Matthew asked.

"Yes," I clarified. "To join the Board."

"A family spell that's graded as exceptional, a large clan at your backing, and a license in a regulated language," Matthew said.

"My understanding, Miss Petrova, is that you don't possess any of those things," Charles added.

I placed a hand against my stomach and drew it up through the center of my chest, the rest of my magic following while I drew it out of me like I'd done when I'd fought Reagol. I circled my heart then slowly extended my right arm.

"E ola," I said, speaking the magic to life. The mana came jutting out as a blazing spear of light. It solidified in my grasp, and I drove it into the ground, where it continued to gleam.

A shocked silence settled on the room as they stared at the smithing I had made from the mana around us. I lifted it above my head so that the Board might get a better look, and the rod hummed quietly.

"I don't have those things, *yet*," I emphasized. "How soon can we grade my family spell? I'm ready."

Charles's face froze in shock. "You shouldn't be able to bring any weapons in past our wards."

"Good thing this isn't a weapon," I said.

"Clearly it is!" Celine shouted. "It's a spear."

"It is," I agreed. "But spears are used for many things—to hunt. To fish. It's as much a thing that gives life as one that takes it away."

"That's not how any of this works!" Matthew argued. "You must schedule a session. Submit the proper paperwork," he sputtered. "We have these procedures for a reason, Miss Petrova. You aren't even a part of LA!"

"Then we'll schedule a session and fill out the paperwork," Haʻaheo said. "And until then, I'll submit an extension on our negotiations."

I let my spell fade away to nothing but sparks as the Lin head joined me in standing, followed by Keanu. The three of us moved to exit, knowing that choosing this path meant that we had a long fight ahead. Beside me, Keanu and Haʻaheo were already plotting our next steps, but all I felt was giddy and very, *very* tired. We'd need to work on recognition, then regulation, to even have a shot at changing the law. But after that, who knew?

I paused at the door, glancing up at Ivy's smithing. I wondered what story it would spin of this meeting and smiled.

Makani's voice sparked in my head, drowning out the uproar of the rest of the court.

You did a good job, Kea.

I scratched my temple, at the place where his voice always made me tingle, then reached back with a single message.

Let's go home.

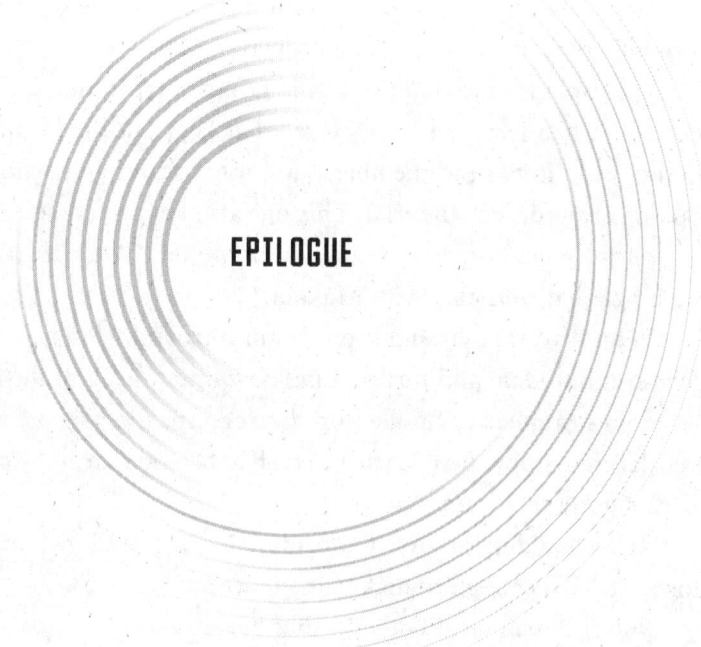

EPILOGUE

I took a deep breath of briny ocean air while lounging on our new lānai. The temperature was dropping by the day as we hurtled toward autumn, but for now, the weather was still suitable for shorts and a T-shirt. I panted as I covered my eyes, sticky sweat streaking down my arms from the day's labor. We were still rebuilding the house, and it was taking much longer than I'd anticipated.

Sisi sat cross-legged next to me, drinking deeply from a jug of lemonade that Nana had made us from fresh lemons off the tree in the backyard. Seasons were funny things after the Flood, and our garden had a particular habit of blooming things out of order. Not that I minded—a glass of fresh lemonade on a summer afternoon was about as close to heaven as we'd get.

Makani came shooting out of the house, screaming at Newt, who was on his tail brandishing a baseball bat. They circled the yard, playing some make-believe game of knights and cowboys until Makani got bored and ran off.

Newt sat down next to us. "Ugh, they're still there," he groaned, looking off at the border of our property.

I sat up and stared ahead at the group camped outside our property. Sora had installed a new ward that kept out the journalists, unauthorized Homestead members, and other scavengers who had been poking around since the trial. This one also kept out magi.

"They'll get bored eventually," I muttered. "After all, all we do is build, garden, and play with Makani."

"Not if your boyfriend keeps coming around." Sisi smirked at me. Her eyes hazed up and turned a milky white. "Speak of the devil."

Sora's familiar car pulled up the road, passing right through the ward. A few stupid people tried to rush in behind him and were thrown back a good three feet.

"He should just move in already," Newt teased me, and I kicked his knee hard enough to make him wince.

"Over Papa's dead body," I shot back.

"Nana would love it," Sisi said.

I pinched her elbow. "Has anyone thought about what *I* want?"

"You mean you *don't* want a live-in boyfriend?" Sisi asked, eyes wide with feigned innocence.

Newt laughed. "Nah, she wants a live-in husband."

I kicked him again. I *didn't* want that, actually.

"Hey, guys!" Sora called as he pulled up on the grass and slammed his car door shut. He opened the trunk and hauled out a stuffed black garbage bag, which he carried up the steps and dumped at my feet. "Special delivery."

"Yippee," I said sarcastically. On cue, we all packed up to move to the back porch and away from prying eyes. Facing the ocean, I hesitantly opened the garbage bag and scowled at the pile of envelopes that lay inside. "I'll add them to my collection."

Ever since Reagol's trial, we had been inundated with letters upon letters from other Homestead heads looking to merge, academics wanting to draw blood samples and stick me under a microscope, and even the occasional unhinged death threat. Newt and Sora began blabbering about computers while I shook the bag as if that would somehow kill the responsibilities that came with it.

"You need to actually read those," Sora chided, massaging my shoulders.

"I know," I said begrudgingly.

"In order to do that, she'd have to open them first," Sisi said, ratting me out with a smirk. Devil-child.

I shrank as Sora's smile flipped. "*Kea*," he warned.

I dragged my fingers through my unruly waves and then tied my hair into a knot. "I will! I will. It's just a lot."

Sora plunked down next to me, fishing through the bag as he scanned the envelopes and then pulled out a smooth white one. "This is your mortgage from the Mahi'ais!"

I hunched over, curling my knees to my chest.

Sora opened it, read the page, and crumpled it up. Keanu had given me a break, but that didn't mean he'd wait forever. I could feel myself getting stiff as his mood darkened like a storm cloud. Newt and Sisi exchanged looks and then coughed uncomfortably.

"I think I need water, Newt. Like, right now. I'm so parched," Sisi said as she stood up, gesturing at him to join her.

"There's lemonade right here," I said, gesturing frantically to the jug. I pleaded with them via telepathic familial communication. *Don't go!*

Newt ignored me. "Yeah, I'm thirsty, too." They both went back inside.

Traitors.

As they left, Sora turned to me, his cherry-red eyes flashing with anger. If he wasn't so pretty, I might actually have the decency to be afraid of him, like any sane person.

"Did you not get enough from solving the case?" he asked lowly. Having successfully completed my task from the Board, Vanessa had made good on her promise, dropping a large sum into our weary accounts.

"We basically had to rebuild from scratch," I explained, throwing my hands up in front of me, which Sora immediately claimed in his own as he began to trace the lines on my palms. My eyes kept glancing down at his beautiful fingers in mine, and I found it harder and harder to concentrate. "Since I donated most of it to the council to buy back the lease on Basilio's old property, we've been—"

He squeezed my hand, and I looked back up at him.

"What did I explicitly tell you to do if something like this happened?"

I faltered under his gaze.

"To tell me right away," he finished.

"I can't just ask you for more," I tried to explain.

"You're my responsibility," he reminded me.

"I don't want to be a burden."

"I said responsibility. As in, I am *responsible* for taking care of you. It's a privilege, not a burden." He touched the top of my nose. "You do make that difficult by withholding these things, though, you know."

"I'm trying not to," I mumbled, looking down.

Sora surprised me then with a quick kiss. A second later, he pulled away and stole my glass of lemonade, taking a deep gulp. As he drank, I noticed that he wasn't wearing a suit. Instead, he had on jeans, steel-toed boots, and a loose gray shirt, a far cry from his usual attire. He hadn't just come to see me, then. He wanted to work.

The fact that Sora had come to help us rebuild after spending all day at Griffith Hall made me even weaker in the knees. Sora had started talking, but I was staring at his mouth so intently that I hadn't heard what he said.

"Sorry, can you repeat that?" I asked.

"I said, we should get married," he repeated.

I pushed him back gently. "No." I'd lost count of how many times he'd brought this up. "We haven't even dated much. I want to enjoy this, *us*, at least for a while."

"How long is that exactly?" he asked.

"I don't know. A year? Two?"

Sora's hand covered his face. "That's a long time." He peeked out at me from between his fingers. "At least let me announce officially that we're engaged?"

"No!" I insisted. "That's basically the same." There were things I wanted to accomplish on my own first.

Sora looked back up at me. "You being my 'girlfriend' is not going to be enough of a deterrent for some of those bottom-feeders out there."

"What do we care what they think? We know that our relationship is more than just some casual thing," I said, loosening the knot on my head. My thick waves fell around my face, reaching down my back, and Sora swallowed, staring at me.

He reached out to tug on a strand of my hair. "It's not about what they *think*, it's about what they might try to *do*."

"You think an LA clan might try to attack us when you're not around?" I asked, suddenly interested as I swatted his hand away.

"Not all danger comes in the form of monsters and magic, Kea," Sora said. He looked to the group at the boundary of our ward, his jaw clenched. "When I came in today, I saw no fewer than four different male heads waiting for you out there. Two from minor clans, one mid-ranked, and one from a major clan that's looking to regain prominence." He turned back to face me. "I'm finding out that I'm susceptible to jealousy."

"You don't need to worry about me," I said, braiding my hair to one side.

He stroked the line of my jaw. "I'll always worry about you."

Oh. My stomach flipped when I stared at his serious expression, coated in the setting sun's orange rays. His long black lashes fluttered, and the afternoon light highlighted the sharp panes of his face.

I watched as Sora's eyes fell down to my neck, then my throat, then lower. He leaned in, and our lips brushed together. In that moment, I was acutely aware of the fact that my family surrounded us from every angle, watching; otherwise, I might have behaved very badly out in broad daylight with this objectively good-looking man.

"Dinner!" Nana Kūlia shouted, sticking her head out the window. "Makani! Get the lovebirds to stop smooching and tell them it's time to eat."

Sora pulled away and took my hand as Makani swarmed us, singing, "Kea and Sora sitting in a tree!"

I grabbed him and kissed his forehead to a chorus of complaints before he broke away and, like fish in a river, darted into the kitchen. Papa slowly came up the steps from the back garden, covered in dirt. It was slow work, restoring fertility to our land, but Papa was managing. The work helped him, too, and every day he looked a little healthier. He shook Sora's hand, took a glance at our interconnected fingers, and walked inside.

When we were alone for a brief moment, Sora whispered in my ear, "I miss seeing you every day."

My stomach fluttered at the low sound of his voice. Between my donation and the house repairs, our clan was trying to make our dollars stretch as far as they could, which meant we'd taken on the brunt of the construction ourselves. It made sleeping at home easier than driving back and forth every day, even though I missed him, too.

"I—it's not practical to always be in the city," I stammered. "I have to wake up early to work on the house."

"I'll be patient," Sora said. He seemed to be talking to himself rather than me. "I wanted to help, too, but I think I came too late." He paused. "I guess I should go, then."

"No. I mean, why? Stay for dinner," I offered.

Inside the house, I could already hear Newt and Makani bickering while Sisi prattled on about the various funny videos she'd collected throughout the day just to show us.

Sora peeked through the window over my shoulder. "I don't know if they want me here."

"Hurry up! The food's getting cold!" Nana hollered. "I didn't slave away for hours to make this just for you two to ignore us and canoodle on the porch all night. I could've *died* from working myself so hard."

"You heard her," I said, laughing and squeezing his hand as I pulled him to the back door. "We're not making out!" I yelled back. "There isn't any privacy here."

The kids made exaggerated kissy noises as we entered the kitchen.

Sora flushed, embarrassed to have been caught, but never one to forget his manners, bowed his head. "Thanks for having me."

Papa Ivan gestured to the table. "Have a seat, son."

Sora sat and stared at the meal, looking bewildered. The room quieted, waiting for his reaction. Finally, his eye drew to the roasted meat in the center of the table and his eyebrows shot up. "Is that—? Can you even *eat* magi?"

I nudged him in the ribs while taking a portion and placing it on his plate. "It's really not that bad."

Sora laughed, and the rest of us joined in, breaking the dam of silence as we settled into our usual squabbles. As dinner passed, the sky darkened and turned an inky black, dotted by bright spots of light over the swelling ocean. My heart and my home were full, and that was more than enough for me.

ACKNOWLEDGMENTS

First and foremost, mahalo nui loa to my amazing agent Jon Cobb. Your belief and guidance pushed me to become a better writer, and I consider myself incredibly lucky to have you at my side.

Mahalo to Amara Hoshijo, who shaped this story into what it is today. Editors are magic, and she is as brilliant as they come. I'd also like to thank everyone on the Saga team who poured their hearts into bringing *The Killing Spell* to the world, and a special shout-out to Lehuauakea for designing this gorgeous cover using the traditional art of kapa printing.

No book is a solo endeavor, so a heartfelt thanks to the people that have kept me sane.

To the Raft: Amanda Helms, A.M. Kvita, Casey Colaine, O.O. Sangoyomi, Samantha Bansil, and S. Hati. Together, we've sailed through calm seas and rough storms. May this journey never end.

To the aptly titled Writers Group: Ann Adams, April Roach, Ari Koontz, B.G. Cane, and Caitin Chisling. We never changed our name, and now, I can't imagine any other.

To the group Pacific Islanders in Publishing who are working to push the needle forward. We deserve to see ourselves in stories, too.

To my class at Waiʻanae High School that I made write books. You shared your stories with me, so I guess it's only fair that I share mine.

Finally, to my family. My Papa Kula, who made clear to us cousins the value of hard work. I miss you. My Nana, who instilled in me the importance of a woman being able to stand on her own. My parents, who let me read in the car as a kid, even though I got sick every time. My sister, Chacha, who is my litmus test for a good story, and the first reader of anything I write. Leinaʻala, who stayed up all night reading my first draft and called me the next day asking me to publish it. Kawena Lei, who helped me fill plot holes and took my official author photo.

I truly cannot name everyone in my ʻohana without filling up a whole other book. So, a warm mahalo to the Kauwes, Ilis, Makaʻikes, Mokulehuas, Aionas, Akaus, Wilsons, Lortzs, Miyahiras, and so many more.

And last, but not least, to my husband, Denis, who first inspired me to learn Russian, and then served as my unpaid translator and language consultant for the next five years. I'd follow you across the world in every lifetime. Я тебя люблю.